ALSO BY RICHARD GODFRAY-HOARE

Echoes of a Boy
If I Had Died Last Summer

*HAPPY READING!*

*Richard*

# Enigma

A Twisted Tale of Love and Magic

Richard Godfray-Hoare

Copyright © 2023 Richard Godfray-Hoare

All rights reserved.

ISBN-13: 979-8-3877-4966-7

Cover design by: Richard Godfray-Hoare

richardgodfrayhoare.com

# DEDICATION

To Scott, my husband, my everything x

# Part One: Patrick

# CHAPTER 1

February 2008

*Oh boy!* The nerves were really kicking in now, for sure. Patrick's palms were sweaty, and his stomach flipped between butterflies and nausea. From where he stood, nervously waiting at the side of the stage, he could see the rows of chairs occupied by his schoolmates. They were transfixed with the current performer on stage, a very confident Year 10 girl who was nailing her rendition of *Leona Lewis's Bleeding Love* – despite her microphone hand being wrapped in a heavily autographed pink plaster cast.

Patrick's mind was racing. *Why did he have to be following this performance? Why was he even taking part in the talent show? What would everyone think?* Not that it mattered, as nobody liked him anyway. Schoolmates, they were not.

He didn't have any mates.

Patrick had just turned fourteen years old and was in Year 9. He had been a pupil at Henry Green Secondary School since the beginning of Year 7, but unlike his classmates, he had not moved up from one of the local primary schools.

Instead, Patrick's family moved house during the summer holidays to a new catchment area. As a result, Patrick had to change his intended secondary school, and none of his previous primary school friends would be going with him. He had hated being the new boy.

Patrick's father, Nigel Morgan, was a vicar, and he had accepted a new post at the rather magnificent parish church of Witford Common. The Witford vicarage that came with the job was a stunning period property. Patrick had enjoyed several sunny weeks of the school holidays exploring the rooms and grounds, accompanied chiefly by his imagination and his dog, Barnaby. Then, one Tuesday towards the end of August, he had to interrupt this play to take a short trip to his new school with his mother. He was briefly shown around the empty classes by the Head of Year 7, and it didn't seem too bad at all. But he was wrong. When Patrick started school just a week or so later, it was awful.

Patrick Morgan had always been a little different from the crowd, but this was apparently less of an issue for primary school children than it appeared for his new secondary school classmates.

To look at, Patrick was a handsome young man who was maturing slightly ahead of the curve of his peers but nothing extreme to warrant undue attention. He had short dark hair with a side parting, a smooth complexion, and a darkening down of fine facial hairs. He was of slim build and average height, although his feet had recently encountered a growth spurt that his body was yet to catch up with, making him a slightly clumsy adolescent as he walked.

Patrick was in the middle set in most subjects, so his intellect was to neither extreme, which can sometimes draw attention. Instead, the ridicule seemed to stem more from his clothing, school bag, and shoes. And, of course, he was also the new boy.

Patrick's parents were thrifty, to say the least, not due to financial constraints but rather because their church work and beliefs governed their behaviour entirely. Patrick's clothes were predominantly sourced from charity shops and, as a result, were a little outdated. Very outdated in some cases. Patrick had no problem with this as he had no real sense of fashion.

It didn't bother him that he didn't have the latest games console or newest mobile phone, either. Patrick enjoyed the outdoors, and he loved his magic. The magic he was about to perform on stage for his hateful peers.

Patrick had been singled out from day one at secondary school. He was routinely mocked and pushed around, the butt of jokes and the victim of many pranks. Individually harmless but collectively draining, although he didn't complain. He kept himself to himself, sat alone during lunch, picked himself up whenever he was tripped over, and kept a smile on his face when, with some relief, he got home at the end of each day.

Patrick's home life was the antithesis of his schooldays. His mother, Kate, made sure her volunteering was worked around Patrick's school day, so she was always at home when he returned from school to greet him with a kiss on the forehead.

While Patrick changed out of his second-hand uniform and into his second-hand casuals, his mother would prepare him a snack of cream crackers, thickly buttered, topped with jam and accompanied by a glass of milk.

Occasionally reminded not to speak with his mouth full, Patrick would swallow his cracker and wipe his milky-moustached top lip onto his sleeve before telling his mum about his day. Not every detail. She didn't need to know he had been forced to run naked from the showers back into the sports hall to recover his belongings. And Kate didn't ask overly probing questions as she knew Patrick was having a tough time, so their conversations danced around the niceties.

Some days Kate had a little gift for her son, usually picked up from the charity shop she volunteered in. Aware her son was due to perform in the school talent show, she had recently picked up a black cloak with a large collar and blood-red lining.

Patrick was always grateful for his gifts and wore

them proudly. Despite the relentless mocking, he remained optimistic in his outlook, although now, as he stood nervously in the wings, he wondered if wearing the black cloak for his performance was a good idea. The intended look was a vaudeville magician, but he feared he looked more like a cheap *Hammer House of Horror Dracula*.

It was too late now. Baby Leona had finished warbling to rapturous applause, the curtain had dropped, and the compère for the afternoon was filling time while the stage was reset. Patrick took his position behind the curtain, and a helper carried out a small table containing his props and placed it beside him. Patrick took a deep breath and slowly exhaled as he listened to the end of his introduction.

'…so, without further ado, please welcome our next performer, Patrick Magic!'

The compère moved aside as the curtain rose to limp applause. Patrick stared out into the crowd, and as he waited for the rising curtain to come to a halt, the clapping stopped, and he could pick up on some whispered sniggering about his cloak. *'What the heck is he wearing?'*

But not everyone was laughing, or at least one person wasn't laughing. Patrick had caught the gaze of a pale-skinned, ginger-haired lad sitting three rows back from the front of the stage. He was smiling, causing his freckled cheeks to dimple. When he noticed Patrick looking at him, he gave a thumbs up and mouthed the words, *'Good luck'*.

Buoyed by this unknown boy's encouragement, Patrick began his routine. 'Good afternoon, ladies and gentlemen,' he bellowed as he stepped forwards on the stage. What happened next would be the stuff of school legend for generations of children to come.

As Patrick walked forwards, somehow, his cloak had become entangled with the legs of the small table carrying his magic tricks. The pace of his stride caused the table to topple over behind him, and as he turned, initially confused as to the source of the crashing noise, he watched in horror as all of his props tumbled to the floor.

Unwrapped packets of cards, pre-prepared for the trick they would perform, spilt across the stage. The three metal cups, again pre-set for their involvement, chimed as they bounced across the stage, spewing a sea of red sponge balls as each expanded to its full size once released from the cup and exposed to the air.

Patrick's opening piece would have been a version of the linking rings trick in which three large metal rings, solid in appearance, are systematically connected and disconnected from each other. These three rings were currently rolling across the stage. Two slowed and came to a rest noisily as they lost momentum and settled similarly to a spinning coin. The third had mustered enough energy to carry itself a little further before plummeting off the front of the stage.

The audience looked on in stunned silence as the final item from the table worked itself to a stop. Ironically the black magician's hat, currently rolling on its brim in a wide circle, centre stage, was planned to be the finale of the act and seemed intent on completing this task.

As the top hat came to rest dead centre of the stage with the opening in full view of the crowd, Patrick just had time to think that he couldn't have placed it better if he had tried before the hidden flap inside fell forward, and two large white ears from the concealed stuffed white rabbit inside flopped out.

'This isn't magic. It's tragic,' a boy shouted, and the audience erupted with roars of laughter.

Stunned by what had just unfolded, Patrick stared into the crowd, unsure of what to do next. This was way beyond recovery.

As he helplessly scanned the laughing faces, he again noticed the ginger-haired boy. He wasn't laughing. Instead, he grinned an awkward but sympathetic smile and then closed his eyes as if to hide Patrick's blushes from further embarrassment. And it was about to get much worse.

The laughter from the crowd faded and was replaced by more concerned whispers and mumblings. Then a boy, possibly the same one who had called out previously, vocalised what everyone else had noticed.

'He's pissed himself!'

Patrick's confusion deepened. *Pissed himself?* Please, no, he thought as he looked down at his crotch. But it was true, and as his eyes fell upon the darkening patch still growing on his grey school trousers, the rest of his senses kicked back in. He could now feel the warmth of the urine on his skin, smell the slightly sweet scent drifting upon the air and hear the tiniest of trickles as a puddle gathered beneath his feet.

He could contain his frustration no more and screamed out.

'Fuuuuuuck!' was Patrick's protracted and pain-filled cry, and as he screamed it out at the top of his voice, one of the stage lights exploded high above his head, raining down sparks to add further effect to the dramatic scene unfolding below.

Patrick released the clasp from the collar of his cloak and let it fall to the ground behind him before running from the stage. He pushed past various stage-hands and refused to stop even as the drama teacher coordinating the show called after him.

\* \* \*

As the whole school community was currently in the auditorium processing what had just unfolded before their eyes, Patrick was able to navigate the corridors with ease. He had sought refuge in the art department and was sitting on the floor at the back of the classroom clutching his knees to his chest and rocking gently back and forth. In hindsight, he probably should have run to a toilet and attempted to sort himself out under the hand dryer, but all he wanted to do right now was hide away.

The talent show had been scheduled for the last lesson on a Thursday afternoon, and the following day was to be an inset day, whatever that actually entailed. Patrick assumed the show would be abandoned and the children sent home. He intended to sit tight and slip away when the coast was clear. The following week was half-term, so at least there would be a period before he would need to face up to events and the undoubted ridicule that would follow.

The thought popped into Patrick's mind that the school may already be calling his mother to let her know there had been an incident and her son had run off. This wasn't a problem as such. Patrick's mother was very loving and caring toward her son and would only be interested in his well-being. But before Patrick could give this further thought, he heard the door to the classroom creaking open.

Someone appeared in the doorway, but from his vantage point on the floor, Patrick could only see them from the waist down. Slightly scuffed boy's school shoes and a pair of grey school trousers similar to Patrick's, albeit newer and dryer. He watched through the desk legs as the boy calmly walked towards his position at the back of the class.

'Are you okay?' the ginger-haired boy asked as he rounded the last desk in the row and came into full view.

'How did you know I was here?' was the first thing Patrick thought to say.

'I followed the wet footprints,' was the immediately retracted reply. 'I am so sorry, that just wasn't funny at all. Sorry.'

'It was quite funny.' Patrick acknowledged the apology and smiled at the boy before him. There was something about him he just warmed to. *Did he know him already?* He certainly didn't, but there was something familiar about him. Obviously, he had noticed him in the auditorium, and it was perfectly feasible he might have seen him around school, but he seemed somehow more familiar. Intriguing.

'Why are you here?' Patrick probed further.

'I brought you these from my locker,' the boy said as he held out a carrier bag towards Patrick, who remained seated on the floor with his knees raised, in part now to hide his damp trousers.

Patrick took the bag and looked inside to find a pair of navy-blue tracksuit bottoms, the standard uniform for PE lessons should the weather be too intemperate for shorts. Puzzled, not by why the boy had brought a change of bottoms but certainly by the kindness of the gesture, he raised his gaze and smiled again.

'I didn't have any spare pants, so you'll have to go commando,' the boy smiled back. 'There are some paper towels in there as well, so you can dry off a bit,' he added.

'I can't get changed here,' Patrick stated.

'Sure you can. I'll turn my back if you like, but I think you're already at maximum points on the embarrassment scale today, so I wouldn't worry too much.'

'I'd still rather not show you my cock,' Patrick joked. 'I don't even know your name yet.'

The boy laughed aloud as he turned his back to Patrick. 'I'm Craig,' he said. 'Craig Newman. I knew I was going to like you.'

When Craig turned his back, Patrick stood up from the floor and undressed. He kicked off his shoes one by one at the heel before breathing in, undoing his belt, and releasing the button and the internal hook and eye that only school trousers seemed to have.

Breathing back out, Patrick made a mental note to ask his mother for a larger size, as his recent growth spurt had rendered these uncomfortably snug. He then pulled down the zip fly, removed his trousers and slipped off his sodden *Calvin Klein* boxer briefs.

Patrick then removed his socks and moved over to the sink, where he wet some of the paper towels, rubbed himself down, and then used the remainder to pat himself dry.

He pulled up the loaned tracksuit bottoms, released the waistband with a slight snap, and packed his damp clothes into the carrier bag.

'You can turn back around now,' Patrick informed, and as Craig did so, he caught sight of the final few tasks being completed. The shoes slipped back onto bare feet without undoing the laces, and the paper towels were collected and put into a bin before Patrick washed his hands.

'Thanks for this,' Patrick said sincerely.

'That's okay. You look cuter in them than I do. You can keep them if you like?' Craig posed a genuine question.

'Erm… sure. Thanks,' Patrick blushed. 'Why are you being so nice to me exactly? People aren't generally very nice to me here,' Patrick said, motioning with his arms to emphasise that by 'here', he meant the school.

Craig moved over to where Patrick was standing and hopped up to a seated position on the counter to the side of the sink.

'I like you. I've noticed you for a few months now, and I thought we could be friends,' Craig explained.

'And you still think that's a good idea after today?' Patrick questioned. 'You'll be hanging around with a laughingstock. What will your friends think?'

'Oh, I don't really have many friends, but people tend to leave me alone. I can handle myself,' Craig said before pointing to Patrick and adding, 'You've got a little drop of blood coming out of your ear.'

Patrick touched his finger to his left ear and then checked the tip for blood. 'For fuck's sake! Could this day get any better?' he cursed while grabbing another paper towel.

'It's only a tiny bit. I reckon you'll live,' Craig comforted. 'It has been a bit of a day, though. What happened?'

With a heavy sigh, Patrick cast his mind back thirty minutes or so to the auditorium carnage. The mechanics of the incident seemed simple. His cloak snagged under the table leg, causing the collapse. Still, he couldn't understand how that had happened.

Before the curtain was raised for his performance, Patrick inspected the table to ensure all his props had been correctly placed and prepared. His cloak had been safely behind him, and he had completed a full circle of the table. It couldn't possibly have been stuck under one of the legs. And as for peeing himself, he was mortified. He had no idea he was even doing it until he heard the boy in the crowd shout out and then glanced down at himself.

As Patrick explained, Craig listened intently, nodding sympathetically in all the correct places.

'Did you notice a spotlight exploded above your head when you shouted fuck?' Craig asked in an attempt to lighten the conversation. 'Maybe you've got real magic powers,' he joked.

'Oh yeah, that's me. The superhero who pisses his pants. A real world-saver.' They both laughed.

'Come on, I'll walk you out of school and make sure nobody bothers you,' Craig offered. He jumped down from the side and started to leave the room without waiting for Patrick's response.

There was nothing to discuss. Patrick was extremely grateful for the offer and grabbed the carrier bag of clothes before hurrying to catch up with Craig. They continued to chatter as they walked, and although some inquisitive looks were received from the students passing by, they managed to leave the premises without incident.

As they walked, they agreed to meet during the half-term holiday. Mobile numbers were exchanged, and after some persuasion, Patrick promised to show Craig some of his magic tricks. Not the ones from the intended show, as he would have to wait until he had retrieved his abandoned belongings for those, but he had plenty more tricks at home.

A little further down the road, they came to a junction where they needed to go their separate ways for the remainder of their journey home.

'You going to be okay from here?' Craig asked.

'Yeah, I'll be fine,' Patrick replied. 'Thanks again for your help. You've been so nice to me.'

Craig grinned, and before Patrick knew what was happening, Craig leaned forwards and kissed him on the cheek.

'See you next week,' Craig called over his shoulder as he walked off.

Patrick stood motionless as he watched Craig disappear around the next corner. *Had he really just been kissed by this boy?* Sure, it wasn't on the lips, just one of those continental-style kisses, but it was a kiss. And Patrick knew from his flushed cheeks and beaming smile that he had liked it much more than he should, even before the realisation he had a stiffy growing in his borrowed tracksuit bottoms.

\* \* \*

Kate Morgan hung up the call and placed the cordless phone back onto its base unit in the hallway. She let out a deep sigh, but before she had time to fully process the information the Head of Year 9 had just imparted, she heard Patrick arriving home from school and putting his key into the door to open it.

Patrick paused briefly at the sight of his mother, hands holding her cheeks and the saddest of looks in her eyes. He pulled the key from the lock and closed the door behind him as his mother rushed over and wrapped him in her arms.

'Oh baby,' she comforted him as she kissed him softly on the forehead.

'Mum!' Patrick protested as he squirmed out of her embrace. 'I'm fine.'

Kate stepped back and looked down at Patrick's legs. More precisely, the borrowed tracksuit bottoms in place of his uniform trousers, her expression alone enough to let Patrick know she wanted to discuss this in more detail.

'I had an accident at school,' Patrick offered as an explanation for his altered attire. 'My stuff got wet,' he added, holding aloft the carrier bag containing his damp socks, pants, and trousers.

'It was more than just a little accident, wasn't it, Patrick?' she asked softly, but using her son's name made it sound more scolding than intended. 'The school has just called,' she added.

Patrick dropped his eyes to the floor, embarrassed to find his mother had been brought up to speed on the afternoon's events. Of course, he knew she wouldn't be mad. She never was, even though he had been wetting the bed regularly over the last three months. All the same, Patrick felt disappointed to have burdened her with yet more worry.

Kate's heart broke to see her son so dismayed. She knew Patrick's life had been torrid for the last couple of years following their move to Witford Common. She knew he was a little quirky, but he was such a sensitive soul. They were an unconventional little family all around.

Being the local vicar's son and an active churchgoer was another oddity, and it seemed school children could be so awful to anyone who deviated from the perceived norm. It seemed every school year needed a communal victim for the bullies to target, if for no other reason than to protect the masses from a share of a similar fate.

Despite the obvious discomfort of his schooldays, Patrick never seemed downtrodden. On the contrary, he was always cheerful and talked about his favourite lessons when he got home each day. Moreover, he was conscientious with his homework and just loved to practice and perform little magic shows for his parents at every opportunity.

Until recently, Kate had rather neglectfully allowed herself to forget her son's struggles. However, they were brought back into focus around three months ago when Patrick had come down to breakfast looking tearfully upset as he informed her he had wet the bed.

A little taken aback, Kate quickly regained her composure and reassured her son not to worry. He was going through many changes at his age, and it was probably just a little accident. It had even crossed her mind that it may have been a wet dream, but when later stripping the bed, it became apparent the discharge was most definitely urine.

This happened again a couple of days later and at regular intervals since. Kate could tell it was getting Patrick down, and his confidence was understandably knocked. She had spoken to the local GP, and they were currently experimenting with no drinks close to bedtime and even sometimes setting the alarm to wake Patrick in the night to go to the toilet.

Their GP also arranged further tests to ensure no underlying health issues, such as a urinary tract infection or neurological problem. So far, nothing untoward had shown up. They had discussed some counselling, but the waiting list for this service was long, so in the meantime, they continued to try and mitigate the problem in other ways, to date, without success. But this was the first time Patrick had ever wet himself during the day.

'Don't worry, sweetheart. We will get it sorted. Do you know what happened?' she wondered if she should have probed further, but the words were out of her mouth before she could check herself.

'I don't know,' Patrick shrugged. 'The magic show was a disaster, and everyone was laughing. I didn't even know I was peeing until some boy shouted out. It was so embarrassing.' Patrick sighed.

'Not to worry, it's the school holidays now. I'm sure it will all be forgotten by the time you go back.'

Neither Kate nor her son believed this for a second,

but it seemed the right thing to say, and Patrick nodded as if he agreed.

'Your teacher said I can pop in tomorrow and collect the things you left behind, so go and pop those tracksuit bottoms off and I will wash them and take them back to the lost property,' Kate instructed, aware they weren't Patrick's own. His were a little too short in the leg, but they were only three pounds from the charity shop.

'Oh, these aren't from lost property,' Patrick smiled. 'Craig gave them to me. He said just to keep them.'

'And who is Craig?' Kate questioned with a raised eyebrow.

'I think I made a friend. No, I definitely made a friend,' Patrick corrected himself and smiled. 'It's been a bit of a weird day, Mum, to be honest, but I think it's going to be all right.'

'Well, there's a turn-up for the books. Now go get changed, and I'll put a wash on. We've got to meet your father for bell ringing practice, and then why don't we go and get pizza? I made a chicken pie, but it will keep until tomorrow. This feels like a pizza day to me.'

Patrick wasn't allowed fast-food often, so he dashed upstairs to get changed before his mother had time to change her mind. It really had been a weird day. An absolutely awful day, the kind you might struggle to get over, but then there was Craig. Patrick couldn't stop smiling when he thought about Craig. This really did feel like the start of something special.

# CHAPTER 2

May 2008

It was just after 8:30 am on a bright warm spring Saturday, and Patrick had finished an early breakfast and headed back upstairs for a shower. Craig would be arriving shortly, and Patrick was running a little late after getting engrossed in an episode of *Sorcerer's Apprentice* while channel-hopping through the Saturday morning kids' TV offerings.

Patrick's room was ensuite, and as he stood under a pounding hot shower watching the shampoo suds rinse down over his toned body and ever-hairier legs, he contemplated how much things had changed of late.

In the months since the incident at the school, Patrick and Craig's friendship had blossomed. The boys would regularly see each other after school and almost every weekend. Sometimes Patrick would make the journey to Craig's, a small council house on the outskirts of town where he lived with his mother, but more often than not, they would meet at the vicarage.

Patrick's family welcomed Craig into their home with open arms as, in fairness, Craig's mother had done in return. However, the vicarage was much more central to the town and all the places the boys enjoyed hanging out together.

The boys had settled into a routine of activities they enjoyed together, ranging from walks around the local area to swimming and cinema trips. However, today they were heading out on the bus to a nearby town to visit the magic shop Patrick had been frequenting for around two years. Magic was everything to Patrick. Well, magic and now Craig too.

Patrick turned off the shower and wiped away the bulk of the residual water from his body with his hands before stepping from the cubical and drying himself more thoroughly with a towel.

He wandered back into the bedroom, where he had laid out his clothes for the day on the bed, and gave his hair one more vigorous rub before discarding his towel. Patrick then picked up his boxer briefs and leaned forward to lift one leg and slip them on.

'Morning, gorgeous. Nice arse!' Craig's voice seemed to bellow from behind.

Startled, Patrick yanked up his underwear and spun around on his heels. On seeing Craig, his initially startled expression turned quickly to anger, and he rushed over and pushed his bedroom door closed. Then, he grabbed Craig by the arm and gripped him tightly.

'What were you thinking? If my mum hears you talking like that, we'll be in so much trouble,' Patrick furiously whispered, tightening his grip.

'Patrick, you're hurting me,' Craig said, but Patrick stared vacantly. 'Patrick!' he said a little louder, and as he tugged his arm away, he managed to snap his friend out of his momentary trance.

'I am so sorry,' Patrick said as he noticed Craig rubbing his arm where small indents had been left from the grip of his nails. He was genuinely puzzled as to what had just happened.

'I don't like it when you get angry like this,' Craig said, his voice cracked with emotion. 'It scares me. And you're bleeding again,' he added, with a nod in the direction of Patrick's left ear.

Patrick moved to his bedside table and pulled a tissue from the box. He held it to his ear for a few moments before discarding it on the side. Then, he moved back over to where Craig remained motionless by the door.

'I'm sorry,' he repeated before leaning forward and kissing Craig on the lips. 'It won't always be like this,' he added, his arms now around his friend's waist, and his hands slipped into the pockets on the rear of Craig's shorts.

They kissed a little more passionately, something they had both improved at since their first brief peck on the street corner in February. Craig placed a hand on the back of Patrick's head, pulling him closer as he kissed deeper, tasting the minty freshness of his recently brushed teeth.

'I love you,' Craig said softly when their mouths parted.

'I love you too,' Patrick said. 'And your bum feels pretty nice as well,' he added as he squeezed it in his hands. 'We can do more than a kiss at some point, Craig. I just need to be really careful.'

'Don't worry about that,' Craig now comforted. 'I will wait as long as you like. There's no rush.'

As if to emphasise Patrick's need for caution, the moment was interrupted by his mum's voice shouting up the stairs. 'Do you boys want a cup of tea before you head out to play?' she asked.

Thankfully she was still oblivious to how her son really liked to play these days.

In unison, the boys declined the offer, and Patrick quickly returned to his bed and finished getting dressed. He also wore denim shorts, similar to Craig's, ones he had insisted his mother buy him from new. He was a little more conscious of his image now that he had a secret boyfriend to impress, but Patrick compromised for the sake of his mother's feelings and pulled on a slightly oversized *Beatles* t-shirt she had picked up for him at a jumble sale.

Trainer socks and a tattered pair of checkerboard *Vans*, and he was good to go.

\* \* \*

When her offer of a hot drink was declined, Kate moved away from the bottom of the stairs and back into the kitchen. She had already filled the kettle, and it was almost to the boil, so she continued to make herself a coffee.

Moments later, she placed the jar of *Tesco Value* instant coffee back on the marble worksurface that topped the hand-finished oak kitchen, stirred the cup, and then placed the used teaspoon into the large Belfast sink in front of the window. She would wash up later.

The kitchen window overlooked a large, well-kept garden, and as Kate took a sip of her coffee, she gazed out at the washing she had hung on the rotary line earlier that morning. It looked dry already, although she had been up at 6:00 am doing chores, and it was a lovely morning. And then she smiled.

There were no bedsheets on the line. Not unusual in itself, as although Kate was a stickler for good housekeeping, even she didn't change the beds daily. The thought only crossed her mind because Craig was in the house, and Patrick had not wet the bed since their friendship had started a few months ago.

Craig was such a lovely boy and had been a godsend for Patrick's confidence. Kate had become aware of some town gossip surrounding an incident several years previously. Something along the lines of an unstable uncle holding Craig hostage, which resulted in him being shot dead by armed police. Very dramatic, if true, but Kate wasn't one for town gossip and was all too aware that the whisperers of Witford could spin many a good yarn.

Since moving into the vicarage, the Morgan family had also been the subject of more than a tall story or two. Reminded of this, Kate was conscious of forming her own opinions, and her assessment of Craig's mother, Lisa, was wholly positive. From their limited interactions, Kate believed Lisa had done a fantastic job as a single mother, and Craig was a testament to that. He would make some lucky lady a lovely husband one day.

Kate's daydreaming was interrupted by the boys clumping down the wooden staircase and back into the hallway. She popped her coffee down on the side and wandered through to catch them before they headed out.

'So, what are you two terrors getting up to today?' she asked.

'We're going to get the bus to the shopping centre,' Patrick replied. 'I want to take a look around the magic shop.'

'And I'm going to get some birthday ideas,' Craig added. 'It's not until July, but my mum wants some ideas. I think she hopes I will have forgotten what I asked for by my birthday so that it will be a surprise,' he laughed.

'Oh yes! Your sweet sixteenth is coming up! How exciting,' Kate beamed, causing Craig to blush.

Patrick rolled his eyes. He was conscious he would

still be only fourteen on Craig's next birthday, and his mother drawing attention to it made him cringe.

Patrick's father initially raised concerns about their friendship's age gap, but Kate dismissed it. There were only eighteen months between them, and Craig was just a year above Patrick in school. Physically they were at a very similar stage of their development, and regardless, Kate would not allow her son's new happiness to be curtailed over such a ridiculous observation.

The concern in Patrick's head was much less ridiculous, to him at least. He was worried Craig would move on and leave him behind in search of a more physical relationship. They had talked about it, and Craig was very reassuring. He understood Patrick was younger and had his parent's religious beliefs to be reconciled. He was more than happy to wait. This was all new to him, too, and the stolen kisses and cuddles were enough. They had recently shared some naughty pictures by MMS, which was exciting, but the kisses and the cuddles were enough for now.

'Can we go now?' Patrick asked, keen to remove himself from this awkwardness.

'Hold on, two ticks. Let me give you some money for lunch.'

Kate had already turned and lifted her handbag from the hall table before she had finished her sentence. She held out a twenty-pound note, and Patrick stepped forwards to take it. Then, before letting go, she leaned in and kissed him on the forehead.

'Mum!' came the usual protest.

'That's right, I'm your mum, and I'll be kissing you no matter if you're fourteen, sixteen, or fifty-two!' she giggled. 'Get you both some lunch, and I don't need any change if you want a sweety too.'

'You are so embarrassing,' Patrick said as he opened the front door, but when he turned around to say goodbye to his mother, he was smiling.

\* \* \*

The retail park was situated on the outskirts of the neighbouring town and was only ten miles away. Even so, with the walk to the bus stop, the wait for the next service, and a village-hopping journey, it had taken them well over an hour from leaving the vicarage to arrive outside the magic shop.

In reality, the magic shop was, in fact, a toy shop. A small independent business owned and run by Geoff, a portly gentleman in his early sixties. A bad case of Dupuytren's contracture had forced Geoff to retire from his magical endeavours, his folded fingers now unable to manage the sleight of hand he had performed professionally for all of his adult life.

However, the foresight to protect his magic career by the insurance of his hands had resulted in a healthy compensation claim, and Geoff had invested his windfall in a local toy shop. Rather than wallow in self-pity, Geoff had maintained a positive outlook and had decided to dedicate a large section of the shop to magic, serious magic.

Geoff was on a waiting list for surgery, but his doctors had been clear with him that he should not expect a return to full function. Accepting his fate, Geoff had channelled his energy into sharing his passion with others and was surprised by how rewarding it now was to enjoy his magic vicariously.

Patrick was a regular visitor, and Geoff had taken him under his wing as a potential protégée. Patrick promised to practice his hardest, and as a reward, Geoff would share tricks and tips from his years of experience. The ultimate promise, though, was to be the backing of Patrick's application to *The Magic Circle* when he reached eighteen years of age, should he still be interested at that point, of course. The application would need to be seconded by someone from within the circle, but Geoff maintained his contacts for just such purposes. He had already introduced Patrick to a few of his friends in preparation.

Geoff spotted Patrick and Craig through the window and waved them both in.

'Hello, boys,' he cheerfully greeted them as they entered the shop.

Patrick had been visiting the store for almost two years, but in recent months he had more often than not been accompanied by Craig. Geoff had noticed it had done wonders for Patrick's confidence, so much so that he had agreed to consider performing at some local events. Patrick would need to build a reputation for himself to assist with his *Magic Circle* application, and the sooner he started, the better was Geoff's advice.

'Morning, Geoff,' they replied in unison. 'Got anything new in?' Patrick added.

'Well, funny you should ask,' Geoff said with mischief in his smile. 'I may just have something you could use in your first show,' he added.

'Oh, I bet!' Patrick rolled his eyes at the suggestion. He knew Geoff was desperate to get him to perform at his first local show. Patrick wanted to but was understandably reticent following the disaster that was his last public display.

'Well, let me show you. I'll lend it to you if you sign up for the Spring Bank Holiday talent show?'

Patrick knew which show Geoff was referring to, and he was very tempted to participate as the show was taking place in the store itself. Patrick knew most of the regular customers, and it seemed a relatively safe environment to attempt another performance. Minus the cloak this time.

'I can't learn a new trick by the twenty-sixth,' he almost gasped. 'That's only like ten days away!'

'You don't have to perform this one, but you can borrow it as a reward. It's a good one,' Geoff winked and beckoned them to follow him to the magic section at the back of the store.

A section of the shop counter in the magic department was covered in black cloth and served as a demonstration area. Geoff placed a small contraption on the fabric that looked a little like a miniature washing mangle before asking Patrick if he had a five-pound note.

'I think I know this one,' Patrick said as he took a note from his pocket and handed it over to Geoff. 'You turn it into a different note. Or a blank piece of paper.'

'Kind of, but there's a little extra with this one,' Geoff grinned.

The boys watched as Geoff flattened out the crumpled note he had been handed and inserted the end into the rollers of the miniature mangle. His twisted fingers restricted most of the magic he could perform, but this one used a prop, and he could just about manage with a bit of patience.

Slowly Geoff wound the handle of the mangle, and the note was drawn almost entirely through to the other side, unchanged. He smiled wider at the puzzled look on the boys' faces.

Geoff then mysteriously waved his hand in the air before appearing to pull a *Sharpie* marker out of his nose, much to the boys' amusement. He handed it to Patrick and asked him to sign the end of the five-pound note that was protruding from the machine. Patrick marked the note with his initials and a small smiley face before placing the lid back on the pen and putting it down on the cloth.

'Are you ready to be amazed?' Geoff questioned.

The boys' leaned in closer as Geoff wound the handle in the reverse direction. The five-pound note gripped by its edge began to move back through the machine, but as it emerged from the other side, it was now a ten-pound note.

Geoff continued to wind the handle until the ten-pound note was fully free from the mangle and fell down onto the cloth to reveal Patrick's initials and smiley face signed across the front of it.

'Wow!' Patrick exclaimed as he lifted the note from the table. He examined it closely, and it was a genuine note with his original marking on it. 'How…' he began to ask but was cut short.

'A magician never tells!' Geoff winked. 'Unless you're on the team for the Bank Holiday show, of course.'

'Okay, I'll do it,' Patrick conceded.

'Marvellous! Well, that isn't actually the end of the trick. You put the note back through, and it turns back into the five-pound note but without a signature. You're supposed to check the serial number at the start to make sure it's the same one at the end, but I forgot to ask you that bit,' Geoff rolled his eyes at his mistake.

'I'll tell you what, you can keep the ten pounds as long as you spend it in the shop today.'

'Thank you,' Patrick smiled. He knew Geoff wouldn't show him the trick's secret in front of Craig. He would have to come back on his own another day, as the magician's code meant everything to Geoff, and Patrick respected that.

The boys routed around the shop for a little while longer before Patrick settled on buying some playing cards. He was trying to learn a few card tricks to add to his growing repertoire of magic. He grabbed a couple of packs of standard bicycle cards along with one marked deck and made his purchase with the gifted ten-pound note and a couple of extra coins.

With a brown paper bag in hand, he and Craig said farewell to Geoff and left the shop. Patrick had promised to pop back in to make arrangements for the show, and he would do this alone so he could be shown the secret of the money mangle. Perhaps tomorrow, after church.

\* \* \*

A glance at the shopping centre clock informed any onlookers that it was almost 12:30 pm. The boys had been wandering around the shops for just over an hour after leaving the magic shop, mostly window shopping and chatting about all sorts of random stuff. The things that seem important when you are a teenage boy.

'Have you heard they are making the *Twilight* book into a movie?' Patrick asked. 'Taylor Lautner is going to be the werewolf.'

'Who?' Craig asked.

'*Sharkboy*!' Patrick explained, clearly expecting Craig to know who he was.

'He's like ten years old!' Craig screwed his face up in disgust.

'He was in *Sharkboy*, but he's a year older than you. And he is fit!' Patrick smiled.

'Oh man, I can't wait to see *The Dark Knight*,' Craig changed the conversation. 'So sad Heath Ledger died, though.'

'Yeah, real bummer. Just like in *Brokeback Mountain*,' Patrick lost his smile.

'He didn't die in *Brokeback Mountain*. It was Jake Gyllenhaal,' Craig corrected.

'No, I meant he was a bummer in it.'

'You idiot!' Craig moaned and punched Patrick softly on the top of his arm. Both boys cracked up laughing at their childish sense of humour.

'Do you fancy something to eat?' Craig suggested. 'I'm starving.'

'*McDonald's?*' the reply, which needed no answer. It was always *McDonald's*.

The food hall was on the top floor of the shopping centre and contained several restaurants and a cinema, as well as the usual atrium of fast-food chains with a shared seating area.

Craig had saved them a table while Patrick had gone to order the food. He returned in only a few minutes carrying a tray stacked with a Big Mac meal and a *McChicken Sandwich* meal, both large but with Diet Coke. With the remainder of the twenty-pound note his mother had given them for lunch, he had bought a large box of chicken nuggets for them to share, and there was still enough left for a couple of *McFlurrys* if required.

They both tucked into their lunch, chatting all the while, with no adults to correct their manners.

'So, you are going to do the show for Geoff?' Craig mumbled around a *McNugget*.

'Yeah, I need to get some experience performing. It

will be okay,' Patrick tried to reassure himself as he wiped a drip of mayonnaise from the side of his chicken sandwich with a chip.

'Can I come and watch?'

Instead of answering, Patrick put the straw of his drink to his mouth and took a long sip. Before his sip was finished, he noticed Craig's eyes widen, his brows rise, and his stare shift over Patrick's shoulder. Then suddenly, Patrick felt a slap across the back of his head and lurched forward, dribbling a little of the cola onto the table.

'Go careful drinking all that,' the voice from behind advised. 'You don't want another accident, pissy pants.'

Patrick could tell instantly through the actions and the sound of the voice that it was Neil Dixon, the school bully and general pain in the arse. Patrick and Craig both got to their feet, Patrick turning to now face his foe as Craig stepped to his side.

Neil was accompanied by two friends whose names did not immediately spring into Patrick's mind. Neil was the tormentor, and they merely bit players in Neil's daily games of name-calling and rib-jabbing.

'Calm down, girls,' Neil mocked. 'I'm not here to disturb your romantic lunch date. Just saying hello to my favourite couple.'

'I didn't know you cared that much. We can have a threesome if you like?' Craig fired back, puffing his chest a little as he spoke, but Patrick curtailed his bravado with an elbow to the ribs.

Neil smiled before quickly leaning forwards to the

right of Patrick and grabbing his brown paper bag from the table.

'What have we got here?' Neil enquired as he peered into the open top of the bag. Then, noticing the playing cards, he held the bag out to Patrick. 'Go on then, show us a trick.'

'Leave us alone,' Craig said as he snatched the bag back.

'It's okay,' Patrick calmly interjected. 'I'll show him a trick.'

With that, Patrick reached into the bag and pulled out a packet of playing cards. All without speaking, he removed the cellophane wrapper, broke the seal, and removed the cards from the box. He pulled out the jokers and the ad cards and discarded them onto the table. He shuffled, ruffle-shuffled, cut, and reshuffled the deck before fanning the cards face down in front of Neil.

'Pick one,' he instructed.

Not usually so compliant, Neil slid a card from the deck and showed it to his two friends. As he did so, Patrick shuffled the cards again and then presented the fanned deck to Neil once more.

'Slide it in wherever you like,' was the next instruction, to which Neil also complied.

Patrick performed another round of theatrical shuffling, a skill he practised regularly, before squaring up the pack. He held the deck between his thumb and forefinger and raised his arm until the bottom card was level with Neil's face.

'Is that your card?' Patrick asked.

'No!' Neil laughed, seeing the Two of Spades before him. 'It was the Queen of Hearts.'

Neil's friends joined in with his sniggering, but the laughter ceased within a fraction of a second, and jaws dropped at what happened next.

Patrick squeezed the deck of cards between his thumb and fingers until it bowed in the middle, and then with a further press, he caused the Two of Spades, closely followed by the remainder of the deck, to flick out and bounce off Neil's face.

Along with Neil's friends, Craig watched on in silence but maintained the wherewithal to prepare himself for Neil's inevitable reaction. But Neil did not react as expected at all. Instead, he stood still, staring directly at Patrick, who did not once break his gaze.

As the moments passed, Neil's face reddened, but this was not the result of a building rage. Instead, his eyes widened, bulging slightly, and tears began to well. He opened his mouth, wide and rounded as if to howl in frustration, but no words came.

Patrick stared blankly at his enemy, giving no reaction whatsoever as Neil's lips began to turn blue and his hands raised up, grabbing at his throat. There was panic and desperation in Neil's expression, and Craig was the only person to react.

Pushing past Patrick, Craig moved around to stand behind Neil and wrapped his arms around his waist. He performed a crude form of the Heimlich manoeuvre, and on the third thrust, Neil coughed up the blockage from his throat. A playing card, folded in quarters with the face showing. It was a saliva-soaked Queen of Hearts.

As Craig released his hold, Neil dropped onto his hands and knees in front of Patrick, gasping air back into his lungs. Patrick used his foot to slide the coughed-up card directly under Neil's face.

'Is that your card?' Patrick asked sarcastically. 'Now fucking leave me alone, you prick!' he added before walking away.

Craig picked up the shopping bag and grabbed a napkin from the table before racing to catch up with his friend.

'Your ear,' he said as he held the napkin out.

Patrick wiped the small trickle of blood from his left ear and discarded the rag in the next bin as they made their way out of the shopping centre and back towards the bus stop.

'What happened there?' Craig eventually asked.

'I'm not sure,' Patrick puzzled. 'But it felt frigging amazing!'

## CHAPTER 3

January 2010

The compère for the evening asked the crowd to put their hands together for Patrick, the young magician who had kept them all entertained with his incredible table magic, and Patrick bashfully took his ovation.

Patrick had been performing on and off all night for the gathered members of the local chamber of commerce, of which Geoff was one. This was their annual Christmas party, always in January to avoid the December trading period, and Geoff had arranged for Patrick to be part of the evening's entertainment.

It had been almost two years since Patrick had been coaxed to perform at the Spring Bank Holiday show in Geoff's shop, but no such coaxing had been required on this occasion. The Spring show had gone amazingly well, and Patrick had caught the bug to be on stage and the centre of attention.

As Patrick took a final bow, he caught sight of Craig standing in the doorway at the back of the hall. *Gosh!* He seemed to get more handsome every time Patrick saw him.

Craig had grown over a foot in the last eighteen months and now stood a head's length taller than Patrick. He had shed his layer of puppy fat and was now almost slightly too slim for his height, his body nowhere near as defined as Patrick's.

His bright ginger hair had rusted a little, and Craig's chin was slightly darkened by stubble, although the remainder of his body was almost blindingly white, with dapples of pink-purple where his rapid growth had left stretch marks on his lower back, hips, and groin.

Patrick adored everything about Craig and even worshipped these imperfections, taking time to kiss them lovingly on the occasions they now managed to carve out alone and naked together.

There had been a short period of anxiety when Craig had announced seven months ago that he was moving to the next town with his mother. Giving up their council house and moving into an apartment block not far from the shopping centre the boys frequented most weekends. Patrick had been terrified it would be the end of their friendship, so much so that he put all his fears and feelings down in the sloppiest of love letters.

He need not have feared. Craig had hugged Patrick

so tightly in the school toilets the next break time after finding the letter in his rucksack during his geography lesson. He reassured Patrick that nothing would change, and their mothers helped to ensure this was true, giving them regular lifts to see each other when the bus timetables did not suffice.

This family support was only required for just over four months as another significant change happened in early October 2009. Craig passed his driving test and became the proud owner of a royal blue 2002 *Peugeot 106*.

This allowed both boys more freedom from their families. They took little road trips to other towns to shop or went on seaside trips filled with ice cream and fish & chips. And often, after dark, they would park up in a secluded layby or down in the lover's field by the river, enjoying kisses and exploring each other's bodies.

Craig had also become Patrick's roadie, and this duty now had him standing at the back of the town hall, waiting for his boyfriend to finish soaking up the adoration.

'I'm sure the rounds of applause get longer every time,' Craig smiled when Patrick eventually came over to his side.

High on the adrenalin from the show, Patrick leaned in and whispered, 'I want you to fuck me next weekend. I think I'm ready.'

Before Craig could respond, he was led by the hand into the car park. Still dazed, he unlocked the car and watched as Patrick placed his rucksack of props into the boot. He slammed it shut and then jumped into the passenger seat to escape the January evening drizzle that had begun to fall. Craig mirrored his movements on the driver's side, fastened his seatbelt, and placed the key in the ignition.

'What did you say?' he finally found the words, but he had heard clearly enough. 'I thought you wanted to wait until your sixteenth birthday?' he added.

'It's only three weeks away, but my parents are away next weekend at a wedding. I'm not going, and they have said you can stay over,' Patrick explained. 'And I really want to. We've been together for nearly two years. The stuff we do is great, but I'm ready to go further. I love you.'

'Oh, man! I love you too!' Craig gushed. 'I've just popped the hardest boner!' Craig dropped his eyes to the protrusion in his jeans, and Patrick's gaze followed.

'Lover's field on the way home?' Patrick suggested. 'I can sort that right out for you,' he added, making a bulge in his cheek with his tongue in a simulation of oral sex.

Craig moaned in anticipation before starting the engine and excitedly pulling away, spinning the car's wheels on the wet tarmac in his eagerness.

\* \* \*

It seemed to have been the longest of weeks, but Patrick had finally finished his last lesson. He escaped the classroom at pace and was almost back home to get changed and wait for Craig to pick him up when he finished college.

As Patrick neared his home, a slight panic set in when he noticed his parents' car still parked on the roadside. He ran the last fifty yards to the front door and clumsily fumbled his key into the lock. As he pushed the door open, he was breathless but reassured to see two small weekend cases sitting at the bottom of the stairs. The plan was still intact.

'Hello, love,' His mother's voice called from upstairs. 'We're running a bit late. How was your day?'

Kate appeared at the top of the stairs, struggling to attach the back to an earring as she descended.

'Have you seen my brown belt?' her husband called from the bedroom.

'Third drawer down,' she replied without breaking her stride.

Patrick had moved into the kitchen and was guzzling down his second pint of water when his mother walked in and continued the conversation she had been repeating all week.

'Now, are you sure you will be okay until Sunday?'

'Yes, Mother,' Patrick rolled his eyes as he wiped his mouth on his sleeve.

'You're not too old for a clip around the ear, you cheeky monkey,' she smiled as she swiped the air with the palm of her hand.

'We will be fine,' he reassured her. 'Craig is picking me up in an hour, and we are going to the early viewing at the cinema. We'll probably bring back a pizza afterwards, and then we plan to stay in for the weekend and watch movies and stuff.'

'Okay. There is money in the bureau if you need anything, and we are only at the end of the phone if you have any problems.'

Patrick raised his eyebrows to let his mother know he knew all this already, and then he excused himself to go upstairs and get changed. He was still upstairs an hour later when he heard his mother opening the door to Craig. Patrick could hear their muffled conversation as he finished brushing his teeth.

'He's still getting ready,' Kate explained. 'Lord knows what he is doing. He's been at it for ages. It smells like a perfume shop up there,' she finished as Patrick wafted down the stairs along with an overpowering scent of *Joop!*

The boys greeted each other with a nod, and Patrick squeezed a pair of trainers onto his feet without undoing the laces.

'Are you heading off now?' his mother asked.

'Yeah, booked the early viewing,' Patrick replied.

'Okay, have fun then. We will be gone when you get back. The spare room is made up for Craig.'

Patrick hugged his mother to reassure her that everything would be okay. 'See you Sunday lunchtime,' were his last words as they left the house, but the final thought that crossed his mind was to remember to ruffle the sheets in the spare room, as Craig certainly wouldn't be sleeping in there.

\* \* \*

Patrick had booked tickets for the new out-of-town multiplex rather than the smaller theatre in the shopping centre they usually visited, and the drive took less than twenty minutes, even with a stop for petrol.

The open-air car park was half empty, and Craig managed to park close to the foyer entrance. They collected their tickets from the automated kiosk before heading to the food counter. A few minutes later, they were taking their seats in the centre of the back row of the near-empty Screen 7, one of the smaller screens that movies were moved to as they came to the end of their run.

'Are you sure you don't want something to eat?' Craig asked. 'You can share this,' he added, holding up a footlong hotdog plastered in onions, ketchup, and mustard.

'I'm okay. I just want a drink,' Patrick declined. 'I douched before we came out. I don't want to eat,' he added nonchalantly.

Craig had just taken a bite of his hotdog and almost choked it down. He had to cough and take a sip of his own drink before he could reply.

'I didn't know you had a douche bulb,' he said, sounding positively impressed.

'I haven't. I used an *Evian* water bottle, the big one with the squirty nozzle on the end.'

'Very resourceful,' Craig commented before they

both burst out laughing.

'I didn't have a clue what I was doing, really,' Patrick confessed. 'I had to google it, but I think I managed okay. I want everything to be perfect,' he blushed a little, and Craig could see it even in the dim movie theatre light.

'You are perfect, Patrick. I bought condoms when we stopped for petrol,' Craig confessed his own preparation for the event. 'This is really happening, isn't it?' he added, and Patrick confirmed with a nod.

The trailers started, and they watched them in silence, both still processing the conversation they had just had, excited and nervous at how the evening would unfold. Then, as the theatre lights dimmed further and the curtains opened a little wider for the main feature, Patrick moved his leg so their knees touched and placed his hand on Craig's thigh. Once Craig had finished eating, he put his own hand over the top of Patrick's, and they interlinked their fingers.

*The Book of Eli* was a film they had both been keen to see, but their minds were elsewhere, and they were both pleased when the end credits began to roll an hour and fifty-eight minutes later. As the lights rose, Craig released Patrick's hand, and they left the cinema, depositing their rubbish on the way back through the foyer, and exited into the early evening darkness.

The journey back to the vicarage was a little awkward, but they made small talk about the film until Craig parked up directly outside the front door.

Patrick turned his key and let them into the hallway

and was relieved to see his parents' travel bags had gone. They both kicked off their shoes, and Patrick went into the kitchen, where the dog was left when the house was empty, while Craig excused himself to use the downstairs toilet.

As Craig returned, Barnaby wandered back in from the garden and was instructed to get back onto his bed. Patrick then led Craig by the hand through to the lounge, shutting the dog back in the kitchen so he didn't bother them.

When they reached the sizeable four-seater sofa towards the back of the room, they released their hands, and Patrick asked Craig to sit down. He then straddled Craig's knees, sitting face-to-face on his lap and began to kiss him. They had kissed many times before, but this time it felt different.

They held the back of each other's heads, desperate for their mouths not to be separated for even a second as their tongues duelled to taste more of each other.

When Patrick did pull back briefly to take a short breath, Craig's hands swiftly dropped and found their way under the rear hem of his jumper. Craig lifted the jumper over Patrick's head in one movement and pulled it free from his raised arms. He repeated the manoeuvre with the t-shirt below and pulled Patrick's naked torso back towards him so they could continue kissing.

Minutes later, Patrick repeated this partial undressing on his friend, but before Craig lowered his arms, Patrick leaned forwards and kissed his armpit. The wispy ginger hairs were moist with sweat, and the scent was acrid with pheromones.

Patrick had discovered early in their explorations that armpits and body hair were a turn-on for him. As he kissed his way from hairy armpit to smooth nipple and then downwards, pressing his lips to Craig's body, he could feel his own penis beginning to bulge in his underwear, still bent downwards but desperate to escape the confines of his clothes.

When his lips arrived at Craig's navel, Patrick paused briefly to give the neat little outie its own oral caress before continuing to kiss his way down yet more wispy ginger hairs that led an enticing path, disappearing into the top of Craig's jeans.

The course of the kissing had caused Patrick to move backwards from his seat on Craig's lap, and he now knelt on the floor between his lover's parted legs. However, the denim would not be the end of this trail, and Patrick quickly undid the belt buckle, popper, and zip, before removing Craig's jeans completely.

Craig wore white *Calvin Klein* briefs, and they hid nothing. His penis was erect and angled upwards and to the right at forty-five degrees along the crease of his groin. The elastic around the leg and the waistband held it firmly in place as Patrick kissed along its entire length until his lips could taste the sweet juice that had leaked from the tip, making a patch of the underwear almost translucent.

The foreplay was over, and Patrick wanted Craig inside him. He pulled the underwear off and lifted Craig's penis away from his body. Craig was uncircumcised, and his glans were half exposed. Patrick pulled the foreskin back further until it fully retracted, and then he placed his lips around the end and pushed downwards, taking as much of Craig's length into his mouth as he could. Craig moaned with pleasure as a slight shudder ran through his body.

Continuing to work slowly up and down Craig's shaft with only his mouth, Patrick used both hands to undo his own trousers and remove them along with his underwear. Moments later, Craig put his hands on each side of Patrick's head and pulled up slightly, indicating he wanted him to stand.

As Patrick rose before him, Craig could see he was rock hard and pointing vertically in youthful exuberance. Craig had begun to trim his pubic hair, not least because it was a ginger frizz, but Patrick had not yet found the need. His balls were still smooth, and he wore just a neat dark patch of hair above the base of the shaft.

Craig slid forwards on the sofa and down onto his knees in front of Patrick. He placed his lips around his friend and took all of him into his mouth. Then, he held his hands on Patrick's buttocks and pulled him in even deeper until his nose pressed into his dark pubic hair, and he could feel Patrick's balls on his chin.

Patrick let out a squeal at the intense pleasure being so deep inside his friend's mouth gave him, and Craig finally released his grip to catch a breath before he gagged. He continued with a gentler blowjob and turned his attention to Patrick's arse.

With a hand still on each buttock, he began to massage them. First, he pulled the cheeks apart slightly and then worked his fingers inwards, a little closer to Patrick's hole with each repetition, before finally hitting the sweet spot.

Patrick's hole was smooth and felt pleasantly moist. It seemed to pulse beneath Craig's fingers, and as he used the tips of each hand to part it slightly, he was surprised at how accommodating it was at first to one and then two fingers.

This was new territory for both of them. They were now putting into practice things they had only ever seen on the internet.

Patrick's knees bent a little at the pleasure he was receiving simultaneously on both sides of his body. Then, concerned his friend's legs may buckle, Craig ceased his fingering and guided him around to sit down on the sofa. As Patrick fell back into the seat, his cock withdrew from Craig's mouth with a comical pop and slapped back vertically against his belly.

'Fuck! This is so hot,' Patrick exclaimed.

'It's about to get a lot hotter, baby,' Craig promised.

Craig pulled Patrick's hips forward until his bottom hung slightly over the front of the sofa, and his body was almost lying on the seat. He then raised Patrick's legs and pushed them back until his knees were almost by his ears. Patrick instinctively took hold of his own calves and held them in this position. He looked down between his legs and saw Craig's eyes staring back at him from just above his scrotum as his tongue went to work rimming his hole.

Craig maintained his stare as he worked his tongue deeper and deeper inside, noting which movements caused Patrick's eyes to roll with pleasure before repeating them.

'Oh, my god! I want you inside me so bad,' Patrick pleaded.

Craig sat back on his haunches and rooted around on the floor for his jeans so he could grab the condoms from his pocket.

'You don't need a condom,' Patrick told him. 'We're both virgins, it's safe, and I just want to feel you.'

Craig was so aroused that he was happy to accept Patrick's logic and avoid further delay in their coupling. He lifted himself onto his knees and shuffled closer to Patrick, who remained prone with his legs in the air.

With one hand, Craig rubbed the precum that had gathered at the tip of his penis over his glans to give some lubrication and then pushed his head against Patrick's hole. He leaned back slightly, giving himself a full view as it slowly slipped inside.

Craig proceeded millimetre by millimetre, checking Patrick's face for any contortions of pain, conscious this was his first time, but Patrick appeared to be enjoying every moment. Craig paused when he was halfway in, pulled back slightly, and then pushed forwards with more force.

Patrick was in ecstasy. He had been a little nervous that this would be a painful experience, assuming the pleasure of anal sex was skewed towards the giver, but he had been wrong. He had read something online about a concentration of nerve endings around the prostate that gave men pleasure, the male G-spot apparently, and he now understood.

He had watched Craig entering him so gently, both of them letting out little groans of pleasure at these new sensations. Craig then paused briefly before pushing his whole length deep inside, and Patrick let out a moan as his penis convulsed and a small amount of semen oozed from the end.

It wasn't a full ejaculation but an intense precursor he had never experienced. Craig also noticed Patrick dribble onto his stomach, so he reached forward, grabbed his friend's penis, and began to masturbate him as they now fucked harder and faster.

'Oh baby, you're so tight. This feels amazing. I don't know how long I can last,' Craig moaned as Patrick closed his eyes and focused on his other senses.

Suddenly everything changed.

Patrick felt Craig's hand pull away from his shaft, and then his penis withdrew without thrusting back forwards. And there was shouting. *Why was there shouting?*

He opened his eyes to see Craig being pulled backwards on his haunches and falling to the floor. Craig pulled his legs to his chest and put his hand up to protect his head as Patrick's father began to rain blows down upon him.

The shouting was a combination of Patrick's

mother's tearful wails from the far end of the room as she stood in the doorway with her hands to her face and the obscenities his father was screaming at Craig in time with every blow.

'You abomination. You fucking disgusting boy. You sodomite. You bastard rapist.' A new variation with every punch to Craig's torso.

Patrick leapt up from the sofa, screaming for his father to stop. He grabbed his shoulder, and Nigel spun around to face his son.

'I will deal with you later…' he spat in rage, but Patrick was already lurching forwards. He clasped his hand around his father's throat, cutting short his words, and then with unnatural strength, he forced his father backwards across the room until his back was against the wall. Then, with further strength still, Patrick lifted his father up onto tiptoes.

'Keep your fucking hands off of my boyfriend!' he said almost calmly as a small trickle of blood ran down his left earlobe.

Kate had lifted a vase from the sideboard and hurled it across the room, intending to hit her son, but instead, it smashed against the wall to the side of her husband.

'Get out of my house. Both of you. Get out of my house now,' she screamed at the boys.

Craig scurried across the floor, gathering their clothes before scampering back into the hallway. Patrick released his father from the chokehold and followed Craig as his mother ran to her husband's side to comfort him.

Expecting to be pursued at any moment, the boys quickly dressed and hurried out of the building and into Craig's car. They were a couple of miles down the road before Craig spoke first.

'I am so sorry. What are we going to do?' he asked and then answered his own question. 'You'll have to stay at mine. We'll have to tell my mum what happened.'

Patrick turned to Craig and smiled. His eyes were still glazed over a little in the trance-like state he seemed to get into in times of stress.

'Pull the car over somewhere. I really need to cum!'

\* \* \*

It was the day of Patrick's sixteenth birthday, and he had not yet seen his parents following the events of almost two weeks ago when the boys had come back to the flat, and Craig had tearfully confessed to his mother what had happened at the vicarage.

Lisa had been disappointed but had comforted them both and agreed Patrick could stay with them while things settled down. Not in Craig's room, though. She was clear about that.

Initially, Kate refused to speak to Lisa when she reached out the following day, accusing her of being complicit in hiding their sons' relationship. However, when Lisa turned up in the charity shop on Monday morning and threatened to have the conversation publicly, Kate agreed to go with her for a coffee.

Lisa assured her she had no idea the boys had been planning anything, as she was also unaware they were in a relationship. Had she ever questioned Craig's sexuality? The thought may have crossed her mind, but she didn't think Craig had acted on it to date, and he didn't seem unhappy or distressed. If he were to be gay, he would tell her in his own time, and it was no big deal as long as he was happy.

Kate could not agree. Patrick was not gay. He was only fifteen, and her son was nearly eighteen, and he must have forced him to do those things. She was glad she had forgotten her wedding fascinator last Friday, coming back to pick it up and catching them before it went on even further behind their backs.

'Your son is sixteen next week, Kate. Craig is only seventeen and a half. That's eighteen months apart, not three years. So don't exaggerate for your own means,' Lisa had said.

'Well, let's see what the police think about him sleeping with a minor, shall we?' Kate threatened.

'While we are at it, shall we see what the local community think about the homophobic Christians who have thrown their fifteen-year-old son out onto the street, shall we?' Lisa sarcastically snapped back.

Kate was horrified at the thought, and her face gave her away. Her eyes dropped, and her tone changed completely.

'Nigel won't have a gay son,' she practically sobbed.

'He won't have him back in the house.'

'Well, you need to talk to Nigel, Kate. This is not the end of the world. And you need to talk to Patrick too,' she spoke softly but was firm. 'It's his sixteenth birthday in a week, he won't have to come back home then if he doesn't want to, and I am sure you don't want to lose him. He's such a lovely boy, Kate. Gay or straight, he is the same boy.'

With the initial tension of the conversation diffused Kate and Lisa were able to talk more calmly. Kate agreed to message Patrick, and she would also speak to Nigel about him coming back home. They finished their coffee, and Kate allowed Lisa to pop back to the vicarage with her to collect a few changes of clothes to take back for Patrick.

Their mothers' coffee morning had been eight days ago, and as promised, Kate had messaged Patrick several times since. First, there was an initial apology for screaming and throwing him out of the house. Then, a change of tone to try and make him understand how shocked they were to walk in and catch them. Next, a heated exchange occurred when Kate implied Craig was to blame entirely. Eventually, she suggested that she and Patrick's father come over on his birthday, and hopefully, he would like to return home with them.

Patrick had agreed, and he really did want to go back home. As great as spending all this time with Craig was, he had been sleeping on the sofa and missed his own bed and belongings. For sure, it was going to be awkward as hell. Being caught having sex was embarrassing enough, let alone it had been with a boy, so now the sexuality conversation would also need to be navigated.

The meeting had been arranged for after school, and Patrick had changed out of his uniform and was waiting for his parents to arrive. Craig had come home from college early for support and was with Patrick on the balcony of the flat, looking down over the small car park waiting for the arrival of Nigel's burgundy Volvo estate.

Patrick's phone vibrated with a text from his mother to say they were nearly there just as they saw the car come around a corner in the distance. Craig wished him good luck with a kiss on the cheek, and Patrick headed off to meet them downstairs.

Nigel parked in a space on the edge of the small playing green that served the blocks of apartments surrounding it on three sides. They were modern five-story affairs, with Lisa's apartment on the fourth floor. She had joined Craig on the balcony and watched as Kate stepped from the vehicle just as Patrick exited the building. They walked towards each other and met halfway down the path.

'Happy birthday,' Kate opened, and Patrick burst into tears. His mother wrapped her arms around him, and they held each other in silence until his sobs had passed.

'Why's dad still in the car?' Patrick asked as he regained composure.

They both turned in the car's direction to see Nigel sitting behind the wheel, staring directly at them but failing to react to Patrick's wave.

'Let's get you home. I've bought steak for tea, and you can open your presents,' Kate put her arm on Patrick's shoulder and moved to walk back to the car.

'What about Dad? Is he okay?' Patrick wasn't ready to move yet.

'I have spoken to him. We know it's not your fault,' Kate explained. 'Dad knows someone at the church you can speak to and get you back on track. Don't worry, we won't involve the police,' she attempted to reassure him.

'You're fucking joking!' Patrick shrugged his shoulder away from his mother's grip. 'Dad's going to pray away the gay. Is that your plan?'

On the balcony, Lisa and Craig became aware the mood had changed, and Patrick's raised voice drew further attention from the parents and children in the playpark in front of where Nigel still sat calmly in his car.

'What's that on your ear? You're bleeding,' Kate said, bizarrely distracted from Patrick's reaction, but another voice called out from the crowd before their conversation could continue.

'Oh, my God! Look up there. There's a man on the roof. I think he's going to jump,' a lady shouted, pointing to the rooftop of the block of flats opposite Lisa's.

Everyone within earshot turned their gaze to where the lady was pointing, and there was, indeed, a man teetering on the edge of the rooftop. He, in turn, was pointing directly at the balcony where Lisa and Craig were standing, mouthing words the crowd below were unable to hear.

In shared confusion, Patrick and his mother quickly looked towards the car. The driver's seat was empty. Nigel was now inexplicably on the roof. They turned back their gaze just as Nigel crossed himself in one final religious act before falling forwards.

The crowds gasped as they watched the man fall to the ground, hitting the concrete below with a gut-wrenching noise before bouncing back up slightly and landing in an unnaturally broken position, with a pool of blood gathering around his fractured skull.

Patrick had witnessed the fall and found himself unable to stop staring at his father's lifeless body as members of the public rushed over to see if anything could be done. Even his mother's screams did not distract him, and he only turned away when Craig arrived at his side a few moments later.

Lisa attempted to comfort Kate, but her screams continued until they were joined by wailing sirens, and a paramedic was required to administer a sedative to calm her.

# CHAPTER 4

April 2019

*Oh boy!* The nerves were really kicking in now, for sure. Not the schoolboy nerves of eleven years ago on that awful day Patrick still couldn't erase from his memory, but good nerves, excited nerves. This was Patrick's big opportunity to get noticed, and he was ready for it.

*Future Stars* was the biggest talent show on television for variety acts, and Patrick had been desperate to audition. He had considered it the previous year, but Craig had talked him out of it, concerned it would change the life they had built together. And they did have a good life. Childhood sweethearts of eleven years now and married for the last two. But Patrick needed to perform, to be seen, and he had worn Craig down into submission with assurances that it would all be okay.

Patrick had never moved back home with his mother following the death of his father. Even if he had wanted to, it would not have been possible. Furthermore, Kate was never released from psychiatric care following the incident. She had suffered a complete breakdown, and Patrick could not visit without sending her into a psychotic frenzy.

Lisa had stepped up and taken Patrick in permanently. After only a week, she had even allowed him and Craig to start sharing a bed after being moved by their relationship when accidentally spying on them.

She had been going to Craig's room to tell them it was bedtime. Craig's door was ajar, and curiosity made her pause and peer through the opening. They were both on the bed, fully clothed, and Craig was cradling Patrick in his arms, and she watched as he cried himself to sleep.

The boys lived with Lisa for over three years before another tragic event occurred in Patrick's life. Geoff passed away.

Patrick was distraught. Geoff had been like a father to him. He was better than his own father, for sure. They would spend hours together practising magic tricks with Patrick as the performer and Geoff as the teacher and observer, picking him up on every detail until his performances were perfect.

After leaving school, Patrick enrolled at a performing arts college to further hone his skills and boost his stage confidence. Geoff had helped him at every stage, putting together his magic shows and encouraging him to get out on the circuit and perform at local events.

Patrick graduated from his course with honours and began working full-time as a performing magician at corporate events, hotels, and holiday camps. He would travel all over to wherever he could find work.

Now able to drive, he would take Craig's car during the week while Craig worked his warehouse job, and in the evenings and at weekends, Craig would join him for company, morale support, and general roadie duties.

Patrick was nineteen, and they had been working this routine for six months, trying to save up a deposit so they could move into their own flat together when the news of Geoff's death came through.

Geoff had been found unresponsive on the floor of his magic shop by the shopping centre security guard early on a Thursday morning. He was rushed to the hospital but pronounced dead on arrival. A week later, the cause of death was confirmed as a massive brain haemorrhage.

The funeral was a small and sombre affair. Geoff had no family, and there was only a small gathering of close friends and a representative from *The Magic Circle*. Patrick thanked each guest for attending as they left and was moved to tears when the man from *The Magic Circle* handed him a letter and explained its contents.

Geoff had submitted his recommendation that Patrick be considered for membership. This had been seconded, and he was now invited to become a fully-fledged member of *The Magic Circle*.

Even from beyond the grave, Geoff was looking out for his protégé, and within a week, Patrick would be dumbfounded once more when he was invited to the reading of Geoff's will. Everything he owned was left to Patrick. This included a generous sum of money, a small two-bedroom house, and the magic business.

Patrick was overwhelmed by the loss of his friend and the unexpected benevolence of his bequeathment. He wasn't sure how he would cope, but Craig supported him and took the lead with the business affairs. He guided Patrick through everything, and within a month, they had moved into their new home.

They also decided to continue trading Geoff's magic shop, so Craig resigned from his warehouse position and started working in the store. Patrick would focus on his performances, and Craig would take over responsibility for his bookings. By all accounts, he became Patrick's manager.

Following the tragedy of Geoff's passing, a whole new life opened up for them. Craig seemed to have an excellent head for business, and their finances were going from strength to strength. Over the coming years, they would be able to afford new cars, and they would sell Geoff's old house and purchase a large, detached property back in Witford Common.

They had pondered the move back to Witford, unsure it was wise given the memories, but it was by far the nicest of the local towns, and their decision worked out just fine.

They were welcomed back into the community with open arms, and aside from the strange feeling Patrick experienced when walking past the vicarage, all was well. More than well, in fact, as on the eighth anniversary of their first meeting at school, a date they celebrated every year, Craig had proposed.

Life was almost perfect. They were surprisingly wealthy, they were sickeningly in love and daily in lust, they had the most beautiful of weddings in the spring of 2017, and they had managed to move on from the traumas of their early relationship without the need for therapy. Life was almost perfect, but not quite.

Patrick had a constant niggle, an itch he needed to scratch. He was confident a psychologist could map the cause back to his disastrous school days and lack of acceptance from his parents, but the result was that he needed to perform. And not to a conference room full of employees at some corporate dinner. He wanted to perform for a real audience. He craved fame.

Craig had initially attempted to dissuade him, unsure they needed to put themselves into the limelight and uncertain how Patrick might take any setbacks. But Patrick was nothing if not persistent, and Craig eventually surrendered, although knowing Craig, he had also recognised an opportunity to be taken.

\* \* \*

Patrick was startled from his thoughts as a hand touched his shoulder from behind. He spun on his heels to see Kevin, the stagehand from *Future Stars*, who had been guiding him and Craig through the day.

'Boo!' Kevin joked when he saw the startled expression on Patrick's face.

'I thought your job was to make me feel more relaxed?' Patrick retorted, but there was humour in his tone. Kevin had been lovely all day. A cute twenty-something blonde wearing skinny jeans and a *Kylie Minogue, Kiss Me Once* tour t-shirt.

'Okay, I've taken Craig to his seat in the audience, and the judges are just on their way back to the auditorium. Stephen will do his piece to the camera, and then you are on. Are you ready?' Kevin asked in his soft, camp, Welsh accent.

'Good to go!' Patrick smiled.

Redlights came on backstage, and silence descended. Patrick took deep breaths and listened as the host introduced the three judges back to the auditorium to rapturous applause. The judges walked in turn to their seats on the raised platform in front of the stage, and the audience quietened.

Someone shouted a ten-second countdown to recording, with the 3... 2... 1... signalled with fingers rather than aloud, and then the host, Stephen, sprang back into life with what would be his link back from the adverts when this was later televised.

Finally, Patrick heard the words '*...and without further ado, please welcome to the stage our next performer.*' He took one final deep breath, walked out to the centre of the stage, and stood on the mark he had been shown earlier in rehearsal.

'Hello there, and what's your name?' the deep, well-spoken voice of Laurence Stokes, the head judge on the panel, asked.

'Hi, I'm Patrick Morgan, but today I will be performing as Enigma. That's the stage name for my magic act.' Patrick nervously replied.

Laurence was rolling his eyes and exhaling in despair almost before Patrick had finished speaking.

'Give the poor guy a chance,' Michelle Martinez interjected on seeing Laurence's reaction. 'I know you don't like magic, but not everyone likes ballet either, and you did okay for yourself,' she added to laughter from the crowd.

Patrick grinned and waited awkwardly under the spotlight during the judge's minor spat before the third of them asked another question.

'How old would you be, Enigma? And what made you decide to audition for us today?'

Kieran Doyle was the older of the three judges, a softly spoken, grey-haired Irish comedian who had found fame on mainstream television twenty years ago. He was a regular on quiz panels and starring in a long-running sitcom, but his enduring appeal, which seemed to have captured the attention of a whole new generation, was the cutting filth of his almost permanent live tour.

'I'm twenty-five. I've been performing magic since I was a young boy, and I really want to bring it to a bigger audience,' Patrick recanted his practised response.

'Okay, well, good luck. Let's see what you've got for us, Enigma!' Kieron was polite but wasn't hopeful, and to soft applause, Enigma began his act.

The trick to be performed was a version of classic coin magic where four coins were placed in the corners of a table and then vanished and reappeared in an alternate corner until all four coins were together. Enigma announced this to the crowd and requested that Laurence join him on stage.

'We may as well have the sceptic up here,' Enigma joked, and the crowd responded with a chuckle.

Laurence made his way onto the stage and joined Enigma beside a small black table where he was now seated. Someone ran from the wings with a second chair, and Laurence took a seat to observe. Enigma then began to explain what was going to happen to the audience, but more specifically to his witness, who would need to be eagle-eyed to try and catch him out. Another chuckle from the crowd. Nervous Patrick was gone, and Enigma was now in control.

The first element of the act was for Enigma to place a large silver coin towards each corner of the black-clothed table. He then put his right hand, palm down, above the coin towards the back right of the table and moved it slightly from side to side before lifting it up again to reveal that the coin was gone. He then theatrically displayed that his hand was empty and received a small ripple of applause from the audience before he continued.

This time he placed his empty hand above the coin to the front right-hand side of the table, wiggled it again, and when he removed it, the first coin reappeared, so there were now two coins together on the cloth. He then quickly repeated this with each of the coins on the left until all four were gathered together in the corner nearest to Laurence. Louder applause was forthcoming.

'How was that?' Enigma asked Laurence. 'Did you see anything suspicious?'

'I mean, you're good, but we've kind of seen it all before,' Laurence shrugged his shoulders as he spoke as if to excuse his honesty.

'Ouch!' Enigma feigned offence, and the audience sympathetically inhaled in unison. 'No, he's right. It's coin magic 101,' he admitted and then went on to demonstrate one of the ways magicians achieved the effect.

Firstly, he lifted the Servante from his lap area behind the table and tipped three coins from it. He then demonstrated how easy it was to slide the coins backwards on the cloth and discard them into the small black bag hidden behind the table.

Next, he focused on the four coins together and explained they had been there all along, three of them initially covered by small flaps of dark cloth that he flipped back and forth to show how invisible it was against the black background. There were a few unimpressed groans from the crowd but further applause at his reveal.

'Nobody likes a cheat,' Enigma suggested. 'Let's try again but make it a bit harder.'

Enigma gathered the coins and discarded the Servante onto the stage floor before removing the black cloth to reveal a glass table below. He again placed one coin towards each corner of the table, handing the three spare coins to Laurence for safekeeping.

'We love to keep stuff up our sleeves too,' Enigma confessed. 'So why don't we lose the sleeves?' With that, he stood up behind the table and unbuttoned and removed his shirt.

Patrick had always been naturally defined, but these days he worked out. His body was toned and muscular, and his low-rise jeans emphasised the v-line below his abs that was disappearing into the waistband of his *Addicted* briefs. His chest was smooth and naturally tanned and sported a tattoo of a magician's top hat, with two protruding bunny ears nestled between pert pectorals.

The audience hooted and wolf-whistled at the striptease, and whereas Patrick would have been embarrassed, Enigma soaked it in. He remained standing until the frenzy abated and then sat down to repeat his coin routine.

'Okay, you can see through the table, and there is nothing up my sleeves,' he reiterated before repeating the trick in its entirety. The same end result but clearly a different, more complex technique, rewarded with rapturous applause.

'Better,' Laurence admitted.

'Better?' Enigma questioned. 'You're a hard man to please,' he joked and, for the first time, looked to the crowd and spotted Craig.

'Shall we take it one stage further?' Enigma addressed the crowd, but his eyes remained locked on Craig. The audience clearly wanted more, and when Craig gave his nod of approval, Enigma continued.

'Take off your trousers,' a voice shouted from the crowd, and the place erupted with more wolf-whistling and laughter.

'Maybe if I get to the final,' Enigma teased. 'But for now, how about we do it one more time, with no hands?'

A hush fell across the crowd, and what happened next would change everything.

Enigma sat upright in his chair and invited Laurence to inspect the coins and the tabletop. He then asked him to place a coin towards each corner as previously. Laurence followed the instructions and confirmed he was happy everything was in order.

'Okay,' Enigma said, taking deep breaths for effect. 'This is going to blow your mind.'

Slowly Enigma placed his hand above the first coin, but this time it was higher in the air leaving the coin in full view of what must have been at least eight thousand prying eyes. He counted down from three, and on zero, he snapped his fingers, and the coin instantly vanished and reappeared at the front of the table.

To gasps from the crowd, Enigma quickly repeated the finger snap for the other two coins, performing the same routine as previously, but this time with the coins in full view. The crowd went berserk on completion of the trick, and Laurence was clearly heard to say, *'What the fuck?'* before rising from his chair and starting the standing ovation Enigma had been craving so badly.

For the next few minutes, the judges gave their stunned appraisals of Enigma's performance before unanimously voting him through to the next round. The adrenaline rush still had him in a slight daze, and the judge's words seemed almost muffled, but he nodded graciously and then ran off stage, picking up his shirt on the way.

'Wow! That was fantastic!' Kevin congratulated him in the wings. 'I think you'll be a real contender in this series. The team want to do some background filming with you before the episode goes to air. I assume that's all okay with you?'

'Oh, for sure, that would be great,' Patrick smiled.

\* \* \*

It had been twelve weeks since Patrick's first audition on *Future Stars,* and he had already been back to film his second performance, but today was the day the first episode was airing on television.

The excitement had been building for a few weeks now as a clip of Patrick and, more specifically, the audience reaction to his finale had been included in the teaser trailers being aired in anticipation of the start of the new series. Even Craig had warmed to the idea of late, and they had decided to host a small party for close friends on the evening of the showing.

They had set up a large flat-screen television in the magic shop for the event, and guests had begun to arrive for pre-show drinks and canapés. Patrick had honoured the production company's request and maintained his silence as to the result of his audition, but he was sure his guests could tell the outcome would be positive from the grin on his face as they all air-kissed and sipped champagne.

The gathered crowd was predominantly made up of Patrick's magic acquaintances, a scattering of regular shop customers, and Craig's mother. A tiny dusting of gay friends made up the remainder, and as Patrick heard another champagne flute breaking in the background, he was pleased they had chosen to host the evening in the shop rather than at their home.

*Future Stars* had been playing in the background with the sound muted while the guests mingled, with Patrick keeping an eye on the time. He had been helpfully informed he was the final performer, featuring just after the last advert break.

Patrick tapped the rim of his champagne flute with the TV remote control to draw attention before turning up the volume just as an advert for *Tena Lady* came on, and he made poorly timed eye contact with Craig's mother. Lisa scowled, but their relationship was strong, and there was humour behind the frown.

The crowd's chatter hushed as the *Future Stars*

theme music sounded, and a voiceover began to describe how it had been a slow day at the auditions, and the judges were hoping the final act would be worth the wait.

Patrick smiled to himself, aware this was theatrical fiction for dramatic effect. His audition had been far from the end of the day, and the editorial team were taking some poetic license with the facts.

He watched himself walk out onto the stage before Laurence Stokes asked him his name, and he replied, *'Hi, I'm Patrick Morgan, but today I will be performing as Enigma. That's the stage name for my magic act.'*

Rather than cut back to the eye roll Laurence had given on the day, which was castigated by Michelle Martinez, the program cut to a background film the postproduction team had pulled together.

There was a cheer from the room as the shopfront came on screen, and we were introduced to Patrick and his partner Craig.

'Partner, not Husband?' Craig tutted at Patrick as he joined him to watch the rest of the show play out.

The short film consisted of an acted-out transaction at the shop counter, Patrick performing some dextrous finger work with some cards and coins, and a voiceover referencing a difficult childhood, including bullying and his father's death, when Patrick was only sixteen. It went on to discuss the development of his interest in magic by Geoff, a father figure and mentor, who had also now passed, leaving him the magic shop in his will.

Patrick had been reluctant to include this information as he did not want to be seen as the sympathy act they always seemed to roll out at the end of each show, trading on some sob story or another, but apparently, it was great television. He squeezed Craig's hand for support just as the show cut back to Patrick's trick, and everyone watched on in silence.

When it was over, Laurence could be heard to say, *'What the…bleep'*, his expletive removed for sensitive ears as they were still before the watershed. The television audience was shown in rapturous applause with a full standing ovation, and the reaction in the room was equally joyous.

They all watched the judges' comments and the confirmation that he was voted through to the next round, and then Patrick muted the sound once more before circling the room, accepting further praise from his guests over yet more champagne.

Everyone was amazed by his performance, but Patrick refused to share the secrets of his trickery, even with his closest *Magic Circle* friends. The guests drifted away over the next couple of hours until only Patrick, Craig, and Lisa remained. The shopping centre closed at 11:00 pm on a Saturday, and they were on the road a little after this. Lisa hadn't been drinking, as she had offered to drop the boys back at their house.

Lisa was offered a coffee before heading home but declined, choosing not to get out of the car. Instead, she would leave them to their celebrations. They waved her away from the kerbside before falling through their doorway, cracking open another bottle of champagne they would drink in bed, and then they fell asleep in each other arms following wild, adrenaline-fuelled sex.

*What a night!*

# CHAPTER 5

July 2019

'Good morning. Welcome back to *The Sunday Review*. I'm Anna Keegan, and alongside me today is Ian Atkinson,' Anna welcomed the viewers back from the commercial break before her colleague continued the link.

'As promised, we have Matt Turner with us this morning to discuss some interesting concerns following the episode of *Future Stars,* which aired yesterday evening,' Ian introduced their guest. 'Hi, Matt. So, what can you tell us?'

'Good morning. Well, what can I say?' Matt began. He joined them via live video link and sat immodestly in front of a bookcase displaying a selection of awards he had received for previous journalistic efforts. 'As you know, *Future Stars* has not been without its share of controversy over the years. However, in their bid to recover the ratings, it would appear they may have sunk to a new low.'

'How intriguing,' Anna intervened. 'We love a bit of scandal with our breakfast on a Sunday morning. Do go on.'

Matt continued, and for the next few minutes, he explained a series of concerns that he had been investigating following the release of the teaser trailers and an early press showing of the episode.

There were rumours of rifts amongst the judges, disappointment at the amount of padding between acts suggesting there was a lack of interest from the public in even auditioning, but the main focus was a concern that the feature act, Patrick Morgan, aka Enigma, was a fraud. A construct of the production company to end the show with the wow factor.

'Oh, my days!' Anna exclaimed in her strong Scottish accent. 'Surely not?'

'Well, maybe not complete fiction, but we can be certain that everything is not as presented in the show,' Matt backtracked slightly. 'We know from several members of the audience that Enigma was not the final act of the day as suggested, and I have been doing a little digging myself. It seems Patrick's childhood was not quite as troubled either, and there are counter-claims that he was, in fact, a bully himself rather than the victim.'

'But Patrick's father did pass away when he was a

teenager. I'm sure that was traumatic in itself,' Ian interjected.

'Yes, of course, I'm sure that was just awful,' Matt conceded before moving on to his next point. 'The biggest accusation, though, is that the show was somehow complicit in faking Enigma's act.'

'Faking how?' Ian continued his questioning, keen to hear some facts.

'Well, as you may have seen, the finale of the act was jaw-dropping. Coins were disappearing and reappearing before our very eyes. Very impressive and worthy of the standing ovation it received. However, we have reviewed this with a panel of independent magic experts. They believe this trick must have been edited for television, as it is just not possible as presented,' Matt smiled as he delivered the revelation.

'Are we sure this isn't just sour grapes? We see plenty of unbelievable feats by magicians. That's the whole point,' Ian scoffed. 'Maybe your panel of experts just don't know how it was done?' he suggested.

'Watch it back yourself. You can click through it frame by frame, and the coins just vanish. It's camera trickery for sure.'

'Interesting indeed,' Anna commented as she began to bring the interview to a close. 'Thanks for that, Matt. We have reached out to the *Future Stars* team, but as yet, they have declined to comment. I'm sure we haven't heard the end of it, though.'

Papers were shuffled, and Anna went straight to the following link, which was an article on how twenty-five per cent of Britons were now opting for plant-based milk.

\*\*\*

Patrick rolled over in bed and opened his eyes to see Craig's side was empty. It took a fraction of a second for his awakening mind to catch up, but he soon remembered it was Sunday, and Craig had left a little earlier than usual to go to the shop and tidy up after last night's party.

Before Craig had left, he had brought Patrick a cup of coffee and suggested he have a lie-in and join him later in the afternoon. Patrick turned back over and reached out for the coffee cup, but it was cold. He must have nodded off, and a glance at his watch on the bedside table confirmed it was now 10:17, and Craig had left well before 9:00 am.

Even before catching a glimpse of the lube and popper bottles beside his coffee cup, Patrick remembered their night of passion. He threw aside the duvet to reveal his naked body, still covered all in the night before, and smiled to himself.

Patrick walked to the ensuite naked and took a pee. He admired his physique in the mirror above the cistern as he did so. Everything looked better in the mornings. His stomach was flatter following a ten-hour fast, and his penis was larger, a combination of the heat from the duvet and residual horniness.

He finished peeing, shook himself, scratched his

balls, and then sniffed his fingers. He needed a shower.

There was a shower in the ensuite, but they had recently refitted the main bathroom, and Patrick preferred to use it, so he walked across the landing and into the newly renovated room.

The floor was matt white marble, with the faintest of veins, and underfloor heating kept it warm to the touch of bare feet. The room was large, previously a double bedroom, and easily accommodated the oversized vanity unit, freestanding bath, and shower enclosure. All the pieces were from Burlington, in white, and finished with Victorian taps in chrome with white ceramics.

In contrast, the walls were finished in *Farrow & Ball Calke Green* paint. This was insisted upon by Craig, whose tastes had grown increasingly expensive over time. Patrick suggested a *Dulux Fresh Sage*, which seemed identical, but Craig had not even graced his suggestion with a reply. The rolling of his eyes was answer enough.

It had been an expensive project, and almost as much had been spent on the artwork, artificial flowers, diffusers, and various other trimmings that had pulled the whole room together into a beautifully serene place to relax while bathing.

Patrick wasn't altogether unhappy with the previous bathroom but bowed to Craig's better judgement on such projects. They had systematically renovated the whole house, and the place looked fantastic. Patrick could not deny it.

Lost in his thoughts under the pounding rainfall showerhead, Patrick hadn't heard either the landline or his mobile ringing, and by the time he stepped out to towel himself down, the calls had desisted.

He pulled on a fresh pair of black *Tommy Hilfiger* briefs he had brought from the bedroom, sprayed deodorant, and then headed back to strip the bed. The cleaner wasn't due until Thursday, and Patrick wanted fresh sheets.

The kitchen had been one of the first projects they had tackled after moving in and was another of Patrick's favourite rooms. They had extended the original area into the garden, adding a wooden framed conservatory they used as a breakfast room. The kitchen had been fully refitted and consisted of a blend of granite-topped wooden cupboards and a selection of freestanding kitchen units. A larder unit, a sideboard, and a freestanding unit housing an oversized Belfast sink.

The centrepiece was a large island containing the cooker, hob, and a secondary breakfast bar area. The cupboards were finished in pale cream, allowing the woodgrain below to show through.

The utility room to the side was a continuation of the kitchen, and Patrick had always thought it unnecessary to fit it to the same standard, but Craig knew best. The salesman in *Miele* must have thought it was his lucky day when they had rolled up and ordered a catalogue of equipment for their kitchen project.

Patrick loaded the bedsheets into the washing machine and returned to the kitchen to make coffee. He almost had it to his lips when he heard the soft ringing of his mobile phone. Instinctively Patrick moved his hand to his trouser pocket to retrieve it, only to realise he was wearing only briefs. The soft ringing was not the muffled sound from within his pocket but rather the distant ring from where he had left it upstairs.

By the time Patrick had reached the bedroom, the ringing had stopped again, but he grabbed his phone to check the caller id. There were seventeen missed calls, the most recent of which was from Craig, and a dozen text messages asking him in various ways if he had seen the news. *What news?*

Patrick was about to call Craig back when he heard the roar of an engine and the scrunching of gravel as a car skidded to a halt on the drive. A quick glance from the window confirmed it was Craig's *TVR*, and Patrick was halfway down the stairs when the front door flew open.

'I knew we shouldn't have gone on that fucking show!' Craig raged.

\* \* \*

Kevin Heath wouldn't usually have been in the office on a Sunday morning, but it was only two weeks until the live finals of *Future Stars*, and his stress levels were through the roof. Cutbacks within the production team had increased everyone's workload, and Laurence Stokes, executive producer and head judge, was almost impossible to please.

The format for the finals was four live shows, airing Monday to Thursday evening primetime, from which two acts would be selected by viewer voting. These eight acts would then perform again on the Saturday grand final and be joined by a further two judges' choices from across the semi-finals.

Everything up to the semi-finals had been pre-recorded, so Kevin knew who the live performers were. Currently, he was trying to shuffle them around on pieces of paper to ensure a decent variety for each of the four shows. Nobody wanted all the dancing dogs on the same night. It was carnage enough as it was.

Kevin was distracted from his task by the ringing of the office phone.

'Kevin Heath, *Future Stars* production office, how can I help?' he greeted on autopilot.

'Oh, hi Kev, it's Jennifer from *The Sunday Review*. What are you doing at work on a Sunday? I was expecting voicemail, to be honest,' she asked.

'No rest for the wicked, babe,' Kevin joked, clearly familiar with Jennifer. 'I don't think I've seen you since the NTAs in January. We should do drinks soon.'

'Sure, love to, but it's not a social call, I'm afraid. I think I'm about to ruin your week,' Jennifer apologised in advance. 'We are about to run an article on *Future Stars*, more specifically, the Enigma episode last night. You're not going to like it.'

'What do you mean? What's happened?' Kevin had no idea what the story may be.

'In a nutshell, the main claim is that the Enigma performance was faked in some way. Collusion, camera trickery, that kind of thing. I'm calling to ask for an official statement from you guys,' she sounded genuinely apologetic.

'That's ridiculous! I was there. I can assure you it was all genuine. It was fucking unreal, actually,' Kevin defended. He remembered the Enigma show well, as both Patrick and Craig had left an impression that day.

'Is that the official press statement?' Jennifer joked.

'How long do I have to get you something?'

'Going to air in about thirty minutes, I'm afraid.'

'Fuck! Laurence is going to shit a load. On top of me probably,' Kevin laughed but was not finding the thought of this funny in the least. 'You'll have to run with the standard nobody available to comment until I get back to you.'

'No problem. Sorry, Kev. I'm sure it will all blow over,' Jennifer tried to comfort him, but Kevin was gone before she had finished her sentence.

The phone call to Laurence went as expected, but once the expletive-laden reaction had ceased, Laurence calmed down and reeled off a list of instructions for Kevin to follow up on. Laurence hadn't achieved his success without navigating the odd scandal or two.

Laurence wanted all eyes on *The Sunday Review* so they knew exactly what was said, and then he wanted the team gathered for a conference call. They would need to release a press statement before the end of the day. If *Future Stars* was going to hit the Monday morning headlines, he intended to exploit the publicity as much as possible.

'And make sure that frigging Enema is on the call too,' was Laurence's final instruction.

'It's Enigma. I'll give him a call after this,' Kevin corrected.

'Well, it should be Enema. He's causing me a pain in the arse!' With that, Laurence hung up.

Kevin tried to call Patrick half a dozen times, but there was no answer. He left a voice message and then rang around the team, briefly explaining the situation before requesting they join a conference call later that morning. He would text out the details.

From the corner of Kevin's eye, he noticed *The Sunday Review* was returning to air following a commercial break. It had been about thirty minutes since Jennifer had called. He turned up the volume on the large wall-mounted television and grabbed a pen and paper, ready to make notes.

\* \* \*

Craig had calmed down considerably since returning home, and he and Patrick had moved out to the summerhouse. Patrick offered to make a pot of coffee, but they had both opted for a beer from the party fridge instead. It was twelve o'clock somewhere.

The summerhouse was a stone-built outhouse that they had restored from near dereliction. The frontage was now mostly glass, with double doors opening outwards onto a raised terrace in front of a perfect lawn.

It was always referred to as the party house, with its French shabby chic interior, a well-stocked fridge, and a thunderous music system. Although, invariably, it was only the two of them partying. Craig wasn't keen on entertaining.

They did have some great nights in there together, though, laughing and dancing the nights away. They loved each other's company, and Craig would make up little dance routines to the latest hits and try and teach them to Patrick, who was not blessed in the dance department. They would drink and giggle the hours away until, more often than not, the pace of the music would slow, and the evening would end with lovemaking.

No such joys today, however.

Patrick had received a voicemail from Kevin letting him know they had an internal meeting scheduled to discuss the breaking news, and they would like to dial him into a conference call around 12:30 pm. The final instruction in the message was to not speak to anyone in the meantime, and Patrick hadn't, with the exception of Craig.

When Craig had arrived home and vented his frustration with his outburst, Patrick had crumbled into floods of tears. Craig was the organiser of the relationship. He did all the practical stuff and rarely got upset with Patrick. The very opposite, in fact. Patrick was the performer who was prone to throwing the occasional diva tantrum. Often unaware of the rage he could muster when the red mist descended.

When Patrick had finally finished sobbing, they reviewed the content of the interview together, which was already doing the rounds on social media, and decided on their course of action.

The only accusation involving Patrick was that of collusion with the production team. This was wholly false, and they would defend this to the hilt. They would give up no secrets about how the trick was performed, and if other "experts" couldn't fathom it out, it was a testament to Patrick's ability. What else could they suggest? Was it really magic?

Everything else reported seemed to be a direct attack on the show itself, its popularity, and the dubious editing technique. Nothing that needed to worry them. Patrick was reassured by Craig's regained composure, and after running through their agreed story once more, they both waited for the call to come in. The clock had just clicked past 12:35 pm when Patrick's mobile began to ring.

'Hello, Patrick speaking,' he answered on speakerphone.

'Hi, Patrick. I'm just going to patch you into the conference call now,' Kevin came back, followed by some clicks, a short silence, and then the echoey sounds of shuffling seats and whispered voices from a distant meeting room.

'Hi Pat, it's Laurence here,' his voice boomed out, seemingly unconcerned with the situation. 'Just wanted to reassure you we are handling the nonsense in the press. You've done nothing wrong,' he added.

'His name is Patrick,' Craig corrected. 'We know we've done nothing wrong. We want to know what you are going to do about the reputational damage you have caused,' he snapped back.

Laurence fell silent, and there were whispers in the background as Kevin informed him it was Craig, Patrick's husband, who had responded. Laurence was not a big fan of surprises.

The production team had gathered thirty minutes before reaching out to Patrick to discuss their response to the news story, and Laurence had been in a foul mood.

They had acquired a recording of the interview from *The Sunday Review,* and the mood in the room calmed as they dissected the facts. They seemed to fall into three areas. Firstly, general criticism of the show's popularity, evidenced by fewer contestants featuring in each episode. To this, they would simply respond with the statistics on the number of auditionees they had processed and a change they intended in the production approach to focus more time on the actual talent, or occasional buffoon, coming through.

Secondly, Patrick's audition was showcased as the end-of-day sob story when there was clear evidence that this was not the case. Okay, they would have to come clean on this one, but it was widely accepted in the industry that shows were edited for a more dramatic impact. With regards to the allegations of bullying, they would question Patrick on this when he joined them on the call.

Thirdly, and the most serious of all, the suggestion that Patrick's act was faked with the full knowledge and assistance of the show's production team. They all knew this to be ludicrous. They filmed the show 'as live', and Laurence himself had been the closeup witness on stage. It was jaw-dropping for sure, unbelievable even, but it had happened. This accusation would be strenuously denied.

'Is there anyone else listening in there I need to be aware of?' Laurence asked when he came back on the line.

'No, it's just the two of us,' Craig reassured.

'Okay, we just have a couple of questions, if that's okay? And then, we will run through our planned response,' he paused for acknowledgement.

'Carry on,' Craig's voice came back.

'With regard to the trick, obviously, we know we were not involved. We are clearly going to deny this, but we wondered if you might want to give a hint as to how it was done. Shut down their experts, so to speak.' was Laurence's first question.

'Certainly not!' Patrick responded instantly. 'I'm in *The Magic Circle*, and I am sharing nothing.'

'Okay, fair enough. That's probably a good response. We can work with that. The second question is a little more sensitive, but I have to ask,' Laurence apologised, pre-empting Patrick's likely response. 'On the pre-recorded video, there was a reference to childhood bullying. Clearly, they have mentioned this may not have been the case, or worse. Did you have anything to add?'

Patrick and Craig had discussed this issue and agreed on their response ahead of the call.

'I don't know whom they have spoken to, but I suspect it is someone from the later years of my secondary school,' Patrick's rehearsed response was a little stiff, but he relaxed more as he went on. 'I had a great time at primary school, but we moved house before I started at secondary, and I was bullied for two years, and I was miserable. It only stopped when I met Craig and finally stood up for myself. They didn't like it,' he finished.

'Perfect,' Laurence accepted. 'Okay, so we are going to pull together a press statement summing this all up. We will fire it over to you for a quick review and then get it issued later this afternoon in time for all the morning headlines. How does that sound?' Laurence asked.

'I'd rather be in the headlines for more positive reasons,' Patrick sighed his frustration.

'There's no such thing as bad publicity, my friend. You'll probably win the whole series. Speak later,' and with that, Laurence hung up the call.

Craig and Patrick kept each other's company for the remainder of the day and chose to ignore the many calls and messages that came through. The press release was sent over to them prior to publication, and they acknowledged they were happy with its content.

It was a warm summer evening, and they spent it drinking and listening to music in the party house. Craig popped back to the main house to answer the door to the takeaway delivery driver, and when he returned to the summerhouse with the pizza, he had stripped down to his underwear.

'I thought we could eat pizza in our pants,' he smiled and winked at Patrick, and before Craig had taken another step, Patrick had removed his t-shirt and was unbuttoning his jeans.

*What a day!*

---PRESS RELEASE---

LSE PRODUCTIONS Ltd

In response to the article aired on *The Sunday Review* on Sunday, 21st July 2019, regarding allegations of impropriety on the television programme *Future Stars*, the management team of LSE Productions Ltd wishes to issue the following statement:

While we accept that the editing of the programme may have been misleading in so much as it implied the performance of Patrick Morgan, performing as Enigma, took place at the end of a day of auditions, we strongly deny all other aspects of the interview.

Patrick Morgan was the victim of bullying during the early years of his secondary education, and this was a very difficult time in his life, compounded by the premature death of his father when he was only sixteen years of age.

With regards to the allegation that Patrick's act was in some way manipulated, this is strenuously denied. Patrick has no connection with the programme or its production team, and his act was aired as performed. Patrick is a proud member of The Magic Circle and reserves his right to keep the technique of his performance private.

We will review our editing procedures to ensure any future programmes are aired more chronologically or with creative disclaimers if required. In the meantime, we can assure all our loyal viewers that *Future Stars* remains the number-one talent show in the UK, and for all of those who were amazed by Enigma's performance, he will be back this Saturday with his second audition, which we can promise will amaze once more.

Laurence Stokes, Executive Producer

---END OF PRESS RELEASE---

# CHAPTER 6

July 2019

It had been a strange week, and Patrick had tried his best to avoid everyone. He had forced himself to work each day but had stayed in the back office and let Craig handle the shop floor. On the advice of the *Future Stars* production company, his corporate performance calendar had already been cleared due to the upcoming live show schedule. It was a condition of the audition process to be available for interviews and other media activities, so this seemed a sensible decision, even more so with hindsight.

Craig was much less sensitive to other people's opinions and had no concerns about facing any potential storm. For Patrick, it had seemed an impossibly long six days, but they were now safely back behind closed doors, snuggled on the sofa and about to watch the next episode of *Future Stars*.

The outcome of the show was already known to them. Patrick had made it to the live finals and would perform again on Tuesday, 6$^{th}$ August, before hopefully making it to the Grand Final on Saturday, 10$^{th}$ August. All the same, he was nervous.

'I'm going to go and sit on the other chair,' Craig announced as he motioned to stand up, allowing Patrick an opportunity to lift his head from Craig's shoulder and avoid collapsing into his empty seat.

'I was enjoying our cuddle.' Patrick poked out his bottom lip in fake distress.

'It's too warm tonight, and you are fidgeting. Don't be so nervous. It will be fine,' Craig tried to reassure him. 'I'm going to grab a bottle of wine. Did you want a glass?'

'Yes, please, and grab the Pringles from the larder,' he shouted after Craig, who was already out of the room.

Patrick rearranged himself on the sofa, now propped up on cushions in place of Craig's body, against one arm of the oversized cream three-seater. When Craig returned, he placed the glass of wine and tube of crisps on a small wooden table to Patrick's left.

'You went for red,' Patrick commented.

'Yeah, so don't spill it!' Craig said, as if spilling white wine would have been acceptable.

One more trip to the kitchen and Craig returned with another glass of wine and the remainder of the bottle. He habitually placed it beside the fireplace before settling on the adjacent cuddle chair. The large open fireplace that, in winter, would warm the bottle currently contained a display of dried flowers for the summer season.

The lounge was relatively small for the size of the house, and they had decorated it with a cosy-cottage feel. The wall housing the fireplace was exposed stonework, and the remaining walls were lightly painted. The furniture was traditional, in light natural tones and wood. There were a couple of pieces of tasteful art on two walls and a well-stocked bookcase on a third. Scatter cushions, vases and candles adorned every surface, and the only thing in the room that didn't fit the style was the large flat-screen television in the corner to the left of the fireplace.

'Oh shit! Here we go,' Patrick exhaled as he turned up the volume, and the title music for *Future Stars* filled the room.

The show began with an introduction from Stephen Lucas, the long-time presenter and former child television star who had achieved his first break after himself winning a legacy talent show. Stephen introduced the judges back to the stage and then reminded the audience of where they were in the process of finding this year's *Future Star*.

Off camera, Stephen explained that the first-round auditions had been completed the previous Saturday with a headline-making show. The camera cut to a full-face shot of Laurence laughing and rolling his eyes.

Patrick turned to Craig and mimicked Laurence's reaction. A video montage then ran, giving a recap of the best and worst of the auditions, ending with the bleeped *'what the fuck'* reaction of Laurence to Enigma's coin trick. The show then cut to a commercial break.

'They are playing silly buggers with the truth again,' Craig commented.

'What do you mean?' Patrick asked, genuinely confused at the observation.

'This show was pre-recorded ages ago. They have edited in the comment about last week's show and used an old reaction from Laurence. That's why it was a closeup of his face. You can't see what he is wearing.'

Craig topped up his glass and poured the remainder of the bottle into Patrick's glass before retrieving a second from the kitchen wine rack. They both grabbed a toilet break and settled down for the rest of the show.

Stephen popped back up on the screen, grinning incessantly, with blindingly white teeth and bottle bronze skin. He welcomed back the viewers and introduced another pre-record of the judges whittling down the successful auditionees to a smaller group who were now to feature on this show.

For the next ten minutes of the programme, the judges debated and argued for the cameras as they slid photographs of the auditionees around on a large tabletop. The aim was to reduce the one hundred and forty-seven faces down to just fifty who would get the opportunity of a second audition.

Patrick felt this was the cruellest part of the process,

although knowing he had succeeded at both this stage and the next made it eminently more watchable. The most brutal part was that two-thirds of the candidates, all of whom had successfully impressed the judges at their audition and had now been gathered in a hotel, were going to be rejected without even an opportunity to perform again.

There were tears, tantrums, and celebrations as groups were pulled back in front of the judges and given the news of their fate until, eventually, there was a roll call of the fifty people who would go forward to the next audition. Then, of course, there had been the usual dramatic ending where the judges decided they had made a mistake, so they recalled an auditionee who had been rejected and told them they would now take the fifty-first place.

Patrick was in one of the successful groups, but thankfully very little attention was given to him at this stage. Craig commented about how awful the shirt Patrick had worn that day was, but Patrick was frankly happy to have just faded into the background. He was desperate for fame, but the last week's exposure had been far from what he had anticipated.

Another commercial break over, and they were into ninety minutes of second auditions in front of a theatre audience and the judging panel. Again, the fifty-one contestants would be thinned down to thirty-two, eight for each of the four live semi-finals.

Some contestants were skimmed through, others featured for a little longer before discovering their fate, and a handful had their full audition televised. Patrick was to be one of the latter.

Unsure where his audition had been placed in the running order, Patrick was glued to the television, nervously waiting his turn, which came about halfway through the show. Finally, his name was announced, and he leapt up from the sofa and covered his eyes.

'I don't think I can watch,' he squealed.

'Don't be a fool. You were there. You know what happened,' Craig bluntly pointed out, and Patrick sat back down and watched as his performance played out.

* * *

This time, Patrick had chosen to perform a card trick of sorts, and as with the previous coin trick, it would build in layers. Patrick began by asking if he could come down from the stage and join the judges, as this was an interactive trick, and they would want to see it close up.

'So today, I am going to do some card tricks with you all. Hopefully, you'll like them,' Enigma said, much more confidently than Patrick ever could have.

Enigma produced a pack of cards from his pocket and performed the standard magician's spiel as he broke the cellophane seal, discarded the jokers, fanned the deck to show new card order, and then shuffled them seven times.

'Seven is apparently the optimum number of times to ensure a thoroughly shuffled deck, although others debate a number anywhere between five and twenty,' he informed the audience.

The cards were fanned again to show the mixed deck, and then Enigma presented them face down and asked Laurence to take a card. Laurence complied and showed the card to the camera and audience behind him to be the Six of Clubs.

'Oh, you don't need to keep it secret,' Enigma said. 'It's the Six of Clubs. They are all the Six of Clubs,' he added as he fanned the deck face up to show that every card was now the Six of Clubs.

Laurence smiled, the audience applauded, and Enigma moved down the line to Michelle.

'Let's try again,' Enigma said, fanning the cards to show a mixed deck again before shuffling them and spreading them out once more face down for Michelle to make her selection.

Michelle took a card and repeated the action of showing it to the camera and audience behind. This time the card was the Nine of Diamonds.

'Okay, this time, can you hold your hand out and place the card face down on the palm,' Enigma instructed and then took Michelle's hand and raised it a little higher to be in clear view.

'Now, what card did you pick?' he asked.

'The Nine of Diamonds,' Michelle replied.

'You can't have,' Enigma questioned. 'I just showed you they are all the Six of Clubs,' he repeated as he fanned the deck to show them all as the Six of Clubs.

Michelle turned over the card in her hand, and it

was indeed now the Six of Clubs. She gasped, and the audience applauded again. Louder this time. Enigma moved another step to his left to face Kieron.

'Okay, your turn. I'll make it simpler this time,' Enigma winked at Kieron.

The deck was reshuffled, but Enigma fanned the pack face-up this time to show a standard mixed deck.

'You can take any card, maybe not the Six of Clubs, though,' Enigma suggested to laughter from the audience.

Kieron ran his fingers across the face-up deck before stopping and pulling out the Three of Hearts.

'Can you place it face down on your palm,' was the next instruction, and Enigma gathered and reshuffled the deck. 'So, what card do you think you have in your hand? He asked.

'Erm… I am going to say the Six of Clubs, I guess,' Kieron answered.

'Well, why would you say that?' Enigma questioned as he nodded for Kieron to turn over the card. 'We all just watched you take the Three of Hearts,' he added as Kieron turned over the card, and it was still the Three of Hearts.

'And that was your totally free choice, right?' Enigma asked while fanning the deck to show they were all now the Three of Hearts. The judges audibly *'wowed'*, and the audience roared with applause.

Enigma took the praise as he bowed his head slightly and waited for the applause to fade.

'Now for the really good stuff,' he teased. 'Have you

all got your mobile phones?'

The judges produced their phones, and Enigma asked them to place them face-up on the desk. A cameraman was on hand to ensure everyone had a good view of everything taking place via the cinema-size screen at the back of the stage.

Enigma took out his phone and handed it to Kieron, asking him to add his number to a blank message and pass it back. Enigma then typed some text into the message and clicked send. Seconds later, the phone in front of Kieron vibrated, and the camera picked up that a new text message had been received from an unknown number.

Enigma shuffled and fanned the deck of cards again and asked Kieron to pick one and show it to everyone. He did so, and he had chosen the Ace of Spades.

'Good card,' Enigma congratulated. 'But you can change it if you want? It's totally your choice.'

'No, no, I'm happy with the ace,' Kieron decided.

'Okay, that's fine, but remember, you could have changed it. Now, why don't you read that text?'

Kieron lifted his phone from the desk and read the new message he had received aloud. 'Ace of Spades.' More applause followed, and Enigma moved back down the line to Michelle.

'I'm not giving you my number,' she said, causing the audience to laugh.

Without speaking, Enigma shuffled and ruffled the pack before fanning the cards and offering them to

Michelle to make her selection. As she reached forwards to pick a card, Enigma snapped the deck back together, making her jump and squeal in surprise.

'Let's do this one differently,' he suggested, handing her the entire deck of cards. 'You take a look through the deck, and you pick any card you like and point it out to the camera. Then just push the pack back together and pop it down on the side. We won't need them again,' he finished.

Michelle complied, and as secretively as she could, she fingered through the cards until she picked one and tapped it with her fingernail. The camera picked up the Eight of Diamonds before Michelle closed the deck and put it back on the table.

'Now, can you open up your phone and go to your photos for me, please? Make sure the camera can see. We're not going to see anything risqué, are we?' he joked.

'Well, maybe,' Michelle joked back as she pressed the icons until she arrived at the thumbnails in her photo gallery. Michelle had already gasped when Enigma asked her to click on the most recent photo and open up the thumbnail so everyone could see. She did so, and a photograph of the Eight of Diamonds was displayed. Applause, applause, applause.

'Oh God,' Laurence blasphemed as Enigma approached him.

'Don't worry. I've saved the best for last, as I know how much you love magic,' Enigma winked. 'Can you just tap your screen for me so we can see your phone?'

Laurence obliged, and his locked home screen was displayed for all to see. The picture was of Laurence when he was much younger, in mid-flight as he leapt across the stage in his ballet tights. It was a famous image from a poster campaign for his debut at a *Royal Ballet* production of *Swan Lake*.

'Oh, it's you,' Enigma didn't sound surprised. 'You didn't consider maybe a picture of your wife? Or kids?' he added, and the audience was laughing again.

'Didn't even cross my mind,' Laurence played along.

'Okay, so this is the big finish. There is no deck of cards, and I am not going to touch your phone. When you are ready, all you have to do is think of any card you like and say it aloud,' Enigma explained.

The cameraman behind Laurence moved a little closer, and the image of the phone was displayed on the screen at the back of the stage for all to see. Enigma nodded to let Laurence know he was ready whenever he was, and a few seconds later, Laurence voiced his choice, the Jack of Hearts.

Almost before his words had finished, the background image on his locked iPhone changed to the Jack of Hearts. There was a momentary silence, the clock display on Laurence's phone clicked over to the next minute, and then the audience erupted into another standing ovation.

\* \* \*

Patrick lowered the volume on the television, downed the last mouthful of wine in his glass, and turned to Craig for reassurance that everything had gone well.

'It was great,' Craig assured him. 'Everyone loves you.'

'The last bit with the picture change, though. Was that too much?' Patrick was genuinely concerned.

'It's impressive, but that's the point. Nobody needs to know how you really did it. They can speculate all they like. We just keep quiet, okay?' Craig emphasised the last instruction, and Patrick nodded in compliance.

'Did you notice they dropped the second backstory film? Probably a good thing, mind. I wasn't comfortable with them filming it in the house anyway.'

'Shall we have another bottle and listen to some music in the garden room?' Craig suggested, and Patrick nodded in agreement. Anything to take his mind off the whole thing was welcome right now.

It was a lovely warm July evening, so they kept the music down low and had the French doors wide open to enjoy the fresh air, although it was currently a little less fresh as Patrick stood on the patio puffing away on a cigarette. He had given up for almost two years but had succumbed in the last week following the stress of the press revelations, and things weren't about to get any easier.

They had been in the garden for just over half an hour when the music cut out, and Patrick's phone began to ring over the Bluetooth speakers. He stubbed out his cigarette and stepped back inside to grab his phone from the tabletop. The caller ID showed Kevin from *Future Stars*.

'Hi, Kevin,' Patrick answered tentatively.

'Hi, mate. I need to update you on a few bits following the show tonight. Is that okay?' Kevin asked, seemingly in good spirits.

'Sure, is everything okay?'

'Oh, it will all be fine. *The Sunday Review* have contacted us as they are going to be running a follow-up article tomorrow morning on us,' Kevin explained. 'Laurence is going on the show live to respond in person, and we want you to join via conference call.'

'Join to do what?' Patrick had panic in his voice, and Craig signalled for him to put the phone on loudspeaker.

'They are convinced there is some collusion going on still because your trick was so good. Laurence is going on to make a point-blank denial, and it would be great to hear the same from you. Clearly, we aren't colluding,' Kevin finished.

'Sure, he'll come on the show,' Craig intervened. 'But this is just to talk about the trick, right? And he won't be telling anyone how it's done. That's our intellectual property,' Craig clarified.

'Of course, that's fine. I assume you have a laptop for the call?' Kevin asked. 'I'll send the details to your email address, and someone from the show will set you up in the morning, sometime between ten-thirty and eleven,' he added before saying a cheery goodbye.

'Why did you agree to that?' Patrick asked Craig, his voice still clearly stressed.

'It will be fine. I've been thinking about it, and we can use this to our advantage,' Craig calmly explained. 'We aren't in cahoots with the show, so you can deny that with a clear conscience, and the publicity is going to be great for your chances in the final.'

'I don't know, Craig. This isn't going the way I was expecting at all. I'm really worried,' Patrick was almost tearful as he spoke.

'When have I ever let you down, baby?' Craig moved in to give Patrick a hug. 'It's all going to be fine. Let's finish this drink and go up for an early night.' Craig squeezed Patrick's buttocks as he spoke, and Patrick's smile was back.

\* \* \*

Laurence had arrived in the studio a good hour before he was due to be on the air, and the atmosphere was amiable. He had met Anna and Ian on previous occasions, promoting his shows and on the annual award circuit, and they exchanged pleasantries in the corridors before the show went on air that morning.

A brief touch-up in hair and makeup and Laurence was placed in the green room to await his call to the morning sofa for his interview. He grabbed a drink and a pastry and worked through some emails, but within ten minutes, he was joined by his co-guest, Matt Turner.

'I believe you know each other?' Jennifer said as she brought Matt into the room. She knew full well that they did and that their public encounters had been fractious over the years. She excused herself, explaining that she needed to get Patrick connected online and ready for the interview and then left them alone. No pleasantries were exchanged this time.

Laurence was renowned for his brutal critiques of guests on his shows, but even he found Matt's style of journalism to be loathsome. He seemed to have built his career, award-winning though it was, through latching on to a small story and then pursuing it relentlessly. The end result was often destructive for those involved – regardless of the seriousness of the misdemeanour or, indeed, the accuracy of the evidence presented. And he was fat. Laurence hated fat people.

They sat in silence until Jennifer returned to take them quietly through into the studio, where off-camera, they waited until the programme paused for a commercial break. A frantic period of activity followed on the studio floor, during which they were ushered to their seats on the sofa opposite their interviewers.

Someone from behind the cameras shouted ninety seconds until back on the air, and Laurence observed as Anna received a final dab of powder to her forehead from a makeup girl. He also noticed a monitor on the floor in front of them with the face and shoulders of a rather nervous-looking Patrick.

A further twenty-second call was made by the floor manager, who had now stepped forward to deliver the countdown, and Anna shuffled in her seat in preparation for her introduction.

'Welcome back, I'm Anna Keegan, and it is Sunday, 28th July. With me on the sofa now, we have Laurence Stokes and Matt Turner, and we are also joined remotely by Patrick Morgan, better known as magician Enigma,' Anna introduced. 'We are following up on last week's controversy around Enigma's performance on *Future Stars* and some subsequent concerns following last night's show too. Matt, if I can turn to you first, what were the issues if you could remind us.'

Matt Turner proceeded to recount his allegations from his previous interview – that he believed Enigma's performance must have been in some way edited to achieve the effect televised. He added that the second performance almost certainly confirmed this suspicion, as it was impossible to update the images of playing cards on the judge's phones without some inside collaboration.

'And obviously, you have already admitted that the editorial sequencing and sob stories in the show are faked for dramatic effect,' Matt added.

'Okay, let me just deal with these in turn,' Laurence jumped in without an invitation from Anna. 'This is not even a story. I am categorically telling you now that there is zero collaboration with Patrick, and his tricks were performed in front of the theatre audience as televised. Patrick is here and can also confirm this,' Laurence paused briefly, and Patrick nodded his agreement on screen.

'With regard to the fakery, as you put it, we did imply that Patrick auditioned at the end of the day, and that was indeed for dramatic effect. This is not uncommon on reality shows, but we will review this practice. However, I would like to add that Patrick was not aware this had been done, and the backstory was certainly not faked. I am sure Patrick can update you on that,' Laurence finished.

At this point, Anna invited Patrick to contribute, and he nervously shuffled in his chair before speaking.

'I don't really understand what is going on, to be honest,' Patrick started. 'I just performed my magic. I am not working with anyone on the show to fake anything, and I did have a troubled childhood. I was bullied, and when I was a little older, I stood up for myself. I don't know what else to say.'

'I have a few more questions,' Matt said as he sat forward on the sofa for a better view of Patrick on the monitor. 'The Press received an early release of last night's show which differed a little from the one televised. Another background film was dropped that featured yourself and your husband at home,' he continued. 'In your 1.6-million-pound home, I should add, with a rather nice *TVR* parked on the drive. I'm a little confused as to your acquired wealth. I believe you do some corporate events, and your council-estate husband works in your magic shop?' Matt was smug with his delivery.

'I... I... was gifted the shop when a very good friend and mentor died. I also inherited a small house at that time. I don't really see what any of this has to do with anything?' Patrick nervously pushed back.

'I have done my research here, and the numbers just don't stack up, Patrick,' Matt continued to push. 'And Geoff wasn't the first important man to die in your life, was he?' Matt was clearly referring to Patrick's father.

'Hang on, please,' Anna interjected. 'This really does feel a little inappropriate, Matt,' but Patrick was not going to let this go unchallenged.

'You mean my father, I assume?' Patrick was clearly getting agitated. 'What has he got to do with anything?'

'I believe you were questioned by the police following his death, and your own mother claims you killed him?' Matt actually smiled after finishing his sentence.

'My father committed suicide on my sixteenth birthday, and my mother, who has actually been in psychiatric care ever since, held me responsible because they were both religious nutters and had recently found out I was gay,' Patrick's voice faltered, and tears began to run down his cheeks. 'Why are you bringing this all up?'

Laurence protested at the line of questioning and stood up, removing his microphone as he did so. Anna quickly announced another short break, and in moments they were off the air.

Matt also moved to stand, but Laurence pushed him back into the sofa.

'What is wrong with you? You fucking nasty prick,' Laurence bellowed, and members of the floor crew ran over to keep the men apart.

'Get him out of the studio,' Anna pointed towards

Matt. 'That was way out of order. You are done on this show,' she added before turning her attention to calming down Laurence.

Calm was restored quickly after Matt was removed from the studio, and Anna managed to convince Laurence to finish the interview in the moments she had left before going back on the air. She opened with an apology for Matt's line of questioning and reassured viewers that Patrick was being offered their full support. She added that anyone else impacted by the discussion could find help on their website before reintroducing Laurence.

'Apologies also to you, Laurence,' Anna offered. 'I know you have something you would like to say related to the original reason for the interview.'

'Thank you, Anna. I must say that was outrageous. That vermin cannot possibly be allowed to get away with his constant unfounded allegations, and we will be taking legal advice,' Laurence opened, referring to Matt but deliberately not using his name. 'I actually came in to address just one issue, the matter of the show's collusion with Enigma. This is also a complete lie, and to try and allay people's concerns, we have put something additional in place for the live semi-finals.'

'Yes, I understand you are bringing in a couple of old adversaries,' Anna questioned, already briefed on this element of Laurence's response.

Laurence went on to explain that Enigma's semifinal performance would be observed live by Cage &

Clerk, a magical double act who were now internationally renowned after famously being dismissed by Laurence as incompetent buffoons who would amount to nothing on one of his early talent shows.

'As you know, Anna, we have not had the most amicable of relationships over the years, and I am sure there is nothing they would like more than to discredit me on live television,' Laurence finished.

'Well, the nation is certainly talking about it, so I am sure viewing figures will be up if nothing else,' Anna began to bring the interview to a close. 'And if I can just thank you for staying with us. We have had many text reactions to the show, and they are very much supportive of Patrick. I can only apologise again,' she finished, and after a short pause for breath, launched straight into the following link.

\* \* \*

Patrick had been blindsided by the change of questioning from Matt and was pleased when the transmission had been cut. Jennifer had called almost immediately to apologise and asked if he had wanted to rejoin the interview with Laurence following the break. However, Patrick declined, still tearfully upset at the mention of his father's death, and the call was ended.

Kevin had also attempted to ring him on his mobile, but Patrick had ignored the call, choosing to watch Laurence's closing interview remarks with Craig instead.

Craig had been listening intently to the whole interview, and when the final section was complete, he sat in silence, rubbing his temples as he considered what had just unfolded. Patrick had seen this kind of reaction before and knew not to speak until Craig had gathered his thoughts.

'I think this is going to be okay,' he finally commented.

'Okay?' Patrick asked. 'He pretty much accused me of killing my own father, and I don't even know where he was going talking about our house and car.' Patrick was on the verge of tears once more.

'Hey,' Craig moved over to comfort Patrick. 'He just made himself look stupid. Nobody thinks you killed your father. The public is on your side. This is good. You might just win this whole show.'

'Win it? I don't think I can do the next show, Craig. I think it's best I just pull out.' Patrick suggested.

'You'll do no such thing,' Craig snapped as he removed his comforting arm from Patrick's shoulders. 'You are doing the show, and we are going big with the performance. I've got a great idea. Trust me,' Craig finished, and Patrick knew the conversation was over, and Craig would have his way.

## CHAPTER 7

August 2019

Patrick and Craig had been at the studio all day, finalising details and performing a dry run of the trick Patrick would be performing live that evening.

The day began with an argument before they had even left the house. Patrick had again suggested he pull out of the competition. He really was feeling uneasy about the whole thing. The Press was clearly out to discredit him, and the trick Craig had demanded Patrick perform seemed unlikely to calm suspicions.

Craig insisted he had a plan and Patrick should not worry, and when Patrick continued to worry, Craig bluntly told him to *'get in the fucking car.'*

The dynamic of their relationship had shifted in recent weeks, and Craig was now the dominant force in a relationship where historically, he had always pandered to Patrick's needs.

The car journey was mostly in silence, but by the time they arrived at the studio, they were talking again. Craig made a faint apology, and Patrick was unable to stay mad. Craig seemed to have the knack of getting into his head, and he could never stay angry at that cute little smile he always pulled.

For the live shows, the production had been switched from the theatres of the auditions to a television studio so they could operate a multi-stage format. Some of the acts, Patrick's being one, required an extensive and precise stage setup, and it was not practical to change this in the time they had available between performances on a live broadcast.

At the previous week's planning session, it had been decided that Patrick would perform as the opening act as his stage setup was the most complex. It consisted of two large vanishing cabinets with doors back and front, each standing on its own Perspex platform roughly six feet above the stage.

The platforms could be rotated to show all sides, and you could clearly see beneath them, demonstrating that no downward escape was possible through a hidden trap door. There were also four Perspex staircases which could be manoeuvred into place, allowing access to the doors on both sides of each cabinet.

The production team had provided dancing boys to assist Patrick in his performance. They were currently performing their routine of swirling around the platforms and moving the staircases into place as part of a final rehearsal. They were dressed in casuals for this practice, but tonight there would be plenty of flesh on show – another of Craig's ideas. Patrick was going big with this one, Craig had insisted. The closeup magic was gone. This was going to make eighties David Copperfield look like a fairground sideshow act.

Patrick half-heartedly completed the rehearsal but stopped short of the final reveal of the trick. Two stand-ins were assisting, but on the night, the renowned Cage & Clerk would be fulfilling these roles in a double-vanishing act with a twist. A twist Patrick was refusing to divulge.

Kevin, the floor manager, encouraged him to put more effort into his performance, but Patrick assured him it would be fine later that evening. He couldn't perform as Patrick. He could only go through the motions, but tonight Enigma would be on stage, and that would be a whole different matter.

With the final rehearsal finished, Patrick and Craig had a little time to themselves in the dressing room. As Kevin left, he said he would be back to give him a thirty-minute warning in roughly an hour.

'We're good, right?' Craig asked when Kevin was out of earshot.

'Yeah, we're good,' Patrick smiled back unconvincingly. 'I thought we might have met Cage & Clerk ahead of tonight, though.'

'I don't think it matters. The less they know, the

better, for sure. You are going to be famous after this, Patrick, I promise you,' Craig had confidence enough for both of them. 'Get yourself changed,' he added, handing Patrick the see-through black mesh muscle vest and skin-tight black jeans he had chosen for him to wear.

'I'm going to look like a stripper in this with all those dancing boys prancing around,' Patrick laughed.

'You'll look just great. The world isn't going to know what's hit it after tonight, Patrick. I think this is all going to work out just fine,' Craig said. 'And go commando in those jeans,' he added before undoing the button on Patrick's trousers and slipping his hand inside. 'Sex sells, big boy!'

\* \* \*

Kevin had returned as promised to give the thirty-minute warning and then again with fifteen minutes left to go. Fortunately, he knocked and waited before entering the room, giving Patrick enough time to tuck himself uncomfortably back into his jeans and for Craig to return to his feet.

'Exciting times!' Kevin declared as his eyes dropped from Patrick's face to the visible erection in his jeans and back again. 'Craig, you'll need to take your seat in the studio. I'll take you through, and then I'll come back for you, Patrick,' he added before turning and leading the way.

Kevin returned several minutes later and took Patrick through to wait on stage in the studio. The floor team were buzzing around, and the audience was informed that they would go live to air in less than five minutes.

It was only moments now until showtime, and Patrick performed a final inspection of the equipment before taking a small foam earplug from his pocket and placing it into his left ear.

The audience was given a ten-second countdown, and then the fun began. The monitors around the studio displayed the show's title sequence coming to an end, and the applause signs were lit. The crowd went wild as the cameras cut to Stephen Lucas on a small stage to the right of where Patrick was waiting to begin his performance, and once he had calmed the cheers, he began his introduction.

The following five minutes were absolute cookie-cutter TV talent show stuff. Each judge was introduced to the stage to their own entrance song before taking their seat on the judging panel. Laurence walked out to *He's the Greatest Dancer* by *Sister Sledge*, Michelle came on to *The Pussycat Dolls, Don't Cha* and Kieron's song was *Bewitched's, C'est La Vie,* which someone had comically positioned to the lyric *Some people say I look like me dad.* The audience exploded into laughter.

Once the judges were seated and the audience had calmed, Stephen continued his opening.

'As you will all be aware, our first act this evening,

Enigma, has not been without some recent controversy,' Stephen began, pausing slightly for the audience's supportive reaction and chants of 'We love Enigma.'

Stephen continued with a summary of the events to date, a blasting critique of *The Sunday Review*, and a reiterated denial of any wrongdoing by the show's team. He then explained that to try and silence the critics once and for all, the internationally renowned Cage & Clerk had been invited to the studio to act as independent adjudicators. The audience applauded once more, and the entrance doors behind Stephen opened again, and the aforementioned Cage & Clerk walked out onto the stage.

'Good evening, gentlemen,' Stephen welcomed them.

'I need to correct your introduction,' Callum Cage said immediately. 'We are not independent adjudicators. We have a grudge. We are here to take Laurence and his show off the air,' Cage was obviously joking, and the audience responded appropriately, but there was an element of truth underlying.

'Yes, yes, I seem to recall Laurence wasn't your biggest fan,' Stephen played along. 'But I believe you've managed to scrape together a career following his dismissal of your talent?'

'We are getting by,' Tristen Clerk spoke next. 'We've had some success being talentless in Europe, Asia, the Middle East, North and South America. Oh, and we managed to blag a little residency in Vegas, so it's paying the bills, at least.'

The audience loved the exchange at Laurence's expense, and Laurence took it all in his stride, smiling and laughing along as he should.

'All joking aside,' Laurence interjected, keen to deflect any further embarrassment. 'Cage & Clerk have clearly had a phenomenally successful career and are well respected around the world. And our fractious history makes them the perfect people to oversee Enigma's next performance.'

'Yes, and we really must get on with the show,' Stephen took back control of the conversation. 'I will just ask you to confirm that you haven't yet met Enigma, and you have no idea what trick he is about to perform?' Stephen waited for both of them to confirm these facts before he continued. 'Okay then, if I can ask you to join Enigma on the main stage, and we can hand over to him for what I am sure is going to be a breath-taking opener to the show.'

Cage & Clerk moved over to where Enigma was awaiting their arrival, and Stephen made one final introduction before music and an explosion of pyrotechnics began the performance.

Enigma stood centre stage with his arms raised, with Cage & Clerk on either side, awaiting further instruction. He was in his tight black jeans, commando as requested, and all too conscious that the combination of pre-show activity with Craig and his current adrenaline level was maintaining a noticeable semi.

His mesh t-shirt, equally tight, made visible the top

hat tattoo on his chest as well as his muscular torso. Before he had a chance to speak his opening line, a male voice from the crowd called out, 'You're so hot,' and Enigma smiled.

'Tonight, the closeup magic is gone,' he shouted above the audience's screams. 'Tonight, we are going big. Tonight, we are going to change the world of magic forever.'

With that, the dancing boys arrived, and the homoerotic dial on the performance was turned up to eleven. Eight male dancers wore matching outfits of black high-laced boots, black PVC hotpants, and a gold neoprene harness supporting a small pair of black feathered wings.

Enigma, Cage, and Clerk moved to one side of the stage, and there followed a synchronised dance routine during which the dancers theatrically manoeuvred the main props of the trick into position. Finally, the two vanishing cabinets atop their raised platforms and the four staircases were whirled around until coming to rest in their final positions.

From stage left to right, there now stood a staircase up to a cabinet platform, followed by two further staircases, one down, then one up to the second platform, and then the final staircase back down to the stage. The only change from the earlier rehearsal was that each piece of equipment appeared solid in construction. The Perspex element was currently hidden from view by black sheets secured on all sides.

To further demonstrate the configuration of the

stage props, Enigma walked up the first set of stairs and entered the side of the box through the first door. The door closed behind him, and he was out of view for no more than a second before the door on the opposite side of the box opened, and he reappeared.

There was soft applause, but the trick had not yet begun.

Enigma continued his journey down the exit steps and then immediately back up again to the second cabinet. He entered and exited as previously before descending the final stairs and returning to Cage & Clerk's side.

'Are you impressed yet?' he asked of them.

'Well, I'm impressed with the dancers. I didn't know where to look,' Clerk replied. 'First,' he added to laughter. Tristen Clerk was an openly gay man, and his humour was not wasted on this audience.

'Okay then, I am only going to perform a single trick tonight, and I want to make sure it's impressive, so let's run a few scenarios by you and see if we can make it a good one,' Enigma explained.

'Sure, sounds good,' Cage answered.

'So, let's say we take one of our dancing dark angels, and he walks up the stairs and into the box and then comes out across the stage from the second box. Would that be impressive?' Enigma asked.

Cage sucked air in through his teeth before replying, 'Well, not really. I mean, we all know there could be a route below the platform through the stairs out of sight of us all. I guess,' he half apologised.

'Okay, good point,' Enigma agreed before moving across the stage and pulling down the black sheets that had been concealing the Perspex makeup of the props. 'How about that? You can see right through the stairs and under the platforms now. Nowhere to hide, right?'

'Hmm, better, but the stage backdrop is very dark,' Clerk took his turn. 'Sometimes you think you are seeing right through, but really you aren't.'

'Boy, you guys are good,' Enigma sighed comically before clapping his hands, and the backdrop of the set was changed from black to a pale-yellow colour. 'And let's get the dancers behind the props while we are at it,' he instructed.

As you now looked at the stage, you could see the full configuration of the props, and they were all clearly transparent, except for the actual vanishing cabinets on top. The eight dancers were merrily gyrating and could clearly be seen behind all of the equipment, and Cage & Clerk seemed much happier with the setup.

'Right, so if I now vanish one of my little angels and he appears on the other side, are you going to be amazed? Will it be inexplicable?' Enigma asked again.

'Well, I can think of another small issue,' Cage offered. 'Sometimes this kind of trick uses a doppelgänger?'

'You are absolutely right, of course,' Enigma conceded. 'How about we use you then? You're not a twin, are you?' he joked. 'In fact, let's use both of you and make this twice as crazy.'

Enigma signalled to someone off-stage that the

main trick was about to commence, and music sounded once more. The dancers continued to gyrate in time, and Enigma first led Cage to the bottom of one staircase before leading Clerk to the one on the opposite side of the stage.

Enigma returned to the centre of the stage and faced the audience with his arms raised.

'Okay, guys, on my signal, I want you to walk slowly up the stairs and into your cabinet. Once the door has closed behind you, just step out from the other side,' Enigma instructed without looking back behind him.

Patrick lowered his arms and called 'go' as if starting a drag car race, and Cage & Clerk began their ascent of the stairs. Patrick didn't move from his position, facing directly into the crowd, and seemed to fall into a trance-like state as he awaited the audience's reaction.

Cage had entered the cabinet on the left of the stage, and Clerk had entered the cabinet on the right. There was a massive explosion of pyrotechnics into the air, and then the audience watched on as the two men exited the cabinets just a second later.

There were gasps of amazement, whoops and squeals of excitement, and a full standing ovation accompanied by thunderous applause by both audience and judges alike. Cage & Clerk had both inexplicably emerged from the opposite cabinet to the one they had entered.

Callum Cage stared directly across the stage at his partner Tristen Clerk. Taking a moment to get his bearings, he quickly realised their positions had been reversed. A look of confusion was evident on both of their faces, but Cage's expression was deeper, more pained.

Tristen Clerk looked on with concern as Cage clutched his chest before he stumbled forwards and fell face forward down the stairs, coming to rest motionless at the bottom.

There were screams from the floor crew to cut the live transmission, and the audience fell silent as they watched the scramble to offer Cage medical assistance on stage.

Patrick had not even turned around. He didn't need to. Instead, he picked out Craig in the crowd and caught his gaze. As their eyes met, Patrick removed the bloodied earplug and threw it to the floor. Patrick was not happy with how this had played out, but Craig seemed to be smiling back at him.

'That couldn't have gone any better.' *Did Craig really just mouth that?*

# Part Two: Craig

# CHAPTER 8

February 2008

Craig had been excited about the school talent show ever since discovering that Patrick, a boy in the year below him that he had been fixating on, would be performing.

Patrick had come onto Craig's radar the previous September, at the start of the new school year. Craig went out of his way to learn more about this handsome dark-haired boy, first discovering his name and then researching a little further.

It turned out Patrick had been at the school from the start of Year 7, and Craig was surprised he hadn't noticed him in the two years since then. Perhaps the last summer holiday had blessed him with a puberty-fuelled growth spurt because he couldn't fail to notice him now.

Whenever Craig looked up, his eyes seemed to pick Patrick out from the crowd. He was a tall, slim, handsome boy with the beginnings of a downy shadow of facial hair and a wonderful smile, despite the challenges he appeared to face at school.

It seemed Patrick was a loner, as was Craig, but where Craig managed to keep himself away from trouble, Patrick seemed to attract it. As a result, Craig often saw him bullied. Nothing too severe, but it could be relentless. He would have loved to have stepped in and helped, but Craig was waiting for the right time.

Craig spent the following months learning as much as he could about Patrick and felt sure he was getting closer to actually engaging with him. So, when he saw the poster on the school noticeboard listing the upcoming performers for the school talent show, he was pleasantly surprised that Patrick's name was amongst them. This was the opportunity he had been waiting for, and he was determined to engineer an interaction.

It was now Thursday afternoon, the day of the talent show, and Craig had rushed to the auditorium to try and get a seat with a good view. He plonked himself down near the centre of the stage, three rows back from the front, tucked the bag he had with him under his seat, and patiently waited for the performances to begin.

The headmaster made a short speech before handing the microphone over to one of the 6th-form students who would be acting as compère for the afternoon's entertainment. The compère fancied himself as somewhat of a comedian and cracked a few jokes, which elicited groans from the audience before he then introduced the opening acts.

The school choir performed first, followed by a street dance routine by one of the afterschool clubs. The school band were next, with a bizarre steel drum performance. The music teacher had been on a once-in-a-lifetime Caribbean holiday the previous year and, on her return, had somehow convinced the school governors that an investment of funds into steel drums was a great way to improve the cultural awareness of the students. It wasn't horrendous, but Craig doubted the students at his Cotswolds comprehensive had quite the same rhythm as their Caribbean counterparts.

The fourth performer was a girl named Alice. She was in Craig's year and some of Craig's classes, but they were not friends. Not that any of Craig's classmates were really his friends, but Alice, in particular, grated on him. He had taken great pleasure in watching her tumble down the school stairs and break her arm the previous month. It was one of the few times her pouting smile was wiped from her face. She was annoyingly good, though, as she belted out her rendition of *Leona Lewis's Bleeding Love*.

Alice finished to rapturous applause, which she milked for what seemed an eternity with her curtseys and sickly smile. Eventually, she exited stage left, and the compère was able to introduce Patrick Magic. The curtain rose, and as Patrick was revealed, murmurs began to run through the crowd mocking the cloak he was wearing.

Craig wanted to cringe himself but managed to maintain a smile as Patrick caught his gaze in the crowd. *Why had he called himself Patrick Magic? And why did he decide to wear the cloak?* Craig knew only too well what it was like to be an outsider. He was pale-skinned, ginger-haired and had only recently begun to shift an excess of puppy fat, but he was skilled in avoiding attention. Patrick needed some guidance.

He mouthed the words '*good luck*', but it was going to take more than luck to see Patrick through the next few minutes. Craig knew this would be painful for Patrick, but it was the opportunity he had been waiting for. The crowd was against him, but Craig was ready to pick up the pieces and be a friend. More than a friend, in time.

Chaos ensued. The sound of props crashing to the stage filled the auditorium as the table behind Patrick collapsed to the floor. The audience fell silent, and Patrick stood motionless as the various items rolling around his feet came to rest.

A voice called out something comical, and there was laughter. Craig could see the utter look of horror on Patrick's face. Their gaze met again, and Craig smiled sympathetically before closing his eyes. It was painful to watch this unfolding.

'He's pissed himself!' a boy's voice called out, and Craig opened his eyes again.

Patrick looked confused and then mortified when he realised he was mid-flow in full view of the whole school. Craig felt for him, but at this stage, there was nothing he could do but watch it play out.

Craig locked his gaze on Patrick once more, focusing to try and get him to look over so he could offer him a sympathetic smile, but Patrick was transfixed on the growing wet patch around his crotch.

'Fuuuuuuck!' was Patrick's protracted and pain-filled cry, and Craig clenched his fists at the sound of it as one of the stage lights exploded high above the stage, raining down sparks to add further effect to the heart-wrenching scene unfolding below.

Craig felt tears welling in his eyes as he watched Patrick release his cloak and run from the stage, gone from sight before the cloak had fully come to rest in the puddle of urine below.

\* \* \*

The auditorium had descended into a cacophony of gasps, laughs, and whispers before one of the teachers called for silence. The curtain had been dropped temporarily, and the decision would be taken to continue with the show, following a short comfort break, as there were still many acts to come who had been practising for weeks for the event.

Before that decision was made, Craig had already left his seat and exited through the rear doors and out into the corridor. A teacher had contemplated stopping him and returning him to his seat, but a determined glare from Craig and she stepped back to the wall and let him pass unchallenged.

Craig paused in the corridor, closing his eyes briefly before wiping away the moisture and deciding to turn left and head to the art department. He was only a minute or so behind Patrick, but Craig had to circle around the auditorium to get to the art block as he had exited the building from the opposite end of the stage.

By the time Craig walked into the art room, Patrick had settled himself on the floor in the back corner. Craig could see the top of Patrick's head rocking slightly back and forth as he slowly began to walk between the desk to the back of the class.

As Craig rounded the final desk, he looked down to see Patrick sitting with his knees pulled to his chest and his arms wrapped around them.

'Are you okay?' Craig asked.

'How did you know I was here?' Patrick responded.

'I followed the wet footprints,' Craig joked, then immediately regretted it. 'I am so sorry, that just wasn't funny at all. Sorry,' he apologised.

'It was quite funny.' Patrick said, and then he smiled, and Craig knew right then that the bonding process he had been waiting months for had begun.

'Why are you here?' Patrick asked.

'I brought you these from my locker,' Craig explained as he held out the carrier bag he'd been carrying towards Patrick.

Patrick took the bag and looked inside and found a

pair of navy-blue tracksuit bottoms. Puzzled, not by why the boy had brought a change of bottoms but certainly by the kindness of the gesture, he raised his gaze and smiled again.

'I didn't have any spare pants, so you'll have to go commando,' Craig smiled back. 'There are some paper towels in there as well, so you can dry off a bit,' he added.

'I can't get changed here,' Patrick stated.

'Sure you can. I'll turn my back if you like, but I think you're already at maximum points on the embarrassment scale today, so I wouldn't worry too much,' Craig said, really hoping Patrick would begin to undress in front of him.

'I'd still rather not show you my cock,' Patrick joked. 'I don't even know your name yet.'

Craig laughed aloud as he politely, albeit a little reluctantly, turned his back to Patrick. 'I'm Craig,' he said. 'Craig Newman. I knew I was going to like you.'

As Craig turned around, he noticed a mirror on the wall, and as Patrick stood up behind him, his torso came into view. Craig stretched himself to full height to try and see lower down in the mirror, but even on slight tiptoe, he could only see just below Patrick's belt buckle.

Even if Craig hadn't known what was happening behind him, he was confident he could have pieced it together from the sounds alone.

One shoe kicked off at the heel, followed by the other. The belt buckle being unfastened, followed by the soft pop of a button slipping out of a buttonhole. The funny click of the metal hook and eye being released from the inside of the slightly too small waistband before the sound of the zip fly being drawn downwards.

Craig stretched even taller as Patrick pulled his trousers down in the mirror, but even at full stretch, he could only see as low as the *Calvin Klein* waistband. Craig was surprised to see Patrick wearing *CK*s and momentarily wondered if they were briefs or boxers as he watched Patrick bend down again and slip them off over his feet.

Aware that Patrick was now naked from the waist down just a few feet behind him, yet frustratingly out of view in the mirror, Craig tried to imagine what he may look like down below.

As Craig daydreamed a scene, there was a ping as each sock was flicked off in turn. Then a pause, and then a tap was running. Presumably, wetting the paper towels for a quick wash down. Next, more paper towels, this time dry ones, being patted over the skin.

Craig quickly glanced back to the mirror. He realised Patrick had walked further away to use the sink, and he now had a clear view of Patrick's bottom. It was smooth, pert, and pale below the dark blue of his school jumper. Craig willed him to turn around, but before he had fully formed the thought, Patrick had already rustled the tracksuit bottoms from the bag and pulled them on.

There was a slight snap as Patrick let go of the waistband and then more rustling as the damp clothes were packed back into the carrier bag.

'You can turn back around now,' Patrick informed.

Craig dropped down from his tiptoes and relaxed the tension in his overstretched body. As he turned, he caught sight of the final few tasks being completed. The shoes slipped back onto bare feet without undoing the laces, and the paper towels were collected and put into a bin before Patrick washed his hands.

'Thanks for this,' Patrick said sincerely.

'That's okay. You look cuter in them than I do. You can keep them if you like?' Craig posed a genuine question.

'Erm… sure. Thanks,' Patrick blushed. 'Why are you being so nice to me exactly? People aren't generally very nice to me here,' Patrick said, motioning with his arms to emphasise that by 'here', he meant the school.

Craig moved over to where Patrick was standing and hopped up to a seated position on the counter to the side of the sink.

'I like you. I've noticed you for a few months now, and I thought we could be friends,' Craig explained.

'And you still think that's a good idea after today?' Patrick questioned. 'You'll be hanging around with a laughingstock. What will your friends think?'

'Oh, I don't really have many friends, but people tend to leave me alone. I can handle myself,' Craig said before pointing to Patrick and adding, 'You've got a little drop of blood coming out of your ear.'

Patrick touched his finger to his left ear and then checked the tip for blood. 'For fuck's sake! Could this day get any better?' he cursed while grabbing another paper towel.

'It's only a tiny bit. I reckon you'll live,' Craig comforted. 'It has been a bit of a day, though. What happened?'

With a heavy sigh, Patrick began to recall the events, and as he explained, Craig listened intently, nodding sympathetically in all the correct places. He was fully aware of what had unfolded, but he allowed Patrick to vent his frustration before deciding to lighten the conversation.

'Did you notice a spotlight exploded above your head when you shouted fuck?' Craig asked. 'Maybe you've got real magic powers,' he joked.

'Oh yeah, that's me. The superhero who pisses his pants. A real world-saver.' They both laughed.

'Come on, I'll walk you out of school and make sure nobody bothers you,' Craig offered. He jumped down from the side and left the room without waiting for Patrick's response.

Craig could hear Patrick behind him, scrambling to gather his belongings and catch up. They continued to chatter as they walked, and although some inquisitive looks were received from the students passing by, they managed to leave the premises without incident.

As they walked, they agreed to meet during the half-term holiday. Mobile numbers were exchanged, and after some persuasion, Patrick promised he would show

Craig some of his magic tricks.

A little further down the road, they came to a junction where they needed to go their separate ways for the remainder of their journey home.

'You going to be okay from here?' Craig asked.

'Yeah, I'll be fine,' Patrick replied. 'Thanks again for your help. You've been so nice to me.'

Patrick looked so sweet and genuinely grateful that Craig had befriended him today. Craig grinned back as he contemplated what he was about to do. He locked Patrick's gaze as he hesitated, but then he went for it, leaning forwards and kissing Patrick on the cheek.

'See you next week,' Craig called over his shoulder as he walked off, not waiting for Patrick's reaction. His mind was racing. *What had he just done? What must Patrick be thinking? Had he ruined the friendship before it had even begun? Should he have kissed him on the lips?*

When Craig turned the next corner and knew he was out of sight, he slipped his hand into his trousers and released his folded erection so it was upright and held flat by his underwear waistband. He hoped Patrick hadn't noticed his bulging trousers as he had turned away. Or maybe he hoped he had. Either way, from Craig's flushed cheeks, beaming smile, and pulsing groin, he realised he had enjoyed the kiss much more than he had ever imagined.

\* \* \*

As Craig turned the front door key and let himself

into his house, he could hear his mother rushing about upstairs.

'Hey mum, I'm home,' he shouted up the stairs, an open staircase in the small lounge the front door opened directly into.

Their home was a tiny two-bedroom council house with an open lounge at the front and a small kitchen-diner to the rear. Upstairs to the front of the house, Lisa had the larger bedroom, roughly the same size as the lounge, and at the back of the house was a small bathroom and Craig's box room, both with windows overlooking a small courtyard garden. It wasn't much, but it was clean and well-kept, and it was perfect for the two of them.

Craig had never known his father, but there was no painful history or secret-keeping. Lisa had been honest with Craig from an appropriate age, and the truth of the matter was that Lisa had fallen pregnant after a one-night stand. Furthermore, she wasn't really sure which one-night stand it had been, as it occurred during a time in her life when the father could have been one of a dozen guys. Although Craig's ginger hair possibly narrowed the field.

'You're home early,' Lisa noted as she ran down the stairs, still buttoning her blouse. She wouldn't normally have bumped into Craig after school as she would have already completed her dash home to get changed out of her care home uniform and into something more casual for her second job at a local hotel.

'We finished early. It was the talent show,' Craig offered as a half-truth explanation. 'And it's an inset day tomorrow before half-term, don't forget,' he added.

'Was the show good?' she asked, now scrambling around in her handbag for lipstick, which she then began to apply in the mirror at the bottom of the stairs.

'Oh, it was something else,' Craig laughed. 'But guess what, I made a friend. We are going to hang out next week, I think,' Craig smiled.

Lisa stopped applying her makeup and turned towards Craig with a look of pleasant surprise on her face.

'That's amazing news,' she beamed.

Craig had been a normal child, whatever normal meant, but at the age of eight, there had been the most traumatic of events for them both. Lisa's brother, Paul, had kidnapped Craig and held him hostage in the local church.

Paul had been a respected local journalist at the time, but he had been acting strangely in the days leading up to the kidnap. Lisa had questioned him about what was wrong, suspicious that something he was investigating was getting out of hand, but Paul dismissed her questions and assured her everything was fine.

Things were clearly not fine. Within the week, Paul had burst into her home early one evening and demanded to know where Craig was. Puzzled, Lisa answered that he was taking a bath, and before she knew it, Paul had raced up the stairs and dragged Craig naked and screaming from the water.

Lisa attempted to stop Paul from descending the stairs with Craig kicking and crying in his grasp, but Paul pushed her backwards, and she fell four or five steps down, jolting her back as she landed. Paul rushed past her and was gone out of the door.

Winded and bruised, Lisa managed to get herself back to her feet, but Paul was out of sight as she scanned up and down the road, screaming her son's name. She quickly returned to the house and called the police, and lights and sirens closed in on her location within minutes. Minutes that felt like hours.

It transpired that Paul had taken refuge in the church. He had somehow managed to arm himself with a handgun and had opened fire on the first officer who had attempted to enter the building. Firearms officers were summoned to the scene, and after a short standoff and then a period of frantic concern, officers stormed the church, and Paul was fatally shot.

Craig had become understandably withdrawn following the ordeal and drifted away from all of his primary school friends over time. He underwent counselling and seemed to be coping well, but he preferred keeping his own company, and even after the move up to secondary school, he had still not built any real friendships. At least none he had ever talked to Lisa about or brought back home over the holidays. This was progress, for sure.

'Does this boy have a name?' Lisa probed further.

'It's Patrick, the vicar's son,' Craig added.

Lisa turned back to the mirror to finish her makeup

and to hide the slight look of surprise that Craig had managed to befriend the only boy at the school with ties back to the church he had been abused in.

'Maybe he can come over for tea next week,' she suggested. 'I've got Tuesday off,' she added before dabbing her lips on a tissue.

'Yeah, maybe,' Craig contemplated.

'Right, baby, I've got to go to work. I've left you some money on the side for chips when the van comes around later. I'll see you in the morning, as I won't be back until gone midnight tonight.' With that, she blew Craig a kiss, pulled on her coat and was out of the door.

Craig kicked off his shoes and headed upstairs to the bathroom. The erection in his underwear persisted, and there was only one way he was going to get rid of it. Craig couldn't stop smiling when he thought about Patrick. This really did feel like the start of something special.

# CHAPTER 9

May 2008

It was just after 8:30 am on a bright warm spring Saturday, and Craig was fifteen minutes into the twenty-minute walk between his house and the vicarage where Patrick lived.

There were several ways to navigate the journey between the boy's homes, with only a minute or two difference between them. Craig had explored each of them over the months and settled on two preferred paths. He chose to stick to the main roads if walking in the dark or on a wet day. That is what he had done when he first made this journey in early winter. Tarmac and streetlights seemed sensible on those occasions. However, walking across the common on a sunny day like today was much more pleasant.

The end of the common was exited using a stile over a drystone wall. Craig wore denim shorts today, so he was careful of the stinging nettles when stepping over. His ginger-haired legs were pale and unsightly enough without also being adorned with the blotches of nettle rash.

The pathway continued to a small footbridge over a stream and onward through the churchyard. Ancient headstones lined the route to the main church gates, and then it was just a short walk down a single-track lane. This lane joined the main A-road through the town, and the vicarage stood opposite the T-junction.

Although not on the grounds of the church itself, the vicarage was in sight of its huge arched oak doors. The vicarage had a similar, scaled version of these doors as its own entrance, and in the early evening sun, they would stand firmly in the shadow of the church spire.

The church in Witford was a large building. Unexpectedly impressive for such a small town, even taking the breath away of the tourists who had travelled solely to take in the history of the place.

Craig didn't remember the whole history of the place, but it had something to do with Cromwell and the execution of some Levellers. There were bullet holes on one of the outside walls, still visible from the seventeenth century, but whenever Craig heard mention of that, he would mumble under his breath that there were much more recent bullet holes on the inside.

Lisa had considered moving away from the area after the incident with her brother at the church, concerned for Craig's mental health, but Craig had protested. So instead, they requested a move to a different council house and began to piece their lives back together.

Craig should probably have had an aversion to the church, but he was okay with it. He'd even been back inside since striking up his friendship with Patrick. It had been a little strange, remembering his uncle standing over him, attempting to crucify him. Craig's left hand had already been nailed to the wooden cross, and as Paul held Craig's right hand in place to do the same, four or five bullets hit his chest, throwing him back into the church's altar.

Seven years on, the scarring on Craig's left hand had almost, but never completely vanished, and it would sometimes itch when he walked past the church. Almost certainly a psychosomatic response rather than anything physical, and Craig scratched at his palm as he exited the church gates and headed down to the vicarage. But not everything that had happened on that day with his uncle had been bad.

Craig's thoughts snapped back to the present as he reached his destination and banged the ornate knocker on the vicarage door. Muffled voices and footsteps closened before the door was opened by Patrick's mother.

'Morning, Craig,' Kate greeted with a smile. 'He's not ready as usual. Just go on up to his room,' she added, stepping aside to let Craig pass.

'Thanks, Mrs Morgan,' Craig said politely before heading up the open staircase from the hallway to the balcony landing.

Craig walked along the landing towards Patrick's bedroom door. It was not his intention to do so quietly, but as he pushed down the handle and slowly opened the door, it became apparent Patrick had not heard him approaching.

Patrick stood naked with his back to the door. His room was ensuite, and he had seemingly just finished his morning shower. His body was dry, but he was giving his hair one last vigorous rub with the towel before getting dressed. Presumably, this towelling action had impaired his hearing.

The sight drew a massive grin across Craig's face. Patrick was the slimmer of the two, almost athletic, although he was not even slightly sporty. With his arms raised to hold the towel, you could see the muscle definition across his shoulders and the bulge of his biceps. Between his shoulder blades was the faint outline of his spine which drew your eyes down, past his slim waist, to his perfect peachy bottom.

Patrick's legs also had some definition around the calves and were covered with a dark down of boyish hair, which faded away just above the knee, but Craig's gaze had fallen no lower than that perfect bottom.

At that moment, Patrick threw his towel onto the bed, picked up his boxer briefs, and leant forward to lift one leg and put them on. As Patrick bent over,

Craig caught a glimpse of his friend's balls hanging between his slightly parted thighs. Suddenly flushed with guilt at his voyeurism, he quickly spoke to alert his friend he had arrived and to avoid any further exhibition.

'Morning, gorgeous. Nice arse!' was all Craig could think to say.

As Patrick yanked up his underwear and spun around on his heels, Craig could see he had clearly startled him. He looked angry as he rushed over and pushed his bedroom door closed before grabbing Craig by the arm and gripping him tightly.

'What were you thinking? If my mum hears you talking like that, we'll be in so much trouble,' Patrick angrily whispered, tightening his grip as Craig locked his gaze in an unblinking stare.

'Patrick, you're hurting me,' Craig said softly after thirty seconds or so in this standoff, but he knew Patrick wouldn't respond as he continued to stare vacantly ahead. 'Patrick!' he said a little louder, and as he tugged his arm away, he broke his gaze, snapping his friend out of his momentary trance.

'I am so sorry,' Patrick said as he noticed Craig rubbing his arm where small indents had been left from the grip of his nails. He was genuinely puzzled as to what had just happened, and this wasn't the first time.

'I don't like it when you get angry like this,' Craig said, his voice cracked with emotion. 'It scares me. And you're bleeding again,' he added, with a nod in the direction of Patrick's left ear.

He watched as Patrick moved to his bedside table and pulled a tissue from the box. He held it to his ear for a few moments before discarding it on the side. Then, he moved back over to where Craig remained motionless by the door.

'I'm sorry,' he repeated before leaning forward and kissing Craig on the lips. 'It won't always be like this,' he added, his arms now around his friend's waist, and his hands slipped into the pockets on the rear of Craig's shorts.

They kissed a little more passionately, something they had both improved at since their first brief peck on the street corner in February. Craig placed a hand on the back of Patrick's head, pulling him closer as he kissed deeper, tasting the minty freshness of his recently brushed teeth.

'I love you,' Craig said softly when their mouths parted.

'I love you too,' Patrick said. 'And your bum feels pretty nice as well,' he added as he squeezed it in his hands. 'We can do more than a kiss at some point, Craig. I just need to be really careful.'

'Don't worry about that,' Craig now comforted. 'I will wait as long as you like. There's no rush.'

As if to emphasise Patrick's need for caution, the moment was interrupted by his mum's voice shouting up the stairs. 'Do you boys want a cup of tea before you head out to play?' she asked.

*If only she knew how her son really liked to play these days*, Craig thought to himself.

In unison, the boys declined the offer, and Craig swiftly pulled back from Patrick's embrace, allowing him to return to his bed and finish getting dressed.

Craig watched as Patrick pulled on a new pair of denim shorts not too dissimilar to his own. He knew Patrick had changed the way he dressed a little since they had met. He liked that Patrick was making more effort for him, copying his style perhaps, but Craig found that flattering.

Patrick then pulled on an oversized *Beatles* t-shirt his mum had picked up at a jumble sale and slipped on a tattered pair of checkerboard *Vans*. Craig smiled. He also liked that Patrick hadn't changed too much.

Craig kissed Patrick once more on the cheek as he leant past him to open the bedroom door, and then they headed downstairs.

'So, what are you two terrors getting up to today?' Kate questioned as she wandered into the hallway, alerted by the boys clumping down the wooden staircase.

'We're going to get the bus to the shopping centre,' Patrick replied. 'I want to take a look around the magic shop.'

'And I'm going to get some birthday ideas,' Craig added. 'It's not until July, but my mum wants some ideas. I think she hopes I will have forgotten what I asked for by my birthday, so it will be a surprise,' he laughed.

'Oh yes! Your sweet sixteenth is coming up! How exciting,' Kate beamed, causing Craig to blush.

Craig noticed Patrick roll his eyes and instantly wished he hadn't mentioned his birthday. Craig knew Patrick was conscious he would still only be fourteen when he turned sixteen. They had talked about it, and Patrick's predominant worry was that Craig would move on and leave him behind in search of a more physical relationship.

This was not the case at all. At this stage, Craig was as naïve as Patrick when it came to sex and relationships, and he was more than willing to respect that Patrick was younger and had his parent's religious beliefs to be reconciled.

Craig wished he could tell Patrick how long he had waited to introduce himself, the things he had done to engineer their first meeting. The nights he had spent imagining them together, but this probably wouldn't have served to reassure him.

Instead, Craig had promised Patrick repeatedly that he was more than happy to wait. This was all new to him, too, and the stolen kisses and cuddles were enough. Although Craig had to confess, the recent escalation of sending each other dickpics was undoubtedly making his physical desires more intense.

'Can we go now?' Patrick asked.

'Hold on, two ticks. Let me give you some money for lunch.'

Kate had already turned and lifted her handbag from the hall table before she had finished her sentence. She held out a twenty-pound note, and Patrick stepped forwards to take it. Then, before letting go, she leaned in and kissed him on the forehead.

'Mum!' came the usual protest.

'That's right, I'm your mum, and I'll be kissing you no matter if you're fourteen, sixteen, or fifty-two!' she giggled. 'Get you both some lunch, and I don't need any change if you want a sweety too.'

'You are so embarrassing,' Patrick said as he opened the front door, but when he turned back to say goodbye to his mother, Craig noticed he was smiling.

\* \* \*

The retail park was situated on the outskirts of the neighbouring town and was only ten miles away. Even so, with the walk to the bus stop, the wait for the next service, and a village-hopping journey, it had taken them well over an hour from leaving the vicarage to arrive outside the magic shop.

Patrick had been visiting the store for almost two years, and when Craig had started to join him on the trips in recent months, he became aware that Patrick had built a strong bond with Geoff, the gnarly-fingered owner.

Craig found Geoff a bit creepy and loathed it when he put his arm around him, resting his crumbling fingers on his shoulder. Craig would smile back all the same. If Geoff was important to Patrick, then he was also important to Craig, for now, at least.

One day, Geoff commented that Patrick had been much more outgoing and confident since meeting

Craig, but despite the compliment, Craig was certain that Geoff didn't like him much either. His lingering stares when the boys would be whispering or giggling suggested he knew they were more than just friends, probably worrying him that Craig would corrupt his protégé.

Geoff spotted Patrick and Craig through the window and waved them both in. Craig couldn't help but think of the *Scary Movie* character and, under his breath, whispered, *'Let me use my strong hand.'* Luckily, Patrick didn't seem to hear.

'Hello, boys,' Geoff cheerfully greeted them as they entered the shop.

'Morning, Geoff,' they replied in unison. 'Got anything new in?' Patrick added.

'Well, funny you should ask,' Geoff said with mischief in his smile. 'I may just have something you could use in your first show,' he added.

'Oh, I bet!' Patrick rolled his eyes at the suggestion. They both knew Geoff was desperate to get him to perform at his first local show.

Craig sided with Geoff on this and was working on getting Patrick to agree, but he was understandably reticent following the disaster that was his last public display. Nevertheless, Craig knew that magic was going to be Patrick's future, even if he didn't quite yet.

'Well, let me show you. I'll lend it to you if you sign up for the Spring Bank Holiday talent show?'

Craig knew only too well the show Geoff was referring to, and he was trying to persuade Patrick to participate as the show was taking place in the store. Patrick knew most of the regular customers, and it seemed a relatively safe environment for him to attempt another performance. Minus the cloak this time.

'I can't learn a new trick by the twenty-sixth,' he almost gasped. 'That's only like ten days away!'

'You don't have to perform this one, but you can borrow it as a reward. It's a good one,' Geoff winked and beckoned them to follow him to the magic section at the back of the store.

Craig went with them and watched as Geoff clumsily fingered his way through his performance on a piece of black cloth that served as a demonstration area on the counter in the magic department.

The trick entailed running a signed five-pound note through a mangle and changing it into a ten-pound note, still bearing the original signature. Craig feigned interest as each step of the trick was performed, but as the big reveal happened, Patrick was clearly more impressed than Craig.

'Wow!' Patrick exclaimed as he lifted the note from the table. He examined it closely, and it was a genuine note with his original marking on it. 'How…' he began to ask but was cut short.

'A magician never tells!' Geoff winked. 'Unless you're on the team for the Bank Holiday show, of course.'

'Okay, I'll do it,' Patrick conceded, and Craig was

suddenly interested again. He'd been working on Patrick for an age to get him to change his mind about another public performance without success, and he seemed to have been persuaded by this simple old trick. Either way, the result was positive.

'Marvellous! Well, that isn't actually the end of the trick. You put the note back through, and it turns back into the five-pound note but without a signature. You're supposed to check the serial number at the start to make sure it's the same one at the end, but I forgot to ask you that bit,' Geoff rolled his eyes at his mistake. 'I'll tell you what, you can keep the ten pounds as long as you spend it in the shop today.'

'Thank you,' Patrick smiled.

Craig knew Geoff wouldn't show Patrick the trick in front of him, some magician's code nonsense, but he wasn't in the mood to wait around on his own, so he stood his ground until Patrick must have decided to take up the offer at a later date.

Craig shadowed Patrick around the shop while he chose a few things to spend his money on, and then, with a brown paper bag in hand, they said farewell to Geoff and left.

\* \* \*

A glance at the shopping centre clock informed any onlookers that it was almost 12:30 pm. The boys had been wandering around the shops for just over an hour after leaving the magic shop, mostly window shopping and chatting about all sorts of random stuff. The things that seem important when you are a teenage boy.

They discussed the new *Twilight* movie that was coming out, and Patrick drooled over Taylor Lautner after pointing out to Craig that he was actually older than them and not still the ten-year-old boy he remembered from *Sharkboy*.

Craig then mentioned his eagerness to see *The Dark Knight* and how sad it was that Heath Ledger had died. Patrick pulled a sad face and referenced him also dying in Brokeback Mountain.

'He didn't die in *Brokeback Mountain*. It was Jake Gyllenhaal,' Craig corrected, but it turned out Patrick was just making a joke about the situation and the character both being a bummer.

'You idiot!' Craig moaned and punched Patrick softly on the top of his arm. Both boys cracked up laughing at their childish sense of humour.

'Do you fancy something to eat?' Craig suggested. 'I'm starving.'

'*McDonald's?*' the reply, which needed no answer. It was always *McDonald's*.

The food hall was on the top floor of the shopping centre and contained several restaurants and a cinema, as well as the usual atrium of fast-food chains with a shared seating area.

Craig saved them a table while Patrick went to order the food. Craig watched his friend across the food hall as he shuffled forward in the queue, staring longingly at the seat of his denim shorts until it was blocked when a rather large lady wearing black leggings stepped in line behind him.

Disturbed by the alternate buttocks now in his line of sight, Craig looked away. As his eyes scanned around, he recognised three faces from school in the distance. They were a way off, but Craig noticed they were heading in his direction. This little gang were sometimes trouble, and Patrick would hate any confrontation, but Craig would handle it if it came to it.

Patrick returned with a tray piled high with food and sat down opposite Craig. They both tucked into their lunch, chatting all the while, with no adults to correct their manners.

'So, you are going to do the show for Geoff?' Craig mumbled around a *McNugget*.

'Yeah, I need to get some experience performing. It will be okay,' Patrick tried to reassure himself as he wiped a drip of mayonnaise from the side of his chicken sandwich with a chip.

'Can I come and watch?' Craig asked, but as Patrick took a sip of his drink, Craig noticed the boys from school had spotted them. His eyes widened, his brows raised, and his stare disappeared over Patrick's shoulder, but it was too late.

Craig looked on as Neil Dixon slapped Patrick across the back of his head, causing him to lurch forward and dribble a little of his cola onto the table.

'Go careful drinking all that,' the voice from behind advised. 'You don't want another accident, pissy pants.'

Surprisingly, Patrick stood up and turned to confront his foe, and Craig quickly stood up and stepped beside him to support, as Neil was accompanied by two friends.

'Calm down, girls,' Neil mocked. 'I'm not here to disturb your romantic lunch date. Just saying hello to my favourite couple.'

'I didn't know you cared that much. We can have a threesome if you like?' Craig fired back, puffing his chest a little as he spoke, but Patrick curtailed his bravado with an elbow to the ribs.

Neil smiled before quickly leaning forwards to the right of Patrick and grabbing his brown paper bag from the table.

'What have we got here?' Neil enquired as he peered into the open top of the bag. Then, noticing the playing cards, he held the bag out to Patrick. 'Go on then, show us a trick.'

'Leave us alone,' Craig said as he snatched the bag back.

'It's okay,' Patrick calmly interjected. 'I'll show him a trick.'

Craig watched intently as Patrick reached into the bag and pulled out a packet of playing cards. All without speaking, he removed the cellophane wrapper, broke the seal, and removed the cards from the box. He pulled out the jokers and the ad cards and discarded them onto the table. He shuffled, ruffle-shuffled, cut, and reshuffled the deck before fanning the cards face down in front of Neil.

'Pick one,' he instructed, focused and confident with Craig by his side.

Not usually so compliant, Neil slid a card from the deck and showed it to his two friends. As he did so, Patrick shuffled the cards once more and then presented the fanned deck to Neil again.

'Slide it in wherever you like,' was the next instruction, to which Neil also complied.

Patrick performed another round of theatrical shuffling, a skill he practised regularly, before squaring up the pack. He held the deck between his thumb and forefinger and raised his arm until the bottom card was level with Neil's face.

'Is that your card?' Patrick asked.

'No!' Neil laughed, seeing the Two of Spades before him. 'It was the Queen of Hearts.'

Neil's friends joined in with his sniggering, but the laughter ceased within a fraction of a second, and jaws dropped at what happened next.

Patrick squeezed the deck of cards between his thumb and fingers until it bowed in the middle, and then with a further press, he caused the Two of Spades, closely followed by the remainder of the deck, to flick out and bounce off Neil's face.

Along with Neil's friends, Craig watched on in silence but maintained the wherewithal to prepare himself for Neil's inevitable reaction. But Neil did not react as expected at all. Instead, he stood in silence, staring directly at Patrick, who did not once break his gaze.

As the moments passed, Neil's face reddened, but

this was not the result of a building rage. His eyes widened, bulging slightly, and tears began to well. He opened his mouth, wide and rounded as if to howl in frustration, but no words came.

Patrick stared blankly at his enemy, giving no reaction whatsoever as Neil's lips began to turn blue and his hands raised up, grabbing at his throat. There was panic and desperation in Neil's expression, and Craig knew he had to do something.

Pushing past Patrick, Craig moved around to stand behind Neil and wrapped his arms around his waist. He performed a crude form of the Heimlich manoeuvre, and on the third thrust, Neil coughed up the blockage from his throat. A playing card, folded in quarters with the face showing. It was a saliva-soaked Queen of Hearts.

As Craig released his hold, Neil dropped onto his hands and knees in front of Patrick, gasping air back into his lungs. Patrick used his foot to slide the coughed-up card directly under Neil's face.

'Is that your card?' Patrick asked sarcastically. 'Now fucking leave me alone, you prick!' he added before walking away.

Craig picked up the shopping bag and grabbed a napkin from the table before racing to catch up with his friend.

'Your ear,' he said as he held the napkin out.

Patrick wiped the small trickle of blood from his left ear and discarded the rag in the next bin as they made their way out of the shopping centre and back towards the bus stop.

'What happened there?' Craig eventually asked.

'I'm not sure,' Patrick puzzled. 'But it felt frigging amazing!'

'How did you get the card folded up and into his throat?' Craig asked, but it was a leading question. Patrick was good, but Craig knew this was beyond Patrick's skill set.

'I didn't. I only meant to flick the cards at him, but then this thought came into my head, and it just kinda happened,' Patrick shrugged.

'You just thought it, and it happened?' Craig asked, sounding a little sceptical.

'I swear,' Patrick insisted. 'It was fucking epic!'

The boys had reached their bus stop and sat themselves down on the bench to await the next service. Craig was silent for a moment while he thought things through a little before deciding to push Patrick further.

'See that window over there?' Craig pointed across the street to the window of a coffee shop. 'See if you can make one of those bags of coffee fall off the shelf,' Craig challenged.

Patrick focused through the window on the bags of coffee stacked on the shelf, unsure exactly what to do other than imagine a bag falling. Craig wasn't looking at the window. Instead, he focused on Patrick, noticing another small drop of blood leak from his left ear just before he leapt up in excitement.

Across the road, the entire shop shelf had collapsed,

spilling coffee bags all over the floor, startling customers and staff alike.

'Holy shit! Did you see that?' Patrick blurted.

'Amazing!' Craig replied, although he sounded less amazed than he might. 'You can't tell anyone about this, Patrick. They'll think you're a freak.'

Patrick calmed down and turned back to Craig.

'You don't think I'm a freak, do you?'

'I think you're freaking amazing, babe. We are gonna do something special with this gift, trust me,' Craig reassured him just as their bus pulled up.

# CHAPTER 10

January 2010

Craig walked into the town hall just as the compère for the evening asked the crowd to put their hands together for Patrick. He had been performing table magic at an event arranged by Geoff, and Craig had come to pick him up at the end of the evening.

It had been almost two years since Patrick had been coaxed to perform at the Spring Bank Holiday show in Geoff's shop, but no such coaxing had been required on this occasion. The Spring show had gone amazingly well, and Patrick had caught the bug to be on stage and the centre of attention.

Patrick was good, too, really good. He had built up an extensive repertoire of tricks, and he had mastered them all the traditional way. Craig had insisted that Patrick did not attempt to use his powers unless they were together, and Patrick would never dream of going against Craig's wishes. That said, he did try once when he was alone in his bedroom, not long after the incident at the shopping centre, but nothing happened.

It had been two years now, and with Craig as his mentor, Patrick would try and perform small tasks, usually moving an object, but it was hit and miss. Honing this skill was proving difficult, and finding a practical and reliable application within his magic routines would take some time, but Craig was very patient with him, and he couldn't have loved Patrick more.

As Patrick stood up from taking his bow, Craig caught his eye from where he stood in the doorway at the back of the hall. Patrick hadn't changed much in the two years since they had met, but Craig still found him so attractive.

Patrick's precocious start to puberty had stalled a little, and Craig, who had been a late starter, had overtaken him in the last eighteen months, now standing a head's length taller than him. Craig had also shed his layer of puppy fat and was enjoying his new slimmer look.

Some commented that he was a little too slim for his height, but Craig loved how he looked. He wasn't as defined as Patrick, and he had a few stretch marks caused by his rapid growth spurt, but he knew he looked good. And everything else had grown, too, taking him well above average in the college locker room.

With newfound confidence, he would happily wander naked from the showers after using the gym, aware of which boys' eyes were taking him in.

Craig was in his first year of college, having chosen it over the sixth form. He wasn't strong academically and had no intention of attending university, so he opted for a more practical BTEC in hospitality management rather than A-levels. Craig had also moved away from Witford Common the previous summer, sending Patrick into a brief panic.

Patrick had written him the sweetest love letter, which he had found in his rucksack during a geography lesson. They had rendezvoused in the toilets at the next break, and Craig had given him a reassuring hug that nothing would change. He was only moving to the next town, his mother giving up their council house and moving into an apartment block not far from the shopping centre the boys frequented most weekends.

The boys' families supported them with lifts when the bus service would not suffice, but within four months, Craig had passed his driving test and had become the proud owner of a royal blue 2002 *Peugeot 106*.

This allowed both boys more freedom from their families. They took little road trips to other towns to shop or went on seaside trips filled with ice cream and fish & chips. And often, after dark, they would park up in a secluded layby or down in the lover's field by the river, enjoying kisses and exploring each other's bodies.

Craig had also become Patrick's roadie, and this duty now had him standing at the back of the town hall, waiting for his boyfriend to finish soaking up the adoration.

'I'm sure the rounds of applause get longer every time,' Craig smiled when Patrick eventually came over to his side.

High on the adrenalin from the show, Patrick leaned in and whispered, 'I want you to fuck me next weekend. I think I'm ready.'

Before Craig could respond, he was led by the hand into the car park. Still dazed, he unlocked the car and watched as Patrick placed his rucksack of props into the boot. He slammed it shut and then jumped into the passenger seat to escape the January evening drizzle that had begun to fall. Craig mirrored his movements on the driver's side, fastened his seatbelt, and placed the key in the ignition.

'What did you say?' he finally found the words, but he had heard clearly enough. 'I thought you wanted to wait until your sixteenth birthday?' he added.

'It's only three weeks away, but my parents are away next weekend at a wedding. I'm not going, and they have said you can stay over,' Patrick explained. 'And I really want to. We've been together for nearly two years. The stuff we do is great, but I'm ready to go further. I love you.'

'Oh, man! I love you too!' Craig gushed. 'I've just popped the hardest boner!' Craig dropped his eyes to the protrusion in his jeans, and Patrick's gaze followed.

'Lover's field on the way home?' Patrick suggested. 'I can sort that right out for you,' he added, making a bulge in his cheek with his tongue in a simulation of oral sex.

Craig moaned in anticipation before starting the engine and excitedly pulling away, spinning the car's wheels on the wet tarmac in his eagerness.

\* \* \*

It seemed to have been the longest of weeks, but Craig had finally finished college and was on his way over to pick up Patrick. He had packed his weekend bag the previous evening, and it was in the boot of his car where Craig now threw in his college rucksack alongside it.

As he closed the boot, he noticed the musty odour from the previous day's gym bag, which he had forgotten to take out and put in the wash. He smiled a little and made himself blush, remembering yesterday's shower incident.

One of the other college students seemed to go out of his way to make sure he was in the gym at the same time as Craig, and his eyes would track Craig's naked exit from the shower and keep locked on to him until he was dressed.

Presumably, the boy thought he was being subtle, but he wasn't. Craig had noticed him again yesterday as he was drying himself off. He also noticed they were alone and, driven by the sexual tension he had been feeling all week in anticipation of the weekend with

Patrick, Craig had dropped his towel on the bench beside himself and asked the stranger if he wanted to suck him off.

The boxershorts-clad boy was on his knees in an instant, deep-throating Craig's seven inches with ease. Then, driven by an uncontrollable desire, Craig pulled him up onto his feet, pulled down his shorts and turned him around before sitting down on the bench. The boy, knowing what was being requested, reached behind himself for Craig's erection and guided it as he lowered himself down inch by inch.

Craig closed his eyes as he was ridden and knew he would be ready to explode in seconds, but he suddenly had a flash of Patrick's face in his thoughts. This was supposed to be Patrick's moment. They had been waiting so long to take each other's virginity, and Craig had a sudden pang of guilt.

He asked the boy to stop, he didn't want to cum inside him, and he got back to his feet, a little confused. Craig still wanted to cum, though, and he motioned for the boy to get back on his knees. He willingly complied, and Craig finished himself off all over the boy's face as the boy wanked and came over his own stomach.

The whole incident lasted no more than two minutes, and both boys were consumed by the moment. Raging teenagers that could cum in a heartbeat, aroused even harder by the risk of getting caught having sex in public. Then when the orgasms were over, their confidence was also drained, and they both wanted to be away from there as quickly as possible.

Craig grabbed his damp towel and offered it to the boy to wipe himself clean. Then they dressed in silence, only catching each other's eyes once when the changing room door opened, and they were joined by three other lads who had come to work out.

Thirty seconds earlier, and they would have been caught. They both smiled at the thought, and as Craig walked past his new acquaintance to leave, he softly whispered, 'I'll be back in on Tuesday if you want to work out together?'

The musty scent of the gym bag, caused by a towel damp with shower water and cum, had sparked instant recall, but Craig pushed it from his mind again. Patrick didn't need to know about it. It hadn't been proper sex. It hadn't meant anything. Craig's conscience was clear for the weekend ahead, and his love for Patrick was as strong as ever.

The drive to the vicarage was traffic-free, and Craig was knocking on the door less than twenty minutes after leaving college. He was a little surprised when Kate answered but was reassured to see their weekend suitcases sitting in the hallway.

'Are you looking forward to the wedding, Mrs Morgan?' Craig asked.

'I very much am, Craig. Thanks for asking,' she smiled back as she ushered him inside. 'We are running a bit late, mind, so forgive me, you'll have to help yourself to a drink if you want one,' she added.

'I'm fine, thank you. I will just wait for Patrick.'

'He's still getting ready,' Kate explained. 'Lord

knows what he is doing. He's been at it for ages. It smells like a perfume shop up there,' she finished as Patrick wafted down the stairs along with an overpowering scent of *Joop!*

The boys greeted each other with a nod, and Patrick squeezed a pair of trainers onto his feet without undoing the laces.

'Are you heading off now?' his mother asked.

'Yeah, booked the early viewing,' Patrick replied.

'Okay, have fun then. We will be gone when you get back. The spare room is made up for Craig.'

Craig watched as Patrick hugged his mother to reassure her that everything would be okay. 'See you Sunday lunchtime,' were his last words as they left the house, but both boys knew Craig wouldn't be sleeping in the spare room.

\* \* \*

The open-air car park of the out-of-town multiplex was half empty, and Craig managed to park close to the foyer entrance. They collected their tickets from the automated kiosk before heading to the food counter. A few minutes later, they were taking their seats in the centre of the back row of the near-empty Screen 7, one of the smaller screens that movies were moved to as they came to the end of their run.

'Are you sure you don't want something to eat?' Craig asked. 'You can share this,' he added, holding up a footlong hotdog plastered in onions, ketchup, and mustard.

'I'm okay. I just want a drink,' Patrick declined. 'I douched before we came out. I don't want to eat,' he added nonchalantly.

Craig had just taken a bite of his hotdog and almost choked it down. He had to cough and take a sip of his drink before he could reply.

'I didn't know you had a douche bulb,' he said, sounding positively impressed.

Patrick went on to explain that he didn't have a proper douche bulb at all. The risk of ordering one of those from *Amazon* and having it discovered didn't bear thinking about. Instead, he had googled the technique and improvised with an *Evian* water bottle.

Impressed by Patrick's ingenuity, Craig confessed his own preparations for the evening's activities. When they had stopped for petrol on the way to the cinema, he had purchased a packet of condoms.

'This is really happening, isn't it?' Craig finished, and Patrick confirmed with a nod.

The trailers started, and they watched them in silence, both still processing the conversation they had just had, excited and nervous at how the evening would unfold. Then, as the theatre lights dimmed further and the curtains opened a little wider for the main feature, Patrick moved his leg so their knees touched and placed his hand on Craig's thigh. Once Craig had finished eating, he put his own hand over the top of Patrick's, and they interlinked their fingers.

*The Book of Eli* was a film they had both been keen

to see, but their minds were elsewhere, and they were both pleased when the end credits began to roll an hour and fifty-eight minutes later. As the lights rose, Craig released Patrick's hand and wiped his sweaty palm on the back of his jeans. They left the cinema, depositing their rubbish on the way back through the foyer, and exited into the early evening darkness.

The journey back to the vicarage was a little awkward, but they made small talk about the film until Craig parked up directly outside the front door. Patrick turned his key and let them into the hallway, and they were both relieved to see his parents' travel bags had gone. After kicking off their shoes, Patrick went into the kitchen where the dog was left when the house was empty, while Craig excused himself to use the downstairs toilet.

As Craig returned, Barnaby wandered back in from the garden and was instructed to get back onto his bed. Patrick then led Craig by the hand through to the lounge, shutting the dog back in the kitchen so he didn't bother them.

When they reached the sizeable four-seater sofa towards the back of the room, they released their hands, and Patrick asked Craig to sit down. He then straddled Craig's knees, sitting face-to-face on his lap and began to kiss him. They had kissed many times before, but this time it felt different.

Craig held the back of Patrick's head as they French kissed, their tongues entwined as they duelled to taste more of each other.

In need of a short breath, Patrick pulled his head back briefly, and Craig took the opportunity to swiftly drop his hands to the rear hem of Patrick's jumper. Craig lifted the jumper over Patrick's head in one movement and pulled it free from his raised arms. He repeated the manoeuvre with the t-shirt below and pulled Patrick's naked torso back towards him so they could continue kissing.

Minutes later, Craig raised his arms aloft, and Patrick took the signal and repeated his partial undressing. Craig noticed Patrick's eyes dart sideways, taking in the sight of his armpits, so he kept his arms raised and nodded permission that Patrick could do as he pleased.

Patrick may have been the younger of the two, but he knew what he liked, and his likes were often on the cusp of fetish. Craig watched on as Patrick leaned forwards and kissed his armpit. He buried his face in the wispy ginger hairs and kissed and licked the sweat, the scent a little acrid with pheromones after a full day at college.

Craig's erection was throbbing as he watched Patrick's kisses track from hairy armpit to smooth nipple and then downwards, pausing briefly to give attention to his outie belly button before carrying on the kisses down yet more wispy ginger hairs that led an enticing path, disappearing into the top of Craig's jeans.

The course of the kissing had caused Patrick to move backwards from his seat on Craig's lap, and he now knelt on the floor between his lover's parted legs. However, the denim would not be the end of this trail, and Craig watched as Patrick quickly undid his belt buckle, popper, and zip.

Craig lifted his hips, allowing Patrick to pull down his jeans and remove them altogether, revealing his bulging white *Calvin Klein* briefs. Craig let out a moan of pleasure as Patrick kissed the outside of his underwear along the entire length of his shaft until his lips came to rest at the tip, which had leaked precum, making the patch of underwear around his helmet damp and translucent.

The foreplay was over. Craig needed to be inside him. He started to pull down the waistband of his underwear, but Patrick took over, pulling it off completely before lifting Craig's penis away from his body and taking as much of it into his mouth as he could. Craig moaned with pleasure as a slight shudder ran through his body.

They had performed oral sex on each other many times before, but it was always the climax of their lovemaking. Knowing that they were going further this time made the sensation feel more intense. As Craig watched his own penis slipping in and out of Patrick's mouth, he knew he wouldn't be able to stop himself from ejaculating if this continued, so he placed his hands on each side of Patrick's head and pulled up slightly, indicating he wanted him to stand up.

As Patrick rose in front of him, Craig noticed he had, at some point, managed to remove his own trousers and underwear and now stood completely naked, his dick rock hard and pointing vertically in youthful exuberance.

Craig slid forwards on the sofa and down onto his knees in front of Patrick. He placed his lips around his friend and took all of him into his mouth. Then, holding his hands on Patrick's buttocks, he pulled him in even deeper until his nose pressed into the small, neat patch of dark pubic hair above his shaft, and he could feel Patrick's soft, smooth balls on his chin.

Patrick squealed at the intense pleasure, and Craig loosened his hold, took a quick breath, and continued with a gentler blowjob. He didn't want Patrick to cum yet, but knowing neither of them would be able to hold out long, Craig turned his attention to preparing Patrick's arse.

For the next minute or so, as he continued the blowjob, Craig tickled and tipped at Patrick's bottom until it was remarkably easy to slip two fingers inside the moist and pulsing hole.

Patrick's knees bent a little at the pleasure he was receiving simultaneously on both sides of his body. Then, concerned his friend's legs may buckle, Craig ceased his fingering and guided him around to sit down on the sofa. As Patrick fell back into the seat, his cock withdrew from Craig's mouth with a comical pop and slapped back vertically against his belly.

'Fuck! This is so hot,' Patrick exclaimed.

'It's about to get a lot hotter, baby,' Craig promised.

Craig pulled Patrick's hips forward until his bottom hung slightly over the front of the sofa, and his body was almost lying on the seat. He then raised Patrick's legs into the air and pushed them back until his knees were almost by his ears, causing Patrick to instinctively take hold of his own calves and hold them in position.

Looking up at Patrick over the top of his scrotum, Craig went to work rimming his hole. He maintained his stare as he worked his tongue deeper and deeper inside, noting which movements caused Patrick's eyes to roll with pleasure before repeating them.

'Oh, my god! I want you inside me so bad,' Patrick pleaded.

Craig sat back on his haunches and rooted around on the floor for his jeans so he could grab the condoms from his pocket.

'You don't need a condom,' Patrick told him. 'We're both virgins, it's safe, and I just want to feel you.'

The briefest image of the boy in the gym slipping down on his unsheathed cock came into Craig's mind, but he pushed it away. He lifted himself onto his knees and shuffled closer to Patrick, who remained prone with his legs in the air.

With one hand, Craig rubbed the precum that had gathered at the tip of his penis over his glans to give some lubrication and then pushed his head against Patrick's hole. He leaned back slightly, giving himself a full view as it slowly slipped inside.

Craig proceeded millimetre by millimetre, checking Patrick's face for any contortions of pain, conscious this was his first time. However, Patrick appeared to be enjoying every moment, and Craig was soon sliding his full length slowly in and out of his friend.

As Craig looked down, turned on by the sight of himself thrusting, Patrick groaned as his penis convulsed and a small amount of semen oozed from the end. It wasn't a full ejaculation but an intense precursor neither had ever experienced.

Aware this would soon be over for both of them, Craig took hold of Patrick's penis and began to masturbate him as they now fucked harder and faster.

'Oh baby, you're so tight. This feels amazing. I don't know how long I can last,' Craig moaned as Patrick closed his eyes and focused on his other senses.

Suddenly everything changed.

Craig felt a hand on his shoulder and was suddenly dragged backwards on his haunches, breaking his contact with Patrick as he fell.

As he looked up from where he lay, Craig could see the beetroot-red face of Patrick's father looking down on him with rage in his eyes. Nigel's fists were clenched, and Craig knew this was going to get ugly, but the intense pleasure he had been feeling only seconds before had crossed the point of no return.

Nigel's eyes widened further, and the veins on his forehead bulged as he looked down to witness Craig's erect penis convulse in a hands-free ejaculation which sprayed spurt after spurt of semen into the air.

Craig pulled his legs to his chest and put his hand up to protect his head as Patrick's father began to rain blows down upon him. In the doorway, Patrick's mother began to wail as Nigel screamed obscenities at Craig in time with every blow.

'You abomination. You fucking disgusting boy. You sodomite. You bastard rapist.' A new variation with every punch to Craig's torso.

Behind them, Patrick leapt up from the sofa, screaming for his father to stop. He grabbed his shoulder, and Nigel spun around to face his son.

'I will deal with you later…' he spat in rage, but Patrick was already lurching forwards.

Craig lowered his hands and watched as Patrick clasped his hand around his father's throat, cutting short his words, and then with unnatural strength, he forced his father backwards across the room until his back was against the wall.

With his head now raised, Craig watched on, realising that Patrick would require more than the initial adrenalin rush to keep his father at bay. Craig willed Patrick to use his power, and with that, Patrick lifted his father up onto tiptoes.

'Keep your fucking hands off of my boyfriend!' he said almost calmly as a small trickle of blood ran down his left earlobe.

Craig noticed the bleeding, and then he saw something in the corner of his eye flying through the air. Kate had lifted a vase from the sideboard and hurled it across the room, intending to hit her son, but instead, it smashed against the wall to the side of her husband.

'Get out of my house. Both of you. Get out of my house now,' she screamed at the boys.

Craig scurried across the floor, gathering their

clothes before scampering back into the hallway. Patrick released his father from the chokehold and followed Craig as his mother ran to her husband's side to comfort him.

Expecting to be pursued at any moment, the boys quickly dressed and hurried out of the building and into Craig's car. They were a couple of miles down the road before Craig spoke first.

'I am so sorry. What are we going to do?' he asked and then answered his own question. 'You'll have to stay at mine. We'll have to tell my mum what happened.'

Patrick turned to Craig and smiled. His eyes still glazed over a little in the trance-like state he seemed to get into when his powers surfaced.

'Pull the car over somewhere. I really need to cum!'

Craig turned into the next side street and pulled the car over, parking it under the darkness of a large tree. While he was manoeuvring, Patrick had already undone his trousers and slipped them down with his underwear. He was rock-hard and began furiously wanking himself.

Craig unfastened his seatbelt and turned towards Patrick to take over the task.

'Faster!' Patrick instructed, pushing his hips into Craig's thrusts. 'Keep going. Oh, fuck! I'm gonna shoot my load.'

With that, Patrick let out a stifled groan as he held his breath and pulsed out a ribbon of semen that hit the front windscreen.

On another occasion, this display would have had both of them giggling, but as Craig reached for a tissue from the glovebox, it didn't feel like a time for humour. He wiped the glass and then turned to offer Patrick a second tissue just as his tears began to flow.

'I fucking hate him!' Patrick cried. 'I fucking hate my father!'

Patrick's tears turned to uncontrollable sobbing, and after Craig pulled up his boyfriend's underwear and jeans, making him decent again should anyone pass by, he held Patrick in his arms until his crying stopped some fifteen minutes later.

\* \* \*

It was the day of Patrick's sixteenth birthday, and he had not yet seen his parents following the events of almost two weeks ago when the boys had come back to the flat, and Craig had tearfully confessed to his mother what had happened at the vicarage.

Lisa had been disappointed but had comforted them both and agreed Patrick could stay with them while things settled down. Not in Craig's room, though. She was clear about that.

Initially, Kate refused to speak to Lisa when she reached out the following day, accusing her of being complicit in hiding their sons' relationship. However, when Lisa turned up in the charity shop on Monday morning and threatened to have the conversation publicly, Kate agreed to go with her for a coffee.

The conversation was heated, but Lisa forced Kate to listen to some home truths, and the end result was that Lisa went back to the vicarage with Kate to collect some clothes and other belongings for Patrick. Kate also agreed she would text Patrick and would speak to Nigel about the possibility of him coming back home.

Their mothers' coffee morning had been eight days ago, and as promised, Kate had messaged Patrick several times since. First, there was an initial apology for screaming and throwing him out of the house. Then, a change of tone to try and make him understand how shocked they were to walk in and catch them. Next was a heated exchange when Kate implied Craig was to blame entirely. Then finally, she suggested that she and Patrick's father come over on his birthday, and hopefully, he would like to return home with them.

The meeting had been arranged for after school, and Patrick had changed out of his uniform and was waiting for his parents to arrive. Craig wasn't happy that Patrick might be returning home and had tried to convince him it would be toxic for their relationship.

All the same, Craig had insisted he came home from college early to support Patrick and was with him on the balcony of the flat, looking down over the small car park waiting for the arrival of Nigel's burgundy Volvo estate.

Patrick's phone vibrated with a text from his mother to say they were nearly there just as they saw the car come around a corner in the distance. Craig wished him good luck with a kiss on the cheek, and

Patrick headed off to meet them downstairs.

Nigel parked in a space on the edge of the small playing green that served the blocks of apartments surrounding it on three sides. They were modern five-story affairs, with Lisa's apartment on the fourth floor. She had joined Craig on the balcony and watched as Kate stepped from the vehicle just as Patrick exited the building. They walked towards each other and met halfway down the path.

Craig couldn't hear the conversation from the balcony, but he watched intently and tried to piece it together in his head. Kate had spoken first, making Patrick cry, and then she wrapped him in her arms as he sobbed for a few moments.

When Patrick stepped back from his mother's embrace, he spoke, and they both turned toward the parked car. Craig also looked over to see Nigel sitting behind the wheel, staring directly at his family but failing to react to Patrick's wave.

The conversation continued, and Kate put an arm on Patrick's shoulder and tried to encourage him towards the car. Craig noticed Patrick stood firm and continued to talk. He wasn't ready to leave yet. He asked a further question before pausing to listen to his mother's reply. Then the rage came.

'You're fucking joking!' Patrick shrugged his shoulder away from his mother's grip. 'Dad's going to pray away the gay. Is that your plan?'

On the balcony, Lisa and Craig had heard Patrick's bellowed response and became aware that the mood had changed. Patrick's raised voice drew further attention from the parents and children in the playpark in front of where Nigel still sat calmly in his car.

Craig took a step forward to better observe the unfolding drama. He noticed that Kate was now pointing at Patrick's ear, confused as to why it was bleeding. But Craig knew why it was bleeding, shit was about to go down, and just then, a voice called out from the crowd.

'Oh, my God! Look up there. There's a man on the roof. I think he's going to jump,' a lady shouted, pointing to the rooftop of the block of flats opposite Lisa's.

Everyone within earshot turned their gaze to where the lady was pointing, and there was, indeed, a man teetering on the edge of the rooftop. He, in turn, was pointing directly at the balcony where Lisa and Craig were standing, mouthing words the crowd below were unable to hear.

Lisa and Craig could only pick out some of the words Nigel was babbling, seemingly some religious text, as he pointed an accusing finger towards their position before crossing himself in one final sacred act and then falling forwards.

The crowds gasped as they watched the man fall to the ground, hitting the concrete below with a gut-wrenching noise before bouncing back up slightly and landing in an unnaturally broken position, with a pool of blood gathering around his fractured skull.

When Craig arrived at his side a few minutes later, Patrick was still staring at his father's lifeless body as members of the public attempted to do what they could. Even his mother's screams had not distracted him, and he only turned away when Craig put his arm around his shoulder and handed him a tissue.

'It will be okay,' Craig whispered, and Patrick took the tissue, all too aware of what it was for.

Lisa had run down the stairs with Craig and was attempting to comfort Kate, but her screams continued until they were joined by wailing sirens, and a paramedic was required to administer a sedative to calm her.

# CHAPTER 11

April 2019

Craig let out a stifled moan as he came inside Kevin, the stagehand who had been guiding him and Patrick through their day, and then another as a shudder of intense sensitivity engulfed his penis as he withdrew.

Kevin pulled up his underwear and skinny jeans, which had been hurriedly yanked down to his knees, and pulled back down his *Kylie Minogue, Kiss Me Once* tour t-shirt, which had been lifted over his head, exposing his smooth, skinny, twenty-something torso.

Craig had already tucked himself away and rezipped, and when Kevin was decent, he opened the door of the prop cupboard they had ducked into for the quick fuck they both knew was going to happen as soon as their eyes met earlier that day.

The coast was clear, so they stepped out and continued their journey to the auditorium, where Kevin was taking Craig to be seated before returning to Patrick, who was waiting in the wings for his performance.

Random sex had become something of a habit for Craig, which, if he had thought about it, he could have traced right back to that first locker room incident at college when he was seventeen. But he tried not to think about it. So instead, he compartmentalised it in his mind as just some harmless hormone fuelled fun.

It certainly wasn't love. Craig had no feelings for these people. It was just sex. Love was what he felt for Patrick. Although he knew it wasn't harmless, really. Patrick would be devastated if he ever found out. They did not have an open relationship, so the cheating had to be accompanied by lies. Not big ones, but regular ones. The hairline ones that could stay hidden for years but, at some point, come together to crack the foundations of a relationship.

Contrary to Craig's sexploits, he really did value the life they had built together. And they did have a good life. Childhood sweethearts of eleven years now and married for the last two.

Patrick had never moved back home with his mother following the death of his father. Even if he had wanted to, it would not have been possible. Kate was never released from psychiatric care following the incident. She had suffered a complete breakdown, and Patrick could not visit without sending her into a psychotic frenzy.

Craig's mother had stepped up and taken Patrick in permanently. After only a week, she had even allowed him to leave the sofa behind and start sharing Craig's bed for reasons Craig was unsure of but was grateful, nonetheless.

The boys lived with Lisa for over three years before Craig had to support Patrick through another tragic event. Geoff passed away.

Selfishly, Geoff's passing came as welcome relief for Craig. Their relationship was fractious, although neither had allowed Patrick to become aware of their mutual dislike of each other.

Patrick, however, was distraught. Geoff had been like a father to him. He was better than his own father, for sure, and Craig would do everything in his power to support him through it.

Patrick was nineteen when the news of Geoff's death came through. Lisa had taken the call. She spoke to Craig, and then they sat down together and broke the news to Patrick, who immediately crumbled into Craig's arms in floods of tears.

Geoff had been found unresponsive on the floor of his magic shop by the shopping centre security guard early on a Thursday morning. He was rushed to the hospital but pronounced dead on arrival. A week later, the cause of death was confirmed as a massive brain haemorrhage.

The funeral was a small and sombre affair. Geoff had no family, and there was only a small gathering of close friends and a representative from *The Magic Circle*.

Craig stood by Patrick's side as he thanked each guest for attending as they left, and he placed an arm around his shoulders when he was moved to tears when the man from *The Magic Circle* handed him a letter and explained its contents.

Geoff had submitted his recommendation that Patrick be considered for membership in *The Magic Circle*, and it appeared this had been approved. Even from beyond the grave, Geoff was looking out for his protégé.

Within a week, Patrick would be dumbfounded once more when Craig accompanied him to the reading of Geoff's will. Everything he owned was left to Patrick. This included a generous sum of money, a small two-bedroom house, and the magic business. Craig was delighted but suppressed the urge to leap from his chair and punch the air.

Overwhelmed by the loss of his friend and the unexpected benevolence of his bequeathment Patrick was in need now more than ever of Craig's support. Craig took the lead with the business affairs and guided Patrick through everything, and within a month, they had moved into their new home.

They also decided to continue trading Geoff's magic shop, and Craig happily resigned from his warehouse position and started working in the store. Patrick would focus on his performances, and Craig would take over responsibility for his bookings. By all accounts, he became Patrick's manager.

From the tragedy of Geoff's passing, a whole new

life opened up for them. Craig seemed to have an excellent head for business, and their finances were going from strength to strength. Over the coming years, they would be able to afford new cars, and they would sell Geoff's old house and purchase a large, detached property back in Witford Common.

They had pondered the move back to Witford, unsure it was wise given the memories, but it was by far the nicest of the local towns, and their decision worked out just fine. They were welcomed back into the community with open arms, and aside from the strange feeling Craig experienced when walking past the church, all was well. More than well, in fact, as on the eighth anniversary of their first meeting at school, a date they celebrated every year, Craig had proposed.

Life was almost perfect. They were surprisingly wealthy, they were sickeningly in love and daily in lust, they had the most beautiful of weddings in the spring of 2017, and they had managed to move on from the traumas of their early relationship without the need for therapy. Life was almost perfect, but not quite.

Where Craig had his itch of extramarital sexual cravings, which he happily allowed any number of strangers to scratch, Patrick also had a constant niggle, an itch he needed to scratch. He was confident a psychologist could map the cause back to his disastrous school days and lack of acceptance from his parents, but the result was that he needed to perform. And not to a conference room full of employees at some corporate dinner. He wanted to perform for a real audience. He craved fame.

*Future Stars* was the biggest talent show on television for variety acts, and Patrick had been desperate to audition. He had considered it the previous year, but Craig had managed to dissuade him, unsure they needed to put themselves into the limelight and uncertain how Patrick might take any setbacks.

However, Craig accepted that Patrick needed to perform and needed to be seen, and the following year he agreed to his application to the show with reassurances from Patrick that it would all be okay, but Craig didn't go into things without some foresight. He had a plan. He would make sure it worked out one way or another, and Craig also realised there was an opportunity here. They were comfortable, but let's face it, those holidays to Mykonos weren't getting any cheaper.

\*\*\*

Craig had been shown to a seat just behind where the judging panel would be sitting, presumably amongst the other performer's relatives, but other than a cursory nod as he shuffled along the row, he made no attempt to engage with any of them.

Not very social at the best of times, it was unlikely Craig would have gone out of his way to initiate a conversation with these strangers, but on this occasion, he wasn't being deliberately standoffish. His mind was elsewhere.

Patrick would be on stage shortly, and his performance would contain more than just his learned sleight of hand. Together they had been honing other skills, the same skills that had forced a card into school bully Neil's throat all those years ago.

The first elements of the trick would be completed the traditional way, and Patrick was more than skilled enough to impress the most diligent of observers. But Patrick was seeking superstardom, and Craig had come up with just the idea to achieve it.

Patrick would use some of the powers they had been honing to stun the audience with something inexplicable. A trick that defied belief. Something clearly observed but mind-bendingly unbelievable. Unless you intended to claim he had actually performed a supernatural feat, you would have no choice but to acknowledge his unequalled skill as a magician.

That was the plan they had been working on, and they had run through the trick successfully multiple times. Craig was confident they could pull it off, but Patrick was very nervous backstage, and Craig just hoped he would calm down enough to step his way through the routine as practised.

The mood in the theatre changed as Kevin walked out from the wings and announced that they were almost ready to begin again following a short break in the performances. A buzz of excitement ensued as the crew returned to their positions, and the audience settled, ready for the next act.

Stephen Lucas, the host of *Future Stars*, returned to

the stage and introduced the three judges back to the auditorium to rapturous applause. The judges walked in turn to their seats on the raised platform in front of the stage, and the audience quietened. Someone shouted out a ten-second countdown to recording, with the 3... 2... 1... signalled with fingers rather than aloud, and then Stephen continued with what would be his link back from the adverts when this was later televised.

Craig leant forward with his elbows on his knees and his hands clasped in front of his mouth as he listened intently to the introductions. He could only imagine how Patrick must be feeling waiting in the wings, but when he finally heard the words '...*and without further ado, please welcome to the stage our next performer*', he was reassured to see Patrick stroll out smiling and stand on his mark, centre stage.

'Hello there, and what's your name?' the deep, well-spoken voice of Laurence Stokes, the head judge on the panel, asked.

'Hi, I'm Patrick Morgan, but today I will be performing as Enigma. That's the stage name for my magic act.' Patrick nervously replied.

Laurence was rolling his eyes and exhaling in despair almost before Patrick had finished speaking.

'Give the poor guy a chance,' Michelle Martinez interjected on seeing Laurence's reaction. 'I know you don't like magic, but not everyone likes ballet either, and you did okay for yourself,' she added to laughter from the crowd.

## Enigma

Craig sat motionless, focused solely on Patrick at this stage, and watched as he grinned and waited awkwardly under the spotlight during the judge's minor spat before the third judge intervened and asked a further question.

'How old would you be, Enigma? And what made you decide to audition for us today?' Kieran asked.

Patrick recited his practised response, and Kieron politely wished him good luck, though with more than a little doubt in his voice, and to soft applause, Enigma began his act.

The trick to be performed was a version of classic coin magic, and as Enigma announced this to the crowd, he requested that Laurence join him on stage.

'We may as well have the sceptic up here,' Enigma joked, and the crowd responded with a chuckle.

Laurence made his way onto the stage and joined Enigma beside a small black table where he was now seated. Someone ran from the wings with a second chair, and Laurence took a seat to observe. Enigma then began to explain what was going to happen to the audience, but more specifically to his witness, who would need to be eagle-eyed to try and catch him out. Another chuckle from the crowd. Nervous Patrick was gone, and Enigma was now in control.

Craig watched on as Patrick ran through the first iteration of his routine. It was a classic coin act, and he performed it flawlessly to ripples of applause in all the correct places.

'How was that?' Enigma asked Laurence when the

trick was complete, and all four coins were now gathered in a single corner of the table. 'Did you see anything suspicious?'

'I mean, you're good, but we've kind of seen it all before,' Laurence shrugged his shoulders as he spoke as if to excuse his honesty. Craig smiled. Laurence couldn't have set up the next element of the act more perfectly, even if he had been asked to.

'Ouch!' Enigma feigned offence, and the audience sympathetically inhaled in unison. 'No, he's right. It's coin magic 101,' he admitted and then went on to demonstrate one of the ways magicians achieved the effect.

Enigma demonstrated how he had hidden three of the coins in the magician's Servante on his lap and then demonstrated how the other coins gathered in the corner had been there all along. Three of them were initially covered by small flaps of dark cloth that he flipped back and forth to show how invisible they were against the black background.

There were a few unimpressed groans from the crowd but further applause at his reveal.

'Nobody likes a cheat,' Enigma suggested. 'Let's try again but make it a bit harder.'

Enigma gathered the coins and discarded the Servante onto the stage floor before removing the black cloth to reveal a glass table below. He again placed one coin towards each corner of the table, handing the three spare coins to Laurence for safekeeping.

'We love to keep stuff up our sleeves too,' Enigma

confessed. 'So why don't we lose the sleeves?' With that, he stood up behind the table and unbuttoned and removed his shirt.

Craig loved Patrick's body. It had always been naturally defined, but these days he worked out, and he was toned and muscular. His low-rise jeans emphasised the v-line below his abs that was disappearing into the waistband of his *Addicted* briefs.

His chest was smooth and naturally tanned and sported a tattoo of a magician's top hat, with two protruding bunny ears nestled between pert pectorals. A homage to his disastrous schoolboy performance, he had chosen to have etched permanently on his body to remind him how far he had come since then.

The audience hooted and wolf-whistled at the striptease, and whereas Patrick would have been embarrassed, Enigma soaked it in. He remained standing until the frenzy abated and then sat down to repeat his coin routine.

'Okay, you can see through the table, and there is nothing up my sleeves,' he reiterated before repeating the trick in its entirety. The same end result but clearly a different, more complex technique, rewarded with rapturous applause.

'Better,' Laurence admitted.

'Better?' Enigma questioned. 'You're a hard man to please,' he joked, and for the first time, he looked to the crowd and spotted Craig.

'Shall we take it one stage further?' Enigma addressed the crowd, but his eyes remained locked on

Craig. This was the point where Patrick would move away from the traditional magic he had spent years perfecting and do something inexplicable. Something he didn't really even understand himself. The crowd clearly wanted more, and when Craig gave his nod of approval, Enigma continued.

'Take off your trousers,' a voice shouted from the crowd, and the place erupted with more wolf-whistling and laughter.

'Maybe if I get to the final,' Enigma teased. 'But for now, how about we do it one more time, with no hands?'

A hush fell across the crowd, and what happened next would change everything.

Enigma sat upright in his chair and invited Laurence to inspect the coins and the tabletop. He then asked him to place a coin towards each corner as previously. Laurence followed the instructions and confirmed he was happy everything was in order.

'Okay,' Enigma said, taking deep breaths for effect. 'This is going to blow your mind.'

Slowly Enigma placed his hand above the first coin, but this time it was higher in the air leaving the coin in full view of what must have been at least eight thousand prying eyes. He counted down from three, and on zero, he snapped his fingers, and the coin instantly vanished and reappeared at the front of the table.

To gasps from the crowd, Enigma quickly repeated the finger snap for the other two coins, performing the same routine as previously, but this time with the coins in full view. The crowd went berserk on completion of the trick, and Laurence was clearly heard to say, *'What the fuck?'* before rising from his chair and starting the standing ovation Enigma had been craving so badly.

Craig leapt from his seat in excitement and joined the ovation. He couldn't have been happier with how the performance had played out, and it had evoked exactly the reaction he had anticipated.

For the next few minutes, the judges gave their stunned appraisals of Enigma's performance before unanimously voting him through to the next round. As Patrick left the stage, picking up his shirt on the way, Craig excused himself from his row in the auditorium and headed backstage.

As Craig arrived, Patrick was finishing a conversation with Kevin about some background filming they would like to carry out before the show aired in a couple of months.

'Oh, for sure, that would be great,' Patrick smiled and then turned to embrace Craig as he approached.

\* \* \*

It had been twelve weeks since Craig's plan had been initiated for Patrick's first audition on *Future Stars,* and he had already been back with Craig to film his second performance, but today was the day the first episode was airing on television.

The excitement had been building for a few weeks

now as a clip of Patrick and, more specifically, the audience reaction to his finale had been included in the teaser trailers being aired in anticipation of the start of the new series. Even Craig had warmed to the idea of late, and they had decided to host a small party for close friends on the evening of the showing.

They had set up a screen in the magic shop for the event, and guests had begun to arrive for pre-show drinks and canapés. The production company had insisted upon secrecy with regard to the result of Patrick's audition, but Craig was sure the guests could tell the outcome would be positive from the permanent grin on Patrick's face as they all air-kissed and sipped champagne.

The gathered crowd was predominantly made up of Patrick's magic acquaintances, a scattering of regular shop customers, and Craig's mother. A tiny dusting of gay friends made up the remainder, and as Craig swept up the second broken champagne flute of the evening, along with a selection of canapé crumbs, he was pleased they had chosen to host the evening in the shop rather than at their home. Not that there were many people in attendance that Craig would actually allow into his home.

*Future Stars* had been playing in the background with the sound muted while the guests mingled, with Patrick keeping an eye on the time and Craig ensuring everyone's glass remained topped up. They had been helpfully informed that Patrick was the final performer on the show, featuring just after the last advert break.

Craig signalled to Patrick, who had inadvertently fallen into deep conversation with one of *The Magic Circle* oddities, that the final adverts had started. Briefly panicked into action, Patrick tapped the rim of his champagne flute with the TV remote control to draw attention before turning up the volume.

The gathered crowds chatter hushed as the *Future Stars* theme music sounded, and a voiceover began to describe how it had been a slow day at the auditions, and the judges were hoping the final act would be worth the wait.

*'What a load of old tripe,'* Craig thought to himself. Patrick's audition had been far from the end of the day. The editorial team were taking more than a little poetic license with the facts, although it further occurred to Craig that they were hardly in a position to take the moral high ground considering the deceit of their own performance.

Craig watched the screen as Patrick walked out onto the stage before Laurence Stokes asked him his name, and he replied, *'Hi, I'm Patrick Morgan, but I will be performing today as Enigma. That's the stage name for my magic act.'*

Rather than cut back to the eye roll Laurence had given on the day, which was castigated by Michelle Martinez, the program cut to a background film the preproduction team had pulled together.

There was a cheer from the room as the shopfront came on screen, and we were introduced to Patrick and his partner Craig.

'Partner, not Husband?' Craig tutted at Patrick as he joined him to watch the rest of the show play out.

Craig and Patrick had been uncomfortable with the small exposé of their private life, although as Craig now watched it back, he could see how it could work to their advantage on the show. Some difficult subjects were discussed around Patrick's early life, including the bullying and death of his father, and Craig felt Patrick squeeze his hand as these were referenced.

It went on to discuss the development of his interest in magic by Geoff, a father figure and mentor, who had also now passed, leaving him the magic shop in his will. Craig returned Patrick's squeeze, and the show cut back to Patrick's trick, and everyone watched on in silence.

When it was over, Laurence could be heard to say, *'What the...bleep'*, his expletive removed for sensitive ears as they were still before the watershed. The television audience was shown in rapturous applause with a full standing ovation, and the reaction in the room was equally joyous.

They all watched the judges' comments and the confirmation that he was voted through to the next round, and then Patrick muted the sound once more before circling the room, accepting further praise from his guests over yet more champagne.

Everyone was amazed by his performance, but Patrick refused to share the secrets of his trickery, even with his closest *Magic Circle* friends. Craig had been vehemently insistent on this, and he was sure Patrick would comply, but he was careful to chaperone him and ensure this was the case.

The guests drifted away over the next couple of hours until only Patrick, Craig, and Lisa remained. Lisa hadn't been drinking as she had offered to drop the boys back at their house, and they were on the road just after 11:00 pm.

Lisa was offered a coffee before heading home but declined, choosing not to get out of the car. Instead, she would leave them to their celebrations. They waved her away from the kerbside before falling through their doorway, cracking open another bottle of champagne, which they would drink in bed, before falling asleep in each other arms following wild, adrenaline-fuelled sex.

*What a night!*

# CHAPTER 12

July 2019

Craig had woken just after 7:00 am and quietly slipped out of the covers leaving Patrick to lie in for a little while. He pulled on yesterday's underwear, which had been discarded on the floor during last night's lovemaking, and headed downstairs for a coffee. He needed a shower, but nothing happened before coffee in Craig's mornings.

It was a lovely clear summer morning, and as Craig pushed open the conservatory doors to the garden, he could feel warmth in the air already. He sat and drank his coffee in the breakfast room while checking through his various phone messages, then made another cup to take up for Patrick.

As Craig entered the bedroom, Patrick stirred and

lifted himself onto his elbows, awake but not yet fully conscious.

'I'm going to head into the shop early. Finish cleaning up from the party last night. Why don't you have a lie-in and head over after lunch?' Craig suggested.

Patrick promptly closed his eyes, rolled over, and collapsed his head back into the pillow, which Craig took as acceptance of his offer. He placed the coffee cup on Patrick's bedside table, noticing the lube and poppers from last night's fun. Craig smiled to himself. He was ready to go again and briefly wondered if Tom was helping out in the shop this morning.

Tom was one of their weekend staff, a slightly geeky seventeen-year-old who was as camp as a row of tents. Not the type of guy Craig would typically go for at all, even for brief relief. Too close to home, and the young lads always tended to catch feelings, which was far too risky when he also worked with Patrick.

The temptation was growing, though, as at a recent after-work bowling event, Craig had found himself next to Tom at the urinals, and his penis was enormous. He swore Tom had leant back a little so he could get a better view, and Craig was slightly relieved when a stranger had entered the toilets as he was certain he would have reached out to touch it if they had been left alone any longer.

Thoughts of Tom drained away, as did the shampoo suds, as Craig took his cold morning shower. He liked to start the day this way, invigorated and refreshed. It was as much a measure of his willpower than anything else, standing under the icy flow for a good five minutes before towelling himself dry.

The morning rituals were complete, and Craig was on the road before eight-thirty and in the shop before nine. First, he gave the floor a hoover to ensure any chards of broken glass were lifted and then filled a bucket with detergent and mopped away a scattering of sticky champagne patches.

\* \* \*

Kevin Heath wouldn't usually have been in the office on a Sunday morning, but it was only two weeks until the live finals of *Future Stars*, and his stress levels were through the roof. Cutbacks within the production team had increased everyone's workload, and Laurence Stokes, executive producer and head judge, was almost impossible to please.

When the phone call from Jennifer came through, Kevin was shuffling pieces of paper with the names of the semi-finalist on them, attempting to pull together a schedule with some variety. Nobody wanted to see all the dancing dogs performing on the same night. It would be carnage enough.

'Kevin Heath, *Future Stars* production office, how can I help?' he greeted on autopilot.

'Oh, hi Kev, it's Jennifer from *The Sunday Review*. What are you doing at work on a Sunday? I was expecting voicemail, to be honest,' she asked.

'No rest for the wicked, babe,' Kevin joked. He had

known Jennifer for years. 'I don't think I've seen you since the NTAs in January. We should do drinks soon.'

'Sure, love to, but it's not a social call, I'm afraid. I think I'm about to ruin your week,' Jennifer apologised in advance. 'We are about to run an article on *Future Stars*, more specifically, the Enigma episode last night. You're not going to like it.'

Jennifer talked him through the allegations, namely that the show was somehow in collusion with Patrick.

'That's ridiculous! I was there. I can assure you it was all genuine. It was fucking unreal, actually,' Kevin defended. He remembered the Enigma show well, as both Patrick and Craig had left an impression that day. Especially Craig, as only in the last couple of days had Kevin been reminded of their backstage encounter when he had received an 'all clear' HIV text from the local GUM clinic.

'Is that the official press statement?' Jennifer joked.

'How long do I have to get you something?'

'Going to air in about thirty minutes, I'm afraid.'

'Fuck! Laurence is going to shit a load. On top of me probably,' Kevin laughed but was not finding the thought of this funny in the least. 'You'll have to run with the standard nobody available to comment until I get back to you.'

'No problem. Sorry, Kev. I'm sure it will all blow over,' Jennifer tried to comfort him, but Kevin was gone before she had finished her sentence.

The phone call to Laurence went as expected, but once the expletive-laden reaction had ceased, Laurence calmed down and reeled off a list of instructions for Kevin to follow up on. Laurence hadn't achieved his success without navigating the odd scandal or two.

Laurence wanted all eyes on *The Sunday Review,* so they knew exactly what was said, and then he wanted the team gathered for a conference call. They would need to release a press statement before the end of the day. If *Future Stars* was going to hit the Monday morning headlines, he intended to exploit the publicity as much as possible.

'And make sure that frigging Enema is on the call too,' was Laurence's final instruction.

Kevin tried to call Patrick half a dozen times, but there was no answer. He left a voice message and then rang around the team, briefly explaining the situation before requesting they join a conference call later that morning.

From the corner of Kevin's eye, he noticed *The Sunday Review* was returning to air following a commercial break. It had been about thirty minutes since Jennifer had called. He turned up the volume on the large wall-mounted television and grabbed a pen and paper, ready to make notes.

\* \* \*

Whilst the floor dried, Craig began to pack away the glasses and empty platters into the boxes the catering company had provided. They could all be returned dirty, a job for Monday, so Craig stacked them in the back office for now. As he was returning to the shop floor at the back of the store, he heard the Sunday help letting themselves in at the front.

'Hi, Chloe,' Craig greeted, actually a little relieved it wasn't Tom. He checked his watch and noted they still had thirty minutes before the store would open at 10:30 am. 'Why don't you pop the kettle on for a cuppa? I'm going to flick the telly on and watch the headlines,' Craig suggested, moving over to the screen they had temporarily installed for Patrick's party night.

As the television came on, Craig's ears pricked up as he caught the tail end of an interview introduction from Ian Atkinson, co-host of *The Sunday Review*.

'... we have Matt Turner with us this morning to discuss some interesting concerns following the episode of *Future Stars,* which aired yesterday evening. Hi, Matt. So, what can you tell us?'

*Some concerns?* Craig turned up the volume and gave his full attention to the remainder of the interview.

'Good morning. Well, what can I say?' Matt began. He joined them via live video link and sat immodestly in front of a bookcase displaying a selection of awards he had received for previous journalistic efforts. 'As you know, *Future Stars* has not been without its share of controversy over the years. However, in their bid to recover the ratings, it would appear they may have sunk to a new low.'

'How intriguing,' Anna Keegan intervened. 'We love a bit of scandal with our breakfast on a Sunday morning. Do go on.'

Matt continued, and for the next few minutes, he explained a series of concerns that he had been investigating following the release of the teaser trailers and an early press showing of the episode.

There were rumours of rifts amongst the judges, disappointment at the amount of padding between acts suggesting there was a lack of interest from the public in even auditioning, but the main focus was concern that the feature act, Patrick Morgan, aka Enigma, was a fraud. A construct of the production company to end the show with the wow factor.

'Oh, my days!' Anna exclaimed in her strong Scottish accent. 'Surely not?'

*What the fuck?* Craig was standing with his jaw open at this revelation when Chloe returned with two cups of tea. She could see something was wrong, but before she had a chance to ask, Craig pointed at the television, and they watched the remainder of the interview together as Craig fumbled for his phone and called Patrick's number.

'Well, maybe not complete fiction, but we can be certain that everything is not as presented in the show,' Matt backtracked slightly. 'We know from several members of the audience that Enigma was not the final act of the day as suggested, and I have been doing a little digging myself. It seems Patrick's childhood was not quite as troubled either, and there are counter-claims that he was, in fact, a bully himself rather than the victim.'

There was no answer from Patrick, and after repeatedly trying, he dropped a text message, *Pick up. Have you seen the news?*

'But Patrick's father did pass away when he was a teenager. I'm sure that was traumatic in itself,' Ian interjected.

'Yes, of course, I'm sure that was just awful,' Matt conceded before moving on to his next point. 'The biggest accusation, though, is that the show was somehow complicit in faking Enigma's act.'

'Faking how?' Ian continued his questioning, keen to hear some facts.

'Well, as you may have seen, the finale of the act was jaw-dropping. Coins were disappearing and reappearing before our very eyes. Very impressive and worthy of the standing ovation it received. However, we have reviewed this with a panel of independent magic experts, and they believe this trick must have been edited for television, as it is just not possible as presented,' Matt smiled as he delivered the revelation.

'Are we sure this isn't just sour grapes? We see plenty of unbelievable feats by magicians. That's the whole point,' Ian scoffed. 'Maybe your panel of experts just don't know how it was done?' he suggested.

'Watch it back yourself. You can click through it frame by frame, and the coins just vanish. It's camera trickery for sure.'

'You have no idea what you are fucking talking about!' Craig yelled at the television, causing Chloe to jump and spill a little of her tea.

'Interesting indeed,' Anna commented as she began to bring the interview to an end. 'Thanks for that, Matt. We have reached out to the *Future Stars* team, but as yet, they have declined to comment. I'm sure we haven't heard the end of it, though.'

'What was that all about?' Chloe asked as Craig turned off the television and frantically continued to try and get Patrick on the phone.

'Go home, Chloe. I need to go. We won't be opening today,' Craig instructed. 'Actually, can you lock up for me, please?' Craig asked, but he was out of the door and heading to the car park without waiting for her reply.

He continued to call and text Patrick from the car as he raced home but had received no response by the time he roared his *TVR* onto the drive, skidding to a halt on the gravel. He flung open the front door to find Patrick halfway down the stairs.

'I knew we shouldn't have gone on that fucking show!' Craig raged, but he could see from Patrick's expression that he was confused and scared.

'What's happened?' Patrick asked, tears beginning to well in his eyes, and Craig knew he would have to calm down. Patrick would need comfort and reassurance. Craig would need to keep a clear head to get them through this.

'Don't worry. It will be okay,' Craig said much more calmly as they met at the foot of the stairs, and Patrick fell into his arms in sobs of tears.

## Enigma

\* \* \*

Patrick had received a voicemail from Kevin letting him know they had an internal meeting scheduled to discuss the breaking news, and they would like to dial him into a conference call around twelve-thirty. The final instruction in the message was to not speak to anyone in the meantime, and Patrick hadn't, with the exception of Craig.

They had both calmed down considerably since Craig had returned home, and he and Patrick had moved out to the summerhouse. Patrick had offered to make a pot of coffee, but they had both opted for a beer from the party fridge instead. It was twelve o'clock somewhere.

Craig plonked himself down next to Patrick on the reproduction Louis XV sofa, and while they waited for the conference call to come through, they reviewed the content of the interview, which was already doing the rounds on social media, and Craig decided on their course of action.

The only accusation involving Patrick was that of collusion with the production team. This was wholly false, and they would defend this to the hilt. They would give up no secrets as to how the trick was performed, and if other "experts" couldn't fathom it out, it was a testament to Patrick's ability. What else could they suggest? Was it really magic?

Everything else reported seemed to be a direct attack on the show itself, its popularity, and the dubious editing technique. Nothing that needed to worry them. Craig made sure Patrick was clear on their story, and then they both waited for the call to come in. The clock had just clicked past 12:35 pm when Patrick's mobile began to ring.

'Hello, Patrick speaking,' he answered on speakerphone.

'Hi, Patrick. I'm just going to patch you into the conference call now,' Kevin came back, followed by some clicks, a short silence, and then the echoey sounds of shuffling seats and whispered voices from a distant meeting room.

'Hi Pat, it's Laurence here,' his voice boomed out, seemingly unconcerned with the situation. 'Just wanted to reassure you we are handling the nonsense in the press. You've done nothing wrong,' he added.

'His name is Patrick,' Craig corrected. 'We know we've done nothing wrong. We want to know what you are going to do about the reputational damage you have caused,' he snapped back.

Laurence fell silent, and there were whispers in the background as Kevin informed him it was Craig, Patrick's husband, who had responded. Laurence was not a big fan of surprises.

The production team had gathered thirty minutes before reaching out to Patrick to discuss their response to the news story, and Laurence had been in a foul mood.

They had acquired a recording of the interview from *The Sunday Review,* and the mood in the room calmed as they dissected the facts. They had broken down the allegations into three main subjects and agreed on a plan of action that they would now talk Patrick through. And Craig, along with him, it would appear.

'Is there anyone else listening in there I need to be aware of?' Laurence asked when he came back on the line.

'No, it's just the two of us,' Craig reassured.

'Okay, we just have a couple of questions, if that's okay? And then, we will run through our planned response,' he paused for acknowledgement.

'Carry on,' Craig's voice came back.

'With regard to the trick, obviously, we know we were not involved. We are clearly going to deny this, but we wondered if you might want to give a hint as to how it was done. Shut down their experts, so to speak.' was Laurence's first question.

'Certainly not!' Patrick responded instantly. 'I'm in *The Magic Circle*, and I am sharing nothing.'

'Okay, fair enough. That's probably a good response, anyway. We can work with that. The second question is a little more sensitive, but I have to ask,' Laurence apologised, pre-empting Patrick's likely response. 'On the pre-recorded video, there was a reference to childhood bullying. Clearly, they have mentioned this may not have been the case, or worse. Did you have anything to add?'

Patrick and Craig had discussed this issue and agreed on their response ahead of the call.

'I don't know whom they have spoken to, but I suspect it is someone from the later years of my secondary school,' Patrick's rehearsed response was a little stiff, but he relaxed more as he went on. 'I had a great time at primary school, but we moved house before I started at secondary, and I was bullied for two years, and I was miserable. It only stopped when I met Craig and finally stood up for myself. They didn't like it,' he finished.

'Perfect,' Laurence accepted. 'Okay, so we are going to pull together a press statement summing this all up. We will fire it over to you for a quick review and then get it issued later this afternoon in time for all the morning headlines. How does that sound?' Laurence asked.

'I'd rather be in the headlines for more positive reasons,' Patrick sighed his frustration.

'There's no such thing as bad publicity, my friend. You'll probably win the whole series. Speak later,' and with that, Laurence hung up the call.

Craig and Patrick kept each other's company for the remainder of the day and chose to ignore the many calls and messages that came through. The press release was sent over to them prior to publication, and they acknowledged they were happy with its content.

It was a warm summer evening, and they spent it drinking and listening to music in the party house. Craig popped back to the main house to answer the door to the takeaway delivery driver, and when he returned to the summerhouse with the pizza, he had stripped down to his underwear.

'I thought we could eat pizza in our pants,' he smiled and winked at Patrick, and before Craig had taken another step, Patrick had removed his t-shirt and was unbuttoning his jeans.

*What a day!*

## ---PRESS RELEASE---

## LSE PRODUCTIONS Ltd

In response to the article aired on *The Sunday Review* on Sunday, 21st July 2019, regarding allegations of impropriety on the television programme *Future Stars*, the management team of LSE Productions Ltd wishes to issue the following statement:

While we accept that the editing of the programme may have been misleading in so much as it implied the performance of Patrick Morgan, performing as Enigma, took place at the end of a day of auditions, we strongly deny all other aspects of the interview.

Patrick Morgan was the victim of bullying during the early years of his secondary education, and this was a very difficult time in his life, compounded by the premature death of his father when he was only sixteen years of age.

With regards to the allegation that Patrick's act was in some way manipulated, this is strenuously denied. Patrick has no connection with the programme or its production team, and his act was aired as performed. Patrick is a proud member of The Magic Circle and reserves his right to keep the technique of his performance private.

We will review our editing procedures to ensure any future programmes are aired more chronologically or with creative disclaimers if required. In the meantime, we can assure all our loyal viewers that *Future Stars* remains the number-one talent show in the UK, and for all of those who were amazed by Enigma's performance, he will be back this Saturday with his second audition, which we can promise will amaze once more.

Laurence Stokes, Executive Producer

---END OF PRESS RELEASE---

# CHAPTER 13

July 2019

It had been a strange week, not to mention a little stressful. However, Craig wasn't directly stressed by the situation per se. He was confident in their approach to the press intrusion and happy to be back working in the store.

Craig was much less sensitive to other people's opinions and had no concerns about facing any potential storm. He had been like this from his school days, and as a result, he was rarely confronted. School bullies just avoided him, and even following the recent press coverage, when it seemed reasonable that a question may be posed, people didn't go there with Craig. The stress he was feeling emanated from Patrick.

Patrick was trying his best to avoid everybody. He

had forced himself to work each day but had stayed in the back office and let Craig handle the shop floor. On the advice of the *Future Stars* production company, his corporate performance calendar had already been cleared due to the upcoming live show schedule. It was a condition of the audition process to be available for interviews and other media activities, so this seemed a sensible decision, although Craig could have done without him under his feet all week.

Patrick was a worrier, and Craig had to reassure him constantly that everything would be okay. It had seemed an impossibly long six days, but they were now safely back behind closed doors, snuggled on the sofa and about to watch the next episode of *Future Stars*.

The outcome of the show was already known to them, but Patrick was restless with nerves all the same.

'I'm going to go and sit on the other chair,' Craig announced as he motioned to stand up, allowing Patrick the opportunity to lift his head from Craig's shoulder and avoid collapsing into his empty seat.

'I was enjoying our cuddle.' Patrick poked out his bottom lip in fake distress.

'It's too warm tonight, and you are fidgeting. Don't be so nervous. It will be fine,' Craig tried to reassure him. 'I'm going to grab a bottle of wine. Did you want a glass?'

'Yes, please, and grab the Pringles from the larder,' he shouted after Craig, who was already out of the room.

By the time Craig returned, Patrick had rearranged

himself on the sofa, now propped up on cushions in place of Craig's body.

'You went for red,' Patrick commented as Craig placed the glass of wine and tube of crisps on the small table to Patrick's left.

'Yeah, so don't spill it!' Craig said, as if spilling white wine would have been acceptable.

One more trip to the kitchen and Craig returned with another glass of wine and the remainder of the bottle. He habitually placed it beside the fireplace before settling on the adjacent cuddle chair. The large open fireplace that, in winter, would warm the bottle currently contained a display of dried flowers for the summer season.

'Oh shit! Here we go,' Patrick exhaled as he turned up the volume, and the title music for *Future Stars* filled the room.

The show began with Stephen Lucas introducing the judges back to the stage and then a reminder of where they were in the process of finding this year's *Future Star*. Off camera, Stephen made a reference to the Enigma controversy, and there was a small video montage shown that had clearly been edited recently.

'They are playing silly buggers with the truth again,' Craig commented when the show cut to a commercial break.

'What do you mean?' Patrick asked, genuinely confused at the observation.

'This show was pre-recorded ages ago. They have edited in the comment about last week's show and used an old reaction from Laurence. That's why it was a closeup of his face. You can't see what he is wearing.'

Craig topped up his glass and poured the remainder of the bottle into Patrick's glass before retrieving a second from the kitchen wine rack. They both grabbed a toilet break and settled down for the rest of the show.

Stephen popped back up on the screen, grinning incessantly, the b-list celebrity treatments carried out on his face and teeth having left him looking in a permanent state of *Instagram* filtered.

For the next ten minutes of the programme, the judges debated and argued for the cameras as they slid photographs of the auditionees around on a large tabletop. Eventually, there was a roll call of the fifty people who would go forward to the next audition. Then, of course, there had been the usual dramatic ending where the judges decided they had made a mistake, so they recalled an auditionee who had been rejected to tell them they would now take the fifty-first place.

Craig was reminded again of how awful Patrick's shirt had been on that day, but luckily there was very little focus on him during the recap of this process.

Another commercial break over, and they were into ninety minutes of second auditions in front of a theatre audience and the judging panel. Again, the fifty-one contestants would be thinned down to thirty-two, eight for each of the four live semi-finals.

Some contestants were skimmed through, others featured for a little longer before discovering their fate, and a handful had their full audition televised. Patrick was to be one of the latter.

'I don't think I can watch,' Patrick squealed when his name was announced, and he leapt up from the sofa and covered his eyes.

'Don't be a fool. You were there. You know what happened,' Craig bluntly pointed out, and Patrick sat back down and watched as his performance played out.

\* \* \*

The second audition process was similar to the first, and Craig had accompanied Patrick during the day of recording. He had been backstage during rehearsals and was once again escorted to his seat in the auditorium by Kevin before the recording of Patrick's performance.

Kevin had paused by a backstage office door and nodded in its direction as an invitation to Craig for a repeat of their first meeting.

'We've got time,' Kevin added when Craig declined the offer, but he had already turned and walked on.

Craig wasn't against the idea, but his mind was preoccupied with the performance Patrick was about to undertake. It required perfect timing, and Craig wanted to be focused. He needed to make sure it looked perfect. The first audition had gone so well, and they needed to keep the momentum.

Comfortably seated with a clear view of the judges' area, Craig watched as Patrick was introduced for his second performance. He began by asking if he could come down from the stage and join the judges, as this was an interactive trick, and they would want to see it close up.

'So today, I am going to do some card tricks with you all. Hopefully, you'll like them,' Enigma said, much more confidently than Patrick ever could have.

Enigma produced a pack of cards from his pocket and performed the standard magician's spiel as he broke the cellophane seal, discarded the jokers, fanned the deck to show new card order, and then shuffled them seven times.

Craig loved the confidence Patrick demonstrated when he was in his Enigma zone, and he was a great magician, but only the first of these tricks would be performed entirely with sleight of hand. The others would require a little bit of Patrick's extra ear-bleeding magic.

The cards were fanned again to show the mixed deck, and then Enigma presented them face down and asked Laurence to take a card. Laurence complied and showed the card to the camera and audience behind him to be the Six of Clubs.

'Oh, you don't need to keep it secret,' Enigma said. 'It's the Six of Clubs. They are all the Six of Clubs,' he added as he fanned the deck once more to show that every card was now the Six of Clubs.

Laurence smiled, the audience applauded, and Enigma moved down the line to Michelle.

'Let's try again,' Enigma said, fanning the cards to

show a mixed deck before shuffling them and spreading them face down for Michelle to make her selection.

Michelle took a card and repeated the action of showing it to the camera and audience behind. This time the card was the Nine of Diamonds.

After asking Michelle what card she had selected, Enigma looked puzzled as he displayed the remaining deck to still all be the Six of Clubs.

Michelle turned over the card in her hand, and it was indeed now the Six of Clubs. She gasped, and the audience applauded again. Louder this time. Enigma moved another step to his left to face Kieron.

With Kieron, Enigma performed a slightly different variation of the trick, allowing Kieron to randomly select the Three of Hearts from a face-up deck.

'Can you place it face down on your palm,' was the next instruction, and Enigma gathered and reshuffled the deck. 'So, what card do you think you have in your hand? He asked.

'Erm… I am going to say the Six of Clubs, I guess,' Kieron answered, trying to get a step ahead of Enigma.

'Well, why would you say that?' Enigma questioned as he nodded for Kieron to turn over the card. 'We all just watched you take the Three of Hearts,' he added as Kieron turned over the card, and it was still the Three of Hearts.

'And that was your totally free choice, right?' Enigma asked while fanning the deck to show they were all now the Three of Hearts. The judges audibly *'wowed'*, and the audience roared with applause.

So far, so good. Patrick was performing exactly to script, and they were hitting the card transitions perfectly. It looked seamless to Craig.

'Now for the really good stuff,' Enigma teased when the applause had faded. 'Have you all got your mobile phones?'

The judges produced their phones, and Enigma asked them to place them face-up on the desk. A cameraman was on hand to ensure everyone had a good view of everything taking place on the cinema-size screen at the back of the stage.

After asking Kieron to enter his mobile number into Enigma's phone, Enigma then sent him a text message. Seconds later, the phone in front of Kieron vibrated, and the camera picked up that a new text message had been received from an unknown number.

Enigma shuffled and fanned the deck of cards again and asked Kieron to pick one and show it to everyone. He did so, and he had chosen the Ace of Spades.

'Good card,' Enigma congratulated. 'But you can change it if you want? It's totally your choice.'

'No, no, I'm happy with the ace,' Kieron decided.

'Okay, that's fine, but remember, you could have changed it. Now, why don't you read that text?'

Kieron lifted his phone from the desk and read the new message he had received aloud. 'Ace of Spades.' More applause followed, and Enigma moved back down the line to Michelle.

'I'm not giving you my number,' she said, causing the audience to laugh.

This trick was going to be similar to the one Enigma had performed with Kieron, but this time he wouldn't send a text. Instead, he was going to use the pictures in Michelle's camera roll.

'Let's do this one differently,' he suggested, handing her the entire deck of cards. 'You take a look through the deck, and you pick any card you like and point it out to the camera. Then just push the pack back together and pop it down on the side. We won't need them again,' he finished.

Michelle complied, and as secretively as she could, she fingered through the cards until she picked one and tapped it with her fingernail. The camera picked up the Eight of Diamonds before Michelle closed the deck and put it back on the table.

'Now, can you open up your phone and go to your photos for me, please? Make sure the camera can see. We're not going to see anything risqué, are we?' he joked.

'Well, maybe,' Michelle joked back as she pressed the icons until she arrived at the thumbnails in her photo gallery. Michelle had already gasped when Enigmas asked her to click on the most recent photo and open up the thumbnail so everyone could see. She did so, and a photograph of the Eight of Diamonds was displayed. Applause, applause, applause.

Craig wondered if these tricks were too subtle. The speed and simplicity of each trick belied just how impossible they were in reality. The audience's reaction was positive, though, so maybe they had pitched it right. Impressive enough to make the live finals but not too crazy to attract any suspicion.

'Oh God,' Laurence blasphemed as Enigma approached him.

'Don't worry. I've saved the best for last, as I know how much you love magic,' Enigma winked. 'Can you just tap your screen for me so we can see your phone?'

Laurence obliged, and his locked home screen was displayed for all to see. The picture was of Laurence when he was much younger, in mid-flight as he leapt across the stage in his ballet tights.

'Oh, it's you,' Enigma didn't sound surprised. 'You didn't consider maybe a picture of your wife? Or kids?' he added, and the audience was laughing again.

'Didn't even cross my mind,' Laurence played along.

'Okay, so this is the big finish. There is no deck of cards, and I am not going to touch your phone. When you are ready, all you have to do is think of any card you like and say it aloud,' Enigma explained.

The cameraman behind Laurence moved a little closer, and the image of the phone was displayed on the cinema-size screen at the back of the stage for all to see. Enigma nodded to let Laurence know he was ready whenever he was, and a few seconds later, Laurence voiced his choice, the Jack of Hearts.

Almost before his words had finished, the background image on his locked iPhone changed to the Jack of Hearts. There was a momentary silence, the clock display on Laurence's phone clicked over to the next minute, and then the audience erupted into another standing ovation.

* * *

'It was great,' Craig assured Patrick after he had lowered the volume and turned to him for reassurance. 'Everyone loves you.'

'The last bit with the picture change, though. Was that too much?' Patrick was genuinely concerned.

'It's impressive, but that's the point. Nobody needs to know how you really did it. They can speculate all they like. We just keep quiet, okay?' Craig emphasised the last instruction, and Patrick nodded in compliance.

'Did you notice they dropped the second backstory film? Probably a good thing, mind. I wasn't comfortable with them filming it in the house anyway.'

'Shall we have another bottle and listen to some music in the garden room?' Craig suggested, realising it was probably best to try and take Patrick's mind off the whole thing.

It was a lovely warm July evening, so they kept the music down low and had the French doors wide open to enjoy the fresh air, although it was currently a little less fresh as Patrick stood on the patio puffing away on a cigarette.

They had been in the garden for just over half an hour when the music cut out, and Patrick's phone began to ring over the Bluetooth speakers. He stubbed out his cigarette and stepped back inside to grab his phone from the tabletop. The caller ID showed Kevin from *Future Stars*.

'Hi, Kevin,' Patrick answered tentatively.

'Hi, mate. I need to update you on a few bits following the show tonight. Is that okay?' Kevin asked, seemingly in good spirits.

'Sure, is everything okay?'

'Oh, it will all be fine. *The Sunday Review* have contacted us as they are going to be running a follow-up article tomorrow morning on us,' Kevin explained. 'Laurence is going on the show live to respond in person, and we want you to join via conference call.'

'Join to do what?' Patrick had panic in his voice, and Craig signalled for him to put the phone on loudspeaker.

'They are convinced there is some collusion going on still because your trick was so good. Laurence is going on to make a point-blank denial, and it would be great to hear the same from you. Clearly, we aren't colluding,' Kevin finished.

'Sure, he'll come on the show,' Craig intervened. 'But this is just to talk about the trick, right? And he won't be telling anyone how it's done. That's our intellectual property,' Craig clarified.

'Of course, that's fine. I assume you have a laptop for the call?' Kevin asked. 'I'll send the details to your email address, and someone from the show will set you up in the morning, sometime between ten-thirty and eleven,' he added before saying a cheery goodbye.

'Why did you agree to that?' Patrick asked Craig, his

voice still clearly stressed.

'It will be fine. I've been thinking about it, and we can use this to our advantage,' Craig calmly explained. 'We aren't in cahoots with the show, so you can deny that with a clear conscience, and the publicity is going to be great for your chances in the final.'

'I don't know, Craig. This isn't going the way I was expecting at all. I'm really worried,' Patrick was almost tearful as he spoke.

'When have I ever let you down, baby?' Craig moved in to give Patrick a hug. 'It's all going to be fine. Let's finish this drink and go up for an early night,' Craig squeezed Patrick's buttocks as he spoke, and Patrick's smile was back.

\* \* \*

Laurence had arrived in the studio a good hour before he was due to be on the air, and the atmosphere was amiable. He had met Anna and Ian on previous occasions, promoting his shows and on the annual award circuit, and they exchanged pleasantries in the corridors before the show went on air that morning.

A brief touch-up in hair and makeup and Laurence was placed in the green room to await his call to the morning sofa for his interview. He grabbed a drink and a pastry and worked through some emails, but within ten minutes, he was joined by his co-guest, Matt Turner.

'I believe you know each other?' Jennifer said as she

brought Matt into the room. She knew full well that they did and that their public encounters had been fractious over the years. She excused herself, explaining that she needed to get Patrick connected online and ready for the interview and then left them alone. No pleasantries were exchanged this time.

They sat in silence until Jennifer returned to take them quietly through to the studio, where off-camera, they waited until the programme paused for a commercial break. A frantic period of activity followed on the studio floor, during which they were ushered to their seats on the sofa opposite their interviewers.

Someone from behind the cameras shouted ninety seconds until back on the air, and Laurence observed as Anna received a final dab of powder to her forehead from a makeup girl. He also noticed a monitor on the floor before them with the face and shoulders of a rather nervous-looking Patrick.

A further twenty seconds call was made by the floor manager, who had now stepped forwards to deliver the countdown, and Anna shuffled in her seat in preparation for her introduction.

'Welcome back, I'm Anna Keegan, and it is Sunday, 28$^{th}$ July. With me on the sofa now, we have Laurence Stokes and Matt Turner, and we are also joined remotely by Patrick Morgan, better known as magician Enigma,' Anna introduced. 'We are following up on last week's controversy around Enigma's performance on *Future Stars* and some subsequent concerns following last night's show too. Matt, if I can turn to you first, what were the issues if you could remind us.'

Matt Turner proceeded to recount his allegations from his previous interview – that he believed Enigma's performance must have been in some way edited to achieve the effect televised. He added that the second performance almost certainly confirmed this suspicion, as it was impossible to update the images of playing cards on the judge's phones without some inside collaboration.

'And obviously, you have already admitted that the editorial sequencing and sob stories in the show are faked for dramatic effect,' Matt added.

Without invitation from Anna, Laurence launched into his defence. He repeated the assertions that had been made in last week's press release, denying all but some slight editing in the sequencing of the auditions. He then suggested Patrick might like to give his own reply with regard to the allegations surrounding his childhood.

At this point, Anna invited Patrick to contribute, and he nervously shuffled in his chair before speaking.

'I don't really understand what is going on, to be honest,' Patrick started. 'I just performed my magic. I am not working with anyone on the show to fake anything, and I did have a troubled childhood. I was bullied, and when I was a little older, I stood up for myself. I don't know what else to say.'

'I have a few more questions,' Matt said as he sat forward on the sofa for a better view of Patrick on the monitor. 'The Press received an early release of last night's show which differed a little from the one televised. Another background film was dropped that featured yourself and your husband at home,' he continued. 'In your 1.6-million-pound home, I should add, with a rather nice *TVR* parked on the drive. I'm a little confused as to your acquired wealth. I believe you do some corporate events, and your council-estate husband works in your magic shop?' Matt was smug with his delivery.

'I… I… was gifted the shop when a very good friend and mentor died. I also inherited a small house at that time. I don't really see what any of this has to do with anything?' Patrick nervously pushed back.

'I have done my research here, and the numbers just don't stack up, Patrick,' Matt continued to push. 'And Geoff wasn't the first important man to die in your life, was he?' Matt was clearly referring to Patrick's father.

'Hang on, please,' Anna interjected. 'This really does feel a little inappropriate, Matt,' but Patrick was not going to let this go unchallenged.

'You mean my father, I assume?' Patrick was clearly getting agitated. 'What has he got to do with anything?'

'I believe you were questioned by the police following his death, and your own mother claims you killed him?' Matt actually smiled after finishing his sentence.

'My father committed suicide on my sixteenth birthday, and my mother, who has actually been in psychiatric care ever since, held me responsible because they were both religious nutters and had recently found out I was gay,' Patrick's voice faltered, and tears began to run down his cheeks. 'Why are you bringing this all up?'

Laurence protested at the line of questioning and stood up, removing his microphone as he did so. Anna quickly announced another short break, and in moments they were off the air.

Matt also moved to stand, but Laurence pushed him back into the sofa.

'What is wrong with you? You fucking nasty prick,' Laurence bellowed, and members of the floor crew ran over to keep the men apart.

'Get him out of the studio,' Anna pointed towards Matt. 'That was way out of order. You are done on this show,' she added before turning her attention to calming down Laurence.

Calm was quickly restored, and Anna went back on screen with an apology to the audience, reassuring them that Patrick was being offered their full support.

'Apologies also to you, Laurence,' Anna offered. 'I know you have something you would like to say related to the original reason for the interview.'

'Thank you, Anna. I must say that was outrageous. That vermin cannot possibly be allowed to get away with his constant unfounded allegations, and we will be taking legal advice,' Laurence opened, referring to Matt but deliberately not using his name. 'I actually came in to address just one issue, the matter of the show's collusion with Enigma. This is also a complete lie, and to try and allay people's concerns, we have put something additional in place for the live semi-finals.'

'Yes, I understand you are bringing in a couple of

old adversaries,' Anna questioned, already briefed on this element of Laurence's response.

Laurence went on to explain that Enigma's semi-final performance would be observed live by Cage & Clerk, a magical double act who were now internationally renowned after famously being dismissed by Laurence as incompetent buffoons who would amount to nothing on one of his early talent shows.

'As you know, Anna, we have not had the most amicable of relationships over the years, and I am sure there is nothing they would like more than to discredit me on live television,' Laurence finished.

'Well, the nation is certainly talking about it, so I am sure viewing figures will be up if nothing else,' Anna began to bring the interview to a close. 'And if I can just thank you for staying with us. We have had many text reactions to the show, and they are very much supportive of Patrick. I can only apologise again,' she finished, and after a short pause for breath, launched straight into the following link.

\* \* \*

Craig had been by Patrick's side, off-screen, during the whole interview and had slammed the lid of the laptop shut just before the show cut to the adverts. He was enraged that they had blindsided Patrick with the change of questioning from Matt.

Jennifer had called back almost immediately to apologise and asked if Patrick had wanted to rejoin the interview with Laurence following the break, but Craig made it very clear to her that Patrick declined.

Kevin had also attempted to ring Patrick on his mobile, but the call was declined. Still tearfully upset at the mention of his father's death, Craig comforted Patrick as they both watched Laurence's closing interview remarks on the small portable TV in the kitchen.

Craig listened intently to every word, and when the final section was complete, he sat in silence, rubbing his temples as he considered what had just unfolded. Patrick had seen this kind of reaction before and knew not to speak until Craig had gathered his thoughts.

'I think this is going to be okay,' he finally commented.

'Okay?' Patrick asked. 'He pretty much accused me of killing my own father, and I don't even know where he was going talking about our house and car.' Patrick was on the verge of tears once more.

'Hey,' Craig spoke softly to Patrick. 'He just made himself look stupid. Nobody thinks you killed your father. The public is on your side. This is good. You might just win this whole show.'

'Win it? I don't think I can do the next show, Craig. I think it's best I just pull out.' Patrick suggested.

'You'll do no such thing,' Craig snapped as he removed his comforting arm from Patrick's shoulders.

'But I did kill my father, Craig. I used to get so angry with my powers. What if I can't keep it under control?' Patrick sobbed.

'You are doing the show, and we are going big with

the performance. I've got a great idea. Trust me,' Craig finished. The conversation was over, and Craig would have his way.

## CHAPTER 14

August 2019

Craig had been with Patrick at the studio all day, finalising details and performing a dry run of the trick he would perform live later that evening.

The day began with an argument before they had even left the house. Patrick was obviously beside himself with worry, and although he never voiced it directly, he was clearly concerned that they would be found out for their deceit. Worse still, his mother's allegations of murder might be revisited, and Patrick knew he was complicit, somehow.

Attempting to reassure him, Craig insisted he had a plan and that Patrick should not worry. The last thing he needed was Patrick's nerve crumbling and bringing everything they had achieved crashing down around them. When Patrick continued to worry, Craig bluntly told him to *'get in the fucking car.'*

The dynamic of their relationship had shifted in recent weeks, and Craig was now the dominant force in a relationship where historically, he had always pandered to Patrick's needs. But, in reality, Craig had always been the manipulator. He just allowed Patrick to believe he was in control.

The car journey was mostly in silence, but by the time they arrived at the studio, they were talking again. Craig made a faint apology, and Patrick was unable to stay mad. Craig seemed to have the knack of getting into his head, and Patrick could never stay angry when Craig turned on his cute little smile.

For the live shows, the production had been switched from the theatres of the auditions to a television studio so they could operate a multi-stage format. Some of the acts, Patrick's being one, required an extensive and precise stage setup, and it was not practical to change this in the time they had available between performances on a live broadcast.

At the previous week's planning session, it had been decided that Patrick would perform as the opening act as his stage setup was the most complex. It consisted of two large vanishing cabinets with doors back and front, each standing on its own Perspex platform roughly six feet above the stage.

The platforms could be rotated to show all sides, and you could clearly see beneath them, demonstrating that no downward escape was possible through a hidden trap door. There were also four Perspex staircases which could be manoeuvred into place, allowing access to the doors on both sides of each cabinet.

The production team had provided dancing boys to assist Patrick in his performance. They were currently performing their routine of swirling around the platforms and moving the staircases into place as part of a final rehearsal. They were dressed in casuals for this practice, but tonight there would be plenty of flesh on show – another of Craig's ideas. Patrick was going big with this one, Craig had insisted. The closeup magic was gone. Coins and cards weren't going to cut it tonight. There was much more at stake than merely Patrick's reputation.

Craig watched on with Kevin as Patrick half-heartedly completed the rehearsal but stopped short of the final reveal of the trick. Two stand-ins were assisting, but on the night, it would be the renowned Cage & Clerk fulfilling these roles in what was effectively a double-vanishing act with a twist. A twist they were refusing to divulge in rehearsals.

Kevin, the floor manager, was unsuccessfully attempting to encourage Patrick to put a bit more effort into his performance, but Craig assured him it would be fine later that evening. Patrick was not a performer. He could only go through the motions, but tonight Enigma would be on stage, and that would be a whole different matter.

With the final rehearsal finished, Craig and Patrick

had some time to themselves in the dressing room. As Kevin left, he said he would be back to give them a thirty-minute warning in roughly an hour's time.

'We're good, right?' Craig asked when Kevin was out of earshot.

'Yeah, we're good,' Patrick smiled back unconvincingly. 'I thought we might have met Cage & Clerk ahead of tonight, though.'

'I don't think it matters. The less they know, the better, for sure. You are going to be famous after this, Patrick, I promise you,' Craig said. *Famous or infamous*, he thought but decided not to share. 'Get yourself changed,' he added, handing Patrick the see-through black mesh muscle vest and skin-tight black jeans he had chosen for him to wear.

'I'm going to look like a stripper in this with all those dancing boys prancing around,' Patrick laughed.

'You'll look just great. The world isn't going to know what's hit it after tonight, Patrick. I think this is all going to work out just fine,' Craig said, with a confidence Patrick clearly didn't share. 'And go commando in those jeans,' he added before undoing the button on Patrick's trousers and slipping his hand inside. 'Sex sells, big boy!'

\* \* \*

Kevin had returned as promised to give the thirty-minute warning and then again with fifteen minutes left to go. Fortunately, he knocked and waited before entering the room, giving Patrick enough time to tuck himself uncomfortably back into his jeans and for Craig to return to his feet.

'Exciting times!' Kevin declared as his eyes dropped from Patrick's face to the visible erection in his jeans and back again. 'Craig, you'll need to take your seat in the studio. I'll take you through, and then I'll come back for you, Patrick,' he added before turning and leading the way.

Craig's seat was with the other acts' friends and family members in a block near the centre of the studio, allowing them a good view of the various performing areas. The floor team were buzzing around, and the audience was informed that they would go live to air in less than five minutes.

A large woman Craig recognised as the mother of a rather obnoxious child comedian sat down beside him, and he politely nodded hello. Her son was very popular with the audience and, on another day, he may have been worried about the competition, but today wasn't going to be about her son or anyone else other than Patrick. Craig was certain of that.

It was only moments now until showtime, and Craig could see Patrick waiting on stage to start his performance once the introductions were made. He was performing a final inspection of the equipment, and then Craig noticed him taking a small foam earplug from his pocket and placing it into his left ear. Reassured that Patrick was still thinking clearly, he settled back in his chair to watch the show.

The audience was given a ten-second countdown, and then the fun began. The monitors around the studio displayed the show's title sequence coming to an end, and the applause signs were lit. The crowd went wild as the cameras cut to Stephen Lucas on a small stage to the right of where Patrick was waiting to begin his performance, and once he had calmed the cheers, he began his introduction.

The following five minutes were absolute cookie-cutter TV talent show stuff. Each judge was introduced to the stage to their own entrance song before taking their seat on the judging panel.

Laurence's and Michelle's songs were almost certainly personally chosen to flatter, whereas Kieron was introduced to *Bewitched's C'est La Vie,* which someone had comically positioned to the lyric *Some people say I look like me dad.* The audience exploded into laughter, although Craig managed to refrain.

Once the judges were seated and the audience had calmed, Stephen continued his opening.

'As you will all be aware, our first act this evening, Enigma, has not been without some recent controversy,' Stephen began, pausing slightly for the audience's supportive reaction and chants of 'We love Enigma.'

Stephen continued with a summary of the events to date, a blasting critique of *The Sunday Review,* and a reiterated denial of any wrongdoing by the show's team. He then explained that to try and silence the critics once and for all, the internationally renowned Cage & Clerk had been invited to the studio to act as independent adjudicators. The audience applauded once more, and the entrance doors behind Stephen opened, and the aforementioned Cage & Clerk joined him on stage.

'Good evening, gentlemen,' Stephen welcomed them.

'I need to correct your introduction,' Callum Cage said immediately. 'We are not independent adjudicators. We have a grudge. We are here to take Laurence and his show off the air,' Cage was obviously joking, and the audience responded appropriately, but there was an element of truth underlying.

'Yes, yes, I seem to recall Laurence wasn't your biggest fan,' Stephen played along. 'But I believe you've managed to scrape together a career following his dismissal of your talent?'

'We are getting by,' Tristen Clerk spoke next. 'We've had some success being talentless in Europe, Asia, the Middle East, North and South America. Oh, and we managed to blag a little residency in Vegas, so it's paying the bills, at least.'

The audience loved the exchange at Laurence's expense, and Laurence took it all in his stride, smiling and laughing along as he should.

'All joking aside,' Laurence interjected, keen to deflect any further embarrassment. 'Cage & Clerk have clearly had a phenomenally successful career and are well respected around the world. And our fractious history makes them the perfect people to oversee

Enigma's next performance.'

'Yes, and we really must get on with the show,' Stephen took back control of the conversation. 'I will just ask you to confirm that you haven't yet met Enigma, and you have no idea what trick he is about to perform?' Stephen waited for both of them to confirm these facts before he continued. 'Okay then, if I can ask you to join Enigma on the main stage, and we can hand over to him for what I am sure is going to be a breath-taking opener to the show.'

Cage & Clerk moved over to where Enigma was awaiting their arrival, and Stephen made one final introduction before music and an explosion of pyrotechnics began the performance.

Enigma stood centre stage with his arms raised, with Cage & Clerk on either side, awaiting further instruction. He was in his tight black jeans, commando as requested, and Craig grinned, knowing he was responsible for Patrick's clearly noticeable semi.

The mesh t-shirt, equally tight, made visible the top hat tattoo on Patrick's chest as well as his muscular torso. Before Patrick had a chance to speak his opening line, a male voice from the crowd seemed to read Craig's mind and called out, 'You're so hot.'

'Tonight, the closeup magic is gone,' Enigma shouted above the audience's screams. 'Tonight, we are going big. Tonight, we are going to change the world of magic forever.'

Craig continued to smile to himself in the crowd. Enigma was doing his thing, and he was right. Tonight, things were going to change forever.

With that, the dancing boys arrived, and the homo-erotic dial on the performance was turned up to eleven. Eight male dancers wore matching outfits of black high-laced boots, black PVC hotpants, and a gold neoprene harness supporting a small pair of black feathered wings.

Enigma, Cage, and Clerk moved to one side of the stage, and there followed a synchronised dance routine during which the dancers theatrically manoeuvred the main props of the trick into position. Finally, the two vanishing cabinets atop their raised platforms and the four staircases were whirled around until coming to rest in their final positions.

From stage left to right, there now stood a staircase up to a cabinet platform, followed by two further staircases, one down, then one up to the second platform, and then the final staircase back down to the stage. The only change from the earlier rehearsal was that each piece of equipment appeared solid in construction. The Perspex element was currently hidden from view by black sheets secured on all sides.

To further demonstrate the configuration of the stage props, Enigma walked up the first set of stairs and entered the side of the box through the first door. The door closed behind him, and he was out of view for no more than a second before the door on the opposite side of the box opened, and he reappeared.

There was soft applause, but the trick had not yet begun.

Enigma continued his journey down the exit steps and then immediately back up again to the second cabinet. He entered and exited as previously before descending the final stairs and returning to Cage & Clerk's side.

'Are you impressed yet?' he asked of them.

'Well, I'm impressed with the dancers. I didn't know where to look,' Clerk replied. 'First,' he added to laughter. Tristen Clerk was an openly gay man, and his humour was not wasted on this audience.

'Okay then, I am only going to perform a single trick tonight, and I want to make sure it's impressive, so let's run a few scenarios by you and see if we can make it a good one,' Enigma explained.

'Sure, sounds good,' Cage answered.

'So, let's say we take one of our dancing dark angels, and he walks up the stairs and into the box and then comes out across the stage from the second box. Would that be impressive?' Enigma asked.

Cage sucked air in through his teeth before replying, 'Well, not really. I mean, we all know there could be a route below the platform through the stairs out of sight of us all. I guess,' he half apologised.

'Okay, good point,' Enigma agreed before moving across the stage and pulling down the black sheets that had been concealing the Perspex makeup of the props. 'How about that? You can see right through the stairs and under the platforms now. Nowhere to hide, right?'

'Hmm, better, but the stage backdrop is very dark,'

Clerk took his turn. 'Sometimes you think you are seeing right through, but really you aren't.'

Once more, the observers played perfectly along with the script, despite having no foreknowledge or rehearsal. Craig could only congratulate himself on his ingenuity and planning that enabled Patrick to perform so smoothly.

'Boy, you guys are good,' Enigma sighed comically before clapping his hands, and the backdrop of the set was changed from black to a pale-yellow colour. 'And let's get the dancers behind the props while we are at it,' he instructed.

As you now looked at the stage, you could see the full configuration of the props, and they were all clearly transparent, except for the actual vanishing cabinets on top. The eight dancers were merrily gyrating and could clearly be seen behind all of the equipment, and Cage & Clerk seemed much happier with the setup.

'Right, so if I now vanish one of my little angels and he appears on the other side, are you going to be amazed? Will it be inexplicable?' Enigma asked again.

'Well, I can think of another small issue,' Cage offered. 'Sometimes this kind of trick uses a doppelgänger?'

'You are absolutely right, of course,' Enigma conceded. 'How about we use you then? You're not a twin, are you?' he joked. 'In fact, let's use both of you and make this twice as crazy.'

Enigma signalled to someone off-stage that the main trick was about to commence, and music sounded once more. The dancers continued to gyrate in time, and Enigma first led Cage to the bottom of one staircase before leading Clerk to the one on the opposite side of the stage.

Enigma returned to the centre of the stage and faced the audience with his arms raised.

'Okay, guys, on my signal, I want you to walk slowly up the stairs and into your cabinet. Once the door has closed behind you, just step out from the other side,' Enigma instructed without looking back behind him.

Craig looked on intently from his seat in the crowd, somewhat surprised at how well Patrick was building up to this trick. He watched as Patrick lowered his arms and called 'go' as if starting a drag car race, and Cage & Clerk began their ascent of the stairs.

Aware the main event was imminent, Craig focused his attention on Patrick. He didn't move from his position facing directly into the audience and seemed to fall into a trance-like state as he awaited the audience's reaction.

Happy that Patrick was correctly focused, Craig turned his attention to the vanishing cabinets just as the doors were closing behind Cage & Clerk.

Cage had entered the cabinet on the left of the stage, and Clerk had entered the cabinet on the right. There was a massive explosion of pyrotechnics into the air, and then the audience watched on as the two men exited each cabinet just a second later.

There were gasps of amazement, whoops and

squeals of excitement, and a full standing ovation accompanied by thunderous applause by both audience and judges alike. Cage & Clerk had both inexplicably emerged from the opposite cabinet to the one they had entered.

*Fuck yes!* Craig had stood with the crowd, not to take any part in the ovation but merely to maintain his view of the stage. This wasn't quite over yet, he was sure.

Callum Cage stared directly across the stage at his partner Tristen Clerk. Taking a moment to get his bearings, he quickly realised their positions had been reversed. A look of confusion was evident on both of their faces, but Cage's expression was deeper, more pained.

Tristen Clerk looked on with concern as Cage clutched his chest before he stumbled and fell face forward down the stairs, coming to rest motionless at the bottom.

There were screams from the floor crew to cut the live transmission, and the audience fell silent as they watched the scramble to offer Cage medical assistance on stage.

Craig turned his attention back to Patrick. He had not even turned around, but he had broken from his trance and was staring back over towards Craig. As their eyes met, Patrick removed the bloodied earplug and threw it to the floor. Craig could tell from his expression that Patrick was unhappy with how this had played out, but Craig smiled back at him.

*'That couldn't have gone any better,'* he mouthed. He

knew Patrick wouldn't understand, but he would understand soon enough.

## CHAPTER 15

August 2019

The drive home could have been more pleasant. Patrick was beside himself with worry about what they had just done, and he would not be calmed by Craig. They picked up Chinese food on the way, but Patrick had no appetite. His head was banging, and he decided to go to bed.

Craig had offered to make Patrick a hot drink, and when he took it upstairs to him, he tried once more to settle his concerns.

'I will sort it out, Patrick. Give me your phone and get some rest. I will go downstairs and call Kevin. I'll get an update on everything. It will all be okay in the morning, you'll see,' he kissed Patrick on the forehead and took his phone off him, so he could get Kevin's number before leaving the room.

The show had been pulled from the air immediately, and the studio cleared of both audience and contestants while paramedics attended to Callum Cage on stage. Craig and Patrick had waited backstage for a short time but were advised to leave and allow the production team to manage the incident.

There would be huge press interest as the collapse had occurred on live prime-time television, not to mention during Enigma's act, but they would deal with it and get in touch as required. The advice from Laurence and Kevin had been to speak to nobody, but Craig had a different plan.

If Patrick had finished his cup of tea, he wouldn't be waking up for a while, but just to be sure, Craig headed out to the garden room to make his phone calls well out of earshot. He started with Kevin and had to call several times before he finally picked up.

'Hi, Patrick. Can I call you back later? Unfortunately, Callum passed away, so it's all gone a bit crazy here right now,' Kevin said when he eventually answered the call from Patrick's number.

'It's not Patrick. It's Craig,' he corrected. 'You're going to need to get Laurence on this call. You really need to hear what I've got to tell you. I'm your get-out-of-jail-free card.'

'I really don't think Laurence can talk right now,' Kevin insisted.

'Kevin, I don't think you understand. Patrick is dangerous. The accusations Matt Turner has been making are true,' Craig explained. 'I want out, and I am ready to talk about it. It will put Laurence and his stupid show in the clear. Callum's death wasn't an accident.'

'What? Oh, fuck! Okay, I'm finding him now. Stay on the line,' Kevin said, and Craig could hear footsteps as he ran off to find Laurence.

\* \* \*

To avoid any unnecessary suspicion, Craig had joined Patrick in bed once plans had been put in motion with Laurence, who had been more than interested in Craig's call, if only out of self-preservation.

Patrick had drained his tea before sleeping and had not stirred all night. He was still fast asleep when Craig snuck from under the covers at 6:00 am to head over to join Laurence at the television studio for the live morning news interview they had arranged the previous evening.

He hoped he hadn't been too heavy-handed with the sedative, as Patrick needed to wake before 8:00 am to keep plans on track. Craig decided to set the alarm on Patrick's phone and leave it on the bedside table, with a note for him to turn on the news. Patrick would be very confused when he awoke, and Craig had a tinge of guilt as he headed out to the car, but there was no other way. This had to be stopped now.

Laurence had already arrived at the studio by the time Craig had been escorted to the set, and they had a short briefing with Ian Atkinson, who would be interviewing them just after the 8:00 am news headlines. During their conversation, he seemed a little sceptical, but he was familiar with the story from his work on *The Sunday Review* and was happy to proceed. In light of Callum's death, this was a major exclusive, regardless of how bizarrely it seemed to be playing out.

Just before going on air Craig received a call from Patrick, which he declined, followed by a text asking where he was and what was happening. Perfect timing.

'Good morning. It's Wednesday, 7$^{th}$ August, and as promised before the news, we are joined today by Laurance Stokes from the now infamous *Future Stars*, and alongside him is Craig Newman, husband of the controversial contestant, Enigma,' Ian introduced.

Patrick was clearly watching as, almost immediately, Craig's wrist vibrated, and he glanced down at his *Apple* watch to see a message reading *What the fuck?*

'As you will no doubt be aware,' Ian continued to the camera. 'Following his collapse on stage last night, Callum Cage, of the magic duo Cage & Clerk, sadly passed away. Laurence, you contacted us as you wanted to share some more information about this incident,' he finished and turned to his guests to await Laurence's response.

'Firstly, Ian, can I just extend mine and the show's deepest sympathy to Callum's family at this absolutely awful time,' Laurence began, and Craig nodded his agreement. 'As you know, there has been some controversy around the performances of Enigma, and I can again state that there has been absolutely no collusion on the part of the show. However, Craig reached out to us yesterday evening, scared for his own safety, and asking if he could speak out.'

'Craig,' Ian asked his next question directly. 'What are you scared of exactly? I believe you are suggesting Callum's death may not have been an accident?' Ian had clear doubt in his voice. He had watched the show, and to the best of his knowledge, Callum appeared to have had a heart attack.

'I am not saying he was murdered,' Craig responded. 'But Patrick is dangerous. He is a great magician, but he also has powers. Last night wasn't a trick, and I think it probably gave Callum a heart attack,' Craig was deliberately vague.

'I am not sure I am following you, Craig. What do you mean he has powers?' Ian questioned.

'The reason some of his tricks seem unexplainable, is that they are. He can make things happen. The coins, the cards, he can just make things disappear and appear again,' Craig was becoming visibly agitated as he spoke, closing his eyes at one point, seemingly to calm himself.

'You are telling us that Patrick has some kind of supernatural powers?' Ian couldn't help but smile as he continued the interview. This would be good for the ratings, if nothing else.

'It started when we were younger. I think the first time was when he got angry with a bully. But he has gotten stronger with it over the years. He uses it to make his magic better but also to steal. The expensive house and cars. It's true what Matt Turner said,' Craig referred back to the original *Sunday Review* allegations.

Laurence remained silent as Craig ranted his fears and concerns. The previous evening when Craig had first explained this all to him, he believed it was the stuff of nonsense, but it was a diversion from the attention the show was receiving. He was happy to facilitate a scapegoat if he could.

'I am not sure I am following you, Craig,' Ian interjected. 'I'm sure you can imagine this is a little hard to swallow. How exactly are you saying it works?'

'He can just make things disappear and then appear again somewhere else,' Craig repeated, then expanded. 'Like with money, he could just imagine that the contents of a cashpoint machine were in the boot of his car, and it would happen.'

'Are you saying Patrick has done this? You have stolen money from cash machines to fund your lifestyle?' Ian began to try and extract some form of facts from this madness.

'You are missing the point,' Craig said. 'He is dangerous. I am worried his mother was right. He might have had something to do with his father's death, maybe even his mentor Geoff. He did rather conveniently inherit everything afterwards,' Craig emphasised.

'These are quite some accusations, Craig. I'm sure the police are going to want to speak to you both once we are done here. So, where does last night's incident with Callum fit into all this?' Ian continued, a little surprised that the producer hadn't come into his ear to ask him to wind up this nonsense.

'I told you. It wasn't a trick. When Cage & Clerk entered the boxes, Patrick used his powers to make them swap places. When Cage walked out and realised he was on the other side of the stage, I guess the shock brought on a heart...'

While Craig had been answering the last question, Ian had put his hand to his earpiece to focus on a frantic message from the previously absent producer. His expression became increasingly puzzled, but when the message was repeated, he cut short the end of Craig's answer to introduce some breaking news.

'Sorry to interrupt you there, Craig, but we seem to have some relevant breaking news coming in from one of our reporters. We have them on the line now. Lynn Mills, what can you tell us?' Ian handed over to a voice that spoke out into the studio.

'Hi Ian, this is Lynn Mills, and I am reporting from a little distance away from the magic shop owned by Patrick Morgan, aka Enigma,' Lynn began her report. 'I just happened to be in the area when reports came through of a hostage situation in the magic store. It is believed Patrick is in the store with as many as five hostages, and more worryingly, armed police are on the scene responding to further reports of shots fired,' she paused to allow Ian a question.

'Do we know who the hostages are, Lynn? Did anyone see them entering the store?' Ian probed.

'Okay, so you are going to think I've gone crazy, Ian,' Lynn excused what she was about to report. 'We know one of the hostages is Matt Turner, the journalist who has recently been trying to expose the Enigma act as a fraud. But he wasn't taken. He was vanished. Matt's wife put in a frantic call to the emergency services less than half an hour ago to say he literally disappeared before her eyes. I have since seen him through the window of the store before we were all moved back behind a police cordon.'

'Vanished, you say?' Ian asked once more in genuine disbelief.

'Yes, inexplicable, but we are receiving further reports of the same. I believe Kevin Heath from the *Future Stars* production team has also vanished, along with your Sunday morning colleague, Anna Keegan,' Lynn reported.

'I told you!' Craig exclaimed as he jumped forward in his seat. 'He's dangerous,' Craig reiterated, and with that, he vanished.

Ian and Laurence looked at the empty seat and then at each other, both confused and concerned, but no more than ten seconds later, Laurence also vanished from the studio.

\* \* \*

Patrick had been woken by his phone alarm a little before 8:00 am. The banging headache with which he had gone to bed was now replaced by a tiresome fog.

As he silenced the alarm, he spotted the note in Craig's handwriting – *Turn on the news. I'm sorry, it's for the best. Please don't be mad, and don't do anything stupid.*

As he turned on the television in the bedroom, he attempted to call Craig. There was no answer, so he sent a text. *Where are you? What's going on?* But the television came on to the right channel just as Ian Atkinson was introducing Craig and Laurence in the studio.

*What the Fuck?* He texted again. *'What on earth is going on?'* he thought to himself, and then he felt a rage building and became aware of that familiar feeling of the first trickle of blood leaking from his ear as his mind began to cloud and his eyes glazed over.

The next Patrick was aware, he was standing at the rear of his magic shop in only yesterday's underwear, all he had awoken in. His arm was raised, and he held a handgun, pointing directly at Matt Turner, who rightly looked frightened for his life as he stood there in the blood-spattered pyjamas he had been wearing when he was vanished from breakfast with his wife.

The blood spattering was a recent addition. Around Matt on the floor were four bodies, all shot and lying dead or dying in pools of blood.

Lisa Newman, Craig's mother, had been shot first. A single bullet dead centre of her forehead, and she fell down onto her back with her open eyes, now staring lifelessly at the ceiling. She wore a smart skirt and blouse, as she had dressed early to head out and meet a friend for coffee, but her feet were still in the *UGG* slippers Craig had bought for her the previous Christmas.

Neil Dixon, the bully from Patrick's secondary school years, had fallen next. Not such a clean shot, as there had been panic in the room once Lisa had died. It had taken two bullets in the back to drop his now overweight frame to the ground, and he currently lay face down, still gurgling a little from his blood-filled mouth. Neil worked nights in a factory, and the police would later find his car in the ditch on a country lane where it had veered when he had been vanished from the wheel. He was alive, but he would not survive.

Kevin Heath slept naked, and after a late night at work following the disastrous Enigma audition, he had still been asleep when he had been vanished and reappeared in the shop. When the shooting started, he dropped to the floor and crouched in a ball with his hands over the back of his head. He still maintained this position, with a stream of blood from the bullet holes in his back now running down the crack of his naked bottom and gathering in a pool around his feet.

Anna Keegan had carved out a successful career in the media and was driven to achieve in every aspect of her life. She had been at the gym toning for her upcoming holiday to the Maldives when she was vanished and reappeared sweating and in full gym Lycra.

When Patrick began to shoot his victims, Anna did the only thing she knew how. She attacked in an attempt to survive, and she nearly made it, but Patrick pulled the trigger as she reached to wrap her hand around the gun.

One of Anna's fingers was removed as the bullet passed through her hand and into her eye socket. Her body fell, twitching on the floor, but the movement was merely from residual electrical pulses in her nerves rather than a sign of possible survival.

Matt Turner had been too scared to run in any direction. If he hadn't already performed his morning ablutions, he may very well have defecated on the spot, but as Patrick turned the gun on him, he seemed to pause, and his expression changed from one of maniacal trance into something a little more confused.

It was at this point that Craig materialised in the store, closely followed by Laurence. There was a brief moment of calm as the four men now present took in the surroundings before Craig spoke.

'What have you done, Patrick?' he asked, but before Patrick could even consider an answer, chaos reigned once more.

From the front of the store, there was an explosion and the sound of shattering glass. Craig turned his head just as three armed police officers came charging into the store through the broken window in response to the recent sound of gunfire.

Craig immediately turned back towards Patrick and watched as his husband pulled the trigger of the pistol he was holding and sent a bullet into the throat of Matt Turner and a second shot into Laurence's shoulder.

Matt dropped to the floor with a colossal thud, where he would soon bleed out, and Laurence was pushed backwards into a wall, where he remained in shock until an ambulance crew was eventually given access to the building.

In response to the renewed gunfire, the armed officers opened fire on Patrick, who was now in clear line of sight. In a move Laurence would later describe as *Matrix*-esque when he was doing the rounds on the chat show circuit, Patrick raised his hand and stopped the police bullets mid-air.

Patrick then clenched his fist, and the bullets dropped to the floor, and the guns were wrenched from the police officer's hands and crashed down amongst the bodies. A second later, the officers were vanished from the store and would shortly radio back into the command centre to let them know they had reappeared in the churchyard in Witford Common.

Amidst the commotion, Craig remained focused. He was determined he would be walking away from this unharmed and untainted by the morning's revelations. By the time Patrick had begun to come down from his latest trance attack, Craig had picked up one of the police firearms and trained it directly at him.

'What are you doing, Craig?' Patrick asked. 'What is happening? Why did you say all those things on the television this morning?' Patrick sounded terrified.

'It's over, Patrick,' Craig said quite calmly but with sadness in his voice.

'You just saw what I did?' Patrick reminded. 'You can't shoot me. I have my powers,' he added, raising his hand to prepare to disarm his husband.

Craig took a step forward and turned slightly so his back was now towards Laurence, who still stood bleeding against the wall.

'You don't have any powers, Patrick,' Craig said softly enough so Laurence wouldn't hear him.

Patrick looked confused as he clenched his fist, and nothing happened. He looked to Craig for the answer just as Craig opened fire and shot four rounds from the semi-automatic weapon into Patrick's chest. Patrick was dead before his body came to rest, and he would never know the truth.

# Part Three: Enigma

## CHAPTER 16

October 2000

For the last twenty-four hours, eight-year-old Craig Newman felt like he had been in a dream, observing himself from a distance. Some would have said nightmare, but Craig didn't feel particularly afraid. It had all happened so quickly. If anything, the aftermath had been more traumatic than the event itself. As he sat in the bath, scrubbing away the doctor's touches, it all seemed too crazy to be true, and it was going to get stranger yet.

At roughly the same time yesterday, Craig had also been in the bath when his uncle Paul had crashed through the door. Although it was unusual for him to come in during bath time, Craig wasn't uncomfortable being naked in front of his uncle. They often went swimming together and would get changed in the same cubicle, and Craig hadn't yet developed the embarrassment that came with adolescence.

'Uncle Paul!' Craig exclaimed as he stood up to greet him, but Craig's smile dropped almost immediately. Something was clearly wrong.

Paul was not smiling. He looked sweaty and frantic, and Craig realised he could hear his mother shouting in the background. Before Craig knew what was happening, Paul had scooped him up from the bath and was heading back downstairs.

Craig let out a screech as Paul grabbed him from the water, and now that he could see his mother screaming on the stairs, he began to kick and cry in confusion, desperate to be released from his uncle's grip.

Lisa attempted to stop Paul from descending the stairs, but Paul pushed her backwards, and she fell four or five steps down, jolting her back as she landed. Paul rushed past her and was gone out of the door.

As soon as they were outside, Paul adjusted his grip on Craig, putting him over his shoulder in a fireman's carry before running down the street. Craig's cries had stopped as his breath was taken by the cold October evening air. His body, still wet from the bath, began to shiver, and he remained quiet and motionless as he tried to process what might be happening.

Ten minutes later, they arrived at the local church, and Paul kicked open one side of the large oak entrance door. As they ran into the church, Craig thought he caught a glimpse of a body slumped over a pew. *Was that the vicar in his clerical robes?* Maybe someone had just left their coat behind after service.

A voice called out from behind them when they were a little further into the church. It was the local PCSO who had been alerted to a commotion by a local passer-by and had subsequently received a radio message following a 999 call from Lisa.

Paul spun on his heels, and Craig watched, albeit upside-down, as he produced a handgun and fired it into the air above the PCSO's head. The officer immediately ducked back out of the church, and Paul turned and continued towards the altar.

Once there, he carefully placed Craig on the front row pew and instructed him to stay there. Craig had no intention of moving, gun or not, and instead, watched on in silence as his crazed uncle leapt onto the altar and tore down the large wooden crucifix that looked down upon the congregation.

The crucifix crashed to the stone floor below, and Paul jumped back down and flipped it over so that Jesus was on his back looking to the heavens. Craig hadn't noticed, but Paul had a small drawstring rucksack on his back, which he now removed and withdrew a claw hammer.

For several minutes, Paul hacked and levered away until Jesus was unceremoniously dismounted from his cross. Paul then removed something else from the rucksack before scurrying over to Craig and pulling him back to the cross by his arm.

At only eight years old, Craig was unable to put up

much resistance. With relative ease, Paul laid Craig on the cross in place of Jesus and then held down his left arm on the crosspiece. He positioned a rusty antique nail on Craig's upturned palm and hammered at it three times until the nail head was almost flush with Craig's pale skin.

Craig let out the most blood-curdling of screams at the sudden piercing pain as the nail penetrated his palm. He broke into sobs and wails, and when Paul swapped sides to stretch out his right arm and repeat the process, Craig began to flail his legs and scream louder for his uncle to stop.

The screams from the church elicited an expedited response from the armed officers who had just arrived outside. The first officer into the church quickly took in the situation before releasing five shots into Paul's chest before he had a chance to bring the hammer down onto the second nail.

Paul's body slumped backwards into the altar before sliding down and coming to rest on the ground alongside the cross. Paul's blood splattering across Craig's face had momentarily silenced his screams, and he turned to face his uncle. Paul had a few more breaths in him before he would be gone, and Craig could see them as they left his body.

The inside of the church was as cold as the October air outside, so it was not peculiar that each breath could be seen, but Craig noticed something strange. These breaths were not the fluffy white vapour that would disperse as quickly as it emerged. These breaths were dark and lingered.

Craig was just about ready to scream again, and as he inhaled, Paul's breath was drawn towards him. He was sure he had taken some of it into his mouth. He could taste it, but it was gone when the armed officer arrived and pushed Paul's body onto its back to check for a pulse.

A period of noisy activity ensued, and several more people gathered to attend to Craig and his uncle. Craig was covered with blankets, and paramedics frantically began CPR on Paul. Lisa was allowed through to comfort her son while a fireman assisted in removing Craig's nailed hand from the cross after he was sedated.

Lisa accompanied Craig in the ambulance, and the nail itself would be removed from his palm during a minor surgery later that evening. She stayed at his bedside throughout the night, and when Craig awoke in the morning, she was surprised at how normal he appeared to be.

After he had eaten a little breakfast, two policewomen came in accompanied by a male doctor, who closed the door to the private room behind him. Some pleasantries were exchanged, and Craig could tell from his mother's responses that this must have been a pre-arranged visit.

'These ladies need to ask you a few questions, Craig,' Lisa explained. 'It's nothing to worry about. Just do your best.'

There followed a series of questions about what had happened the previous evening, but Craig wasn't sure what had happened other than the fact that he had been taken by his uncle and his hand had been hurt. His mind was still fogged by the anaesthetic.

Then, one of the ladies began to ask questions that embarrassed Craig in front of his mother. He fell silent, and his face reddened as she asked if his uncle had touched him on his private parts.

Craig didn't know what to say. He had been picked up naked from the bath and then gripped, carried, and thrown over his uncle's shoulder. He had then been held down on the cross. *Did his uncle's hand brush against his bits at any point? Is that what she meant?*

Lisa nodded to Craig to encourage him to answer the ladies' questions.

'I don't know,' was his timid reply, and this seemed to stir a response from the doctor, who began to put on a pair of surgical gloves and grab some things from the tray he had carried in with him.

'Do we really need to do this?' Lisa asked as the policewomen moved to leave the room.

'It's for the best,' the doctor explained. 'We need to make sure there is no harm done, and it's best to gather any evidence in case your brother pulls through.'

*Pulls through?* Craig thought. *Was his uncle still alive?* And for the next ten minutes, as the doctor took blood samples and swabs from his mouth, genitals, and anus, all in full view of his mother, Craig wished the breaths he had seen rolling from his uncle's mouth had been his last. In fact, he wanted there to be no breath left in his uncle's body at all.

Two floors below, in the intensive care unit, Paul's heart monitor flatlined. Nurses pushed past the police guard on the door, and the crash trolley was pulled to the bedside, but nothing more could be done.

Craig had overheard someone in the corridor outside his hospital room telling his mother that Paul had died. She had cried, and Craig could hear her crying again now in her bedroom as he sat in the bath, scrubbing away the doctor's touches.

Washing with one hand was awkward. Lisa had secured a sandwich bag over his bandaged hand with an elastic band to stop it from getting wet and offered to wash him, but Craig was adamant in his refusal. He didn't want anyone else touching him today.

With a bar of soap clasped in his good hand, Craig rubbed a lather all over his torso. Then, as he shifted his body so he could kneel and gain access to his lower regions, Craig slipped, letting go of the soap to grab the side of the bath and steady himself.

The soap shot across the bathroom floor and came to rest under the towel rail. Craig sat himself back down and stared at the soap and then at the palm of his hand, and the soap was back in his grasp.

*'That was strange,'* he thought.

\* \* \*

Craig had become understandably withdrawn following the ordeal and drifted away from all of his primary school friends over time. He underwent counselling and seemed to be coping well, but he preferred keeping his own company, and even after the move up to secondary school, he had still not built any real friendships.

Lisa assumed this was all a result of her brother's maniacal attack on her son, which in a roundabout way, it was, but not in the way she imagined. Craig had been keeping his distance from people, not through fear or shame. He was keeping his distance because he was keeping secrets.

It had taken some time before Craig was able to repeat the telekinesis he had performed in the bathroom that day, but eventually, he learned not only to repeat it but how to hone his new skill.

At an age when many would brag of such powers, Craig was careful not to divulge the secret. Initially, he feared more medical probing if it was discovered, and latterly he realised he could take much better advantage of his abilities if they remained unknown. And besides, he somehow just knew he could never allow this power to be discovered, whatever the cost.

By the time he was in secondary school, he had built a small repertoire of skills. Teleportation of inanimate objects, such as the original soap bar, was the simplest to perform but had little practical use. He might make the remote control for the television appear in his hand from the coffee table rather than reaching for it, but even this could only be performed when he was alone.

Craig progressed from performing this on an object

in front of him to being able to teleport something he knew was elsewhere, albeit out of sight. This was much more useful, and he had used it for such practicalities as retrieving his PE kit from where he had left it on the end of his bed and making it appear in his school locker. Detention avoided.

Once, Craig had mischievously stolen a chocolate bar from the local newsagents using this technique, but suddenly concerned he might be caught, he discarded it unopened in a nearby bin. A pang of conscience he would learn to ignore in time.

The harmless practising of these abilities went on for several years, and it was only as Craig moved into his teens that his experimenting became a little more nefarious. At first, by accident when he had been startled by a beetle scurrying across the kitchen floor.

He intended to vanish it and make it reappear outside in the garden. The vanishing worked fine, but when Craig checked outside the backdoor, expecting the beetle to be continuing its scurry down the garden path, he saw the remnants of a bloodied beetle carcass. It seemed transporting the living was more difficult than chocolate bars.

Craig now had a new focus. It would take several months of trial and error, mangling various mice, squirrels, rabbits, and birds, before he would manage to teleport a living creature successfully.

The secret seemed to be to give much deeper thought to the process rather than simply imagine the creature in a new location. Craig would focus his thoughts on the integrity of the whole animal. Its feathers or fur, its internal organs, the blood in its veins. He had no idea of the precise anatomy of any of his experimental subjects, but that didn't seem to matter. Focusing on the desired end result appeared enough to facilitate survivable transportation.

Once Craig mastered a skill and could reliably repeat it at will, he would seek a practical application that wouldn't draw too much attention, to himself at least. For example, one summer, while walking through a relatively quiet street, he noticed a dog that had been left alone in a locked car. Aware of the dangers of heatstroke in such situations, Craig decided to remove the dog out onto the street.

Craig very quickly realised he hadn't thought this through at all. Although he was a safe distance away so as not to be seen by any passers-by or in any immediate danger from the dog, he very quickly realised the dog wasn't going to sit on the kerb and patiently await the return of its owner.

In seconds, the dog had bolted into the road, causing an approaching car to slam on its brakes to avoid a collision. Unfortunately, the car behind was either too close, or the driver was less vigilant, as he didn't manage to stop and ploughed into the back of the now stationary vehicle. Both drivers leapt out into the street in a rage whilst Craig and the dog scurried away as the men argued it out.

Craig was more cautious with his activities for several months afterwards until a chance encounter with a boy from the year below him at the start of the new school year. This encounter would send his fifteen-year-old heart reeling and lead him to take his skills in a dangerous and sinister direction.

His intentions were honourable. Craig had noticed this boy one lunchtime, being pushed around by Neil Dixon. He didn't recall ever seeing him before, but on this occasion, once he had picked himself up from being shoved to the ground, the boy made eye contact with Craig and smiled.

Craig was instantly obsessed and went out of his way to learn more about this handsome dark-haired boy. He was experiencing feelings he had never felt before, and they felt good. He had such a cute smile, and Craig needed to know more about him.

He attempted to make some subtle enquiries in the classroom, but his questions were not subtle at all. It was well known that Craig would barely speak to anyone, so his sudden interactions were suspiciously out of character.

Alice, one of his least favourite classmates, made some teasing remark about him fancying Patrick, the vicar's son, but Craig was able to stop this escalating with a simple stare. Another skill of his mind that he had developed was to prevent people from thinking about him. He had used this technique successfully to keep himself off the radar of the likes of Neil Dixon.

Alice wasn't a bully, but she was annoying. She seemed to walk around in a permanent state of readiness for yet another pouting selfie, which she apparently posted all over her *Myspace* and *Facebook* pages, not that Craig was a follower. She would get her comeuppance.

Early the following year, after another attempt to embarrass him in the school corridor, Craig would watch Alice walk away, and just as she reached the top of the stairwell, he would transport a small bird that had been passing the window outside into her hair. Then, in a frantic flap of hands and wings, Alice would lose her footing and fall down the stairs, resulting in a broken arm.

For now, though, Alice had revealed the name of his muse, and it gave Craig something to work with. After school that afternoon, at a safe distance, Craig had followed Patrick, and he did indeed walk home to the local vicarage. From his vantage point in the lane opposite, Craig stood and watched for a while to see what else he could ascertain.

Through a window into the vicarage hallway, Craig could see Patrick shrug off his coat and hang it on a coat rack. Another slight pause while he presumably kicked off his shoes, and then Patrick disappeared upstairs in socked feet.

A moment later and a light went on in an upstairs room, and Craig saw Patrick appear near the window. His arms were raised, his school jumper was discarded, and his shirt was unbuttoned and removed. Craig was wishing he had a higher vantage point for this impromptu striptease when Patrick stepped forwards and drew his curtains together.

Craig spent the following months learning as much as he could about Patrick. Whenever Craig looked up, his eyes seemed to pick Patrick out from the crowd. He was a tall, slim, handsome boy with the beginnings of a downy shadow of facial hair and a wonderful smile, one he managed to wear despite the torrid time he seemed to be having at school.

It seemed Patrick was a loner, as was Craig, but where Craig managed to keep himself away from trouble, Patrick seemed to attract it. As a result, Craig often saw him bullied. Nothing too severe, but it could be relentless. He would have loved to have stepped in and helped, but he was waiting for the right time.

Then one night early in December, Craig lay awake in bed, scheming how he might take control of this situation and encourage some reciprocation of attention. Whether his mind was fogged by teenage lust, or perhaps Craig's mind had been destined to be this twisted following his partial crucifixion all those years ago, he devised a plan.

Patrick was already being bullied at school, and Craig intended to use his powers to break down Patrick's confidence even further, and when he was at an all-time low, he would step in and fix him.

Craig didn't waste any time putting his plan into action, and the following evening when his mother had left the house to start her night shift at a local hotel, Craig snuck out into the darkness and headed along to the vicarage.

The journey took a little longer than usual, as Craig was creeping cautiously in the shadows, keen not to be seen if possible. However, the roads were quiet, and the journey went without incident. Finally, just before midnight, Craig was again standing in a doorway on the corner of the lane opposite the vicarage.

The vicarage was in darkness, upstairs and down, and Craig took a couple of deep breaths in preparation before attempting something he had only practised briefly earlier that evening. He teleported himself from where he stood on the street corner into Patrick's bedroom.

Craig had chosen to reappear in front of the window where he had often watched Patrick partially undress before closing his curtains. This seemed likely to be a clear area of the floor for him to reappear on without risking knocking anything over and causing a disturbance.

He had chosen well, and as Craig's eyes adjusted to the darkness, illuminated a little by a streetlight on the other side of the curtains, he could see Patrick was soundly asleep on his bed. At some point in the night, Patrick had rolled onto his back, kicking away the duvet, and he now lay there topless and in light grey jogging bottoms.

Craig stood motionless, almost frightened to breathe for fear of disturbing the house. He quickly took in as much information about the room as he could. He noted an open door that led to an ensuite shower room, as well as memorising where the larger pieces of furniture were.

He would be able to control events remotely going forwards, but for this first time, he needed to be present to surveil the scene. That's how it seemed to work. When he was satisfied he had enough information to conjure up this image again, he turned his focus to Patrick, who still lay soundly asleep on the bed.

The next stage was an awful thing to do to anyone, and Craig would repeat it every couple of days or so for almost three months. He sighed softly, disappointed in himself, but it was part of a bigger plan that he was sure would have a happy ending.

Focusing his stare on Patrick's groin, it took only a few seconds before the material darkened, and a circle of urine began to grow on the front of his joggers.

Craig had first learnt this trick while once again in the bath. He needed to pee and had the idea to transport the urine into the toilet as it left his body. It was the strangest sensation, feeling the flow but seeing nothing, only hearing the sound of splashing in the bowl across the room.

He refined this trick by learning to extract the urine directly from the bladder, and it was this technique Craig now used to cause Patrick to wet the bed. The growing warm patch was causing Patrick to stir, and he moved his head on the pillow and adjusted his position.

Concerned he might get caught, Craig extracted himself from the bedroom and back down to the street corner opposite. He stayed there for a few minutes and noticed Patrick's bedroom light turn on. Craig felt awful as he walked back home, but he was committed to his plan. He considered teleporting himself back home, but Craig didn't like to overuse his abilities, and the fresh air would probably do him good.

The chain of events had begun.

# CHAPTER 17

February 2008

Craig had been excited about the school talent show ever since discovering that Patrick would be performing. This was the opportunity he had been waiting for to take his plan to the next phase.

It had been around ten weeks now that he had been inducing Patrick to wet the bed, and Craig could tell Patrick was suffering as a result.

Although he had always been a loner, subject to regular playground pushing and shoving, Patrick usually brushed it off and carried on with a smile. But of late, that beautiful smile, which had first captured Craig's attention, was gone. Instead, Patrick's head would now drop, and he would slope away, looking desperately sad.

Craig was shocked Patrick could even muster the confidence to participate in the talent show, but his name was on the list. When Craig had seen it the previous week, his conscience gave Patrick some slight reprieve by leaving five days between nocturnal accidents. Craig hoped this might act as some subliminal encouragement that things were about to improve.

Whether it had worked or not, it was now Thursday afternoon, and Craig was sitting in the auditorium awaiting the start of the show. He had taken a seat three rows back from the front and roughly in the centre of the stage so he would have a good view of the performances.

On the way to the auditorium, Craig had stopped at his locker to grab his PE kit tracksuit bottoms, which he had stuffed into a plastic bag along with some paper towels he had picked up in the toilets. He would need these shortly, but for now, the bag sat neatly on his lap and on top of it was a small leaflet they had been handed on entry to the hall, containing the running order for the show. Patrick was listed as the fifth to perform. Craig tucked the carrier bag under his seat and settled for the performances.

Craig sat through the headmaster's introduction, the 6th-form compère's attempts at comedy, the school choir, a dance routine, and the school band's steel drum performance. Broken-armed Alice was fourth, singing *Leona Lewis's Bleeding Love*, and then it was time for Patrick's magic routine.

Alice finished to rapturous applause, which she

milked for what seemed an eternity with her curtseys and sickly smile. Eventually, she exited stage left, and the compère was able to introduce 'Patrick Magic' to the stage. The curtain rose, and as Patrick was revealed, murmurs began to run through the crowd mocking the cloak he was wearing.

Craig wanted to cringe himself but managed to maintain a smile as Patrick caught his gaze in the crowd. *Why had he called himself Patrick Magic? And why did he decide to wear the cloak?* Craig knew only too well what it was like to be an outsider. He was pale-skinned, ginger-haired and had only recently begun to shift an excess of puppy fat, but he was skilled in avoiding attention. Patrick really did need some guidance.

He mouthed the words *'good luck'*, but it was going to take more than luck to see Patrick through the next few minutes. Craig knew this would be painful for Patrick, but it was the opportunity he had been waiting for.

Just before Patrick stepped forwards, Craig took his opportunity and used his mind to place the back of Patrick's cloak under the leg of the prop table behind him. The cloak tugged as Patrick walked forwards, but it wasn't enough alone, so Craig focused further and toppled the whole table over.

Chaos ensued. The sound of props crashing to the stage filled the auditorium as the table behind Patrick collapsed to the floor. The audience fell silent, and Patrick stood motionless as the various items rolling around his feet came to rest.

A voice called out something comical, and there was laughter. Craig could see the utter look of horror on Patrick's face. Their gaze met again, and Craig smiled sympathetically before closing his eyes, partly to concentrate, partly because he didn't want to watch what was about to happen.

'He's pissed himself!' a boy's voice called out, and Craig opened his eyes and promised himself that he would never do that to Patrick again.

Patrick looked confused and then mortified when he realised he was mid-flow in full view of the whole school. Craig felt for him, but at this stage, there was nothing he could do but watch it play out.

Craig locked his gaze on Patrick once more, focusing to try and get him to look over so he could offer him a sympathetic smile, but Patrick was transfixed on the growing wet patch around his crotch.

'Fuuuuuuck!' was Patrick's protracted and pain-filled cry, and Craig suddenly thought of one more thing that could add even more drama. He clenched his fists and forced one of the stage lights to explode high above the stage, raining down sparks on Patrick below.

Craig felt tears welling in his eyes as he watched Patrick release his cloak and run from the stage, gone from sight before the cloak had fully come to rest in the puddle of urine below.

\* \* \*

The auditorium had descended into a cacophony of

gasps, laughs, and whispers before one of the teachers called for silence. The curtain had been dropped temporarily, and the decision would be taken to continue with the show, following a short comfort break, as there were still many acts to come who had been practising for weeks for the event.

Before that decision was taken, Craig had already left his seat and exited through the rear doors and out into the corridor. A teacher had contemplated stopping him and returning him to his seat, but a single glance from Craig and she stepped back to the wall and let him pass unchallenged.

Craig knew precisely where Patrick had run off to, another functional ability he had acquired. Pausing briefly in the corridor to wipe away the moisture in his eyes, Craig then headed straight to the art department.

By the time he arrived, Patrick had settled himself on the floor in the back corner of one of the classrooms. Craig could see the top of Patrick's head rocking slightly back and forth as he slowly began to walk between the desks to the back of the class.

As Craig rounded the final desk, he looked down to see Patrick sitting with his keens pulled to his chest and his arms wrapped around them.

'Are you okay?' Craig asked.

'How did you know I was here?' Patrick responded.

'I followed the wet footprints,' Craig joked, then immediately regretted it. 'I am so sorry, that just wasn't funny at all. Sorry,' he apologised.

'It was quite funny.' Patrick said, and then he

smiled, and Craig knew right then that the bonding process he had been waiting months for had begun.

Craig handed Patrick the carrier bag with his tracksuit bottoms in, and he gratefully accepted this act of kindness.

'I didn't have any spare pants, so you'll have to go commando,' Craig smiled back. 'There are some paper towels in there as well, so you can dry off a bit,' he added.

'I can't get changed here,' Patrick stated.

'Sure you can. I'll turn my back if you like, but I think you're already at maximum points on the embarrassment scale today, so I wouldn't worry too much,' Craig said, really hoping Patrick would begin to undress in front of him.

'I'd still rather not show you my cock,' Patrick joked. 'I don't even know your name yet.'

Craig laughed aloud as he politely, albeit a little reluctantly, turned his back to Patrick. 'I'm Craig,' he said. 'Craig Newman. I knew I was going to like you.

As Craig turned around, he noticed a mirror on the wall, and as Patrick stood up behind him, his torso came into view. Craig spent the next few minutes stretching every sinew of his body in an attempt to gain height so he could see further down in the mirror.

Even on tiptoes, his efforts only afforded him a glimpse as low as Patrick's *Calvin Klein* waistband. Craig was surprised to see Patrick wearing *CK*s and momentarily wondered if they were briefs or boxers as he watched Patrick bend down again and slip them off over his feet.

Aware Patrick was now naked from the waist down just a few feet behind him, yet frustratingly out of view in the mirror, Craig tried to imagine what he may look like down below. No sooner had the thought crossed his mind than he heard a tap running and realised Patrick must have walked further away to use the sink.

Craig quickly glanced back to the mirror to find he had a clear view of Patrick's bottom. It was smooth, pert, and pale below the dark blue of his school jumper. Craig willed him to turn around, but before he had fully formed the thought, Patrick had already rustled the tracksuit bottoms from the bag and pulled them on.

'You can turn back around now,' Patrick informed.

Craig dropped down from his tiptoes and relaxed the tension in his overstretched body. As he turned, he caught sight of the final few tasks being completed. The shoes slipped back onto bare feet without undoing the laces, and the paper towels were collected and put into a bin before Patrick washed his hands.

'Thanks for this,' Patrick said sincerely.

'That's okay. You look cuter in them than I do. You can keep them if you like?' Craig posed a genuine question.

'Erm… sure. Thanks,' Patrick blushed. 'Why are you being so nice to me exactly? People aren't generally very nice to me here,' Patrick said, motioning with his arms to emphasise that by 'here', he meant the school.

If only you knew, Craig thought as he moved over to where Patrick was standing and hopped up to a seated position on the counter to the side of the sink.

'I like you. I've noticed you for a few months now, and I thought we could be friends,' Craig explained.

'And you still think that's a good idea after today?' Patrick questioned. 'You'll be hanging around with a laughingstock. What will your friends think?'

'Oh, I don't really have many friends, but people tend to leave me alone. I can handle myself,' Craig said before pointing to Patrick and adding, 'You've got a little drop of blood coming out of your ear.'

Patrick touched his finger to his left ear and then checked the tip for blood. 'For fuck's sake! Could this day get any better?' he cursed while grabbing another paper towel.

'It's only a tiny bit. I reckon you'll live,' Craig comforted. 'It has been a bit of a day, though. What happened?'

With a heavy sigh, Patrick began to recall the events, and as he explained, Craig listened intently, nodding sympathetically in all the correct places. He was fully aware of what had unfolded, but he allowed Patrick to vent his frustration before deciding to lighten the conversation.

'Did you notice a spotlight exploded above your head when you shouted fuck?' Craig asked. 'Maybe you've got real magic powers,' he joked, but this wasn't accidental. Craig was planting a seed. And the drop of blood on Patrick's earlobe, presumably caused by the falling spotlight glass, had given him another idea.

'Oh yeah, that's me. The superhero who pisses his

pants. A real world-saver.' They both laughed.

'Come on, I'll walk you out of school and make sure nobody bothers you,' Craig offered. He jumped down from the side and left the room without waiting for Patrick's response.

Craig could hear Patrick behind him, scrambling to gather his belongings and catch up. They continued to chatter as they walked, and although some inquisitive looks were received from the students passing by, they managed to leave the premises without incident.

As they walked, they agreed to meet during the half-term holiday. Mobile numbers were exchanged, and after some persuasion, Patrick promised he would show Craig some of his magic tricks.

A little further down the road, they came to a junction where they needed to go their separate ways for the remainder of their journey home.

'You going to be okay from here?' Craig asked.

'Yeah, I'll be fine,' Patrick replied. 'Thanks again for your help. You've been so nice to me.'

Patrick looked so sweet and genuinely grateful that Craig had befriended him today. Craig grinned back as he contemplated what he was about to do. He locked Patrick's gaze as he hesitated, but then he went for it, leaning forwards and kissing Patrick on the cheek.

'See you next week,' Craig called over his shoulder as he walked off, not waiting for Patrick's reaction. His mind was racing. *What had he just done? What must Patrick be thinking? Had he ruined the friendship before it had even begun? Should he have kissed him on the lips?*

When Craig turned the next corner and knew he was out of sight, he slipped his hand into his trousers and released his folded erection so it was upright and held flat by his underwear waistband. He hoped Patrick hadn't noticed his bulging trousers as he had turned away. Or maybe he hoped he had, and Craig suddenly had the idea to use his mind-power to pull a little blood into Patrick's penis, just enough to cause him to wonder why this boy's kiss had aroused him so.

* * *

Both boys arrived home smiling that day, and each told their mother about their new friendship. Kate and Lisa received the news with equal surprise and excitement. Their sons didn't have friends, which was concerning. This was welcome news indeed.

Patrick's evening began at bell-ringing practice, waiting for his mother and father to finish their session, followed by a trip to a local pizzeria.

Craig popped out to the mobile chip shop when he heard the van tooting its horn at the end of the road and then decided to crash on the sofa and watch *Hot Fuzz*. He had received the DVD for Christmas and had already watched it several times, but he fancied a laugh and nothing that required too much concentration tonight.

Later that evening, when both boys had gone to bed and were lying awake thinking through the events of the day, it was Patrick who blinked first. He sent Craig a text.

*Thanks again, Craig.
I can't believe such a
shitty day ended so well x.*

Was the kiss at the end too much?

*No problem, Patrick. It did end
well. Do you want to meet up
tomorrow and do something? x*

*Yeah, sounds good. I'll text
you tomorrow. Night x*

*Goodnight xxx*

Sleep came quickly that night, and Patrick was pleased to wake up dry in the morning, something that would become the new normal, and he and his mother would both later attribute to his meeting Craig.

Keen not to seem too desperate, Patrick refrained from messaging Craig as soon as he woke up. Instead, he washed and dressed and then headed down for some breakfast.

Today was an inset day leading into next week's half-term, and both of Patrick's parents had already left the house for their usual Friday commitments. But, as Patrick made toast, he noticed his mother had left a note on the kitchen message board, a standard communication tool for their family business. The note informed him that Barnaby, the dog, had been fed, but he needed to be taken for a walk later.

After four slices of toast and two glasses of orange juice, Patrick pulled on his coat and harnessed up Barnaby, ready for his walk. He headed across the road and through the churchyard to the common on the other side of the river before letting Barnaby of the lead for a run around the field.

After five minutes of madness doing zoomies up and down the length of the field, Barnaby began to circle. Patrick knew the signs, so he pulled a poop bag from the plastic holder attached to the handle of the dog lead in preparation. As he did so, his mobile phone beeped in his pocket, notifying him of a new text message. The message was from Craig.

*Morning. How you doing?*
*What you at?*

*I'm good. Just walking*
*the dog on the rec. You?*

*I can be there in 10mins*
*if you want company.*

*Sure, I'll head up*
*to the playpark end.*

*Great. See you soon x*

While Patrick had been texting, Barnaby had returned to his side. Patrick looked up but realised he had lost track of where the dog had deposited his business. He had no intention of hunting for it, so he stuffed the poop bag into his pocket and reattached Barnaby's lead before heading to the far end of the recreation ground to await Craig's arrival at the playpark.

The park was empty, and Patrick decided to wait on the swings. He swayed gently back and forth, scuffing his trainers on the grass below, while Barnaby wandered around on his extending lead. There were two points which Craig could enter the park from, and Patrick regularly looked up to check both.

Craig made it there in just over the ten minutes he had suggested in his text and had clearly run all the way. Craig had shot into the park through one of the end gates and then slowed his walk to catch his breath as he covered the last fifty yards to the swings.

As Patrick watched Craig strolling over, they smiled at each other, and Patrick immediately felt the same stirring in his loins he had experienced after yesterday's kiss on the cheek. *What was going on? Was he going to pop a boner every time they met?*

This would indeed be the case for the next week at least. Craig would make certain of it, just to be sure.

Craig could only stay for an hour that first Friday as his mother had taken the day off and arranged a visit to her ageing father. They spent the time walking and chatting, both keen to know more about each other.

They covered a myriad of subjects. How long had they lived in Witford? Where were they born? What was their favourite film? Favourite TV show? Favourite subject at school? Did they do any sports? Did they have any hobbies? Many, many things.

The question on hobbies raised the subject of Patrick's interest in magic, and Craig once more asked if he would show him some tricks. He promised he would, and when Craig passed on his mother's invitation for him to come over for tea on Tuesday, Patrick agreed to bring something.

By Tuesday evening, the boys were giggling and carrying on as if they had been lifelong friends. They had seen each other every day. They had been to the cinema on Saturday to watch the newly released *Jumper*, followed by the first of what would be many *McDonald's* meals together.

On Sunday, they had taken Barnaby out for a three-hour walk off into the surrounding countryside. It was cold, and there was speculation of some snow showers later in the week, but they wrapped up warm and constantly talked the whole journey.

On the way back, they stopped at a local café for hot chocolate stacked with marshmallows and cream, and when Craig took a sip, leaving cream all over his top lip and nose, Patrick burst into laughter before picking up a napkin and gently wiping Craig's face clean. Craig blushed. *Was Patrick catching feelings?* God, he hoped so.

Monday afternoon, they had arranged to go swimming. This wasn't an activity Patrick or his family did other than on holiday, but Craig went weekly, so Patrick agreed and that morning had dug out his least embarrassing pair of holiday swimming shorts. They were navy, covered in pineapples, and a little tighter than the previous summer, but they were fine.

He needn't have worried. They undressed in separate cubicles, and as they both exited into the communal area, Patrick's eyes widened when he saw Craig in his shape-hugging royal blue Speedos. Little did he realise he would shortly see him out of them too.

They swam and fooled around in the pool for almost an hour before deciding to get out and grab a snack in the foyer cafeteria.

The pool in Witford was aged and undergoing a programme of renovations but had yet to reach the desired state of a unisex changing facility. Individual cubicles had been installed for privacy, replacing the open hooks and benches from a less paranoid era, but the showers in the male changing area were still communal.

The boys were alone, and Patrick followed Craig's lead as he grabbed his towel from the locker and headed to the shower area. There were five shower heads with towel hooks on the side wall near the entrance. They hooked their towels and took the two showers closest to them. After an initial burst of cold water, the showers warmed nicely, and they began to rinse the chlorine from their hair as they chatted about plans for the rest of the week.

Just as Patrick turned towards Craig and asked him what they would be having for tea the following day, Craig bent forwards and removed his swimming trunks. He held them to the shower head to rinse them, scrunched them to remove the excess water, and threw them onto the floor below the towels. Craig then turned to answer, but Patrick wasn't really listening. He couldn't help but stare, and Craig couldn't help but notice.

'You not rinsing yours off?' Craig smiled.

'I couldn't if I wanted to. You've just given me a hardon,' Patrick grinned back. He always turned to humour when embarrassed.

Craig dropped his own eyes, and from the bulge in Patrick's shorts, he could tell he was only half joking. The pineapple on the front seam definitely looked a little distorted, and Craig knew this time it was nothing he had forced. It seemed Patrick really did like him the same way, and concerned he may also quickly stiffen, Craig turned off his shower, grabbed his towel and trunks, and headed back to get changed.

In the cafeteria, they grabbed a can of cold drink and a chocolate bar each, which they took with them as they walked home. Patrick had suggested he walk back with Craig so he could see where his house was for the following evening. They said goodbye at Craig's front gate, and then Patrick walked back home via the recreation ground. He smiled all the way.

Lisa had pulled together Cornish pasty, chips, and beans for their tea the following day, and Patrick had eaten it all, thanking her afterwards.

'You are more than welcome, my lovely,' Lisa said. 'What a polite young man you are, nothing like my Craig,' she added, glaring at him as he wiped his last chip around the plate, mopping up the remaining drops of bean juice.

'It was delicious, mummy. May we please be excused from the table?' Craig mocked in a posh accent before getting up from his seat and beckoning Patrick to follow him upstairs to his room.

Craig's room was small, with a single bed, a side table, a built-in wardrobe, and a small desk, but it was immaculate. Patrick had never seen it before but imagined nothing was out of place.

Books were neatly lined on a shelf, and a couple of *Star Wars Lego* sets were built and displayed on the windowsill. On the bedside table were a drinks coaster, a lamp and an alarm clock, and a paperback whose bookmark gave away that Craig had almost finished it. It was *The Kite Runner by Khaled Hosseini*. Patrick made a mental note to check it out.

Craig's school bag was hung over the back of the desk chair, and on the desk itself, a pen pot stood neatly at the back next to a *Bose* docking station holding Craig's *iPod*. Craig hit play, and *Rhianna* continued where she had left off, inviting all listening to share her umbrella.

Patrick was invited to sit on the bed, which he was surprised to see had a teddy bear resting on the pillow. He did so, sitting with his back against the wall, and then Craig joined him, sitting close enough for their sides to be touching.

They stayed like this, chatting and listening to music for over two hours before Patrick had to head home. Lisa had popped in once to offer them a drink, and the only other eyes on them that evening were from the posters of *Enrique Iglesias* and *Kylie Minogue* pinned to the wall opposite.

They were learning so much about each other in such a short period, and the rest of the week would bring more of the same. On Wednesday and Thursday, they would spend a few hours together kicking around in the park, and Patrick would show Craig a couple of card tricks using a deck he always carried in his pocket.

Craig had forgotten to ask when they had been at his for tea, and Patrick didn't like to remind him, but it came up again in conversation, and Patrick was always prepared.

On Friday, Patrick's mother returned the offer to join them for tea, but rather than eat at the house, they all travelled to a local fish and chip restaurant to dine. Craig was dropped off on the way home, and it would be another couple of weeks before he saw the inside of the vicarage and got to analyse Patrick's bedroom in daylight.

Saturday brought another trip to the cinema and another swimming session, and on Sunday, Craig had agreed to join Patrick at church for the morning service. Patrick had no idea how big of a deal it was for Craig to re-enter the church building, and Craig only agreed because he wanted to spend as much time with his new friend as he could.

Their final hour together of the school holiday was spent once more in the park, sitting on the swings. Patrick seemed a little anxious, and Craig guessed it was due to their imminent return to school.

'Don't worry too much, Patrick,' Craig tried to reassure. 'We've seen people around from school this week, and nobody has said anything,' he pointed out.

'Yeah, I noticed that. I'm surprised, to be honest,' and Patrick genuinely was.

'I'll leave a bit earlier tomorrow and come and meet you. We can walk into school together. Nobody bothers me,' Craig said, and Patrick accepted the offer.

And nobody did bother them. Neil Dixon continued to be a dick, but he was like that with most people. Patrick wasn't being particularly singled out.

## CHAPTER 18

February 2010

As Craig looked down from the fourth-floor balcony of his mother's flat to where Patrick was in a heated conversation with his mother, he knew this day would not end well.

It was Patrick's sixteenth birthday, and his parents had come over to speak to him about returning home following their rather graphic discovery of his homosexual relationship with Craig.

From the body language below and from the fact that Nigel had chosen to stay in his car and let his wife speak to Patrick alone, Craig reasonably assumed the discussion was not going well. He shrugged his shoulders when his mother stepped out onto the balcony to join him, asking how it was going as she did so.

Craig felt no guilt that their relationship was now out in the open. Patrick had been terrified for two years of what would happen when his god-fearing parents found out, and it was making him miserable and causing them both frustration that they were unable to be open about their love for each other.

With this in mind, Craig knew he had to take some action to bring this to a head, and when he found out Patrick's parents were going to be away for a wedding and Patrick had suggested they take the opportunity to fuck for the first time, he hatched a plan.

It was a simple plan. When Craig had been at the vicarage earlier that fateful evening to pick up Patrick for the cinema, he had noticed Kate had her wedding fascinator in a box on the entrance hall table, ready to pack into the car. Craig would simply make it vanish from the vehicle at some point during what he knew would be an almost two-hour car journey and return it to the entrance hall table.

Kate would obviously notice its absence on arrival at the hotel and send Nigel back for it either later that evening or early in the morning, as she certainly would not attend the wedding without it. Craig intended to be discovered asleep in bed with their son. It wasn't a perfect plan, but with a fair wind, it might work. Nothing ventured, nothing gained.

As it turned out, happenstance would ensure Craig's desire to be outed would be achieved in the most dramatic way imaginable.

While Patrick and Craig were at the cinema watching *The Book of Eli*, neither really concentrating as their minds were racing with thoughts of the imminent passing of their respective virginities, events elsewhere were beginning on a timeline to catastrophe.

Nigel and Kate had been on the road for just over an hour when Kate was minded to glance over her shoulder to the backseat of the car.

'Nigel, where is my fascinator?' she quizzed.

'It's on the back seat, Kate,' he replied confidently, unaware Kate was staring at the empty back seat.

'No, Nigel, it jolly well is not,' Kate sighed aloud before instructing her husband to pull the car over in the next layby.

Kate checked in the boot, despite Nigel's insistence that he had placed the box on the backseat, before ringing back to the house phone to check with Patrick if it was still sitting on the table in the hall. There was no answer at home and, remembering the boys had left for the cinema before they got on the road, there seemed to be little point disturbing Patrick on his mobile.

'Right, we will have to go back for it.'

It wasn't a question, and Nigel knew better than to protest. So instead, he spun the car around in the road and headed back home. They would arrive at the house just fifteen minutes after the boys had returned from the cinema.

Craig had never confessed it, but he had heard Patrick's parents put their key in the door when they arrived back at the house. It wasn't exactly according to plan, but it would have the desired effect.

Patrick's eyes were closed, focusing on his pleasure, and Craig raised his voice to cover the sound of the now fast-approaching footsteps.

'Oh baby, you're so tight. This feels amazing. I don't know how long I can last,' Craig moaned just before he felt Nigel's hand on his shoulder, dragging him backwards on his haunches.

As he looked up from where he lay, Craig could see the beetroot-red face of Patrick's father looking down on him with rage in his eyes. Nigel's fists were clenched, and Craig knew this was going to get ugly, but the intense pleasure he had been feeling only seconds before had crossed the point of no return.

Craig locked his stare and grinned as Nigel's eyes widened, and the veins on his forehead bulged when he looked down to witness Craig's erect penis convulse in a hands-free ejaculation which sprayed spurt after spurt of semen into the air.

Knowing his grinning face and vulgar display had enraged Nigel further, Craig pulled his legs to his chest and put his hand up to protect his head as Patrick's father began to rain blows down upon him. In the doorway, Patrick's mother began to wail as Nigel screamed obscenities at Craig in time with every blow.

'You abomination. You fucking disgusting boy. You sodomite. You bastard rapist.' A new variation with every punch to Craig's torso.

Behind them, Patrick leapt up from the sofa,

screaming for his father to stop. He grabbed his shoulder, and Nigel spun around to face his son.

'I will deal with you later...' he spat in rage, but Patrick was already lurching forwards.

Craig lowered his hands and watched as Patrick clasped his hand around his father's throat, cutting short his words. This was a perfect opportunity for Craig to use his powers to give Patrick control of the situation and change the dynamic of their father/son relationship.

Thinking quickly, Craig used his mind to force them both across the room until Nigel's back was against the wall. He then caused Patrick to lift his father by the throat until he was on tiptoes.

Convinced he was using his own abilities, Patrick confidently and calmly spoke to his father.

'Keep your fucking hands off of my boyfriend!' he said as a small trickle of blood ran down his left earlobe.

Craig always remembered to make Patrick's ear bleed. It was a trigger he had used for the last two years to convince Patrick that the powers were his own. The idea had come to him after Patrick's ear had been genuinely cut by the falling glass from the stage spotlight Craig had made explode during his disastrous school magic show.

It had been almost two weeks since Kate had flung a vase across the room, breaking up the fight and screaming for both of the boys to leave the house, and as Craig looked down at her from the balcony, he knew he was about to do something much worse. Something that Patrick would believe was of his own making, but it needed to be done, and Craig would be there to support Patrick through the aftermath, as he always had.

Craig couldn't hear the conversation from the balcony, but he watched intently and tried to piece it together in his head. Kate had spoken first, making Patrick cry, and then she wrapped him in her arms as he sobbed for a few moments.

When Patrick stepped back from his mother's embrace, he spoke, and they both turned toward the parked car. Craig also looked over to see Nigel sitting behind the wheel, staring directly at his family but failing to respond to Patrick's wave. God, how he hated that man.

The conversation continued, and Kate put an arm on Patrick's shoulder and tried to encourage him towards the car. Craig noticed Patrick stood firm and continued to talk. He wasn't ready to leave yet. He asked a further question before pausing to listen to his mother's reply. Then the rage came in Patrick's raised voice and Craig's violent response.

'You're fucking joking!' Patrick shrugged his shoulder away from his mother's grip. 'Dad's going to pray away the gay. Is that your plan?'

Craig was incensed when he heard his lover's words. Kate and Nigel hadn't come to apologise. They had come to steal Patrick away and drag him through some form of faith-poisoned conversion therapy.

Nigel was still sitting calmly in his car when Craig

vanished him, making him reappear instantly on the roof of the apartment block opposite. He simultaneously induced the trance-like state in Patrick that he always evoked when Patrick's pseudo-powers were to be linked to anger, along with a small trickle of blood from his left ear.

'Oh, my God! Look up there. There's a man on the roof. I think he's going to jump,' a lady shouted, and as she pointed upwards, everyone within earshot turned their gaze to where Nigel now stood on the roof edge.

Nigel, in turn, was pointing directly at the balcony where Lisa and Craig were standing, mouthing words the crowd below were unable to hear.

Initially shocked at his inexplicable appearance on the rooftop, Nigel stumbled to gain a footing. He immediately noticed Craig staring at him from the balcony opposite, and his religious inclination led him to conclude that Craig was the source of this evil.

Lisa and Craig could only pick out some of the words Nigel was babbling, seemingly some religious text, as he pointed an accusing finger towards their position. Lisa turned to ask her son what was happening and noticed Craig grinning back directly at Nigel and nodding his head.

Nigel crossed himself in one final religious act before falling forwards, pulled by an unseen force he wasn't strong enough to resist. The crowd gasped as they watched him fall to the ground, hitting the concrete below with a gut-wrenching noise before bouncing back up slightly and landing in an unnaturally broken position with a pool of blood gathering around his fractured skull.

Lisa would question Craig about his behaviour at some point as something didn't feel right, and this wasn't the first time she had thought it. She was paranoid that her son was more deeply wounded by her brother's abduction of him when he was a child, but for now, her first reaction was to run downstairs with Craig and comfort Kate and Patrick.

Patrick had witnessed the fall and found himself unable to stop staring at his father's lifeless body as members of the public rushed over to see if anything could be done. Even his mother's screams did not distract him, and he only turned away when Craig arrived at his side a few moments later.

'It will be okay,' Craig whispered as he put his arm around Patrick and handed him a tissue to wipe the blood from his ear.

Lisa attempted to comfort Kate, but her screams continued until they were joined by wailing sirens, and a paramedic was required to administer a sedative to calm her. She had been screaming at Patrick, accusing him, in no uncertain terms, of murder.

A police officer had stayed close to Patrick, unsure if these allegations were true until several onlookers confirmed he had been on the ground during the whole event, and it seemed a clear case of suicide.

Once Kate was sedated and led away to an ambulance, Patrick was allowed to return to the flat with Lisa and Craig, although he was informed there would be a need for a more formal statement in due course.

When they were alone, Craig once more tried to console Patrick, who was beside himself with grief and guilt over what had happened.

'I killed him,' Patrick sobbed when Lisa left them alone to put the kettle on.

'Don't you ever say that again,' Craig grabbed Patrick's shoulders and scolded him. 'He jumped. He was never going to allow you to be happy, Patrick. It is not your fault.'

And it truly wasn't Patrick's fault. This was all Craig's doing. Craig had spent the last two years successfully planting seeds and manipulating Patrick into believing he had some form of supernatural abilities, and Patrick believed it without question.

\* \* \*

Craig had been secretive for years about his abilities, precociously aware they would attract too much attention if ever discovered. However, he knew they were somehow connected to the events that had taken place with his uncle, and nobody spoke well of him.

The nature of his abilities presented slowly over a number of years, and Craig would practice them in private and, to begin with, only use them for small, innocuous tasks.

It was unlikely a coincidence that the experiments became more nefarious with the onset of puberty. As secondary school went on, Craig would accidentally disembowel many a small creature while trying to master the art of transporting a live animal. Not to mention honing his ability to pee into the toilet bowl while still lying in bed, a skill which also lent itself to ejaculation when the need arose.

The real change came when Craig was fifteen and first met Patrick. In desperation to win Patrick's affection, Craig concocted his disturbing bedwetting scheme, which concluded with Patrick's public humiliation on the school stage. But still, all of these actions were carried out in secret.

The first time Craig exposed his powers was in May 2008 when the boys visited the shopping centre one Saturday morning. It happened quite by chance when Craig's guard had been down, but he quickly regained composure and controlled the situation to his advantage.

They had spent the morning in Geoff's magic shop, which happened far too often for Craig's liking, but Patrick was obsessed with his magic, and Geoff was somewhat of a father figure and a mentor to him.

Craig and Geoff were not keen on each other. Nothing had ever been said, but their minds had been set in the short time they had known each other.

Geoff accepted that Patrick was much more outgoing and confident as a result of Craig's friendship, but there was something he didn't like that he just couldn't put his finger on.

Craig knew exactly what he didn't like about Geoff.

He was an old man paying far too much attention to a young boy. But, of course, Craig knew nothing untoward was going on. Still, it was an easy stereotype to label Geoff with, and it masked the underlying issue that Craig was, in fact, jealous of anyone and everyone who courted Patrick's attention.

On this particular day, Craig found Geoff even more creepy than usual, practically bribing Patrick with the offer of a free magic trick if he would agree to perform at the Spring Bank Holiday show Geoff had arranged in the coming weeks.

Patrick was understandably reticent following his disastrous performance at the school show, but to Craig's surprise, he agreed with barely any resistance. Although Craig agreed it was a good idea for Patrick to perform in public again, he had wanted to be the person to encourage him over his nerves, not Geoff, the gnarly-fingered paedophile.

By the time Geoff had finished, Craig had lost interest. He knew Geoff wouldn't show Patrick the secret of the trick in front of him, some magician's code nonsense, but he wasn't in the mood to wait around on his own, so he stood his ground until Patrick must have decided to take up the offer at a later date.

Craig shadowed Patrick around the shop while he chose a few things to spend his money on, and then, with a brown paper bag in hand, they said farewell to Geoff and left. They wandered around the shopping centre for another hour or so before deciding to get some lunch.

Lunch was always *McDonald's*, and Craig saved them a table while Patrick went to order the food. Craig watched his friend across the food hall as he shuffled forward in the queue, staring longingly at the seat of his denim shorts until it was blocked when a rather large lady wearing black leggings stepped in line behind him.

Disturbed by the alternate buttocks now in his line of sight, Craig looked away. As his eyes scanned around, he recognised three faces from school in the distance. They were some way off, but Craig noticed they were heading in his direction. This little gang were sometimes trouble, and Patrick would hate any confrontation, but Craig would handle it. He could easily influence them to walk by without noticing them.

But when Patrick returned with a tray piled high with food and sat down opposite Craig, they both tucked into their lunch, chatting all the while, and Craig momentarily forgot he was supposed to be safely steering the bullies aside.

'So, you are going to do the show for Geoff?' Craig mumbled around a *McNugget*.

'Yeah, I need to get some experience performing. It will be okay,' Patrick tried to reassure himself as he wiped a drip of mayonnaise from the side of his chicken sandwich with a chip.

'Can I come and watch?' Craig asked, but as Patrick took a sip of his drink, Craig noticed the boys from school had spotted them. Patrick noticed Craig's eyes widen, his brows raise, and his stare disappear over his shoulder. Then suddenly, felt a slap across the back of his head, causing him to lurch forward and dribble a little of his cola onto the table.

'Go careful drinking all that,' the voice from behind advised. 'You don't want another accident, pissy pants.'

It was Neil Dixon, the school bully and general pain in the arse. He would usually avoid Craig, but Patrick had been a target on his radar from the start of secondary school.

Surprisingly, Patrick stood up and turned to confront his foe, and Craig quickly stood and stepped beside him to support, as Neil was accompanied by two friends.

'Calm down, girls,' Neil mocked. 'I'm not here to disturb your romantic lunch date. Just saying hello to my favourite couple.'

'I didn't know you cared that much. We can have a threesome if you like?' Craig fired back, puffing his chest a little as he spoke, but Patrick curtailed his bravado with an elbow to the ribs.

Neil smiled before quickly leaning forwards to the right of Patrick and grabbing his brown paper bag from the table.

'What have we got here?' Neil enquired as he peered into the open top of the bag. Then, noticing the playing cards, he held the bag out to Patrick. 'Go on then, show us a trick.'

'Leave us alone,' Craig said as he snatched the bag back.

'It's okay,' Patrick calmly interjected. 'I'll show him

a trick.'

It was good that Patrick had grown in confidence, but as Craig watched him come to the end of his trick, which was not a trick at all, but just an excuse to flick the whole deck of cards into Neil's face, Craig realised he needed to take action to stop Neil punching Patrick in the face.

In a fraction of a second, Craig had devised a distraction he thought would at least stop Neil from immediately lashing out at Patrick. Neil had just revealed his card to be the Queen of Hearts, so Craig imagined this card to be folded in half and then half again and inserted into Neil's mouth.

As the last of the playing cards bounced off Neil's face and fluttered to the ground, Neil's friends watched in stunned silence, awaiting Neil's inevitable reaction. But Neil did not react as expected at all. Instead, he stood in silence, staring directly at Patrick, who did not once break his gaze.

As the moments passed, Neil's face reddened, but this was not the result of a building rage. His eyes widened, bulging slightly, and tears began to well. He opened his mouth, wide and rounded as if to howl in frustration, but no words came.

Patrick stared blankly at his enemy, giving no reaction whatsoever as Neil's lips began to turn blue and his hands raised up, grabbing at his throat. There was panic and desperation in Neil's expression, and Craig realised the card must have lodged in his throat.

Pushing past Patrick, Craig moved around to stand

behind Neil and wrapped his arms around his waist. He performed a crude form of the Heimlich manoeuvre, and on the third thrust, Neil coughed up the blockage from his throat. It was a playing card, folded in quarters with the face showing. It was a saliva-soaked Queen of Hearts.

As Craig released his hold, Neil dropped onto his hands and knees in front of Patrick, gasping air back into his lungs. Patrick used his foot to slide the coughed-up card directly under Neil's face.

'Is that your card?' Patrick asked sarcastically. 'Now fucking leave me alone, you prick!' he added before walking away.

Craig picked up the shopping bag and grabbed a napkin from the table before racing to catch up with his friend.

'Your ear,' he said as he held the napkin out.

Until now, Craig hadn't been sure why he had latched on to the bleeding ear from when he had first met Patrick in the art room after his school stage catastrophe, but he had been using it as a trigger in the subsequent months.

Even earlier that same day, when Patrick had been annoyed when Craig had commented on his naked bottom when he had walked in on him dressing, Craig had made his ear bleed when Patrick grasped his arm, concerned his mother may overhear and catch them out.

Suddenly Craig put the pieces together in his mind. He could make Patrick believe he had his own powers, and the bleeding ear was a sign that they had been used, regardless of Patrick being conscious of the fact.

Craig realised he could use his powers vicariously, for his own advantage, without risk of exposure. Patrick could become his lover and his subterfuge, but Craig would have to act quickly to secure this narrative.

Patrick wiped the small trickle of blood from his left ear and discarded the rag in the next bin as they made their way out of the shopping centre and back towards the bus stop.

'What happened there?' Craig asked.

'I'm not sure,' Patrick puzzled. 'But it felt frigging amazing!'

'How did you get the card folded up and into his throat?' Craig asked, keen to make Patrick try and explain the unexplainable.

'I didn't. I only meant to flick the cards at him, but then this thought came into my head, and it just kinda happened,' Patrick shrugged.

'You just thought it, and it happened?' Craig asked, but he knew he didn't sound as surprised as he should as he continued to lead Patrick to the wrong conclusion.

'I swear,' Patrick insisted. 'It was fucking epic!'

To avoid losing momentum, Craig decided to push Patrick a little further. When they reached their bus stop and sat themselves down on the bench to await the next service, Craig set Patrick a little challenge.

'See that window over there?' Craig pointed across the street to the window of a coffee shop. 'See if you can make one of those bags of coffee fall off the shelf.'

Patrick focused through the window on the bags of coffee stacked on the shelf, unsure exactly what to do other than imagine a bag falling. Craig wasn't looking at the window. Instead, he focused on Patrick, causing another small drop of blood to leak from his left ear just before making the entire shop shelf collapse, spilling coffee bags all over the floor and startling customers and staff alike.

'Holy shit! Did you see that?' Patrick blurted out as he leapt up in excitement.

'Amazing!' Craig replied, although he sounded less amazed than he might. 'You can't tell anyone about this, Patrick. They'll think you're a freak.'

Patrick calmed down and turned back to Craig.

'You don't think I'm a freak, do you?'

'I think you're freaking amazing, babe. We are gonna do something special with this gift, trust me,' Craig reassured him just as their bus pulled up.

In reality, they didn't do anything very quickly at all. Craig remained extremely cautious that Patrick's abilities must not become exposed, similar to the paranoia Patrick felt about their relationship becoming discovered. As a result, their experimenting with Patrick's newfound powers moved at a similar pace to their sexual exploration.

Craig continued to insist that Patrick should only attempt to use his powers when they were together, and he kept this promise with the exception of one obviously unsuccessful attempt when he was alone in his bedroom not long after the incident at the shopping centre.

By the time almost two years had passed from the shopping centre incident and the lead-up to Patrick's father's death, they had only tried to perform small tasks, usually moving an object, but it was hit and miss.

Patrick believed it was just the natural difficulty of honing an unexplainable skill, but Craig was simply managing his progression at a slow pace.

In the meantime, Patrick was becoming increasingly proficient in performing his magic tricks the old-fashioned way. He was now performing at various corporate events and private parties, often chaperoned by Craig, who had learnt to drive shortly after moving with his mother to a new apartment.

Finding a practical and reliable application within Patrick's magic routines would take some time, but Craig was very patient. He would know when the time was right to make the most of the situation. His key focus to date had been convincing Patrick that it was his skill they were developing, and Craig continued to reinforce the triggers of a trance-like state and a bleeding ear every time they were seen to succeed.

Craig would also do this when Patrick became angry, leading him to believe he had tripped out and perhaps squeezed his arm too hard or scared him with his shouting. Craig was crafting a narrative where Patrick was the alpha male with unique skills, and Craig was his compliant partner, only there to love and guide him.

And Craig did love him so much, and he truly believed that he was doing the best for both of them. So, when Patrick had asked that they wait until his sixteenth birthday before they had full penetrative sex, Craig had been happy to comply.

In the same time frame as the development of the powers, their relationship had moved on as well, albeit still in secret. Within a short period of their initial meeting, they settled into a regular routine of stealing kisses and cuddles at every opportunity. Then, after a couple of months, Craig was pleasantly surprised when he opened an MMS message to find a picture of Patrick holding his erection.

Craig replied with a picture of his penis flopped on his cum covered stomach, and so began a regular exchange of images of them enjoying themselves, thinking about each other.

Of course, after a period of sexting, both boys were motivated to go further, and they discussed the idea of trying mutual masturbation. This soon became their second regular release, and by the time Craig was driving, they were ready to park up in dark laybys or down in the lover's field in his royal blue 2002 *Peugeot 106* and take turns to give each other blow jobs.

They both knew the next step would be anal sex, and after experimenting with fingering each other during their oral sessions, it seemed that Patrick was the most receptive to the sensations this gave. He promised this would happen on his sixteenth birthday, a milestone he felt he should respect, and they both agreed this was sensible.

It was Patrick who suggested they break this promise a little early, as his parents were going away for a wedding two weeks before his birthday, giving them the perfect opportunity to make love in private and in comfort.

Craig was so turned on in anticipation that he had fallen at the last hurdle and had sex in the gym changing room just a day before their planned mutual deflowering. He was so mad with himself, but in equal measure, Craig was angry with Patrick's parents for making their son so scared to be himself.

This loathing led Craig to concoct his next plan of engineering the return of Patrick's parents so they would catch them in bed together. Convinced this was the best thing to do for all involved, Craig hadn't anticipated that they would be discovered mid-coitus or the ferocity of Nigel's reaction.

This, in turn, led Craig to take further action two weeks later when Nigel and Kate came to try and take his lover away and brainwash him with conversion therapy.

Nigel would be killed, and as Craig had done such an excellent job with his conditioning, Patrick would assume responsibility. It was cruel, but Craig knew it was for the best. Now all he needed to focus on was making sure Patrick held his nerve in the face of his mother's unbelievable accusations.

# CHAPTER 19

April 2019

So much had changed for Patrick and Craig in the nine years following Nigel's assumed suicide.

The initial aftermath had been horrendous. Patrick had never moved back home with his mother following the death of his father. Even if he had wanted to, it would not have been possible. Kate was never released from psychiatric care following the incident. She had suffered a complete breakdown, and Patrick could not even visit without sending her into a psychotic frenzy.

Kate had maintained her accusation that Patrick had killed her husband, and the police had rightly followed up on this line of enquiry. Patrick was called in for informal questioning, and Lisa was allowed to accompany him as his responsible adult.

The interview just turned out to be a formality of taking a statement from Patrick on the events of the day. The police already had several witness statements that placed Patrick on the ground with his mother when his father jumped. Clearly, he could not have pushed his father from the roof, and the sad reality was that his mother was suffering a mental breakdown in which she had directly linked Patrick's homosexuality as the cause of suicide.

When the police officer made this blunt suggestion, Patrick immediately burst into tears. Lisa scolded the officer's tactless observation and insisted that the interview was over and that they would be leaving.

Lisa had been fantastic, stepping up and taking Patrick in permanently in the absence of any extended family. Craig had also been of great comfort to Patrick, and they had even been allowed to start sharing a room, often accompanied by Barnaby, Patrick's dog, whom Lisa had also taken into her home.

Barely a week after Nigel's funeral, Barnaby had been the cause of another, smaller heartbreak when he had been run over while they were out walking. Barnaby usually walked so well off his lead, and Patrick had only looked away for a second at something Craig had pointed out in the distance.

Tyres screeched, and there was an awful thud, and when the boys looked to the source, Barnaby was lying in the road, seemingly intact but struggling to take his final breaths. Patrick held Barnaby as he passed, and Craig held Patrick as he sobbed.

The boys lived with Lisa for over three years before Craig had to support Patrick through yet another traumatic event. Geoff passed away.

Much to Craig's dismay, Geoff had also stepped up and offered great support and guidance to Patrick when it had become clear his mother would be unable to be released from psychiatric care.

Knowing how important he was in Patrick's life, Lisa had even begun to ask Geoff around to the house on occasion, and Patrick would spend time alone with him working on a trick, or sometimes Geoff just joined them for a meal.

Craig despised this intrusion into his life, but Patrick was broken and had thrown himself into his magic as a coping mechanism. In addition, Patrick refused to discuss any more attempts to practice his powers, enraged that Craig could even suggest it after what had happened. Craig apologised for his insensitivity but made sure Patrick was aware his ear was bleeding once his shouting had stopped.

Weeks rolled into months, the months into a year, then two, then three. Slowly, Patrick began to heal, in so much as you ever can, and their relationship remained strong. Craig had even grown to like Geoff a little more, although their relationship was still fractious on occasion.

Patrick had started to work in the magic shop on weekends, and when he had finished college, he would work there full-time, performing his magic at events in the evenings. Geoff had started to back away from the home visits, realising they were spending too much time together and recommending Patrick focus his spare time on Craig.

Never one to miss an opportunity, Craig embraced the change and recommended they book their first holiday together, a little trip to Barcelona for a long weekend. He told Patrick he had saved a little money from his warehouse job so that it could be his treat, a belated eighteenth birthday present.

Patrick was dumbfounded when they arrived in Spain and were chauffeur driven in a limousine to the W Hotel Barcelona, where they were shown to the suite they would be staying in for the next three nights.

'Jesus!' Patrick had exclaimed as he stood on their sea view balcony. 'How much did you frigging save?'

'Never you mind,' Craig said as he wrapped his arms around Patrick's waist from behind. 'There is nothing I wouldn't do for you, baby,' and he meant it, including using his mind force to steal almost ten thousand pounds from a G4 security box.

Craig had been thinking about using his powers to steal for years but had never found the courage. The one attempt with a chocolate bar as a boy had filled him with paranoia that he would be found out. It seemed this was much less of a concern now. After all, he'd gotten away with murder.

One afternoon he had been sitting in the car park after grabbing a few groceries on the way home from work and noticed a G4 security guard collecting a cashbox from the supermarket. In seconds he had imagined the contents of the lockbox into the boot of his car, and when he arrived home, he had to grab a holdall from the house into which he would stuff what turned out to be almost ten thousand pounds in used notes.

The holiday was amazing. Three days of sun, sea, sex, and sangria, not all in equal measure. When they did venture out of the bedroom, Patrick had insisted they pay a visit to *El Rei de la Màgia*, reputedly Europe's oldest magic shop. He wanted to buy Geoff a gift to thank him for all he had done for him over the years.

It was during the weekend after their return from Spain that Craig was tempted into another twisted development. His mind had a knack for concocting the most devious schemes, masking themselves as necessities to provide a better future for Patrick. This was all for Patrick.

Patrick wanted to give Geoff the gift he had bought in Barcelona, so they travelled together on Saturday morning to the shop. Geoff had practically broken into tears just on seeing the branded bag Patrick had brought for him, let alone the joy he felt when he reached inside and pulled out a beautifully boxed magic trick. A souvenir replica of one of the original tricks the founder, Joaquín Partagás, had learned when he had travelled to South America prior to first opening *El Rei de la Màgia*.

While they gushed over the trick, unboxing it and unfolding the instructions to the English print, Craig excused himself to the bathroom in the back office. He peed and washed his hands and then headed back through the office towards the shop floor again, but for some reason, he paused to take in some papers he had noticed sitting on Geoff's desk.

The paperwork was a signed copy of Geoff's will, presumably with the original document sealed in the stamped envelope addressed to his solicitor that sat alongside it on the desk.

A quick skim-read revealed everything had been left to Patrick. This included Geoff's house, the shop, and all remaining funds and possessions. Craig's mind was racing. *How long after someone changed their will would it not seem suspicious should they drop dead?*

Craig decided six months seemed reasonable, although that would coincide almost exactly with Patrick's nineteenth birthday. So instead, he settled on eight months, feeling that was a big enough gap from the anniversary of Nigel's death for Patrick to cope with.

Geoff had been found unresponsive on the floor of his magic shop by the shopping centre security guard early on a Thursday morning. He was rushed to the hospital but pronounced dead on arrival. A week later, the cause of death was confirmed as a massive brain haemorrhage.

Manifesting a fatal blockage in blood flow to Geoff's brain had been easy, even from the comfort of his warm bed, with Patrick snuggling against him. So that was two murders now, three if you included Barnaby. Craig just couldn't help mind-shoving that little bastard dog in front of a car after coming home from college and discovering he had taken a shit on his duvet.

Although devastated by the loss, Patrick had taken Geoff's death remarkably well. Perhaps as Geoff was older, with failing health, or maybe he was already numbed by the previous losses in his life.

The funeral was a small and sombre affair. Geoff had no family, and there was only a small gathering of close friends and a representative from *The Magic Circle*. Craig stood by Patrick's side as he thanked each guest for attending as they left, and he placed a comforting arm around his shoulders when Patrick was moved to further tears when the man from *The Magic Circle* handed him a letter and explained Geoff's last act before passing had been to arrange Patrick's membership of *The Magic Circle*.

Within a week, Patrick would be dumbfounded once more when he was invited to the reading of Geoff's will. Everything he owned was left to Patrick. This included a generous sum of money, a small two-bedroom house, and the magic business. Craig was delighted the will he had seen was still in place but managed to suppress the urge to leap up from his chair and punch the air.

Patrick was overwhelmed by the loss of his friend and the unexpected benevolence of his bequeathment. He wasn't sure how he would cope, but Craig supported him and took the lead with the business affairs. He guided Patrick through everything, and within a month, they had moved into their new home.

The move could not have come too soon. Living with Lisa for so long was straining their relationship. Craig couldn't bear another embarrassing conversation with his mother in which she asked them to make less noise at night in the bedroom, and there was something else. Lisa would sometimes look at Craig in an odd way, a stare that said *I know what you are*, but she couldn't have known.

They also decided to continue trading Geoff's magic shop, so Craig happily resigned from his warehouse position and started working in the store. Patrick would focus on his performances, and Craig would take over responsibility for his bookings. By all accounts, he became Patrick's manager.

From the tragedy of Geoff's passing, a whole new life had opened up for them, and they had gone from strength to strength. Craig seemed to have an excellent head for business, and their finances were improving all of the time.

The occasional loss of a G4 security box didn't seem to be making the news, probably as they were preoccupied with their many other failings hitting the headlines during that period. And Craig had new ways of bolstering funds. For more significant sums, he had been known to dip into a cashpoint machine or two. For smaller sums, it was easy to empty the wallets of a few drunk guys at the end of a night out. They would almost certainly believe they had overspent when they woke with a hangover the following day.

One of Craig's favourites, though, was to take from

the bad guys. It helped with his conscience, what little there was left of it. Drug dealers were prime pickings.

Craig had to venture a little further for this, but once a target was identified, it was like taking candy from a baby. In fact, quite often, he took the candy too. Craig was partial to the occasional line of cocaine or an MDNA bomb, and surprisingly it was Patrick who had first encouraged him to try it when they were watching Tulisa at the 2015 Brighton Pride festival.

Drug dealers were good for all kinds of things: money, drugs, and even guns, as it turned out, but Craig wouldn't need a gun for a few years yet.

Over the coming years, they would be able to afford new cars and lovely holidays, and they would sell Geoff's old house and purchase a large, detached property back in Witford Common.

They had pondered the move back to Witford, unsure it was wise given the memories, but it was by far the nicest of the local towns, and their decision worked out just fine. They were welcomed back into the community with open arms, and aside from the strange feeling Craig experienced when walking past the church, all was well. More than well, in fact, as on the eighth anniversary of their first meeting at school, a date they celebrated every year, Craig had proposed.

Life was almost perfect. They were wealthy, they were sickeningly in love and daily in lust, and they had the most beautiful of weddings in the spring of 2017. They had managed to move on from the traumas of their early relationship without the need for therapy.

Life was almost perfect, but not quite.

From the day Craig had half-cheated on Patrick with the lad in the gym changing rooms when they were both teenagers, he had continued to have additional sexual needs. He couldn't have explained it if he had tried. His love life with Patrick was amazing, but he would still pop a boner at the sight of a cute lad, and once it was up, it was only coming down one way.

Where Craig had his extramarital sexual cravings, which he happily allowed any number of strangers to satisfy, Patrick also had a constant niggle, an itch he needed to scratch. He was confident a psychologist could map the cause back to his disastrous school days and lack of acceptance from his parents, but the result was that he needed to perform. And not to a conference room full of employees at some corporate dinner. He wanted to perform for a real audience. He craved fame.

*Future Stars* was the biggest talent show on television for variety acts, and Patrick had been desperate to audition. He had considered it the previous year, but Craig had managed to dissuade him, unsure they needed to put themselves into the limelight and uncertain how Patrick might take any setbacks.

However, Craig used this as an opportunity to accelerate the exploration of Patrick's powers. They had returned to it a few times over the years, Craig keen to maintain the façade he had created, but Patrick was understandably nervous to try too much.

Patrick was remarkably receptive when Craig suggested they try and work something subtle into one of Patrick's already impressive magic routines, something that would leave the audience amazed.

They both set to work enhancing an already impressive coin routine, and the wheels were set in motion for Patrick to apply for next year's *Future Stars* auditions. Craig accepted that Patrick needed to perform and needed to be seen, and Craig also realised there was an opportunity here. They were comfortable, but let's face it, those holidays to Mykonos weren't getting any cheaper.

\* \* \*

The day Patrick had been longing for had finally arrived. He stood nervously in the wings of the theatre, going over his routine in his head, determined to make it as good as he possibly could. Patrick was totally unaware that Craig had just unloaded in Kevin, the stagehand, and equally unaware it was Craig who would be in control of the magic too.

Craig had been shown to a seat just behind where the judging panel would be sitting, amongst the other performer's relatives, but other than a cursory nod as he shuffled along the row, he made no attempt to engage with any of them.

Not very social at the best of times, it was unlikely Craig would have gone out of his way to initiate a conversation with these strangers, but on this occasion, he wasn't being deliberately standoffish. His mind was elsewhere.

Stephen Lucas, the host of *Future Stars*, returned to the stage and introduced the three judges back to the auditorium to rapturous applause. The judges walked in turn to their seats on the raised platform in front of the stage, and the audience quietened. Someone shouted out a ten-second countdown to recording, with the 3… 2… 1… signalled with fingers rather than aloud, and then Stephen continued with what would be his link back from the adverts when this was later televised.

Craig leant forward with his elbows on his knees and his hands clasped in front of his mouth as he listened intently to the introductions. He could only imagine how Patrick must be feeling waiting in the wings, but when he finally heard the words '…*and without further ado, please welcome to the stage our next performer*', he was reassured to see Patrick stroll out smiling and stand on his mark, centre stage.

'Hello there, and what's your name?' the deep, well-spoken voice of Laurence Stokes, the head judge on the panel, asked.

There followed a sarcastic exchange between Laurence and Michelle Martinez before Kieron Doyle, the nicer of the three judges, calmed them and allowed Patrick to begin his act.

Patrick took a deep breath and retreated within himself, allowing Enigma, the confident showman, to surface. Enigma invited a reluctant Laurence to the stage to act as a witness, and so the performance began.

Craig watched intently as Patrick delivered a masterful display of genuine sleight of hand. The first iteration of his routine was a classic coin act, and he performed it flawlessly to ripples of applause in all the correct places.

'How was that?' Enigma asked Laurence when the trick was complete, and all four coins were now gathered in a single corner of the table. 'Did you see anything suspicious?'

'I mean, you're good, but we've kind of seen it all before,' Laurence shrugged his shoulders as he spoke as if to excuse his honesty. Craig smiled. Laurence couldn't have set up the next element of the act more perfectly, even if he had been asked to.

'Ouch!' Enigma feigned offence, and the audience sympathetically inhaled in unison. 'No, he's right. It's coin magic 101,' he admitted and then went on to demonstrate one of the ways magicians achieved the effect.

After demonstrating how he had performed the trick by revealing the magician's Servante hidden behind the table on his lap, and the small flaps of black cloth, which flipped back and forth to reveal additional coins beneath, Enigma discarded these gimmicks.

There were a few unimpressed groans from the crowd but further applause at his reveal.

'Nobody likes a cheat,' Enigma suggested. 'Let's try again but make it a bit harder.'

Enigma then removed the black cloth to reveal a

glass table below and again placed one coin towards each corner of the table, handing the three spare coins to Laurence for safekeeping.

'We love to keep stuff up our sleeves too,' Enigma confessed. 'So why don't we lose the sleeves?' With that, he stood up behind the table and unbuttoned and removed his shirt.

The audience hooted and wolf-whistled at the striptease, and whereas Patrick would have been embarrassed, Enigma soaked it in. He remained standing until the frenzy abated and then sat down to repeat his coin routine.

'Okay, you can see through the table, and there is nothing up my sleeves,' he reiterated before repeating the trick in its entirety, again with only the use of his sleight-of-hand skills. The result was the same but clearly, a different, more complex technique, rewarded with rapturous applause.

'Better,' Laurence admitted.

'Better?' Enigma questioned. 'You're a hard man to please,' he joked, and for the first time, he looked to the crowd and spotted Craig.

'Shall we take it one stage further?' Enigma addressed the crowd, but his eyes remained locked on Craig. *Were they really going to do this?*

Craig gave his nod of approval to continue. This was the moment of no return, where Patrick would move away from the traditional magic he had spent years perfecting and do something inexplicable. Something he didn't really even understand himself.

Of course, Craig understood only too well. As long as Patrick followed their endlessly practised routine, Craig would ensure the real magic happened in all the right places. Patrick needed this, and it was better for everyone if he believed it too. Craig didn't have the same craving for superstardom that Patrick did. He was happy to use his power vicariously, safe in anonymity, benefiting from any success, but protected by plausible deniability should anything go wrong.

'Take off your trousers,' a voice shouted from the crowd, and the place erupted with more wolf-whistling and laughter.

'Maybe if I get to the final,' Enigma teased. 'But for now, how about we do it one more time, with no hands?'

A hush fell across the crowd, and what happened next would change everything.

Enigma sat upright in his chair and invited Laurence to inspect the coins and the tabletop. He then asked him to place a coin towards each corner as previously. Laurence followed the instructions and confirmed he was happy everything was in order.

'Okay,' Enigma said, taking deep breaths for effect. 'This is going to blow your mind.'

Craig focused his full attention as Enigma placed his hand above the first coin, but this time it was higher in the air leaving the coin in full view of what must have been at least eight thousand prying eyes. Enigma counted down from three, and on zero, he snapped his fingers, and the coin instantly vanished and reappeared at the front of the table.

It was seamless. Craig couldn't have been happier with the timing, and the gasps from the audience confirmed that the desired impact had been achieved.

Enigma quickly repeated the finger snap for the other two coins, performing the same routine as previously, and Craig ensured the coins disappeared and reappeared in the correct places.

The crowd went berserk on completion of the trick, and Laurence was clearly heard to say, *'What the fuck?'* before rising from his chair and starting the standing ovation Patrick had been craving so badly.

Craig leapt from his seat and joined the ovation, surprised by his own excitement and almost forgetting to trigger the trickle of blood in Patrick's ear that continued to convince him he was the master of these powers.

For the next few minutes, the judges gave their stunned appraisals of Enigma's performance before unanimously voting him through to the next round. As Patrick left the stage, picking up his shirt on the way, Craig excused himself from his row in the auditorium and headed backstage.

As Craig arrived, Patrick was finishing a conversation with Kevin about some background filming they would like to carry out before the show aired in a couple of months.

'Oh, for sure, that would be great,' Patrick smiled and then turned to embrace Craig as he approached.

The thing neither of them realised was that they had

succeeded only in triggering a series of events that would ultimately lead to Patrick's death in just over three months' time.

## CHAPTER 20

July 2019

It had been twelve weeks since Craig's plan had been initiated for Patrick's first audition on *Future Stars,* and he had already been back with Craig to film his second performance, but today was the day the first episode was airing on television.

The excitement had been building for a few weeks now as a clip of Patrick and, more specifically, the audience reaction to his finale had been included in the teaser trailers being aired in anticipation of the start of the new series. Even Craig had warmed to the idea of late, and they had decided to host a small party for close friends on the evening of the showing.

The production company had insisted upon secrecy with regard to the result of Patrick's audition, but Craig was sure the guests could tell the outcome would be positive from the permanent grin on Patrick's face as they all air-kissed on arrival for the pre-show drinks and canapés.

Craig had changed his mind about the party, and as he was sweeping up the second broken champagne flute of the evening, along with a selection of canapé crumbs, he thought to himself he would rather have been anywhere else than here right now.

The evening seemed to drag on for an unbelievably torturous length of time, but eventually, Patrick's performance aired, and Craig felt some slight relief when he heard Laurence's *'What the fuck?'* moment, although his expletive had been removed for sensitive ears as they were still before the watershed.

They all watched the judges' comments and the confirmation that Enigma was voted through to the next round, and then Patrick muted the sound once more before circling the room, accepting further praise from his guests over yet more champagne.

Everyone was amazed by his performance, but Patrick refused to share the secrets of his trickery, even with his closest *Magic Circle* friends. Craig had been vehemently insistent on this, and he was sure Patrick would comply, but he was careful to chaperone him and ensure this was the case.

The guests drifted away over the next couple of hours until only Patrick, Craig, and Lisa remained. The shopping centre closed at 11:00 pm on a Saturday, and they were on the road a little after this. Lisa hadn't been drinking, as she had offered to drop the boys back at their house.

Lisa was offered a coffee before heading home but declined, choosing not to get out of the car. Instead, she would leave them to their celebrations. They waved her away from the kerbside before falling through their doorway, cracking open another bottle of champagne, which they would drink in bed, before falling asleep in each other arms following wild, adrenaline-fuelled sex.

What a night!

\* \* \*

The following morning Craig headed back into the shop to finish cleaning up from the previous night's party while Patrick stayed in bed before spending the morning pottering around the house. He intended to head over to the shop around lunchtime, but elsewhere, events were unfolding that would throw their Sunday into chaos.

Kevin Heath wouldn't usually have been in the office on a Sunday morning, but it was only two weeks until the live finals of *Future Stars*, and his stress levels were through the roof. Cutbacks within the production team had increased everyone's workload, and Laurence Stokes, executive producer and head judge, was almost impossible to please.

When the phone rang, and he took the call from Jennifer Lewis, an old friend and production team member on *The Sunday Review*, his heart sank. She hadn't called with good news.

'I think I'm about to ruin your week,' Jennifer apologised in advance. 'We are about to run an article on *Future Stars*, more specifically, the Enigma episode last night. You're not going to like it.'

'What do you mean? What's happened?' Kevin had no idea what the story may be.

'In a nutshell, the main claim is that the Enigma performance was faked in some way. Collusion, camera trickery, that kind of thing. I'm calling to ask for an official statement from you guys,' she sounded genuinely apologetic.

'That's ridiculous! I was there. I can assure you it was all genuine. It was fucking unreal, actually,' Kevin defended. He remembered the Enigma show well, as both Patrick and Craig had left an impression that day.

'Is that the official press statement?' Jennifer joked.

'How long do I have to get you something?'

'Going to air in about thirty minutes, I'm afraid.'

'Fuck! Laurence is going to shit a load. On top of me probably,' Kevin laughed but was not finding the thought of this funny in the least. 'You'll have to run with the standard nobody available to comment until I get back to you.'

'No problem. Sorry, Kev. I'm sure it will all blow over,' Jennifer tried to comfort him, but Kevin was gone before she had finished her sentence.

After an expletive-laden phone call to Laurence in which Kevin was given a list of instructions, including the setting up of a conference call after the interview had aired so they could dissect it and agree on a response, Kevin tried to call Patrick.

Patrick wasn't answering his phone, so Kevin left a voice message and then rang around the team to explain the situation.

From the corner of Kevin's eye, he noticed *The Sunday Review* was returning to air following a commercial break. It had been about thirty minutes since Jennifer had called, so he turned up the volume on the large wall-mounted television and grabbed a pen and paper, ready to make notes.

As the conversation between Kevin and Jennifer took place, Craig arrived at the magic shop and started cleaning up. He had already swept and mopped the floor when the Sunday helper arrived.

'Hi, Chloe,' Craig greeted. He checked his watch and noted they still had thirty minutes before the store would open at ten-thirty. 'Why don't you pop the kettle on for a cuppa? I'm going to flick the telly on and watch the headlines,' Craig suggested, moving over to the screen they had temporarily installed for Patrick's party night.

As the television came on, Craig's ears pricked up as he caught the tail end of an interview introduction from Ian Atkinson, co-host of *The Sunday Review*.

'… we have Matt Turner with us this morning to discuss some interesting concerns following the episode of *Future Stars,* which aired yesterday evening. Hi, Matt. So, what can you tell us?'

*Some concerns?* Craig turned up the volume and gave

his full attention to the remainder of the interview.

'Good morning. Well, what can I say?' Matt began. He joined them via live video link and sat immodestly in front of a bookcase displaying a selection of awards he had received for previous journalistic efforts. 'As you know, *Future Stars* has not been without its share of controversy over the years. However, in their bid to recover the ratings, it would appear they may have sunk to a new low.'

'How intriguing,' Anna Keegan intervened. 'We love a bit of scandal with our breakfast on a Sunday morning. Do go on.'

Matt continued, and for the next few minutes, he explained a series of concerns that he had been investigating following the release of the teaser trailers and an early press showing of the episode.

There were rumours of rifts amongst the judges, disappointment at the amount of padding between acts suggesting there was a lack of interest from the public in even auditioning, but the main focus was concern that the feature act, Patrick Morgan, aka Enigma, was a fraud. A construct of the production company to end the show with the wow factor.

'Oh, my days!' Anna exclaimed in her strong Scottish accent. 'Surely not?'

*What the fuck?* Craig was standing with his jaw open at this revelation when Chloe returned with two cups of tea. She could see something was wrong, but before she had a chance to ask, Craig pointed at the television, and they watched the remainder of the interview together as Craig fumbled for his phone and called Patrick's number.

'Well, maybe not complete fiction, but we can be certain that everything is not as presented in the show,' Matt backtracked slightly. 'We know from several members of the audience that Enigma was not the final act of the day as suggested, and I have been doing a little digging myself. It seems Patrick's childhood was not quite as troubled either, and there are counterclaims that he was, in fact, a bully himself rather than the victim.'

There was no answer from Patrick, and after repeatedly trying, he dropped a text message, *Pick up. Have you seen the news?*

'But Patrick's father did pass away when he was a teenager. I'm sure that was traumatic in itself,' Ian interjected.

'Yes, of course, I'm sure that was just awful,' Matt conceded before moving on to his next point. 'The biggest accusation, though, is that the show was somehow complicit in faking Enigma's act.'

'Faking how?' Ian continued his questioning, keen to hear some facts.

'Well, as you may have seen, the finale of the act was jaw-dropping. Coins were disappearing and reappearing before our very eyes. Very impressive and worthy of the standing ovation it received. However, we have reviewed this with a panel of independent magic experts, and they believe this trick must have been edited for television, as it is just not possible as presented,' Matt smiled as he delivered the revelation.

'Are we sure this isn't just sour grapes? We see plenty of unbelievable feats by magicians. That's the whole point,' Ian scoffed. 'Maybe your panel of experts just don't know how it was done?' he suggested.

'Watch it back yourself. You can click through it frame by frame, and the coins just vanish. It's camera trickery for sure.'

'You have no idea what you are fucking talking about!' Craig yelled at the television, causing Chloe to jump and spill a little of her tea.

'Interesting indeed,' Anna commented as she began to bring the interview to an end. 'Thanks for that, Matt. We have reached out to the *Future Stars* team, but as yet, they have declined to comment. I'm sure we haven't heard the end of it, though.'

'What was that all about?' Chloe asked as Craig turned off the television and frantically continued to try and get Patrick on the phone.

'Go home, Chloe. I need to go. We won't be opening today,' Craig instructed. 'Actually, can you lock up for me, please?' Craig asked, but he was out of the door and heading to the car park without waiting for her reply.

He continued to call and text Patrick from the car as he raced home but had received no response by the time he roared his *TVR* onto the drive, skidding to a halt on the gravel. He flung open the front door to find Patrick halfway down the stairs.

'I knew we shouldn't have gone on that fucking show!' Craig raged, but he could see from Patrick's expression that he was confused and scared.

'What's happened?' Patrick asked, tears beginning to well in his eyes, and Craig knew he would have to calm down. Patrick would need comfort and reassurance. Craig would need to keep a clear head to get them through this.

'Don't worry. It will be okay,' Craig said much more calmly as they met at the foot of the stairs, and Patrick fell into his arms in sobs of tears.

\* \* \*

While Craig and Kevin had been glued to the interview, both trying frantically to get hold of Patrick, Patrick had been blissfully unaware that things were unravelling. He had showered and then gone downstairs with the laundry, leaving his phone in the bedroom.

It was only when he had heard it ringing in the distance that he returned to the bedroom to pick it up, and realised there were seventeen missed calls, the most recent of which was from Craig, and a dozen text messages asking him in various ways if he had seen the news.

Patrick was about to call Craig back when he heard the roar of an engine and the scrunching of gravel as a car skidded to a halt on the drive. A quick glance from the window confirmed it was Craig's *TVR*, and Patrick was halfway down the stairs when the front door flew open.

Once Craig had explained what had happened and Patrick had finally stopped crying, they went through his phone messages from Kevin. Patrick had received a voicemail letting him know the production company had an internal meeting scheduled to discuss the breaking news. They would like to dial him into a conference call at around twelve-thirty.

They had both calmed down considerably since Craig had returned home, and he and Patrick had moved out to the summerhouse. Patrick had offered to make a pot of coffee, but they had both opted for a beer from the party fridge instead.

While they waited for the conference call to come through, they reviewed the content of the interview, which was already doing the rounds on social media, and Craig decided on their course of action.

The only accusation involving Patrick was that of collusion with the production team. This was wholly false, and they would defend this to the hilt. They would give up no secrets as to how the trick was performed, and if other "experts" couldn't fathom it out, it was a testament to Patrick's ability. What else could they suggest? It was really magic?

Everything else reported seemed to be a direct attack on the show itself, its popularity, and the dubious editing. Nothing that needed to worry them. Craig made sure Patrick was clear on their story, and then they both waited for the call to come in. The clock had just clicked past 12:35 pm when Patrick's mobile began to ring.

'Hello, Patrick speaking,' he answered on speakerphone.

'Hi, Patrick. I'm just going to patch you into the conference call now,' Kevin came back, followed by some clicks, a short silence, and then the echoey sounds of shuffling seats and whispered voices from a distant meeting room.

'Hi Pat, it's Laurence here,' his voice boomed out, seemingly unconcerned with the situation. 'Just wanted to reassure you we are handling the nonsense in the press. You've done nothing wrong,' he added.

'His name is Patrick,' Craig corrected. 'We know we've done nothing wrong. We want to know what you are going to do about the reputational damage you have caused,' he snapped back.

There followed a tetchy exchange in which Laurence asked them a few questions before explaining how they were going to manage the response.

'Okay, so we are going to pull together a press statement summing this all up. We will fire it over to you for a quick review and then get it issued later this afternoon in time for all the morning headlines. How does that sound?' Laurence asked.

'I'd rather be in the headlines for more positive reasons,' Patrick sighed his frustration.

'There's no such thing as bad publicity, my friend. You'll probably win the whole series. Speak later,' and with that, Laurence hung up the call.

Craig and Patrick kept each other's company for the

remainder of the day and chose to ignore the many calls and messages that came through. The press release was sent over to them prior to publication, and they acknowledged they were happy with its content.

The only thing preying on Craig's mind when he had reviewed it was that the second audition had already been pre-recorded, so they had no opportunity now to tone down the act and avoid any further suspicion.

Craig decided to put it to the back of his mind. The show was only a week away. They would know the impact soon enough. Patrick would only worry if he mentioned anything, so Craig kept his thoughts to himself.

It was a warm summer evening, and they spent it drinking and listening to music in the summerhouse. Craig popped back to the main building to answer the door to the takeaway delivery driver, and when he returned with the food, he had stripped down to his underwear.

'I thought we could eat pizza in our pants,' he smiled and winked at Patrick, and before Craig had taken another step, Patrick had removed his t-shirt and was unbuttoning his jeans.

*What a day!*

---PRESS RELEASE---

LSE PRODUCTIONS Ltd

In response to the article aired on *The Sunday Review* on Sunday, 21st July 2019, regarding allegations of impropriety on the television programme *Future Stars*, the management team of LSE Productions Ltd wishes to issue the following statement:

While we accept that the editing of the programme may have been misleading in so much as it implied the performance of Patrick Morgan, performing as Enigma, took place at the end of a day of auditions, we strongly deny all other aspects of the interview.

Patrick Morgan was the victim of bullying during the early years of his secondary education, and this was a very difficult time in his life, compounded by the premature death of his father when he was only sixteen years of age.

With regards to the allegation that Patrick's act was in some way manipulated, this is strenuously denied. Patrick has no connection with the programme or its production team, and his act was aired as performed. Patrick is a proud member of The Magic Circle and reserves his right to keep the technique of his performance private.

# CHAPTER 21

July 2019

It had been a strange week, not to mention a little stressful. Craig wasn't directly stressed by the situation per se. He was confident in their approach to the press intrusion and was happy to be back working in the store. The stress he was feeling emanated from Patrick.

Craig was much less sensitive to other people's opinions and had no concerns about facing any potential storm. Since his school days, Craig had been able to mind-bend people into avoiding him, and he still used the technique when required.

Just this morning, one of the local fishwives had popped into the shop, clearly trying to catch a snippet of gossip, as Craig had no recollection of her having an interest in magic or ever having visited before. As she stood with a puzzled expression, confused even as to why she had come into the store and tongue-tied when she tried to find any words, Craig just smiled politely as he fucked with her mind.

Patrick, on the other hand, was trying his best to avoid everybody. He had forced himself to go to work each day but had stayed in the back office and let Craig handle the shop floor. Patrick was a worrier, and Craig had to reassure him constantly that everything would be okay.

It had seemed an impossibly long six days, but eventually, they found themselves safely behind closed doors, snuggled on the sofa and about to watch the next episode of *Future Stars*.

The outcome of the show was already known to them. Patrick had made it to the live finals and would perform again on Tuesday, 6$^{th}$ August, before hopefully making it to the Grand Final on Saturday, 10$^{th}$ August. All the same, he was nervous.

Annoyed by his fidgeting, Craig removed himself from Patrick's embrace on the sofa and grabbed a bottle of wine from the kitchen. Patrick shouted after him to also bring Pringles, and when Craig returned, he placed the glass of wine and tube of crisps on a small wooden table to Patrick's left.

'You went for red,' Patrick commented.

'Yeah, so don't spill it!' Craig said, as if spilling white wine would have been acceptable.

One more trip to the kitchen and Craig returned with another glass of wine and the remainder of the bottle, which he habitually placed beside the fireplace, even though it was unlit, before settling on the adjacent cuddle chair.

'Oh shit! Here we go,' Patrick exhaled as he turned up the volume, and the title music for *Future Stars* filled the room.

The show began, and Stephen Lucas introduced the judges back to the stage before reminding the audience of where they were in the process of finding this year's *Future Star*.

Off camera, Stephen explained that the first-round auditions had been completed the previous Saturday with a headline-making show. The camera cut to a full-face shot of Laurence laughing and rolling his eyes, which Patrick mimicked.

'They are playing silly buggers with the truth again,' Craig commented when the video montage ended, and the show cut to its first commercial break.

'What do you mean?' Patrick asked, genuinely confused at the observation.

'This show was pre-recorded ages ago. They have edited in the comment about last week's show and used an old reaction from Laurence. That's why it was a closeup of his face. You can't see what he is wearing.'

Craig topped up his glass and poured the remainder of the bottle into Patrick's glass before retrieving a second from the kitchen wine rack. They both grabbed a toilet break and settled down for the rest of the show.

Stephen popped back up on the screen, grinning incessantly, with blindingly white teeth and bottle bronze skin, to welcome back the viewers and introduced another pre-record of the judges whittling down the successful auditionees to a smaller group who were now to feature on this show. Craig hoped that the magic of television editing would shift the focus from Patrick's performance.

For the next ten minutes of the show, the judges debated and argued for the cameras as they slid photographs of the auditionees around on a large tabletop.

After tears, tantrums, and celebrations, they had finally settled on fifty-one. It should have been fifty, but of course, there had been the usual dramatic ending where the judges decided they had made a mistake, so they recalled an auditionee who had been rejected and told them they would now take the fifty-first place.

Patrick was in one of the successful groups, but thankfully very little attention was given to him at this stage. Just a brief glimpse of him in a line-up of four people as they were told they had made it through. *Hopefully, no one watching would remember Patrick's godawful shirt that day*, was Craig's only thought.

Another commercial break over, and they were into ninety minutes of second auditions in front of a theatre audience and the judging panel. Again, the fifty-one contestants would be thinned down to thirty-two, eight for each of the four live semi-finals.

Unsure where his audition had been placed in the running order, Patrick was glued to the television, nervously waiting his turn, which came about halfway through the show. When his name was finally announced, he leapt up from the sofa and covered his eyes.

'I don't think I can watch,' he squealed.

'Don't be a fool. You were there. You know what happened,' Craig bluntly pointed out, and Patrick sat back down and watched as his performance played out.

Some contestants had been skimmed through, others featured for a little longer before discovering their fate, and a handful had their full audition televised. It seemed Patrick was to be one of the latter.

Craig remembered the day of the recording well. It had taken place about six weeks after the first audition when he and Patrick were still blissfully unaware of the furore that would ensue.

They had created a series of card tricks, two for each judge, which started conventionally with a sleight of hand force of the Six of Clubs onto Laurence when he believed he was making a free choice from a shuffled deck.

It was a simple enough trick, well within Patrick's capabilities. Laurence smiled, the audience applauded, and Enigma moved down the line to Michelle.

From this point on, the tricks would use Enigma's mind powers, or more accurately, Craig's powers timed perfectly with Patrick's actions to convince him he was doing it himself.

Michelle had chosen the Nine of Diamonds, and the trick was to change it back to the Six of Clubs used in the previous trick. This also looked to be just a simple sleight of hand deception. However, the more observant would have noticed that after Michelle had selected the Nine of Diamonds and placed it face down on the palm of her hand in full view of cameras and audience alike, it was never touched again by Enigma.

Watching this back now, Craig wondered if Matt Turner and his 'panel of independent magic experts' would be watching the whole show back on freeze-frame looking for precisely this kind of detail. Luckily, with the way the show had been edited with camera shots cutting away, it was hard to know the card had not been touched unless you had been in the audience that day.

The third trick with Kieron, although very similar in appearance to the last, had taken some planning on Craig's part. In this version, Kieron had a free choice from a face-up deck and selected the Three of Hearts. This time instead of changing the Three of Hearts back to the Six of Clubs, Enigma would reveal that the whole deck was now the Three of Hearts.

Easy enough for Enigma, all he had to do was imagine the deck to all be the Three of Hearts, and when he turned it over, it would be, somehow. But, in reality, Craig could only swap objects from one place to another. So, in preparation for this trick, he secretly purchased fifty-two decks of cards and sorted them into fifty-two piles of each card number.

When Kieron made his genuinely free choice, Craig swapped the deck in Patrick's hand with the deck of

Three of Hearts he had pre-sorted and hidden in a box in the boot of his car.

Next, Enigma worked his way back along the line performing tricks that required using the judge's phones, all of which they declared had not been out of their possession at any point.

Kieron received a text containing the name of his freely chosen card before he had even selected it. Likewise, Michelle chose a card randomly from a face-up deck only to discover a picture of it already stored in her phone's photo library.

Many modern magicians would use smartphones in their routines these days. There were varying methods to deceive your onlookers, many using links to data or pictures that can be changed in real-time, giving the appearance that the image has been there all along.

Not on this occasion. Kieron genuinely received the text, and the photo was physically on Michelle's phone. Craig had just done a little mind switcheroo with the words he quickly typed following Kieron's selection and replaced whatever the last picture had been on Michelle's phone with one of the fifty-two pictures Craig had previously taken with his own phone camera in preparation.

The same fifty-two photos were also used to change the wallpaper on Laurence's phone the instant the words 'Jack of Hearts' had left his mouth.

There was a momentary silence, the clock display on Laurence's phone clicked over to the next minute, and then the audience erupted into another standing ovation.

Craig had wondered on the day if these tricks were too subtle. The speed and simplicity of each trick belied just how impossible they really were, but the audience's reaction was positive, so maybe they had pitched it right. Impressive enough to make the live finals but not too crazy to attract any more scathing accusations.

'It was great,' Craig assured Patrick after he had lowered the volume and turned to him for reassurance. 'Everyone loves you.'

'The last bit with the picture change, though. Was that too much?' Patrick was genuinely concerned.

'It's impressive, but that's the point. Nobody needs to know how you really did it. They can speculate all they like. We just keep quiet, okay?' Craig emphasised the last instruction, and Patrick nodded in compliance.

In reality, Craig was concerned, but sharing his concerns with Patrick would not help at all.

'Shall we have another bottle and listen to some music in the garden room?' Craig suggested, deciding it was best to try and take Patrick's mind off the whole thing.

It was a lovely warm July evening, so they kept the music down low and had the French doors wide open to enjoy the fresh air, although it was currently a little less fresh as Patrick stood on the patio puffing away on a cigarette. He had given up for almost two years but had succumbed in the last week following the stress of the press revelations, and things weren't about to get any easier.

They had been in the garden for just over half an hour when the music cut out, and Patrick's phone began to ring over the Bluetooth speakers. He stubbed out his cigarette and stepped back inside to grab his phone from the tabletop. The caller ID showed Kevin from *Future Stars*.

Patrick answered with a tentative hello, and Kevin, seemingly in good spirits, dropped the news that *The Sunday Review* would be running another story on him in the morning, and they would like him to join Laurence on the interview.

Panicked, Patrick put the phone on loudspeaker so Craig could hear the remainder of the conversation.

'They are convinced there is some collusion going on still because your trick was so good. Laurence is going on to make a point-blank denial, and it would be great to hear the same from you. Clearly, we aren't colluding,' Kevin finished.

'Sure, he'll come on the show,' Craig intervened. 'But this is just to talk about the trick, right? And he won't be telling anyone how it's done. That's our intellectual property,' Craig clarified.

'Of course, that's fine. I assume you have a laptop for the call?' Kevin asked. 'I'll send the details to your email address, and someone from the show will set you up in the morning, sometime between ten-thirty and eleven,' he added before saying a cheery goodbye.

'Why did you agree to that?' Patrick asked Craig, his voice still clearly stressed.

'It will be fine. I've been thinking about it, and we

can use this to our advantage,' Craig calmly explained. 'We aren't in cahoots with the show, so you can deny that with a clear conscience, and the publicity is going to be great for your chances in the final.'

'I don't know, Craig. This isn't going the way I was expecting at all. I'm really worried,' Patrick was almost tearful as he spoke.

'When have I ever let you down, baby?' Craig moved in to give Patrick a hug. 'It's all going to be fine. Let's finish this drink and go up for an early night,' Craig squeezed Patrick's buttocks as he spoke, and Patrick's smile was back.

*＊＊*

Patrick had not slept well and had been downstairs drinking coffee since just after 8:00 am. Craig joined him just over an hour later and insisted they have breakfast, despite Patrick's protest that he did not have an appetite this morning.

Craig baked some croissants straight from the freezer and halved a grapefruit for them to share. They chatted while Craig was preparing everything but noticeably avoided the elephant in the room, Patrick's pending interview on *The Sunday Review*.

Eventually, Patrick blinked first and once more voiced his nervousness, but Craig cut him short with a scolding reminder to stick to their story. They were not colluding with the show in any way, and they would not be sharing their magic secrets with anyone.

They finished breakfast, and Craig cleared away the dishes while Patrick set up his laptop on the table in the conservatory in preparation for the call from Jennifer, which came in at around 10:45 am.

Jennifer was reassuringly calming as they exchanged pleasantries, and she talked him through the Skype setup from the link he had been emailed. Patrick had been sitting with his back to the garden, but the light behind was throwing him into darkness, so Jennifer asked if he could move seats.

Craig moved to the seat where Patrick had been, he would be observing proceedings from off-screen, and Patrick now sat with his back to the kitchen. He had been asked to remain there as they may be cutting to him at any time over the next ten minutes or so.

In the studio, Laurence was relieved to finally be taken through to the set after spending an awkward half-hour in a silent green room with Matt Turner.

They stood off-camera until the programme paused for a commercial break. A frantic period of activity followed on the studio floor, during which they were ushered to their seats on the sofa opposite their interviewers.

Someone from behind the cameras shouted ninety seconds until back on the air, and Laurence observed as Anna received a final dab of powder to her forehead from a make-up girl. He also noticed a monitor on the floor before them with the face and shoulders of a rather nervous-looking Patrick.

A further twenty seconds call was made by the floor

manager, who had now stepped forwards to deliver the countdown, and Anna shuffled in her seat in preparation for her introduction.

'Welcome back, I'm Anna Keegan, and it is Sunday, 28th July. With me on the sofa now, we have Laurence Stokes and Matt Turner, and we are also joined remotely by Patrick Morgan, better known as magician Enigma,' Anna introduced. 'We are following up on last week's controversy around Enigma's performance on *Future Stars* and some subsequent concerns following last night's show too. Matt, if I can turn to you first, what were the issues if you could remind us.'

Matt Turner proceeded to recount his allegations from his previous interview – that he believed Enigma's performance must have been in some way edited to achieve the effect televised. He added that the second performance almost certainly confirmed this suspicion, as it was impossible to update the images of playing cards on the judge's phones without some inside collaboration.

'And obviously, you have already admitted that the editorial sequencing and sob stories in the show are faked for dramatic effect,' Matt added.

'Okay, let me just deal with these in turn,' Laurence jumped in without an invitation from Anna. 'This is not even a story. I am categorically telling you now that there is zero collaboration with Patrick, and his tricks were performed in front of the theatre audience as televised. Patrick is here and can also confirm this,' Laurence paused briefly, and Patrick nodded his agreement on screen.

'With regard to the fakery, as you put it, we did imply that Patrick auditioned at the end of the day, and that was indeed for dramatic effect. This is not uncommon on reality shows, but we will review this practice. However, I would like to add that Patrick was not aware this had been done, and the backstory was certainly not faked. I am sure Patrick can update you on that,' Laurence finished.

Anna invited Patrick to contribute at this point, and off-screen, Craig nodded and put his thumb up in encouragement for Patrick to say his piece. Patrick nervously shuffled in his chair before speaking.

'I don't really understand what is going on, to be honest,' Patrick started. 'I just performed my magic. I am not working with anyone on the show to fake anything, and I did have a troubled childhood. I was bullied, and when I was a little older, I stood up for myself. I don't know what else to say.'

'I have a few more questions,' Matt said as he sat forward on the sofa for a better view of Patrick on the monitor. 'The press received an early release of last night's show which differed a little from the one televised. Another background film was dropped that featured yourself and your husband at home,' he continued. 'In your 1.6-million-pound home, I should add, with a rather nice *TVR* parked on the drive. I'm a little confused as to your acquired wealth. I believe you do some corporate events, and your council-estate husband works in your magic shop?' Matt was smug with his delivery.

Craig stood up at the table on hearing Matt's questions, and his rage nearly carried him to the screen to intervene on Patrick's behalf, but Patrick had already begun to respond.

'I... I... was gifted the shop when a very good friend and mentor died. I also inherited a small house at that time. I don't really see what any of this has to do with anything?'

'I have done my research here, and the numbers just don't stack up, Patrick,' Matt continued to push. 'And Geoff wasn't the first important man to die in your life, was he?' Matt was clearly referring to Patrick's father.

'Hang on, please,' Anna interjected. 'This really does feel a little inappropriate, Matt,' but Patrick was not going to let this go unchallenged.

'You mean my father, I assume?' Patrick was clearly getting agitated. 'What has he got to do with anything?'

'I believe you were questioned by the police following his death, and your own mother claims you killed him?' Matt actually smiled after finishing his sentence.

Matt Turner hadn't hit his peak weight of twenty-two stone by putting in lots of legwork on his enquiries. However, he had ventured out to visit Patrick's mother in her secure home when he had uncovered there had been allegations made about Patrick's involvement at the time.

It was clear from the police reports that Patrick had been firmly on the ground when his father had fallen from the roof, and it was even more apparent when

Matt spoke to Kate that she was a complete fruitcake.

Kate was more than happy to talk about the incident even after all these years, desperate, in fact, eager that this new stranger might help her finally get justice for her husband's murder.

Luckily for Matt, it took very little investigative prowess to establish that Kate was insane. She babbled and contradicted herself, and even when Matt pointed out that she had said Patrick was with her on the ground when her husband fell, she couldn't see the contradiction of the statement that Patrick had pushed him off.

The truth, however, did not need to stand in the way of a good story. Patrick and Craig's finances were definitely suspect, and he would get to the bottom of that in time, but until then, he would cast his aspersions and see what stuck.

'My father committed suicide on my sixteenth birthday, and my mother, who has actually been in psychiatric care ever since, held me responsible because they were both religious nutters and had recently found out I was gay,' Patrick's voice faltered, and tears began to run down his cheeks. 'Why are you bringing this all up?'

Craig lunged forwards and slammed the laptop closed, and back in the studio, Laurence protested at the line of questioning and stood up, removing his microphone as he did so. Anna quickly announced another short break, and in moments they were off the air.

Matt also moved to stand, but Laurence pushed him

back into the sofa.

'What is wrong with you? You fucking nasty prick,' Laurence bellowed, and members of the floor crew ran over to keep the men apart.

'Get him out of the studio,' Anna pointed towards Matt. 'That was way out of order. You are done on this show,' she added before turning her attention to calming down Laurence.

Calm was restored quickly after Matt was removed from the studio, and Anna managed to convince Laurence to finish the interview in the moments she had left before going back on the air. She opened with an apology for Matt's line of questioning and reassured viewers that Patrick was being offered their full support. She added that anyone else impacted by the discussion could find help on their website before reintroducing Laurence.

'Apologies also to you, Laurence,' Anna offered. 'I know you have something you would like to say related to the original reason for the interview.'

'Thank you, Anna. I must say that was outrageous. That vermin cannot possibly be allowed to get away with his constant unfounded allegations, and we will be taking legal advice,' Laurence opened, referring to Matt but deliberately not using his name. 'I actually came in to address just one issue, the matter of the show's collusion with Enigma. This is also a complete lie, and to try and allay people's concerns, we have put something additional in place for the live semi-finals.'

'Yes, I understand you are bringing in a couple of

old adversaries,' Anna questioned, already briefed on this element of Laurence's response.

Laurence went on to explain that Enigma's semi-final performance would be observed live by the internationally respected magicians Cage & Clerk.

'As you know, Anna, we have not had the most amicable of relationships over the years, and I am sure there is nothing they would like more than to discredit me on live television,' Laurence finished.

'Well, the nation is certainly talking about it, so I am sure viewing figures will be up if nothing else,' Anna began to bring the interview to a close. 'And if I can just thank you for staying with us. We have had many text reactions to the show, and they are very much supportive of Patrick. I can only apologise again,' she finished, and after a short pause for breath, launched straight into the following link.

\* \* \*

Patrick had been blindsided by the change of questioning from Matt and was pleased when Craig cut the conference call. Jennifer had called back almost immediately to apologise and asked if he had wanted to stay on the interview with Laurence following the break, but Craig made it very clear to her that Patrick refused.

Kevin had also attempted to ring him on his mobile, but Patrick had ignored the call, still tearfully upset at the mention of his father's death. He watched Laurence's closing interview remarks with Craig comforting him instead.

Craig had been listening intently to the whole interview, and when the final section was complete, he sat in silence, rubbing his temples as he considered what had just unfolded. Patrick had seen this kind of reaction before and knew not to speak until Craig had gathered his thoughts.

'I think this is going to be okay,' he finally commented.

'Okay?' Patrick asked. 'He pretty much accused me of killing my own father, and I don't even know where he was going talking about our house and car.' Patrick was on the verge of tears once more.

'Hey,' Craig moved over to comfort Patrick. 'He just made himself look stupid. Nobody thinks you killed your father. The public is on your side. This is good. You might just win this whole show.'

'Win it? I don't think I can do the next show, Craig. I think it's best I just pull out.' Patrick suggested.

'You'll do no such thing,' Craig snapped as he removed his comforting arm from Patrick's shoulders.

'But I did kill my father, Craig. I used to get so angry with my powers. What if I can't keep it under control?' Patrick sobbed.

'You are doing the show, and we are going big with the performance. I've got a great idea. Trust me,' Craig finished, and Patrick knew the conversation was over, and Craig would have his way.

# CHAPTER 22

August 2019

Craig's day had not started well, as his mother had called, and they ended up having a blazing row.

Lisa had cut straight to the chase and asked what was going on with Patrick's performances, whether Craig was involved, and did it have anything to do with her brother all those years ago.

'What do you mean?' Craig asked, gobsmacked, and genuinely intrigued as to how his mother had managed to pull such an accurate theory together.

'Something isn't right, Craig, I just know it,' Lisa insisted. 'Your uncle wasn't right, and I have been worried about you ever since he did those things. Strange things have happened, Craig, and I am worried about you.'

'What strange things, mother? What are you talking about?' Craig was confused.

'You became so withdrawn after Uncle Paul took you, which was understandable, but it was more than that. There was your PE kit, and I would hear things in the night that didn't make sense. Noises in the toilet but nobody there. I thought I was going mad, but I am not sure now,' Lisa was rambling a little.

'My PE kit?' Craig asked. 'You are not making any sense, mum.'

'I was in your room one morning after you had gone to school, and your PE kit was still on the end of your bed. I tidied up a bit, and when I turned around, it was gone,' she explained.

Craig immediately remembered the time he had forgotten his PE kit and had vanished it from his room to have it reappear again in his locker at school. And the bathroom noises must have been when he sometimes used the trick of going to the toilet without getting out of bed. *How had he been so stupid?* Craig thought he had always been so careful with his abilities.

'Listen to yourself. You sound insane,' Craig said calmly, needing to take control of this situation. 'I was withdrawn because your brother tried to kill me. Are you trying to suggest it gave me magic powers?'

'I don't know, Craig, I am just upset. Why are they saying all these things about Patrick? And you have done very well for yourselves financially since Patrick's father and Geoff died. You didn't like either of them. I know you didn't,' she sounded accusatory again.

'Okay, Mother, you need to stop this and calm down. Are you accusing me of vanishing my PE kit or murdering people?' Craig raised his voice angrily as he spoke. 'I have got to go with Patrick today as it is his live semi-final performance tonight. I will come and see you tomorrow and talk about all this, but please don't speak to anybody. Patrick is upset enough already,' he added more calmly.

Lisa seemed at least temporarily appeased by Craig's offer to visit her the next day, and their telephone call ended just as Patrick came downstairs. Patrick enquired who had been on the phone out of habitual politeness, but before Craig had responded, he had moved back to audibly worrying about the day's events.

Craig had been attempting to reassure him all morning not to worry. The last thing he needed was Patrick's nerve crumbling and bringing everything they had achieved crashing down around them. With the added stress of his mother's call, Craig's patience had worn out.

'Just get in the fucking car!' he yelled, and Patrick complied.

The dynamic of their relationship had shifted in recent weeks, and Craig was now the dominant force where historically, he had always pandered to Patrick's needs. But, in reality, Craig had always been the manipulator. He just allowed Patrick to believe he was in control.

The car journey was mostly in silence, but by the

time they arrived at the studio, they were talking again. Craig made a faint apology, and Patrick was unable to stay mad. Craig seemed to have the knack of getting into his head, and he could never stay angry at that cute little smile he always pulled.

For the live shows, the production had been switched from the theatres of the auditions to a television studio so they could operate a multi-stage format. Some of the acts, Patrick's being one, required quite an extensive and precise stage setup, and it was not practical to change this in the time they had available between performances on a live broadcast.

At the previous week's planning session, it had been decided that Patrick would perform as the opening act as his stage setup was the most complex. It consisted of two large vanishing cabinets with doors back and front, each standing on its own Perspex platform roughly six feet above the stage.

The prop guys on the show had been exceptional when presented with the challenge of pulling together such an elaborate setup. Laurence had questioned why Patrick didn't already have some of this equipment if it was one of his show-stopper tricks, and Craig explained that their version required an overhaul, too tired and damaged for the glamour of such an illustrious show.

Laurence's ego readily accepted the logic. It made sense that a corporate circuit magician would struggle to compete with the might of his production. Patrick just glared at Craig, taken aback by the ease at which he had just lied. There was no tattered equipment. This was a brand-new trick straight from Craig's imagination.

Patrick was wholly uncomfortable about it, but Craig would not be reasoned with and was usually right in the end, so Patrick agreed to play along. He had even surrendered to Craig's choice of costume, a see-through black mesh muscle vest and skin-tight black jeans.

'I'm going to look like a stripper in this with all those dancing boys prancing around,' Patrick laughed.

'You'll look just great. The world isn't going to know what's hit it after tonight, Patrick. I think this is all going to work out just fine,' Craig said, with a confidence Patrick just didn't share. 'And go commando in those jeans,' he added before undoing the button on Patrick's trousers and slipping his hand inside. 'Sex sells, big boy!'

Patrick stripped naked and pulled the vest over his head. He stood in front of the mirror and noticed his top hat and bunny ears tattoo showed through the mesh, giving the appearance that it was imprinted on the shirt. With the tattoo and his well-defined torso, he had to concede he looked pretty hot, while lower down in the mirror's reflection, his penis began to enlarge in agreement.

Quickly grabbing for his jeans, Patrick pulled them over his feet and upwards, but Craig had already noticed his stirring. He turned Patrick towards him while the tight black jeans were still wedged halfway up his thighs and dropped to his knees.

Kevin had returned as promised when there were fifteen minutes left before Patrick's performance. Fortunately, he knocked and waited before entering the dressing room, giving Patrick enough time to tuck himself uncomfortably back into his jeans and for Craig to return to his feet.

'Exciting times!' Kevin declared as his eyes dropped from Patrick's face to the visible erection in his jeans and back again. 'Craig, you'll need to take your seat in the studio. I'll take you through, and then I'll come back for you, Patrick,' he added before turning and leading the way.

Craig's seat was with the other acts' friends and family members in a block near the centre of the studio, allowing them a good view of the various performing areas. The floor team were buzzing around, and the audience was informed that they would go live to air in less than five minutes.

A large woman Craig recognised as the mother of a rather obnoxious child comedian sat down beside him, and he politely nodded hello. Her son was very popular with the audience and, on another day, he may have been worried about the competition, but today wasn't going to be about her son or anyone else other than Patrick. Craig was going to make certain of that.

It was only moments now until showtime, and Craig could see Patrick waiting on stage to start his performance once the introductions were made. He was performing a final inspection of the equipment, and then

Craig noticed him taking a small foam earplug from his pocket and placing it into his left ear. Reassured that Patrick was still thinking clearly, he settled back in his chair to watch the show.

The audience was given a ten-second countdown, and then the fun began. The monitors around the studio displayed the show's title sequence coming to an end, and the applause signs were lit. The crowd went wild as the cameras cut to Stephen Lucas.

Stephen Lucas was the consummate master of ceremonies, and he seamlessly ran through his opening sequence, introducing each judge in turn to their own entrance music.

Once the judges were seated and the audience had calmed, Stephen continued his opening by addressing the controversy surrounding Enigma, who was to be the opening act of the evening. Stephen summarised the events to date with a blasting critique of *The Sunday Review* and a reiterated denial of any wrongdoing by the show's team.

He then explained that to try and silence the critics once and for all, the internationally renowned Cage & Clerk had been invited to the studio to act as independent adjudicators. The audience applauded once more, and the entrance doors behind Stephen opened, and the aforementioned Cage & Clerk walked out onto the stage.

There was a somewhat cringeworthy, not to mention obviously rehearsed, exchange between them aimed primarily at embarrassing Laurence and then

Cage & Clerk were asked to confirm they had not yet met Enigma and were entirely in the dark as to the performance that was about to take place.

Cage & Clerk then moved over to where Enigma was awaiting their arrival, and Stephen made one final introduction before music and an explosion of pyrotechnics began the performance.

Enigma stood centre stage in his figure-hugging black outfit with his arms raised while the audience wolf-whistled, and a male voice from the crowd called out, 'You're so hot!'

'Tonight, the closeup magic is gone,' he shouted above the audience's screams. 'Tonight, we are going big. Tonight, we are going to change the world of magic forever.'

Craig smiled to himself. Enigma was doing his thing, and he was right. Tonight, things were going to change forever.

The routine unfolded perfectly, just as they had rehearsed it all day. The dancing boys arrived, all wearing matching outfits of black high-laced boots, black PVC hotpants, and gold neoprene harnesses supporting a small pair of black feathered wings. The homoerotic dial on the performance was officially turned up to eleven.

Once the dancers had completed their routine of parading the various pieces of equipment around the stage and then arranging them in line for the trick that was about to be performed, Enigma theatrically walked up the first set of steps, through the vanishing cabinet and down the steps on the other side. He repeated with the second cabinet before returning to where Cage & Clerk stood watching.

'Are you impressed yet?' he asked of them.

'Well, I'm impressed with the dancers. I didn't know where to look,' Clerk replied. 'First,' he added to laughter from the audience.

'Okay then, I am only going to perform a single trick tonight, and I want to make sure it's impressive, so let's run a few scenarios by you and see if we can make it a good one,' Enigma explained.

'Sure, sounds good,' Cage answered.

Enigma then went on to run through the intention of the trick. One of the dancing boys would enter the first cabinet and be magically transported to the second cabinet on the other side of the stage. A discussion ensued about how impressive this would be, and Cage & Clerk were invited to comment.

Each time his adjudicators suggested a potential method for achieving this magical feat, Enigma removed the possibility. Covers were pulled away to reveal Perspex, the stage lighting was changed, and the dancing boys relocated their gyrating to behind the equipment. It was now clear to see that the entire configuration of props was transparent, except for the vanishing cabinets on top.

The final observation from Cage was that Enigma could be using a concealed doppelgänger to achieve the effect.

'You are absolutely right, of course,' Enigma conceded. 'How about we use you then? You're not a twin, are you?' he joked. 'In fact, let's use both of you and make this twice as crazy.'

This was it. It was time for Craig to focus.

Enigma signalled to someone off-stage that the main trick was about to commence, and music sounded once more. The dancers continued to gyrate in time, and Enigma first led Cage to the bottom of one staircase before leading Clerk to the one on the opposite side of the stage.

Enigma returned to the centre of the stage and faced the audience with his arms raised.

'Okay, guys, on my signal, I want you to walk slowly up the stairs and into your cabinet. Once the door has closed behind you, just step out from the other side,' Enigma instructed without looking back behind him.

Craig looked on intently from his seat in the crowd, somewhat surprised at how well Patrick was building up to this trick. He watched as Patrick lowered his arms and called 'go' as if starting a drag car race, and Cage & Clerk began their ascent of the stairs.

Aware the main event was imminent, Craig hazed Patrick's mind into a trance-like state, forced a trickle of blood from his ear, and then turned his attention to the vanishing cabinets just as the doors were closing behind Cage & Clerk.

Cage had entered the cabinet on the left of the stage, and Clerk had entered the cabinet on the right. There was a massive explosion of pyrotechnics into the air, and then the audience watched on as the two men exited the cabinets just a second later.

There were gasps of amazement, whoops and squeals of excitement, and a full standing ovation accompanied by thunderous applause by both audience and judges alike. Cage & Clerk had both inexplicably emerged from the opposite cabinet to the one they had entered.

*Fuck yes!* Self-praise may be no recommendation, but Craig knew what he had just accomplished was beyond good. He stood with the crowd, not to take any part in the ovation but merely to maintain his view of the stage. This wasn't quite over yet, he was sure.

Callum Cage stared directly across the stage at his partner Tristen Clerk. Taking a moment to get his bearings, he quickly realised their positions had been reversed. A look of confusion was evident on both of their faces, but Cage's expression was deeper, more pained.

Tristen Clerk looked on with concern as Cage clutched his chest before he stumbled and fell face forward down the stairs, coming to rest motionless at the bottom.

There were screams from the floor crew to cut the live transmission, and the audience fell silent as they watched the scramble to offer Cage medical assistance on stage.

Patrick had not even turned around. He didn't need to. Instead, he picked out Craig in the crowd and caught his gaze. As their eyes met, Patrick removed the bloodied earplug and threw it to the floor. Craig could tell from his expression that Patrick was unhappy with how this had played out, but Craig smiled back at him.

*'That couldn't have gone any better,'* he mouthed. He knew Patrick wouldn't understand, but he would understand soon enough.

\* \* \*

The drive home was even more unpleasant than the drive to the studio had been after their argument that morning. Patrick was beside himself with worry about what they had just done, and he would not be calmed by Craig. They picked up Chinese food on the way, but Patrick had no appetite. His head was banging, and he decided to go to bed.

Craig had offered to make Patrick a hot drink, and when he took it upstairs to him, he tried once more to settle his concerns.

'I will sort it out, Patrick. Give me your phone and get some rest. I will go downstairs and call Kevin. I'll get an update on everything. It will all be okay in the morning, you'll see,' he kissed Patrick on the forehead and took his phone off him before leaving the room.

Downstairs, Craig served himself a plate of their takeaway Chinese and grabbed a beer from the fridge. He hadn't lost his appetite and was starving after barely eating all day. He swallowed down a final sweet and sour chicken ball with the last of his beer and then set about putting the final pieces of his plan into action.

If Patrick had finished his cup of tea, he wouldn't be waking up for a while, but just to be sure, Craig headed out to the garden room to make his phone calls well out of earshot. He started with Kevin and had to call several times before he finally picked up.

'Hi, Patrick. Can I call you back later? Unfortunately, Callum passed away, so it's all gone a bit crazy here right now,' Kevin said when he eventually answered the call from Patrick's number.

'It's not Patrick. It's Craig,' he corrected. 'You're going to need to get Laurence on this call. You really need to hear what I've got to tell you. I'm your get-out-of-jail-free card.'

'I really don't think Laurence can talk right now,' Kevin insisted.

'Kevin, I don't think you understand. Patrick is dangerous. The accusations Matt Turner has been making are true,' Craig explained. 'I want out, and I am ready to talk about it. It will put Laurence and his stupid show in the clear. Callum's death wasn't an accident.'

'What? Oh, fuck! Okay, I'm finding him now. Stay on the line,' Kevin said, and Craig could hear footsteps as he ran off to find Laurence.

Although totally confused, Laurence couldn't have been more relieved when Craig had explained his offer to throw Patrick under the proverbial bus for everything that had taken place. He agreed to Craig's request to appear on television with him the following morning, without Patrick's knowledge, and when their call ended, Craig had no doubt Laurence would follow through on his promise to make the arrangements.

There was no going back now, but Craig knew he was doing the right thing, however painful it would be. The only thing that mattered was protecting himself from suspicion. He had known from age eight that he could never allow his powers to be discovered, whatever the cost.

The plan was elaborate but had a simple aim. First, implicate Patrick and then remove all witnesses to the contrary.

Craig would go on live television and act as the victim. The poor downtrodden boyfriend who had spent a lifetime in fear of his partner's truly supernatural abilities. Matt Turner's accusations were all true.

He would confess that Patrick had used his abilities to cheat at the tricks on the show. The coins, the cards, and the phone tricks were all done using his psychic powers. Craig would also tell them Patrick had stolen money this way, but even more worryingly, he suspected that Patrick's mother's accusations of murder might also be true.

They had been dismissed as unbelievable madness, but Craig was now convinced Patrick had something to do with it. And Geoff too. Craig would suggest it was far too convenient that Patrick's mentor had died only weeks after revealing the contents of his will to them both. And now there had been another death live on television after another impossible trick by Enigma.

If the interviewer probed too far into why Craig had not spoken up previously, he would hide behind the veil of fear. Patrick was too powerful. Craig had tried to stop him and even suggested they withdraw from the show, but Patrick's ego was out of control. He believed he could do anything.

Craig was all too aware this would be hard for anyone watching the show to believe, let alone the respected journalist conducting the interview, and that is where the second half of his plan came into play. Of course, he would need to get his timings right, but the vanishing of Patrick's adversaries and their reappearance for execution in the magic shop should prove convincing enough.

The list had already been decided in Craig's mind. Matt Turner, Kevin Heath, Anna Keegan, Neil Dixon, and his own mother, Lisa, seemed likely candidates for Patrick's wrath. Craig would also be vanished from live television along with Laurence to complete the list.

When this was all over, Patrick would have murdered five of them with a gun he must have acquired at some point, but fortunately, Craig would manage to overpower him and save himself and Laurence, who would be a convenient witness to his bravery. Obviously, Patrick was not going to be able to survive.

\* \* \*

To avoid any unnecessary suspicion, Craig joined Patrick in bed once his plan had been put in motion with Laurence.

Patrick had drained his tea before sleeping and had

not stirred all night. He was still fast asleep when Craig snuck from under the covers at 6:00 am to head over to join Laurence at the television studio for the live morning news interview they had arranged the previous evening.

He hoped he hadn't been too heavy-handed with the sedative. Patrick needed to wake before 8:00 am to keep plans on track. Craig decided to set the alarm on Patrick's phone and leave it on the bedside table, with a note to turn on the news. He would be very confused when he awoke, and Craig had a tinge of guilt as he headed out to the car, but there was no other way. This had to be stopped now.

Laurence had already arrived at the studio by the time Craig had been escorted to the set, and they had a short briefing with Ian Atkinson, who would be interviewing them just after the 8:00 am news headlines. During their conversation, he seemed a little sceptical, but he was familiar with the story from his work on *The Sunday Review* and was happy to proceed. In light of Callum's death, this was a major exclusive, regardless of how bizarrely it seemed to be playing out.

Just before going on air Craig received a call from Patrick, which he ignored, followed by a text asking where he was and what was going on. It was perfect timing, and from that moment, things unfolded exactly as Craig had envisaged, and in around twenty minutes, he would see his husband again for the last time.

When Craig materialised in the store, closely followed by Laurence. There was a brief moment of calm as the four men now present took in the surroundings.

Lisa, Neil, Kevin, and Anna were already dead or dying on the floor. Laurence gasped at the sight and clasped his hand to his mouth while Craig surveyed the results of his own creation. Although he had controlled Patrick's mind to action these executions, his power did not work in such a way that he had observed it himself, although he was aware of how it must have unfolded.

Anna and Neil were of no consequence. Neil had always been a bully, and Anna had taken her own delight in trying to expose a scoop which had ultimately destroyed them all. They were merely pawns in this game and supported the narrative Craig was trying to create.

Kevin was just in the wrong place at the wrong time. Craig was playing himself to be the feeble victim of this whole tale, and fucking Kevin in a backstage storeroom wasn't really in keeping with that image, so he, unfortunately, had to be removed as a witness.

And then there was his mother. Craig had to turn away as soon as he saw her body. *Why had he been so careless as to cause her suspicion?* Nevertheless, his powers had to be protected even over his own mother's life. Somehow, he had always known that.

'What have you done, Patrick?' he asked for Laurence's benefit as a witness, but before Patrick could even consider an answer, chaos reigned once more.

From the front of the store, there was an explosion and the sound of shattering glass. Craig turned his head just as three armed police officers charged into the store through the broken window in response to the recent sound of gunfire.

Craig immediately turned back towards Patrick and mind-forced his husband to pull the trigger of the pistol and send a bullet into the throat of Matt Turner and a second shot into Laurence's shoulder.

Matt dropped to the floor with a colossal thud, where he would soon bleed out, and Laurence was pushed backwards into a wall, where he remained in shock until an ambulance crew was eventually given access to the building.

In response to the renewed gunfire, the armed officers opened fire on Patrick, who was now in clear line of sight. In a move Laurence would later describe as *Matrix*-esque when he was doing the rounds on the chat show circuit, Patrick raised his hand and stopped the police bullets mid-air.

Patrick then clenched his fist, and the bullets dropped to the floor, and the guns were wrenched from the police officer's hands and crashed down amongst the bodies. A second later, the officers were vanished from the store and would shortly radio back into the command centre to let them know they had reappeared in the churchyard in Witford Common.

Patrick was in a state of complete confusion. He still had no idea that Craig was controlling him and had been for their whole life together. From Patrick's point of view, it was undeniably all his own doing, even if he couldn't understand it and felt like a helpless observer in his own body.

Amidst the commotion, Craig remained focused. He knew he would be walking away from this unharmed and untainted by the revelations of the morning, and by the time Patrick had begun to come down from his latest trance attack, Craig had picked up one of the police firearms and had it trained directly at him.

'What are you doing, Craig?' Patrick asked. 'What is happening? Why did you say all those things on the television this morning?' Patrick sounded terrified.

'It's over, Patrick,' Craig said quite calmly and with sadness in his voice.

'You just saw what I did?' Patrick reminded him, suddenly confident he could somehow control the situation. 'You can't shoot me. I have my powers,' he added, raising his hand to prepare to disarm his husband.

Craig took a step forward and turned slightly so his back was now towards Laurence, who still stood bleeding against the wall.

'You don't have any powers, Patrick,' Craig said softly enough so Laurence wouldn't hear him.

Patrick looked confused as he clenched his fist, and nothing happened. He looked to Craig for the answer just as Craig opened fire and shot four rounds from the semi-automatic weapon into Patrick's chest. Patrick was dead before his body came to rest, and he would never know the truth.

More armed officers who had observed the finale from the shopfront now entered the premises as Craig dropped his weapon and ran forwards. He dropped to his knees, pulled Patrick's lifeless body into his arms, and held him tightly as he began to wail in grief.

Craig's body was pierced with heart-breaking pain. The man he loved was gone. This wasn't how it was supposed to be. Patrick was everything he had ever wanted from the first moment he laid eyes on him in the school playground.

*What was this power he had been afflicted with? Why was it more important than everything else?*

## CHAPTER 23

July 2021

Craig placed a white rose upon the grave and then used a couple of the wet wipes he had brought in his pocket to clean the summer dust from Patrick's headstone. He didn't often visit Patrick's grave, even though he still lived in what had been their home. Two lockdowns had made it difficult, although Craig secretly found it a welcome excuse to avoid Witford churchyard.

It was typical that Patrick would be buried at the sight where all Craig's troubles had begun. He had considered changing the funeral arrangements, but Nigel had secured the family plot years before when he had been the church vicar, and Craig didn't have the energy at the time to set about undoing his long-laid plans.

In truth, Craig doubted Patrick's body was even in

the coffin.

The aftermath of the magic shop massacre had been intense and prolonged but bizarrely discreet. The expected press intrusion did not materialise. And as the investigation developed and Craig was routinely questioned at length, it became apparent he was not being spoken to by regular police investigators.

Nobody would explicitly confirm or deny anything, but it seemed clear to Craig that some form of gagging order had been invoked, and the investigation was now under the control of a government agency.

It was understandable. The implications of having people among us with inexplicable abilities were far-reaching, but Craig was surprised the tabloid press could be silenced so easily. Perhaps they had been placated with another story. He had heard that was how attention was sometimes diverted, and barely two weeks after Patrick's rampage, the headlines were filled with pictures of Prince Andrew enjoying some downtime at Jeffrey Epstein's mansion back in 2010.

A true conspiracy theorist might even have suggested that the outbreak of COVID-19 later that year had been engineered to give the world something more pressing to focus on rather than the fear of some superhuman race living amongst them, but Craig was far from this fanciful.

There had been a time delay on the transmission of the morning news that day, 7$^{th}$ August 2019, just time enough for unwanted swearwords to be bleeped the intention, but when Craig and Laurence had vanished from the couch, a quick thinker in the gallery had cut the shows feed. As a result, very few people were even aware it had happened. It was a result for the authorities and Craig, as it had turned out.

The reports that Matt Turner had vanished in front of his wife's eyes had already been aired when Lynn Mills had reported live from outside the magic store, but this would never be corroborated.

For the vast majority, this was a tragic mass shooting by a contestant who had been found to be cheating on a talent show. Even Craig's accusations during the interview would be brushed over, and the production crew would be spoken to. This story was over. Somebody somewhere was making sure of that.

For Craig, it went on a little longer. Presumably, the authorities were trying to establish if he had indeed been a victim of Patrick or if he was somehow complicit. This was easily addressed, Craig's powers were more than capable of diverting people's suspicions, but he hardly needed to as he had been meticulous in his planning. Even the note left at Patrick's bedside on the morning of the shooting was deemed evidence in support of his claim, and Craig was relieved when he was finally allowed to return home from the secure location they had detained him in.

Craig had been concerned he may never be allowed to leave, perhaps held prisoner indefinitely to avoid the risk of exposure, but a different approach was taken. Craig was bribed.

He had already confessed to benefiting from the

proceeds of Patrick's purported robberies, and early enquiries had supported the fact that their joint finances were dubious, to say the least. These proceeds from crime would ordinarily be seized, and Craig would be subject to prosecution, but all this would be waived for his silence.

Laurence must also have come to some arrangement as, despite appearing on every chat show or radio show that would have him, his retelling of events was conveniently cleansed. No supernatural connotations at all, just a purified account aimed at publicising himself and the next season of *Future Stars*, which had already been commissioned and would give the contestants whose live shows had been cancelled, the opportunity to recompete fairly.

Once released, Craig was minded to leave well enough alone, but he continued to pursue the investigating team until they finally agreed to release Patrick's body to him for burial. Craig was convinced they would have been experimenting on his corpse, attempting to find signs of divergence, and he couldn't bear the thought of Patrick being dissected in a lab somewhere.

But the release process raised even more suspicions in Craig's mind. On top of the extended timescale, the appointed undertaker – not appointed by Craig – had informed him that the casket would be sealed and there would be no opportunity for Craig to see his husband prior to this taking place.

Craig was unsure if it was because the body was not

in there or if they had disfigured Patrick so much during the post-mortem, but he was sure something was being hidden from him. He momentarily considered using his abilities to check the coffin's contents but decided he would rather not know. It would serve no real purpose, as Craig could not risk exposing himself by confronting anybody with his findings. Instead, he had vowed to take a period of abstention, and except for a bit of mind-fogging during his interviews, Craig would keep this promise to himself for almost two years.

After the funeral, and before the world went crazy with the impact of the pandemic, Craig had decided to sell the magic shop and take a bar job locally. Craig didn't need the money as his bank account was still very healthy with the ill-gotten gains he had been allowed to retain for his silence. And it would have been much easier to hide away from the world, but Craig was constantly strategising and felt that appearing in public, earning a wage, and outwardly trying to support himself after suffering such adversity would maintain the narrative, possibly even endear some sympathy.

Craig also reached out to Kate, who remained in psychiatric care, too far gone to be exonerated and rehabilitated, although the coverup of events never afforded her this opportunity. Neither was Craig motivated by Kate's well-being. It was just another selfish outward gesture, the sorrowful son-in-law attempting to build a bridge.

The announcement of a complete lockdown in March 2020 was a welcome reprieve from the façade of Craig's grieving widower life. He threw himself into gardening to pass the time and occasionally leave the house, as garden centre visits were still permitted under lockdown rules.

Craig also began to read, usually accompanied by a glass of wine or two in the garden, enjoying the unseasonal weather in his newly manicured solace.

It was almost a shame when Craig was eventually called back into work, albeit offering restricted services before the chaotic debacle of 'Eat Out to Help Out'. It was hardly a surprise that a second circuit-breaker lockdown was in place before Christmas, closely followed by another in the New Year.

Craig made the most of them all until he again had to return to work and attempt to police 'groups of six' and a myriad of other madness, until arriving at today, 19$^{th}$ July 2021 – Freedom Day.

All remaining restrictions were lifted, and some form of normality could return to life, and Craig intended for this to also be a trigger point for something new for himself. He hadn't yet decided what this was to be. Perhaps he would finally sell the house and move away for a fresh start, or maybe just a new venture locally.

Today though, he had committed to only two things. First, after finishing his early shift, he would visit Patrick's grave, tidy it a little, and allow himself some closure. After that, he was having sex, and Craig knew exactly who with.

Garry Mardy was a thirty-nine-year-old front-of-house manager at another of the local hotels who had moved to the area just after the first lockdown. At ten years older than Craig, he wouldn't have ordinarily triggered a romantic interest, but Garry looked and carried himself much younger than his years.

With a haircut that was apparently fashionable again, although in another era it would have been referred to as a basin cut your mother may have inflicted upon you with her *Tupperware*, and a wardrobe made up almost exclusively of skinny jeans, polo shirts and *North Face* jackets, Garry was carrying off fashionable with ease. Of course, he wasn't perfect, a little too short for his weight, but nothing excessive and very much doable in Craig's eyes.

With no sign of grey and a hair colour that looked natural even if, in fact, it wasn't, Craig had initially mistaken him for around the same age when they had first met in the summer of 2020.

Craig had almost sensed the eyes upon him when Garry had come in for a drink one evening after work. He sat alone at one end of the bar, and every time Craig glanced over, he would be greeted with a smile. Nothing more than that on the first night and several after, but eventually, they got chatting.

Garry hadn't moved far. He had previously been around forty minutes away in Swindon. He hadn't been lucky enough to qualify for the furlough scheme, so he had been let go by his previous employer and had come to the area searching for work.

A few more encounters later and Craig received a

friend request on Facebook. 'Interested in Men', Craig had noticed while browsing Garry's sparsely completed 'About info'. Suspicions were confirmed, but Craig wasn't ready to go there just yet.

As their friendship grew over the subsequent months, they discovered a shared penchant for the occasional line of cocaine to accompany the Friday night drinks and live music on offer in another of the local establishments, but aside from the occasional innuendo or lewd comment at the urinals, no advances were made by either party.

Craig refused to use his influence to coerce Garry to act, and he still did not feel ready for a relationship. Despite the final circumstances, Craig had truly loved Patrick, and his loss had left a physical aching that Craig felt duty-bound to suffer for an appropriate period.

Bizarrely, or perhaps respectfully, Garry had never asked Craig about Patrick. He must have known as it was not a secret around town, but the questions never came. Craig once considered raising it himself, but what would he say? It was time to let go and move on from Patrick.

So that morning, during a quiet period on his breakfast shift, Craig decided to send Garry a message.

*Hi, it's Freedom Day!*
*Fancy fucking later to*
*celebrate?*

That was it. Totally unsolicited and with no magic influence popping Garry a boner when he read it. This was good old-fashioned romance at its best. Well, sexting, at least.

> *Fuck yes! I thought you'd never ask. How about getting smashed and making it chemsex? I've got ketamine x*

*Well, that went well*, Craig thought, *and a kiss too!* So, plans were made, and after visiting Patrick's grave with a single white rose, part a show of love and part a goodbye, Craig had arranged to meet Garry in the bar at around 7:00 pm.

Showered and prepared for fun, Craig arrived early only to find Garry had arrived earlier still. They drank and chatted amongst themselves, as well as with other friends who came and went throughout the evening. Fairly standard for a Saturday night, although slightly busier as people embraced their new freedoms.

Several pints in, Garry excused himself to the toilets, and when he returned, he signalled for Craig to check his phone. Craig had received a picture message of a toilet roll sitting on the cubical windowsill. Aware of its meaning, he smiled and headed to the toilet himself.

Craig pissed first and then rolled up a five-pound note and snorted the line of cocaine Garry had left for him hidden on the side. He'd have another three lines between drinks before they decided to leave and take this night to the next level.

Once outside, Garry led them off in the direction of his place. They would have to go there as he hadn't brought the ketamine with him, and he was really horny for it, he had said, reaching to the side and placing his hand on Craig's crotch to emphasise the point.

They walked for around fifteen minutes before turning into a road Craig recognised only too well, and as they approached his mother's old council house, he pointed to the door.

'Don't tell me you live in there,' he slurred as he spoke.

'No,' Garry replied. 'I live in a flat around the corner. Why?' he asked.

'Oh, it doesn't matter. Just take me home and get me naked, lover boy.' Craig did feel drunk. He hoped he would still be able to perform.

Garry's flat was tiny. Craig plonked himself down on the two-seater sofa in the lounge, and Garry went to the kitchen to grab them both another beer. A few minutes later, Garry returned with two bottles in one hand and a small chopping board in the other, on which he had prepared a line of ketamine for Craig.

'What about you?' Craig asked.

'I just did mine in the kitchen,' Garry replied as he put the board on the coffee table, passed Craig a beer, and pulled a curled note out of his pocket for Craig to use.

They sat together on the sofa listening to music, and by the time Craig had finished his beer, he could feel himself really beginning to trip out.

'Okay, I'm high,' he declared. 'Are we doing this?'

'Let's go through to the bedroom. I wanna play,' Garry smiled and then led the way.

The bedroom was roughly the same size as the lounge, and even in his dazed state, Craig was able to make a few observations. Firstly, it was immaculately clean and neatly kept, as the lounge had been.

Craig's eyes were then drawn to the large mirror on the ceiling above the bed and then to the bed itself, which was a simple metal bed frame. The type that squeaked a lot when in action, he thought to himself.

Then Garry's hands were on his shoulders, turning him around so they were face to face at the foot of the bed. Craig moved forwards to kiss him, but Garry had already untucked his t-shirt and lifted it over Craig's now raised arms.

Garry then pushed Craig backwards, so he collapsed on the mattress. The sudden movement sent Craig's head spinning even more than it already was, and he only briefly caught sight of himself in the ceiling mirror before blacking out.

When Craig came back around, he was still on his back on the mattress, although he seemed to have shifted position a little. His arms were outstretched, perpendicular to his sides, just slightly higher than his head, and as he regained focus on the mirror above his head, he noticed he was restrained.

Still confused and tripping from the evening's intoxications, Craig checked each arm in turn. One wrist was restrained by the cord from a dressing gown tied around the bedpost and the other by a leather belt. A glance downwards revealed it was his own belt, and his jeans were now unbuttoned and unzipped.

Garry still stood at the end of the bed smiling up at him, and Craig was reassured he must have only zoned out for a short period.

'Welcome back to the party,' Garry said as he peeled Craig's socks from his feet.

Still totally spaced out, Craig didn't even attempt to reply. Instead, he simply smiled back and watched as Garry leaned forwards and tugged his jeans down his legs and off over his feet.

Craig's briefs were bulging, neither the drugs nor the alcohol impairing his erection, it seemed. As Garry repeated his action and removed Craig's underwear, his released penis made an audible slap as it bounced upwards and came to rest on his stomach.

'You have no idea how long I have waited for this moment,' Garry said.

'Fuck! It is so hot,' Craig mumbled. 'Suck me off,' he almost begged.

'Oh, I'm afraid that isn't going to be happening,' Garry replied, and for the first time, it occurred to Craig that Garry seemed much more lucid than he was.

Craig was in no state to make any sense of what was happening and continued looking down across his own naked body as Garry grabbed the base of the mattress and tugged it out from underneath him.

It took a bit of a struggle for Garry to remove the mattress from the bed in the space he had to manoeuvre, but in a moment or two, he had managed to free it and rest it vertically against the end wall.

During the removal process, Craig's body had dropped down and come to a stop on a rigid wooden structure hidden beneath the mattress. Looking up at the mirror, he saw himself lying naked and restrained upon a large wooden cross.

Garry moved around to Craig's side and picked up a cloth wrap from the dresser. As he unwrapped it, revealing an ancient-looking hammer and half a dozen large handmade nails, he spoke softly as he continued his task.

'You can't imagine how hard it was to get my hands on this cross. Do you recognise it? You've been in this position once before when you were a boy,' Garry explained.

Craig's mind was muddled, and he couldn't shake it at all. Nothing was making any sense. He was still fully erect from previous anticipations, yet something was clearly awry with this whole situation.

'Now, this is probably going to hurt a little, but the ketamine should help,' Garry sympathised as he held the first nail in place on Craig's left palm and then hammered it almost exactly through the small scar Craig had carried since he was eight years old.

Remarkably Craig barely flinched as Garry walked around to the other side of the bed. Instead, he was trying desperately to focus his mind. He was trying to vanish Garry away to another location, any location, but his powers weren't working.

Maybe a smaller feat was achievable, so he attempted to vanish the hammer and nail away that Garry now held hovering above his right palm. Craig focused on the tools but could only watch as Garry hammered the second nail deep into the wood below his hand. A small stream of blood surfaced, and there was some pain this time.

'What are you doing?' Craig asked, still unable to offer any resistance. He didn't even have the strength to kick his legs as Garry moved down to his feet to complete the crucifixion.

'I am finishing something that should have happened years ago,' Garry answered as he hammered a nail through Craig's left ankle and secured it to the base of the cross.

'Did you know it's a matter of great theological debate as to whether they used three or four nails for a crucifixion,' he calmly informed Craig. 'I am going to use four as it's a bitch to try and do both feet with one nail. Trust me. I've tried.'

'Who the fuck are you?' Craig wailed through the increasing pain but was distracted by a strange black mist that had begun to escape his mouth.

'It doesn't matter who I am, Craig. It's time for you to leave this world, but I was a friend of your Uncle Paul's, and I want you to know that he was a good man.'

With that, Garry brought down the hammer on the fourth nail, and the blackness escaping Craig's mouth grew thicker as, finally, his earthly life was ceremoniously extinguished.

# ACKNOWLEDGEMENTS

**Paula Newman & Kirsten Curry –** Thank you both for your time and feedback when proofreading for me. Sometimes you need a good honest friend to tell you what you already know, just to be sure. Oh, and the mistakes, I definitely need you for that too. Who even knew *discreet* and *discrete* were two different words? ☺

**Troye Sivan –** I think I became aware of Troye Sivan when I googled him after watching the film *Spud* several years after its original release date. This led to his music, and I became an instant fan despite being a generation above his target audience, maybe two. My husband then bought me a ticket to see his *Bloom* tour in Paris, which was unfortunately cancelled as Troye was suffering from a sore throat following the previous night's concert in Amsterdam *(singing-related, I assume)*. We had a lovely time in Paris regardless, and I still love Troye's music and films. If you are a fan and were paying attention, you will have noticed that I dropped in a Troye lyric in Chapter 5, *"covered all in the night before"*, taken from his song *Animal*. I hope that's all right, Troye. I figured you owed me. ☺

Printed in Great Britain
by Amazon